HIGHLAND CHAMPION

Keira looked into Liam's eyes and noticed that they were more blue than green again. It was a sign of his desire, she realized, and she felt her blood warm in response. No other man had ever looked at her in such a way. Keira cocked one brow in a silent question and challenge.

Liam nearly growled in response to Keira's unspoken challenge, his whole body taut with the need to taste again the sweet heat of her mouth. For reasons he did not even dare to guess at, Keira was not going to retreat. It was his chance to show her the passion they could share.

The first touch of his lips against hers made Keira feel so hot and needy, she had to clutch at his broad shoulders to steady herself. She heard him groan softly and felt him wrap his strong arms around her. The feel of his lean body pressed so close made Keira shiver with delight.

Why not? her reckless self whispered in her mind. Who would know? Did she not deserve a little joy? Why not grab a little pleasure while she could, fleeting though it might be . . .

Books by Hannah Howell

Only For You

My Valiant Knight

Unconquered

Wild Roses

A Taste of Fire

Highland Destiny

Highland Honor

Highland Promise

A Stockingful of Joy

Highland Vow

Highland Knight

Highland Hearts

Highland Bride

Highland Angel

Highland Groom

Highland Warrior

Reckless

Highland Conqueror

Highland Champion

Published by Zebra Books

HANNAH HOWELL

HIGHLAND CHAMPION

ZEBRA BOOKS
KENSINGTON PUBLISHING CORP.

ZEBRA BOOKS are published by

Kensington Publishing Corp.
850 Third Avenue
New York, NY 10022

ISBN 0-7394-6138-9

Printed in the United States of America

To my grandson Benjamin:
Be happy. Be safe. Be healthy.
Grab life by the throat and live it well.
And, never forget that you are loved.
Gran.

THE MURRAY FAMILY LINEAGE

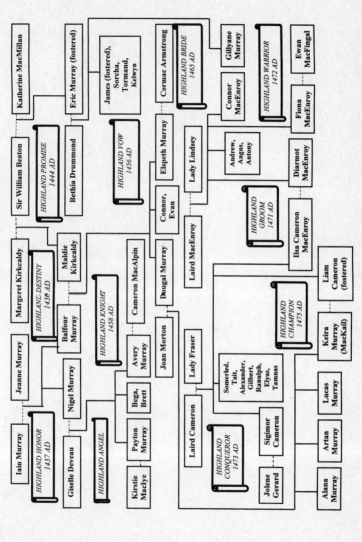

CHAPTER 1

Scotland, Spring 1475

What was an angel doing standing next to Brother Matthew? Liam thought as he peered through his lashes at the couple frowning down at him. And why could he not fully open his eyes? Then the pain hit, and he groaned. Brother Matthew and the angel bent closer.

"Do ye think he will live?" asked Brother Matthew.

"Aye," replied the angel, "though I suspicion he will wish he hadnae for a wee while."

Strange that an angel should possess a voice that made a man think of firelit bedchambers; soft, unclothed skin; and thick furs, Liam mused. He tried to lift his hand, but the pain of even the smallest movement proved too much to bear. He felt as if he had been trampled by a horse. Mayhap several horses. Very large horses.

"He is a bonnie lad," said the angel as she gently smoothed one small, soft hand over Liam's forehead.

"How can ye tell that he is bonnie? He looks as if someone staked him to the ground and rode over him with a herd of horses."

Brother Matthew and he had always thought alike in many ways, Liam recalled. He was one of the few men Liam had missed after leaving the monastery. He now missed the touch of the angel's soft hand. For the brief time it had brushed against his forehead, that light touch had seemed to smooth away some of his pain.

"Aye, he does that," replied the angel. "And yet, one can still see that he is tall, lean, and weel-formed."

"Ye shouldnae be noticing such things!"

"Wheesht, Cousin, I am nay blind."

"Mayhap not, but 'tis still wrong. And, he isnae at his best now, ye ken."

"Och, nay, that is for certain. Howbeit, I am thinking that his best is verra good, aye? Mayhap as good as our cousin Payton, do ye think?"

Brother Matthew made a very scornful noise. "Better. Truth tell, 'tis why I ne'er believed he would stay with us."

Why should his appearance make someone think him a bad choice for the religious life? Liam did not think that was a particularly fair judgment, but could not seem to give voice to that opinion. Despite the pain he was in, his thoughts were clear enough. He just seemed to be unable to voice them or to make any movement to indicate that he heard these people discussing him. Even though he could look at them through his lashes, his eyes were obviously not opening enough to let them know he was awake.

"Ye dinnae think he had a true calling?" asked the angel.

"Nay," Brother Matthew replied. "Oh, he liked the learning weel enough, was verra quick and bright, but we could only teach him so much here. We are but a small monastery, nay a rich one and nay a great teaching place. I think, too, that he found this place too quiet, too peaceful. He missed his family. I have met his kinsmen, and I can understand. A large, loud, somewhat, weel, untamed lot of men they are. The learning offered eased that restlessness in Liam for a while, but it wasnae enough in the end. The quiet routine, the sameness of the days began to wear upon his spirit, I think."

Liam was a little surprised at how well his old friend knew and understood him. He had been restless, still was, in some ways. The quiet of the monastery, the rigid schedule of the monastic life had begun to press in upon him and feel more smothering than comforting. He *had* missed his family. For a moment, he was glad that he seemed unable to speak for he feared he would be asking for them now like some forlorn child.

" 'Tis hard," said the angel. "I was most surprised that ye settled into the life so verra weel. But ye have a true, deep calling, dinnae ye?"

"Aye, I do," Brother Matthew replied softly. "I did e'en as a child. But, ne'er think I dinnae miss all of ye, Keira. I did and do most painfully at times, but there is a brotherhood here, a family of sorts. Yet, I will probably visit again soon. I have begun to spend a great deal of time wondering how the bairns have grown, if everyone is still hale and strong, and many another sort of thing. Letters dinnae tell all."

"Nay, they dinnae." Keira sighed. "I have missed them all too, and I have been gone for but a six month."

Keira, Liam repeated the name in his mind. A fine name. He tried to move his arm despite the pain and felt a twinge of panic when it would not respond to his command. When he realized he was bound to the bed, his unease grew even stronger. Why would they do that to him? Why did they not wish him to move? Were his injuries so dire? Was he wrong to think he had been given aid? Had he actually been made a prisoner? Even as those questions spun through his mind, he fought past his pain enough to tug against his bonds. A groan escaped him as that pain quickly and fiercely swept through his body from head to toe. He stilled when a pair of small, soft hands touched him, one upon his forehead and one upon his chest.

"I think he begins to wake, Cousin," Keira said. "Hush, sir. Be at peace."

"Tied." Liam hissed the word out from between tightly gritted teeth, the pain caused by speaking that one small word telling him that his face had undoubtedly taken a severe beating. "Why?"

"To keep ye still, Liam," Brother Matthew said. "Keira does-nae think anything is broken, save for your right leg, but ye were thrashing about so much, it worried us some."

"Aye," agreed Keira. "Ye were beat near to death, sir. 'Tis best if ye remain verra still so as not to add to your injuries or pain. Are ye in much pain?"

Liam muttered a fierce curse at what he considered a very stupid question. He heard Brother Matthew gasp in shock. To his surprise, he heard Keira laugh softly.

" 'Twas indeed a foolish question," she said, laughter still tinting her sultry voice. "Ye dinnae seem to have a spot upon ye that isnae brilliant with bruising. Aye, and your right leg was broken. 'Tis a verra clean break, and I have set it. After three days, there is still no sign of poison in the wound or in the blood, so it should heal verra weel."

"Liam, 'tis Brother Matthew. Keira and I have brought ye to the wee cottage at the edge of the monastery's lands. The brothers wouldnae allow her to tend to your wounds within the monastery, I fear." He sighed. "They werenae too happy with her presence e'en though she was weel hidden away in the guest quarters. Brother Paul was particularly agitated."

"Agitated?" Keira muttered. "Cousin Elspeth would say he—"

"Aye," Brother Matthew hastily interrupted, "I ken what our cousin Elspeth would say. I think she has lived too long amongst those unruly Armstrongs. She has gained far too free a tongue for a proper lady."

Keira made a rude noise. "My, but ye have become verra pi-ous, Cousin."

"Of course I have. I am a monk. We are trained to be pious. Now, I can help ye give Liam some potion or change his ban-dages if ye wish, but then I must return to the monastery."

"Ah, weel then, best see if he needs to relieve himself," Keira said. "I will just step outside so that ye can see to that. Now that he is waking, 'tis best, I think. I shall just run up to the monastery's garden and collect a few herbs. I shall be but a few moments."

"What do ye mean *now* that he is waking?" demanded Brother Matthew, but then he grunted with irritation when the only reply he got was the door closing behind Keira as she hurried away. "Wretched wee lass."

"Cousin?" Liam asked, realizing that not only was his throat injured but his jaw and mouth as well.

"Cousin? Oh, aye, the lass is my cousin. One of a vast horde of cousins, if truth be told. A Murray, ye ken?"

"Kirkcaldy?"

" 'Tis what I am, aye. Her grandmother was one too. Now, I do fear that nay matter how gentle I am, this is going to hurt."

It did. Liam was sure he screamed at one point, and that only increased his pain. He welcomed the blackness when it swept over him, as he suspected the continuously apologizing Brother Matthew did.

"Oh, dear, he looks a wee bit paler," Keira said as she set the herbs she had collected down on a table and moved to stand at the side of the small bed Liam was tied to.

"He still suffers a great deal of pain, and I fear I added to it," said Brother Matthew.

"Ye couldnae help it, Cousin. He is better, nay doubt about it, but such injuries will be slow to heal. There truly isnae a part of this mon that isnae hurt. 'Tis a true miracle that only his leg was broken."

"Are ye certain that he was only beaten? Or that he was e'en beaten at all?"

"Aye, Cousin, he was beaten. I have nay doubt about that, but he could have been tossed off that hill, too. Some of these injuries could be from the rocky slope his body would have fallen down and the equally rocky ground he landed on. I dinnae suppose he was able to tell ye what happened to him, was he?"

"Och, nay. Nay. He spoke but a word or two, then made a painful cry, and has been like this e'er since." Brother Matthew shook his head. "I wish I could understand this. Who would do such a terrible thing to the mon? I ken I havenae seen that much of the mon o'er the years since he left here, but he really wasnae the sort of mon to make enemies. Certainly nay such vicious ones."

Keira idly tested the strength of the bonds that held Liam still upon the bed and carefully studied the man. "I suspect jealousy is a problem he must often deal with."

Brother Matthew frowned at his cousin. She seemed far too interested in Liam Cameron, revealing more than just a healer's interest in a patient. A healer surely did not need to touch her patient's hair as often as Keira did Liam's thick, dark copper hair. Liam was certainly not looking his best, might well have lost a little of his beauty due to this vicious beating, but there was clearly enough allure left in his battered body and face to draw Keira's interest.

He tried to see Keira as a woman grown, not simply as the cousin he had played with as a child. His eyes widened slightly as he began to see that his cousin was no teasing child now, but a very attractive woman. She was small and slight, yet womanly, for her breasts were well shaped and full, and her hips were pleasingly curved. Her hair was a rich, shining black, and it hung in a thick braid to well past her tiny waist. That hair made her fair skin look even purer, soft milk white with the blush of good health. Keira's oval face held a delicate beauty, her nose being small and straight, with a hint of strength revealed in her small chin, and her cheekbones being high and finely shaped. What would catch a man's interest were her eyes. Set beneath gently arched dark brows and trimmed with thick, long lashes were a pair of deep green eyes. Those wide eyes bespoke innocence, but their depths held all the womanly mystery that could so intrigue a man. He was a little startled to realize that her mouth, slightly wide and full of lip, held the same contradictions. Her smile could be the epitome of sweet innocence, but Brother Matthew suddenly knew men of the world would quickly see the sensuality there as well. He suddenly feared it had been a serious error in judgment on his part to allow her to tend to a man like Liam Cameron.

"Ye have a rather fierce look upon your face, Cousin," Keira said as she moved to begin preparing more salve for Liam's injuries. "He willnae die, I promise ye. He will just be a verra long time in healing."

"I believe ye. 'Tis just that, weel, one thing Liam did find hard to abide about the monastic life was, weel, was . . ."

"No lasses to smile at." She grinned at the severe frown he gave her for it sat so ill upon his boyishly handsome face. "I think, just as with our cousin Payton, this mon has a way with the lasses. Aye, and he need do nay more than smile at them."

"I dinnae think he e'en needs to smile," grumbled Brother Matthew.

"Nay, probably not. Come, Cousin, dinnae look so troubled. He is no danger to me now, is he? Aye, and e'en when he is healed enough to smile again, he can only be a danger to me if I wish him to be. Ye cannae think that with the kinsmen I have, I havenae been verra weel taught in the ways of men." She glanced toward Liam. "Is he a bad mon then? A vile, heartless seducer of innocents?"

Brother Matthew sighed. "Nay, I would ne'er believe such a thing of him."

"Then there is naught to fret o'er, is there? 'Tis best if we worry o'er our many other troubles. They are of more importance than whether or nay I can resist the sweet smiles of a bonnie lad. I have been here nigh on two months now, Cousin. There has been nary a sign of my enemy so I think, soon, I must try to get home to Donncoill."

"I ken it. I am fair surprised none of your kinsmen have come round. 'Tis odd that they wouldnae start to wonder on how long ye have stayed at a monastery or e'en why the monks would allow it."

Keira pushed aside the pinch of guilt she felt for allowing him to continue to believe she had contacted her family when she had not. " 'Tisnae so verra unusual for guests, male or female, to linger in the guest quarters, and I paid weel for the privilege."

She smiled and patted his arm when he flushed with embarrassment over that hard truth. "It has been worth it. I needed to hide and mend my wounds, needed to o'ercome my grief and fear, and needed to be certain that when I did go home, I wasnae leading that murderous bastard Rauf right to the gates of Donncoill."

"Your family would protect ye, Keira. They would feel it their duty, their right, and willnae be pleased that ye denied them."

Keira winced. "I ken it, but I will deal with it. I also had to decide what to do. Duncan pulled a vow from me, and I had to think hard on how to fulfill it and how much it might cost me to do so."

"I ken that willnae be easy. Rauf is cunning and vicious. Yet ye swore to your husband ye would see to it that his people didnae suffer under Rauf's rule if he failed to win the battle that night. He failed. He died that night, Keira, so your vow to him is much akin to one made at a mon's deathbed. Ye have to do all ye can to fulfill it." He kissed her cheek and started for the door. "I will see ye in the morning. Sleep weel."

"Ye too, Cousin."

The moment he was gone, Keira sighed and sat down in the little chair next to Liam Cameron's bed. Her cousin made it all sound so simple. She dearly wished it were. The vow she had made to her poor, ill-fated husband weighed heavily on her mind and heart. So did the fates of the people of Ardgleann. Duncan had cared deeply for his people, a mixed lot of gentle and somewhat odd souls. It distressed her to think of how they must be suffering under Rauf's rule. She prayed for them every night, but she could not fully dispel the guilt she felt over running away. Although some of what Duncan had asked of her did not seem right, the people of Ardgleann could no longer wait for her to debate the moral complexities of it all. It was time, far past time, to do something.

She idly bathed Liam with a soft cloth and cool water. He did not really have a fever, but it seemed to make him rest more quietly. He was a strong man, and she felt certain he would continue to recover. By the time he was able to tend to himself, she had better have decided what to do about Ardgleann and Rauf. Once she knew why Liam had been hurt and was certain that no enemy hunted him still, she would leave him in the care of the monks and face her own destiny.

Keira felt an immediate pang at the thought of leaving the man and almost laughed at the absurdity of it. He was a mass of bruises, and had barely said three words in as many days. She supposed that she felt some odd bond with him because she had been the one to find him. In truth, she had been drawn to him by a strange blend of dreams and compulsion. It had been a little frightening for although similar experiences had oc-curred in the past, she had never seen things so clearly or felt as strongly. Even now, she could not shake the feeling that there was more to it all than helping him recover from his in-juries.

"Foolishness," she muttered and shook her head as she pat-ted him dry with a soft rag.

Perhaps she should send word to his people, she thought as she began to make a hearty broth to feed to him when he woke again. From what her cousin had told her, Sir Liam's kinsmen were more than capable of protecting him. Keira quickly dis-carded the idea for the same reason she had given her cousin when he had suggested sending for the Camerons. Sir Liam might not want that, might be reluctant to pull his family into whatever trouble he had gotten himself. She could sympathize for she too hesitated to involve her family in her own troubles.

That, too, was foolish, she suspected. She had done nothing wrong, had not caused the trouble or invited the danger. If one of her family were in such trouble, she would be ready and eager to ride to his or her side. Which is why he or she would hesitate to tell her about it, she suddenly thought and briefly grinned. It was instinctive to try to keep a loved one safe. When her family found out the truth, they would be angry, perhaps even a little offended or hurt, but they would understand, for they would know in their hearts that they would have done the very same thing.

And, she told herself as she sat down at the small table near the fire, if this man was as close to his family as her cousin implied, he would do the same. The last time she had seen her cousin Gillyanne, she had heard a few tales about the Camerons. Even though the tales had been told to amuse everyone, they had revealed that the Camerons were probably as close a family as her own. There was also Sir Liam's manly pride to consider. It would undoubtedly bristle at the implication that he could not take care of himself. No, Keira decided, it was not a good idea to send for his people without his permission.

After a meal of bread, cheese, and cold venison, Keira took a hasty bath. She then settled herself upon a pallet made up near the fire. Keira stared into the flames and waited for sleep to come. She hated this time of the night, hated the silence, and hated the fact that sleep was so slow to come, leaving her alone in the silence with her memories. Try as she might, she could not shake free of the grip of those dark memories. She could only suppress them for a while.

Duncan had been a good man, passingly handsome and gentle. She had not loved him, and she still felt guilty about that, even though it was hardly her fault. At nearly two and twenty, however, she had decided she could wait no longer for some great, passionate love to stroll her way. She had wanted children and a home of her own. Although she loved her family deeply, she had begun to feel an increasing need to spread her wings, to walk her own path. Marriage did not usually free a woman, but all her instincts had told her that Duncan would never try to master her. He had wanted a true partner, and knowing how rare that was, she had accepted him when he had asked her to be his bride.

She could still recall the doubts of her family, especially those of her grandmother Lady Maldie and her cousin Gillyanne. Their special gifts had told them that she did not love the man she was about to marry. They had sensed her unease, one she could not explain even to herself. Keira was not sure it was a good thing that they had not pressed her on that, and then roundly scolded herself. They had respected her choice, and it had been *her* choice.

Why she had felt uneasy from the moment she had accepted Duncan's proposal of marriage was still a puzzle to her. Keira had smothered that unease and married him. Within hours of marrying him, the first hint of trouble between them had begun, and within days of reaching Ardgleann, the trouble with Rauf had begun. She had thought that explained all those odd feelings she had suffered, but now she was not so sure. Every instinct she had told her that the puzzle was not yet solved.

Just as she began to relax, welcoming the comfort of sleep, a harsh cry from Sir Liam startled her. Keira tugged on her gown and hurried to his side to find him straining against his bonds, muttering furious curses at enemies only he could see. She stroked his forehead and spoke softly to him, telling him over and over where he was, who cared for him now, and that he was safe. It surprised her a little when he quickly grew calm again.

"Jolene?" he whispered.

Keira wondered why hearing him speak another woman's name should irritate her as much as it did. "Nay, Keira," she said as she placed her hand over his to try to stop him from tugging at his bonds.

"Keira," he repeated and grasped her hand in his. "Aye. Keira. Black hair. Confused me. Thought I was home. At Dubheidland."

"Ah. She is your healer?" Keira tried to wriggle her hand free of his grasp, but he would not release her, so she sat down in the chair at his bedside.

"Sigimor's wife. Lady of Dubheidland. Thought I was home."

"So ye said. I can give ye something to ease the pain, if ye wish it."

"Nay. Thought I was caught again."

She could see that it pained him to speak, but she could not resist asking, "Do ye remember what happened to you?"

"Caught. Beaten. Thrown away. You found me?"

"Aye, me and my cousin Brother Matthew."

"Good. Safe here."

"Aye, ye will be." She tried yet again to wriggle her hand free of his, but failed.

"Stay." He heaved a sigh. "Please. Stay."

Keira inwardly cursed the weakness that caused her to heed that plea. She carefully shifted her seat closer to the bed so that she could sit more comfortably as she waited for him to release her hand. After a few moments of silence, she wondered if he had gone back to sleep, but his grip upon her hand remained firm. To her surprise, he began to stroke the back of her hand with his thumb. The warmth that gesture stirred within her was a little alarming, but she could not bring herself to stop him.

This was not good, Keira thought. The light brush of a man's thumb over her hand should not make her feel warm. True, it was a very nice hand, the fingers long and elegant, but it was too benign a caress to stir any interest. Or, it should be. She looked at his battered face and sighed. To all the troubles she already had, she realized she now had to add one more. A man she did not know, a man whose face was so bruised and swollen it would probably give a child the night terrors, could stir her blood with the simple stroke of his thumb.

CHAPTER 2

Liam opened his eyes, feeling an odd spark of anticipation mingled with his pain. He was just wondering what he could possibly be looking forward to, since being awake meant being far too aware of all the pain he was in, when he realized he was holding someone's hand. He hoped he was not clinging to Brother Matthew. The hand was too small and too soft, he decided. Liam had the fleeting thought that somehow that small hand was soothing him in body and in spirit. Then he remembered the woman.

Cautiously, he turned his head, even as he struggled to remember her name. Keira, he whispered as he saw the lovely, delicate hand resting in his and a thick, gleaming black braid draped over his wrist. The chair was pulled up hard against the bed, and Keira was sleeping half in the chair and half on his bed. He recalled being tied down, but either he had dreamt that, or she had loosened the bonds on all but his right leg. Her cheek was resting on his stomach, and he fleetingly cursed the bedcovers that separated them. Liam looked at the hand he held close to his chest and wondered how long he had kept the woman captive. He felt guilty for having forced her into such an uncomfortable position, knowing she would ache when she awoke, but he was still reluctant to release her.

She looked as innocent as a child as she slept. Yet, in the sensuous curve of her mouth, there was the hint of a passionate nature. She was beautiful in a way that grew more evident the longer one looked at her. When she entered a room, men might give her a brief, curious glance, but they would soon find themselves looking again and again until she firmly held their interest with the purity of her features—her beautiful skin; her thick, long hair; and the delicate, feminine curves of her slim body. Liam suddenly recalled the sound of her voice, a soft, sultry music, and knew she would only have to speak to firmly catch the attention of any man.

He felt her hand move in his and resisted the urge to clutch it tighter. She placed her hand over his heart, and her neatly curved brows lowered as she frowned. If he did not know better, he would think she could tell he was awake simply through that touch. Slowly, she lifted her head and looked at him. Liam looked into her sleep-softened deep green eyes and felt an odd twist in his heart, as if she had reached into his chest and pinched it. Pain was making him delirious, he decided.

Keira slowly sat up, wincing at the many aches she had gained by sleeping in such an awkward position. She blushed a little as she met his gaze, embarrassed to have been found with her head on his stomach and her hand upon his chest. Recalling how he had refused to release her even as he slept, her embarrassment eased.

His eyes were not quite so swollen today, although he wore a livid mask of bruises. Those eyes were surely tools of seduction, she mused. Well shaped, surrounded by lashes almost feminine in their length and thickness, they were an intriguing and beautiful blend of blue and green. She had once seen water that color. Shaking herself free of her fascination, she idly rubbed her back as she studied his color.

"Ye look improved," she said.

"Do I? I still feel weel trodden on," he replied, wincing a little as his bruised mouth protested the movement.

"And so ye shall for a while yet, but soon, ye will be cursing that leg for keeping ye abed."

"Was it a bad break? I ken ye spoke of it last time I awoke, but I cannae remember much."

"Nay, 'tisnae bad. Ye were lucky. A verra clean break, and the bone didnae come out through your skin. Howbeit, ye will need to be verra careful. 'Tis why I shall continue to tie that leg down whilst ye sleep. It must set firm, ye ken." She stood up and brushed down her skirts. " 'Tis difficult to say just how long that will take."

Just as she was wondering how to ask if he needed any personal assistance, Brother Matthew arrived. Keira breathed a sigh of relief as she left the small cottage. Dealing with an unconscious man could be done with a measure of calm. A wide awake man with beautiful eyes was another matter altogether. Even when he was no more than a limp, occasionally moaning, body, she had not been able to be completely impersonal. She doubted any woman could be while tending to such a handsome man. She did not want him noticing her appreciation, however. That could bring her the kind of trouble she had no time for now.

After a quick visit to the bushes, she stood by the well and washed as much of herself as she could without completely disrobing. Ever since she had caught Brother Paul spying on her, she had been careful. Worse, he seemed to think it was all her fault he was having difficulty controlling his sinful thoughts and urges.

Keira sighed and started back to the cottage. She had the sinking feeling she was going to be having similar troubles. Knowing that no woman alive could remain immune to the allure of a man like Liam Cameron did not make her feel all that much better. She still felt the sting of her husband's lack of desire for her. The very last thing she needed was to expose herself to that humiliation again.

Liam cursed fluently as Brother Matthew helped him back to bed and then apologized to the monk. He slumped against the pillows the man plumped up behind him and waited for the pain to ease a little. Brother Matthew efficiently washed the sweat from Liam's body while he sprawled there as weak and helpless as an infant. It was humiliating, but Liam had to admit that he felt better afterward.

"Keira will return soon," said Brother Matthew. "If ye are willing, she will feed you."

"Aye, I am feeling hungry," Liam murmured.

"A good sign. I confess, when we first found ye, I held out little hope that ye would survive."

"Just how *did* ye find me? I dinnae think I was attacked on the monastery's lands."

"Nay, but not so verra far away either." Brother Matthew smiled. "My cousin has a gift, as do many of the Murrays, though 'tis something we keep secret, for some dinnae see it as a gift from God. Keira had a dream, ye ken. A dream told her what had happened and where to find ye. God wasnae ready to take ye yet."

"I dinnae think He will e'er want me, old friend. I have followed few of the monk's ways since leaving this place."

"That does not surprise me." Brother Matthew smiled when Liam frowned. "Dinnae take insult, my friend. I meant none. Some men can be true believers, yet there is an earthiness within that makes the monk's or priest's life a poor choice. Sadly, not all of us have the choice to return to their old life as ye did. They make poor men of the church, and oftimes, give the rest of us a bad name. We suffer for their sins. 'Tis the same with the nuns. If forced, I believe ye would have been verra successful within the church and done your best to hold to your vows, but ye wouldnae have been happy. 'Tis no fault or sin. After all, there has to be someone to heed God's word to go forth and multiply. Aye?"

"True enough, and dinnae worry. As far as I ken, I havenae multiplied yet. Aye, I ken that, too, is considered a sin, but, I think, a wee one. My laird, my cousin Sigimor, frowns upon the breeding of bastards. As do I. God's truth, I would like to have a wife, but I am without lands and nay verra rich."

"And, mayhap, havenae found one who can see beyond your bonnie face."

"Aye, there is that, though it sounds vain to say so. Howbeit, this face may nay be so verra bonnie any longer."

" 'Twill heal. Keira said naught was broken there, although she felt certain the ones who beat you were trying hard to damage it. She was most astonished that your nose wasnae broken."

Hearing her cousin's words as she entered the cottage, Keira said, "I suspicion they found it difficult to strike a target that wouldnae stand still. And then, they tried to kill ye, aye?"

"I am nay sure about that," Liam replied. "By the time I fell to the rocks, I was so dazed I cannae say for certain if they pushed or I just fell."

"If ye fell, 'twas because they were beating on ye and caused that misstep. How many?"

"Four."

"Ye are verra fortunate to still be breathing."

"I dinnae think they intended to kill me. Nay so quickly, leastwise. They would have come down the hill after me to finish me, but they didnae. 'Tis that which makes me doubt murder was intended."

"That may be. Of course, they may have simply decided that ye were dead or soon would be, so why trouble themselves. There was little chance ye would be found where ye lay."

"True. My horse?"

"In the stables," Brother Matthew replied. "All of your belongings were safe. So, not a robbery either."

"Mayhap," said Liam, "although they could have exhausted themselves trying to catch Gilmour. The beast shies from strangers, especially men, and can outrun most other horses."

"He was there when we found ye," said Keira as she moved to the fire to heat up some hearty broth for him. "A loyal beast."

"Ye had no trouble with him?"

"Och, nay. He was a wee bit uncertain about my cousin at

first, but I had a wee talk with him. He wasnae going to leave ye. Nay, not e'en when we brought ye in here. I had to bring him inside so that he could see that ye were settled safely. Still, it took nearly two days to convince him to go to the stables."

"Ye brought Gilmour inside?"

"Aye, he was fretting." She turned her attention to mixing him a tankard of cider strengthened with healing herbs.

Liam looked at a grinning Brother Matthew and laughed softly. That hurt, but he ignored the pain. For the first time since waking up in the cottage, he felt sure he would live. He did not believe he would be so amused if he had one foot in the grave.

"Ah, weel, ye are laughing," said Keira as she set the tankard of herbed cider down on the small table by his bed. " 'Tis a good sign." She sat on the edge of the bed with a bowl of broth in her hands. "A dying mon doesnae find too much to laugh about."

"Unless he is too dim of wit to ken he is dying," Liam drawled.

He swallowed the broth she spooned into his mouth. It was thin but rich with the flavor of herbs and vegetables. Liam did hope it would not be long, however, before he could eat something that required chewing. The fact that the simple chore of swallowing the broth and the drink exhausted him made him realize that it would be many days before he was recovered enough to actually argue over what he was being fed. He sagged against the pillows as she took the empty bowl and tankard away.

"Liam, do ye ken who did this to you?" asked Brother Matthew.

"I have my suspicions," Liam replied, "but I am nay sure. Things were said as they beat me, but I think it may be a while ere I recall any of it. There isnae much chance that will help, though."

"An old enemy, mayhap? One of your clan's?"

"Nay, I think not."

"Weel, 'twill come to ye, I am certain. Do ye want us to send word to your family?"

"Nay, not yet, not until I am more certain of who did this and why. I dinnae wish to lead trouble to their door." He frowned. "Mayhap I should leave here."

"And go where, my friend? Nay, ye will stay here until ye are healed enough to travel. Now rest. Naught helps a body to heal as much as sleep does."

Liam nodded faintly in reply and closed his eyes. When he heard Brother Matthew and Keira move away, he opened his eyes just enough to watch them. He felt weak, but was not quite ready to go to sleep. His pain had been eased by whatever herbs Keira had put in the food, and he wanted to savor that for a little while. He was also curious about this woman who had saved his life because of a dream she had had. Although he believed in such things, more or less, and Brother Matthew clearly accepted it, Liam felt a need to remain wary. There was no ignoring the cold fact that if she had not found him because of some vision, the only other possibility was that she had known about the attack. He loathed the idea that she had had any part in it, but one thing he had learned in his time at the royal court was that it was dangerous to trust anyone too quickly. That was especially true concerning bonnie lasses who could stir a man's lusts.

"Do ye need help in the garden today, Cousin?" Keira asked as she took the pot of broth off the fire and set her pot of mutton stew in its place.

"I think ye must needs stay here, dinnae ye?" Brother Matthew sat at the small table set near the fire. "If it willnae be too much trouble, I did bring some clothes that need mending."

"Nay, 'tis no trouble," she assured him as she sat down across the table from him. "'Twill give me something to do whilst he sleeps. Aside from a wee bit of cleaning, tending my mutton stew, and having a bath, there isnae much else for me to do."

"Have ye finished all that needlework ye were doing? Ye were making some gifts, aye?"

"Aye. I finished the shift for Mama. I must needs decide what to put on the one for Grandmere. And there are months left in which to finish those. S'truth, if I hadnae bought all the linen and thread from Lady Morrison, I wouldnae be making gifts now anyway. And all of that lovely lace," Keira murmured and shook her head. "I felt most guilty o'er how little I paid for it all."

"She needed the coin, and ye didnae cheat her. Many would have once they kenned how desperate she was. She was most thankful for what ye gave her." He glanced at the pot upon the fire. "Mutton stew, did ye say?"

Keira laughed. "Aye. Plan to sup with me now, do ye?"

"Aye. When 'tis a choice of what is fed to us at the monastery and your mutton stew, I fear my will to resist temptation is verra weak. Mayhap a game of chess, too?"

"Do ye think losing to me will be penance enough for enjoying my stew?"

"Such arrogance." Brother Matthew tsked and shook his head. "I could win."

"Aye, ye might," she murmured, and they both grinned.

"Weel, I had best return to the monastery," he said as he stood up. "Do ye need me to come back here, say, at about midday?"

"To tend to him?" she asked as she followed him to the door, and he nodded in reply. "Nay, I can manage him. I did before."

Brother Matthew frowned and hesitated just outside the door. " 'Tisnae right."

"I am a healer, Cousin. He is a battered mon who still has one leg tied down on the bed. And I tended him myself ere he woke. Go, tend to your work. I will be fine. Why, I shall probably e'en find time to make some honey-sweetened oatcakes."

"Wicked lass to toss such temptation before a mon of the cloth," he said, shaking his head again as he turned away.

Keira laughed then, and leaving the door open so she could hear if Liam should call out, she began the tedious chore of drawing the water for her bath from the well. It was undoubtedly improper to even think of bathing with a man sharing the tiny cottage with her, but she felt a strong need to bathe. A blanket or two hung up around the tub should provide her with enough privacy. Thinking of Brother Paul, she decided she would also bar the door.

Liam blinked and bit back a groan as full awareness of his various injuries returned upon waking. He could not recall falling asleep. One moment, he was listening to Keira and Brother Matthew talk, and the next he was rousing from a deep sleep. He suspected whatever she put into the cider or even the broth not only eased his pain but also nudged him into sleep, whether he willed it or not.

Glancing around the dimly lit cottage, he wondered how long he had slept. Keira sat near a tiny window at the rear of the cottage, sewing what appeared to be a woman's shift. A quick glance at the neatly folded monks' robes set on a stool by the door told Liam that he had slept long enough for her to finish that chore.

He studied her as she sat so quietly plying her needle and tried to recall all he had overheard before falling asleep. She and Brother Matthew had sounded just like the cousins they claimed to be, speaking of people they both knew and teasing each other. Liam felt a pinch of guilt over his wariness. The woman had obviously been caring for him for days. If she meant him harm, she had clearly had ample opportunity to inflict it. No one would have questioned it if he had not survived his injuries. After all she had done for him, he would not be foolish to trust her.

There was, however, at least one thing that made him hesitate to trust in her. Why was she living here in a tiny cottage on the grounds of a monastery? From what little had been said, Liam got the feeling she had been living here for a while. Even though her cousin was here, it was an odd place for a woman to take refuge. Why did she not return to her family? Everything he had ever heard about that clan told him the Murrays were closely bonded and deeply loyal to each other. He doubted there was much they would not forgive or help her with.

Brother Matthew seemed to have no qualms about her or her tale, but Liam was well aware of the man's sweet nature and naïveté. The man could also be blinded by the fact that this pretty little woman was blood kin to him. Liam knew he would find it difficult to remain wary, especially when he looked into those big green eyes. Or glanced at that tempting mouth. Or heard that seductive voice. Liam inwardly cursed. It was going to be very difficult indeed.

He shifted his body in a vain attempt to get more comfortable and realized his broken leg was propped up on several cushions and still secured to the bed. A moment later, he also realized that his movement had drawn Keira's attention. He watched as she set aside her sewing and moved toward him. That was something else he had better not do too often if he wished to remain sharp of mind and cautious, he thought ruefully, for she had an almost sultry grace to her walk.

"I think ye are a fast healer, Sir Liam," Keira said as she looked him over.

"I dinnae feel much healed," he said as he studied his broken leg.

"Nay, I suspect all those aches and pains ye suffer now hide the truth from ye, but I can see it in the color of that bruising and in the amount of the swelling. Both have eased more swiftly than in other people I have tended, and that is good. E'en your leg isnae as troubled by swelling as others I have tended."

"Why is it still tied to the bed then? And why have ye set it up on those cushions?"

" 'Tis tied so that ye dinnae move it too much as ye rest. Not only could the pain that would cause disturb the rest ye need, but ye could also easily destroy what healing has begun. 'Tis raised like this to ease the swelling, but I think that willnae be so verra necessary soon. Oh, ye will still have to rest it a lot and

raise it like this from time to time for several weeks yet but unless ye do something verra foolish, I think ye will soon be using
that leg again. 'Twill be weak at the start, but nay more than
that."

Liam muttered a curse, then muttered an apology for his
language, then sighed. "How many weeks?"

"Six or more until we can remove the slats and the wrappings.
I cannae say how long after that until ye can use it with the same
ease and grace ye did before. That is up to ye, but I think it willnae be that long for ye are young, strong, and healthy. Ye willnae be left with a limp if ye take care," she added, softly reminding him of his good fortune.

"I ken it. I am verra fortunate indeed. 'Tis still an irritation."
He met her smile with a faint one of his own as she helped him
sit up against the pillows she hastily set behind his back. "I
think there are some monks who must be resting their heads
on a verra flat bed." She chuckled, and the low, husky sound
stirred a dangerous warmth inside him.

"Some do anyway as they feel such soft pillows are a sinful in
dulgence, but, aye, there are few spare ones at the monastery
just now."

"I dinnae suppose 'tis time for Brother Matthew to arrive, is
it?" Liam asked, aware of a pressing need and reluctant to have
this blood-stirring woman assist him in such a personal chore.

"Ah, nay, but one of the lads is here. He brought some hay
for your horse. I will fetch him for ye."

The moment she left, Liam closed his eyes and recited every
curse he could think of. It might be wise to cease trying to
remain wary and use all his willpower to keep himself from
reaching for her. He could not recall any woman who had
stirred his lusts as swiftly and fiercely as this one did. Worse, she
was not even trying to do so. There was not even the smallest
hint of flirtation in her manner. She gave him no coy looks, no
soft flatteries, and no inviting smiles, but despite the pain he
was in, he wanted her as he had never wanted a woman before.

Keira returned with a thin boy who had not yet grown into

his feet and hands. She introduced young Kester and then hurried away. Liam watched the youth stare after her and heard him sigh. Obviously, the boy was old enough to suffer an infatuation with a woman. Liam supposed he ought to find some comfort in that for it revealed that he was not the only one bewitched by Keira. However, he thought grimly when the boy finally turned his way, Kester was not gambling with his life.

CHAPTER 3

A fortnight of deception, Keira mused as she finished collecting herbs from the monastery garden and started back toward the cottage. That was how she saw the time she had spent with Sir Liam Cameron. To be completely fair to herself, she supposed she could say it was more like ten days of deception, for Liam had been mostly unconscious, then resting, for four days. It was as his mind had begun to clear and they had actually begun to talk to each other about more than his injuries that the deception had truly begun.

She shook her head over her own foolishness. Deception was necessary. In a way, it was an act of self-preservation. She had to keep herself at a distance from him in any way that she could. It was impossible to leave him as he still needed care, but in all other ways, she had to keep a wall between them. If she revealed any of her confused but intensifying feelings for him and he responded in even the smallest way, she feared she would be lost. The man was proving to be all she could ever want, but he was far above her touch.

There was also Ardgleann and its people to consider. To help them, she had to hold fast to a lie. Duncan had made her swear to it shortly before his death. That was not a vow she could risk breaking. There was not even any room for compromise, a way for her to get what she was craving more each day and yet keep her vow to her murdered husband.

Setting her basket down as she neared the well by the cottage, Keira went to clean herself of the dirt she had accumulated while collecting herbs from the garden. She had felt compelled to work in the garden for a while in payment for the herbs she harvested, and it showed. What little vanity she possessed would not allow her to go into the cottage where Sir Liam rested without at least attempting to look her best.

"Foolish woman," she muttered to herself as she drew up a bucket of water.

"Aye, that ye are. Ye thought ye could continue to tempt a mon to madness and nay pay the consequences."

Keira silently cursed as she turned to face Brother Paul. The man looked flushed, a little wild-eyed, and dangerous. She was neatly trapped between him and the well, armed with only the rag she had just dampened to clean herself. This, she thought, could be unpleasant for he did not look as if he was in the mood to listen to reason.

Liam sat on the edge of the bed and scowled at the cottage door. He was restless. Most of his other injuries had healed, but his broken leg kept him trapped. Although he had spent the morning hobbling around on his crutch, hoping to gain some semblance of grace while using it, he was not tired. He was bored. There was nothing to do and no one to talk to, so he sat there wondering when Keira would return. It was a sad end for a man who had never had to wait upon any woman before, he mused, and briefly smiled at the vanity of such thoughts.

Holding himself at a safe distance from Keira was proving as difficult as he had thought it would be, and it was not because she was the only woman around. She fascinated him as much as she aroused him. It was a dangerous combination. The more he watched her, the more beautiful she became. He knew she was holding fast to some secrets, and he wanted to know each and every one.

The fact that she was trying to keep a distance from him as

well was not helping him all that much. Instead, it worked to intrigue him. Liam knew she was not doing so intentionally, but that air of mystery around her kept pulling at him, tempting him to step over the boundaries he had set for himself. Even reminding himself that he had little to offer a woman like her did not rein in his growing interest. For one brief moment, when he had learned that she was a widow, he had even considered becoming her lover for a while, but had forced that tempting plan out of his head. Widow she may be, but Keira was a woman one married. Although he had heard that the Murrays allowed their women to choose their husbands, he doubted they would smile upon a poor, landless knight.

Even as he wondered why the thought of marriage kept tripping through his mind, he heard a noise outside. At first, he thought Kester had returned with Keira, following her like some faithful puppy, as was his habit. Then he realized that the voices were raised, for he would not be able to hear them through the door otherwise. He was just wondering if he ought to limp to the door to see who Keira might be arguing with or if he would soon have other company to deal with when he heard a brief, feminine screech.

Cursing softly over how awkward he still was with his new crutch, Liam made his way to the door. He opened the door, stepped outside, and nearly bellowed out the rage that swept over him. A monk had Keira pinned to the ground. Liam caught sight of Kester in the distance, but the boy tripped and fell as he hurried to help Keira. When he saw the monk was struggling to pull up Keira's skirts, Liam forgot about his injured leg, forgot about his pain, and hurried toward the wrestling couple.

Keira could not believe how quickly Brother Paul had gotten her pinned to the ground. One minute they had been arguing, the next she was beneath him. He smelled strongly of ale and sweat, and was proving to be far stronger than she would have expected him to be.

"Brother Paul, remember who ye are!" she cried as she struggled to keep him from mauling her. "What about your vows?"

"I am a mon first," he muttered as he tried to pull up her skirts yet not lose his grip on her. "I have prayed for guidance and strength until my knees bled from the kneeling on them, but still ye tempt me. I have set harsh punishments for myself, but still ye haunt my dreams. I have tried so hard—"

Brother Paul was suddenly removed from on top of her, his sentence ending abruptly in a strangled gurgle. Keira stared in wonder as Liam held the man several inches off the ground with one hand. Liam's beautiful face was hardened by fury while Brother Paul's was white with fear.

"Ye obviously didnae try hard enough," Liam said, shaking the man slightly. "Ye are an idiot. And if ye e'er touch the lass again, ye will be a *dead* idiot."

Keira was just scrambling to her feet when Liam flung the terrified monk aside. She gaped as Brother Paul landed hard on the ground several feet away and sprawled there, gasping like a fish out of water. As she turned to stare at Liam, Kester stumbled up to them.

"M'lady! Are ye hurt?" asked Kester.

"Nay, just a wee bit bruised," she replied, smiling at the youth to ease his obvious concern. When she looked at Liam again, she suddenly became aware of the fact that he had rushed to her rescue and manhandled Brother Paul on his broken leg. "Och, Sir Liam, ye should ne'er have rushed out here! I thank ye, but ye could have damaged your leg."

" 'Tis already damaged." Liam's anger was fading, and he was becoming acutely aware of the intense pain in his broken leg.

"I meant ye could have ruined whate'er healing there has been."

"Ah, weel, ye may be right." He realized he had dropped his

crutch as he had reached for the monk and looked around for it. " 'Tis verra clear it doesnae like being stood on."

Keira quickly picked up his crutch and handed it to him, then moved to his other side to give him even more support. The man was suddenly very pale, and there was a faint sheen of sweat upon his face. He had to be in agony, but he made no sound.

"Kester, see that Brother Paul returns to the monastery," she said to the boy as she began to help Liam back into the cottage.

"Aye, m'lady." A scowling Kester moved toward the groaning monk. "There will be a dire penance to pay for this."

The boy seemed quite pleased about that possibility, Keira thought, then hoped he was right. Brother Paul deserved some punishment for trying to force himself upon an unwilling woman and, worse, for convincing himself that it was all her fault. She doubted he would be punished for that latter idiocy, however. There were undoubtedly many at the monastery who would agree with him.

As soon as she had helped Liam onto the bed, Keira began to remove the bindings and wooden slats from his broken leg. The fact that he remained still, his arm flung over his eyes and his breathing a little ragged, told her that he was in a great deal of pain. She prayed he had not undone all of the healing that had begun.

When she found no sign of further injury to his leg, she breathed a heavy sigh of relief. He had obviously caused himself a great deal of pain, but he had not actually hurt his leg. Keira glanced at him, but he still had his eyes covered. His breathing had eased a little, and she wondered if he had swooned. She knew she could ease his pain, but she was a little reluctant to reveal her skill. Then she scolded herself over her fears. The man had already been told that she had found him because of a vision, and he had not cried her a witch. There was also the chance he would not even realize what she had done. After one last glance at his face, she placed her hands upon his leg and closed her eyes, sensing where the pain was the worst and working to ease it.

Liam felt Keira's small, soft hands upon his leg and peered at her from beneath his arm. The touch of her hands smoothed away the worst of his pain. There was a growing warmth and a strange, not wholly unpleasant tingling. His eyes widened as he realized she knew exactly what was happening to him, what her touch could do, as she stood there with her eyes closed and an intense look of concentration on her sweet face. A brief twitch of fear rushed through him, a superstitious fear of the miraculous, that he quickly dismissed. Even though he felt a little dizzy when she finally took her hands away, he knew deep in his soul that she could never hurt him, or anyone, that she truly was a healer.

He forced himself to hold fast to the pose of being nearly unconscious as she slipped her arm beneath his shoulders and poured cool, sweet cider down his throat. It was not all that difficult for he did feel dazed. She looked pale, and was trembling faintly. Liam watched her stumble over to the small table by the fire. His eyes widened as she gulped down cider and slathered honey over pieces of bread, shoving them into her mouth so fast her cheeks bulged slightly. He suddenly felt a craving for the food she was devouring so rapidly.

"Do ye think I might have some of that?" he asked.

Keira was so startled she nearly choked on the honey-drenched bread she was eating like a starved piglet. Then she felt the heat of a fierce blush burn her cheeks. She was standing before a beautiful man she desired with her mouth so full of food she could barely chew it and honey dripping off her chin. It was impossible to act as if nothing was unusual about her gluttony, but she decided to try anyway. Wiping the honey from her chin with a rag, she quickly spread some honey on a few pieces of bread, set them on a wooden plate, and took it to him. It was not until she handed it to him that she realized he could not have been unconscious while she had worked to ease his pain, that there was a good chance he knew what she had done. Although she saw no fear or condemnation in his eyes, she waited tensely for him to say something. She stood torn between the hope that he knew what she had done and accepted it and the hope that he had not noticed anything strange at all.

"Why are ye limping?" Liam asked as he savored the taste of the rich, honey-sweetened bread.

Inwardly cursing, Keira tried to think of a reasonable explanation for her sudden limp. When she eased a person's pain, it often flowed into her, and she had not yet fully mastered a way to remove it. That was not something she could tell him, however. She still clung to the small hope that he did not really know what she had done.

"Just a wee bruising from being roughly tossed to the ground by Brother Paul," she replied, pleased with her response until she saw the glint of amusement in his fine eyes.

"Ah, foolish me. I had wondered if in taking the pain from my leg, it had somehow entered yours. 'Tis odd that 'tis the right leg, too. Just like mine."

"One only has two legs. Nay much choice as to which gets injured." He knew, Keira thought, and wondered why she was still trying to deny her gift, especially since her evasions seemed to be amusing him so much.

"True." Liam finished the last of the bread, then idly licked the sticky honey from his fingers before asking, "Why cannae ye just take that pain away as ye did mine?" He had to bite back a laugh when she planted her small fists upon her gently rounded hips and glared at him.

Liam's amusement abruptly faded when he saw that behind her anger lurked fear and cursed himself for an idiot. Of course she would be afraid. Although her cousin had spoken of her vision, he had also stressed that the Murrays were cautious in the revealing of the gifts their clan was so heavily blessed with. There was danger in possessing such skills. Too many saw them as sorcery or the devil's work. The very last thing he wanted was for Keira to be afraid of him.

"Poor wee Keira," he murmured, "ye need not fret that I will be making the sign to ward off evil. Aye, when I kenned what ye were doing, I felt a wee tickle of superstitious fear, but I killed it. My cousin's wife kens your clan weel and has made it her duty to banish such nonsense from our heads and hearts."

Keira felt herself relax. "Who is your cousin's wife?"

"Fiona, once a MacEnroy. Connor MacEnroy's sister. He is wed to a cousin of yours, I believe."

"Aye, to our Gilly. I have met Fiona. She has a true skill at healing."

"Aye, that she does. So, do ye take in the pain?"

Sitting down on the bed, for she suddenly felt very tired, Keira nodded. "It has to go somewhere, doesnae it? I havenae yet mastered a way to rid myself of it. It doesnae last so verra long. Sometimes if I can, I think of standing in the rain or beneath a gentle waterfall, letting the cool water wash it all away."

She closed her eyes and struggled to fill her mind with the vision of herself standing naked beneath a gentle fall of water. Breathing slowly, she let the sensation of being cleansed fill her mind and body. Little by little, she felt the ache in her leg ease. Right behind that relief came a feeling of utter exhaustion.

"So, ye truly had a vision of me?" Liam asked, a little astonished at how the pinched look of pain slowly faded from her face.

"Aye," Keira replied, too tired to even open her eyes to look at him. "I just wish it had warned me of the attack upon you. We may have been able to stop it."

"Ye saved me from dying. 'Tis enough. Do ye often have visions?" When she did not reply, he looked more closely at her and realized she had gone to sleep sitting up. "Och, poor wee lass."

Cautiously, not wishing to make the bed move too much, Liam sat up. He gently grasped Keira by her shoulders to help settle her more comfortably upon the bed. She nearly fell into his arms, her body so limp and boneless he would think her dead except that he could see that she was still breathing. When he leaned back against the pillows, tucking her up against his side, she murmured something that sounded very much like a very courteous thank you. He then nearly groaned aloud when she wrapped her arm about him and nestled even closer, her soft cheek pressed against his shoulder. Every lustful urge he had sprang to attention, as did one certain mindless, impertinent part of his body.

Keira Murray MacKail was soft and warm, and she smelled nice. Lavender and, he grinned, a touch of honey. He was failing so miserably in remaining only distantly courteous to her, he wondered why he did not just give up. The idea appealed to him, as she did. Too much so. He now believed God had sent her a vision, one allowing her and Brother Matthew to save his miserable life. He could trust her. That did not, however, change any of the other reasons why he had felt it best to keep some distance from her. She was far above the reach of a cousin of a minor laird who was, in many ways, not much more than a common man at arms. He simply could not believe the Murrays' habit of allowing their women some choice in the matter of gaining a husband extended to one such as him.

"Keira!" Brother Matthew called as he hurried into the cottage.

Liam silenced the man with one sharp move of his hand. As Brother Matthew approached the bed, Liam noticed how the look of concern upon the man's face began to change into an expression of dark suspicion, and he sighed. It stung a little that his old friend would think him capable of seducing a woman who cared for him so well, but Liam suspected even the cloistered monks may have heard a few tales about him.

"She fell asleep sitting on the edge of the bed," Liam explained and fixed the frowning monk with a cool, unwavering stare, "after she had eased the pain in my leg."

"Putting salve upon your leg shouldnae weary her so."

So, they were more secretive about her healing hands than her visions, Liam mused. "Nay, no salve. Her hands." It was probably for the best that this particular Murray kinsman was a cloistered monk, Liam decided, for Brother Matthew's face was far too easy to read. "Come, old friend, we may nay have seen much of each other these last few years, but do ye truly think I could condemn the lass for her gift or nay have the sense to ken that it must be kept a very closely guarded secret?"

Brother Matthew sighed and rubbed a hand over his eyes. "Nay, of course ye wouldnae."

"Nor would I seduce a weelborn lass such as she, a new widow, and one who nay doubt sits higher above the salt than I e'er will." Liam smothered a pinch of guilt, for it was not a complete lie. He had every intention of trying to hold fast to that gallant attitude, but he was beginning to think that fate was working against him.

"Forgive me for the insult." Brother Matthew shook his head.

"None taken. I will confess that I havenae been verra saintly since I left here." Liam shared a brief grin with his old friend. "Nay, I mean her no harm. I but forgot to take care of my broken leg. When I saw that fool pinning her to the ground, I was so enraged I acted as if I had two good legs."

"He will be harshly chastised, though mayhap not as harshly as we might like. Did he hurt her?"

"Nay, though he handled her roughly enough to leave bruises. He was struggling to toss up her skirts when I saw them and rushed to play the hero. After I tossed him aside and the anger began to fade, the pain was excruciating. She did whate'er it is she does with those wee hands, ate like a piglet, then fell asleep in the midst of a conversation. She took the pain into herself," he murmured with a lingering wonder.

"Aye, 'tis how it often works. It takes her a while to cast it aside, and then she sleeps hard for a few hours. We are cautious about her visions, but such things are acceptable to many people. Healing hands, the ability to ease pain with a touch?" Brother Matthew shrugged. "That too often stirs dangerous fears and whispers of sorcery. I think her husband kenned about her gift, though she hasnae said so. I believe it is one reason he sought to wed her."

"He was unweel?"

"Och, he looked hale enough, but he was a troubled mon. She was told so by those of our clan who can sense such things, but she married him anyway. Keira can be stubborn. I ken I may worry o'er her too much. She is one of my favorite cousins, and these last few months have been verra trying for her. Aye, and she faces more trials in the months ahead. She is strong, but mayhap, too tender-hearted and nay verra worldly."

"Did she love her husband weel then?"

"I think she would have if they had been given more time, or at least, cared for him weel and been a good wife to him. She chose him because she was o'er twenty and had ne'er been much moved by any mon. She craved a family of her own, ye ken. Sadly, they were wed but three months, and he left behind no child."

"How did he die?"

"Murdered by Rauf Moubray, who also did her some harm. She managed to escape, but swore to her husband ere he died that she would help the people of Ardgleann, would wrest the land from Rauf's thieving hands."

"The mon set a heavy burden upon her wee shoulders by making her promise such a thing. How could he expect this fey lass to do that? I have heard of Rauf Moubray—dark tales of brutality."

"And probably all true. As for how she can fulfill her vow to her poor, ill-fated husband? I dinnae ken, and neither does she, especially as she is loathe to drag her family into this trouble." Brother Matthew lightly touched Keira's thick hair. "At such times, I can almost regret my calling for I am nay a warrior, I have few fighting skills to lend her, and yet I would like to be her champion."

"Then I *will* be," said Liam and tried not to be insulted by Brother Matthew's obvious look of surprise.

"Ye have a broken leg, Liam."

" 'Twill heal. She willnae be rushing off to save Ardgleann on the morrow, will she?"

"Weel, nay, but—"

"I owe the lass my life. The least I can do is try my best to make sure she doesnae get herself killed trying to fulfill the vow her husband pulled from her." He winked at Brother Matthew. "Aye, and I rather like the idea of being a champion. Mayhap, in years to come, someone will compose a song about me." He chuckled along with his friend.

" 'Twill make me rest more easily kenning that a strong mon stands by her in the battle ahead."

"Then 'tis settled."

"Aye, between us. Ye may find that wee lass isnae so quick to agree. As I said, she can be stubborn."

"So can I, my friend. So can I."

CHAPTER 4

An odd scraping and thumping noise came from just beyond the cottage door. Liam looked across the table at Keira and smiled. She was concentrating very hard on the chessboard set between them, plotting a move that would probably defeat him yet again. He wanted to drag her across the table and kiss those lips she was gently worrying with her teeth. What few scraps of resistance he still clung to after a month of being with her day and night were rapidly shredding. His growing feelings for her refused to be cowed.

"I believe Kester has just stumbled by for a visit," he said, grinning when she gave him a stern frown, for the silent scold was belied by the laughter in her beautiful eyes.

Keira stood up, moved one of the finely carved chessmen, and said, "Checkmate."

As she walked to the door, she grinned when she heard Liam softly curse. He had not beaten her yet, but he was good enough to present a real challenge. She doubted he would be pleased if she told him so. It might also sound very vain, she thought as she opened the door to find Kester brushing the dirt from his robes.

Kester smiled at her, and she smiled back. He was going to be a big, handsome man when he finally grew into those feet he kept tripping over. She also had the strongest feeling that Kester did not really want to become a monk, that he would do his best but would never be really happy. That bothered her, but as yet, she had no ideas of what, if anything, she could do about it. If nothing else, she had far too many concerns of her own to deal with, troubles that left her with neither the wit nor the strength to deal with someone else's.

"M'lady, someone has come looking for Sir Liam," Kester said, his dark blue eyes wide with curiosity.

"Who?" demanded Liam as he moved to stand behind Keira.

"A woman named Maude, Lady Maude Kinnaird."

Liam cursed softly, his anger enhanced by the way Keira tensed. "Has anyone told her I am here?"

"Not as yet, but I fear someone will soon. Is she your enemy?"

"Nay, she is but a nuisance. I believe her husband is, however."

"Her husband?" Keira turned to face Liam. "She is wed, yet she chases ye about the country?"

Liam found it a little daunting to be stared at by Keira and Kester, both looking shocked. It was also irritating to see the glint of censure in their eyes. He did not have the time to explain matters, however, nor did he feel particularly inclined to. He briefly savored a few very dark thoughts about Lady Maude Kinnaird, who seemed unable to understand the word nay, then the sound of approaching horses drew his gaze beyond Keira.

"Someone told her, curse their eyes!" He yanked Kester inside, nudged Keira out of the way, and slammed the door shut. "Bar it," he ordered and limped over to retrieve his sword from where it had been set upon a heavy chest at the foot of the bed.

Keira turned from barring the door and gaped when she saw Liam donning his sword and scabbard. " 'Tis just a woman! Do ye often greet your cast aside lovers with a sword?"

"She isnae my lover," Liam snapped.

"Ah, weel, sir, at the monastery she said—" began Kester.

"I dinnae care what the woman said. I begin to think she is mad."

"Liam, m'love!" called a woman from just outside the door. "I ken ye are in there!"

For a brief moment, Keira saw a very beautiful face peering in the small window by the door. Then Liam slammed the thick shutters closed on both the cottage windows. Kester hurriedly lit a candle on the table to ease the sudden darkness. Keira winced as the pounding started on the door, loud and a little frantic.

"Liam, my sweet prince, please speak to me! How can ye treat me so unkindly after all we have meant to each other?"

"We havenae meant a cursed thing to each other," Liam replied. "Not now. Not ever."

Compared to the woman's strident voice, Liam's tone seemed almost pleasant, but Keira could hear the hard, cold bite of anger. She rubbed her forehead as a sharp pain started between her eyes. She wanted to blame the woman's pounding on the door for the rapidly blooming ache in her head, but she knew it was born of far more complicated things.

"I have left my husband for ye, sweet Liam!"

"Curse it, woman, I ne'er asked ye to do that!"

" 'Tis the only way we can be together. I have money. We can flee to France!"

This, Keira decided, was a sign that it was far past time for her to leave the shelter of the monastery. She had let this man slip into her heart. Keeping a distance had not shielded her at all. Listening to this woman speak so fulsomely of her love for Liam and hearing his cold, angry replies made Keira wonder if she had actually been drawn to a man who did not really exist except in her imaginings. This was certainly not the smiling, teasing man she had come to know, nor the gallant knight who had ignored his pain to save her from Brother Paul. She was ashamed that she had allowed herself to forget the needs of the people of Ardgleann, to convince herself constantly that Sir Liam still needed her care just so that she could remain close to him. It was obvious he could choose from a vast array of women to care for him and shelter him. Keira grabbed her saddle packs and began to pack her things.

"Jesu, Maude, will ye just go away?" Liam lightly pounded his head against the wall and wondered if the madness that seemed to have taken possession of Maude was now afflicting him.

"Ye have a woman in there, dinnae ye? How can ye turn from all we shared with such ease? How can ye break my poor heart so? But I shall forgive ye, my dearest love. I wasnae here to comfort ye after ye were hurt, so I ken I bear some of the blame for your fall from grace."

"Ye daft woman, I fell from grace years ago. Fell so hard and fast I am surprised the ground didnae shake." Liam heard some men laugh and realized Maude had a few of her personal guard with her. Then he grasped the full import of her words. "How did ye ken I had been hurt, Maude?" he demanded, and abruptly, Maude was silent. "Maude, how did ye ken I was hurt?"

"The monks told me," Maude replied.

Liam looked at Kester, who shook his head, and then he frowned at the door. "I ask again, Maude, how did ye ken I was hurt?"

"Robert taunted me with the tale, Liam! He tormented me day and night with talk of how badly he had hurt ye, of how he had seen to it that ye would ne'er beguile a lass with your beauty again. I had to come to ye, to help ye! Can ye nay see that?"

What Liam could see was that Maude was lying. He was almost certain of it. Ignoring her continued pleas to let her inside so that she could make amends for her husband's crimes against him, Liam turned to look at Keira and nearly gaped. She was busy stuffing all of her things into her saddle packs, which had sat in a far corner of the cottage, untouched, for the entire time he had been there.

"Keira, what are ye doing?" he demanded.

"Leaving," she replied. "Ye are weel able to care for yourself now, and if ye need anything, 'tis evident ye can find all the aid

ye need. I have a vow to fulfill, and 'tis past time I saw to the doing of it."

"*That* isnae aid," he said, pointing toward the door. "That is
the reason I was near beaten to death and left to rot."

"Then, mayhap, ye shouldnae have meddled with another
mon's wife."

"I didnae meddle with her!"

"Nay? She just imagines that ye are her love? Her sweet
prince? 'Tis all in her head, is it?"

It was, but Liam could see that Keira was in no mood to listen. Even Kester, who had lately taken to dogging his heels like
a faithful, adoring puppy, looked doubtful. Liam could not
really blame them for their disbelief. He was in the middle of
this insanity and still had trouble believing it. Nothing he said
or did dissuaded Maude from her rabid pursuit of him. It
would sound undoubtedly vain if he said so, however.

"Liam! Ye must let me in now! Robert is coming!"

Liam cursed and moved to the front window. He cautiously
opened one of the heavy, iron-banded shutters just enough to
peer out and cursed again. The burly Laird Kinnaird could be
seen rapidly approaching the cottage, six equally large men
riding hard at his heels. For a woman who claimed to love him,
Maude was doing a very fine job of getting him killed. He
slammed the shutter closed as Laird Kinnaird reined in before
the cottage.

There was a part of Liam that wanted to break something,
wanted to have a long, exhausting temper tantrum. He had
spent the last fortnight wooing Keira with a patience he had
never used before, winning her trust, and gently pulling confi-
dences from her. It was wrong of him, of course, but he had
not been able to stop himself. He had even planned to try and
steal a kiss this very night. All his work was for naught now, and
he was a little surprised at how furious that made him, furious
and heartsore. Glancing at Keira, Liam rather doubted she
would even shed a tear for him now if Laird Kinnaird gutted

him on the threshold of the cottage they had shared for a month.

"Cameron, ye bastard!" bellowed Laird Kinnaird. "Cease cowering in there, and come out to face me like a mon!"

Keira frowned at the door. Angry and hurt though she was, the arrival of this enraged husband made her afraid for Liam. She told herself it was because Liam was in no condition to fight anyone, that her sense of fairness was offended. It was a lie, but she tried her best to cling to it.

"I mean to make sure ye have naught left to cuckold another mon!"

The way both Kester and Liam paled slightly and glanced at Liam's groin would have been amusing if the threats being hurled were not so heartfelt. Keira knew she could not simply walk away and leave him to his fate. The woman was, to Keira's way of thinking, as guilty as Liam, but no one was threatening to maim her. Although Lady Maude's arrival had revealed a side of Liam she did not like and had shattered the few dreams she had been foolish enough to indulge in, Keira knew she would hate herself forever if she did not do all she could to save him.

"Best ye leave now," she said.

"If I step out that door, I am a dead mon," said Liam, "or will soon wish to be." Liam could not believe Keira truly meant to usher him coldly out of the cottage to face the raging Laird Kinnaird.

Something heavy crashing against the door made Keira wince. The little cottage was built of stone, and the door was of thick, iron-banded oak, but she did not think it could take too much of that sort of punishment. She tossed aside the sheep-skin rug upon the floor, revealing a hatch door set into the floor. Beneath it was a tunnel that would lead them to the stables. She looked up at Liam, idly wondering how she could have been so stupid as to ignore the possibility that such a handsome man could be a licentious swine.

"Hurry and collect your things, my sweet prince," she said.

Liam gritted his teeth against the urge to demand Keira never call him that again and hurriedly gathered up his belongings. "Where does that lead to?"

"The stables. This cottage was built to withstand a great deal, but the ones who built it kenned that it wasnae impregnable. So, a way to flee whilst the attackers weary themselves trying to break in."

"If we ride out of the stables we are sure to be seen. That could put ye in danger as weel."

"Then 'tis a verra good thing there is a back way out of the stables, aye?" Although Liam had become quite good with his crutch, Keira suddenly realized he would have great difficulty getting down the small wooden ladder into the tunnel. "Kester, take Sir Liam's things for him. Ye and I will go down first so that we may be ready to help him if he stumbles upon the ladder."

It was on the tip of his tongue to proclaim loudly that he did not require the help of a small woman and a too thin boy just to climb down a ladder, but Liam bit back the caustic words. One look at the ladder told him it was not going to be possible to climb down nimbly with his stiff right leg. He tossed his crutch down to Kester and carefully began to climb down, gritting his teeth against the pain every time he had to put weight on his bad leg. Once at the bottom, he leaned against the ladder and willed away the pain. He had no time for it now. The sound of Laird Kinnaird working hard to batter down the door was almost deafening.

"We had better shut the hatch door," Keira said when Liam finally moved away from the ladder. "It can be weel secured from this side. That will slow down any pursuit."

"I will close it after ye leave," said Kester. "And cover it o'er again."

"Nay, Kester, 'tis too dangerous. That mon out there sounds nearly blind with rage. Ye must come with us. Ye can flee to the monastery from the stables."

"E'en blind with rage, no one will mistake me for Sir Liam, if only because my hair is brown, nay red. Ye go, m'lady, and I will hold their attention here. 'Twill give ye a better chance of fleeing unseen."

"Lad, at some point e'en that fool will ken that 'tis too quiet in the cottage," said Liam.

"Oh, that fool will think that ye are still within, Sir Liam," said Kester, and then he grinned.

Keira knew Liam was probably staring at Kester with as much amazement as she was, but she could not tear her gaze from the boy in order to confirm that. Kester had sounded just like Liam. The fact that Kester's voice usually ranged from high to low several times in a sentence when he spoke made it all the more astonishing.

"How did ye do that?" she finally asked.

Kester shrugged. "I just do it. I can mimic most of the monks. 'Tis just a wee game I play."

"Keep playing it, lad," said Liam. " 'Tis a true skill ye may find some use for one day. I am just nay sure that ye will be too safe playing that game now. Laird Kinnaird isnae too sane at the moment."

Kester frowned. "I willnae stand near the door. 'Twill give the mon a wee bit of time to look about and see that I am nay you."

"Ye do that," said Keira, "and as soon as that door looks to crack open, ye start yelling in your own voice. That will certainly make him look about, for 'twill make him think that there are several people inside."

"Aye, m'lady, I will do that," agreed Kester.

Keira watched as the boy scrambled up the ladder. When the hatch door was shut, she hastily beat back a sudden wave of fear. She truly hated small, dark places. She especially hated small, dark places under the ground. They reminded her a little too much of the grave. The light from the lantern did not penetrate the dark all that well. She shook her head when she heard Kester yell something extremely obscene at Lord Kinnaird in Liam's voice.

"I am certain he didnae learn *that* in a monastery," she muttered.

"I wouldnae be too certain of that. None of the monks were born there, after all," said Liam.

"Weel, if Kester isnae careful, when Sir Kinnaird finally stumbles inside, he will be fair to frothing at the mouth after having had to endure so many insults."

"The lad will be fine. He may nay be able to walk two yards without tripping o'er his own feet, but he is quick-witted. Now, lead on. It may yet occur to that bellowing laird that someone should stand guard in the stable."

Keira started down the tunnel, alarm at that possibility spurring her onward. She closed her mind to the tight quarters of the tunnel, to the pervasive smell of damp earth and thought only of the opening at the other end. There lay freedom. She just wished it meant freedom from Liam. Keira knew he would be at her side for a while yet, and she suspected he would reside in her heart and mind for many years to come.

Once at the end of the tunnel, Keira handed Liam the lantern. She climbed the ladder to the hatchway and carefully lifted the door just enough to peer around the stables. To her relief, there was no sign of any of Laird Kinnaird's men, and even better, it appeared that Kester had almost completely shut the stable door after attending to the animals that morning. There was little chance that anyone besieging the cottage would be able to see her and Liam in the stables. She hurried to climb out of the tunnel, then after setting down all she carried, knelt by the tunnel opening to take Liam's belongings as he handed them up to her.

Liam inwardly cursed as he had to be helped up the final step of the ladder by Keira. Although he was deeply grateful for all of her help and knew he owed her his life, he was weary of being an invalid. He knew a great deal of his irritation at the moment was because it was his problem that had sent them fleeing the comfort of the cottage, yet he had to depend upon a boy and a tiny lady to extract him from it. Once inside the stable, he quickly gathered up his things and hurried to ready his horse as Keira covered their route of escape. This much, at least, he could do for himself, he thought crossly.

As Keira moved to saddle her dark gray mare in the stall next to Liam's horse, Gilmour, she said quietly, "There is a way out at the rear of the stables. Once outside, there are, oh, five yards or so of open space before ye enter the wood. A few more yards after that, and the wood grows thick enough to hide us."

"Mayhap we should lead our horses o'er that more open ground," said Liam.

Keira glanced at his right leg, still swathed in linen bandages and wooden slats. He wore breeches with the right leg sliced open to just above the knee. Over the bandages and wood he wore an odd sort of deerskin boot one of the monks had sewn for him. The foot of the boot had been made a little too big to allow for swelling, and the shaft of the boot was simply two flaps of leather brought up front and back and tied onto his damaged leg with lengths of rawhide. It all worked to make it nearly impossible for Liam to bend his leg at the knee.

"If we were to be seen doing that, we would have to mount quickly, and I think ye will find that ye cannae do that," she said.

Liam looked down at his strapped up leg, thought about how he needed to move to mount his horse, and silently repeated every curse he could think of. He had gotten so good at managing his everyday needs that he had deluded himself into thinking he was self-sufficient. Now he knew he could not adequately defend himself, or others, from an enraged husband or even mount his horse without assistance. He might be able to forgive Maude for the beating he had suffered, but he doubted he would ever forgive her for this constant battering of his pride, this seemingly unending helplessness.

"Aye, ye are right," he replied, unable to keep all of his anger out of his voice. "S'truth, I think ye will have to help me mount." He led his horse out of the stall and waited for her to give him a hand.

Keira led her mare out of her stall, then moved to give Liam help in mounting. She beat down the sympathy she felt for him by reminding herself of the reason why he was so injured. The punishment had been too harsh, but a man had to expect some retribution from a husband he had wronged. Keira knew a lot of her anger was born of hurt, of feeling like a complete fool. One glimpse of Lady Maude's stunningly beautiful face had been more than enough to harshly remind her of her own lack. For a brief time, she had actually begun to believe his pretty words and sweet smiles were for her alone, that they had truly meant something. The truth was bitter. A man who could win a woman like Lady Maude could never really be stirred by a woman like her.

Once Liam was settled in the saddle, Keira said, "I must needs shut the door after we leave, so just ride into the wood. Dinnae wait for me until ye are deep into the shelter of the trees."

Liam hesitated only a moment before nodding. He had feared that Keira might try to leave him now, setting her own trail, but her words implied that she would ride with him for now. After having to be helped into the saddle, he was hard-pressed to believe he could still be her ally, her champion, but he knew that sense of defeat would pass. If nothing else, he could help her gather the men she would need to retake Ard-gleann.

Ducking to pass through the door she had opened, Liam made his way toward the wood, waiting tensely for any outcry every step of the way. Once sheltered within the trees, he watched Keira carefully make her way toward him and breathed a sigh of relief when she reached his side unseen by Kinnaird and his men. Whatever Kester was doing, it was working to keep all attention fixed upon the cottage.

"We shall ride to my cousin's keep Scarglas," he told her.

"I intended to return to my kinsmen," Keira said.

"Nay alone, and until this leg of mine heals, I am hindered in my ability to protect ye. Scarglas is but three days ride from here. Mayhap more if we run into any trouble. There will be men to escort ye home there, and supplies for the journey."

It made sense, too much sense to argue with, so Keira nodded. "Lead on."

Liam began to do just that, hiding his face in case his expression revealed the relief he felt over her acceptance of his plan. Taking her to Scarglas was a good plan, but it would also give him time alone with her. He would probably need every moment of that time to ease her anger and regain the ground he had lost owing to Maude's arrival at the cottage. By the time they reached Scarglas, he wanted her to have told him of the challenge she faced and to have accepted his part in the battle ahead. He also hoped to renew his wooing, to regain her trust. One glance at her face told him that might prove to be the hardest battle of all.

CHAPTER 5

Keira glanced over at Liam and silently cursed. The man looked so pale she was surprised he was still in the saddle. Her anger and disappointment had obviously smothered the healer in her for a while for she had not taken a moment since fleeing the cottage to consider what a long, hard ride might cost him. Even she was feeling a bit sore, and she was not suffering from any injuries. Since he had taken the lead in their flight from the enraged Lord Kinnaird, she wondered why he had said nothing about the pain he was so clearly suffering. Manly pride, she supposed, and shook her head over such foolishness.

"I think 'tis time we stopped for the night," she said.

" 'Tis still light enough to ride," Liam said, although he ached to get off his horse and rest his leg.

"Aye, but ye look ready to fall out of that saddle."

Liam hated the fact that she could see how he suffered with each movement Gilmour made. "Nay, I—"

"Sir Liam, I am nay strong enough to catch ye if ye start to fall or move ye from wherever ye land, and a fall could cause serious damage to your leg. Ye are but a fortnight from having all of that binding off. Do ye truly wish to start at the beginning again?"

He gave her an ill-tempered grunt in reply. "About an hour from here, there is a wee village. We can rest there."

She knew it was all the concession he would make, so Keira said nothing more. Men could become stubborn when their pride was at stake. There was a chance that if she pushed the man too hard, he would try to ride even further than the next village, and she had no wish to spend the coming night keeping a vigil over his unconscious body or resetting his leg. Instead, she decided just to keep a very close watch on him until they reached their destination. She just hoped the man had the good sense to give up before he swooned.

By the time they rode into the little village, Liam could barely see straight. He reined in before a small alehouse that let rooms to travelers and fought the urge to let himself just fall to the ground. Taking slow deep breaths, he pushed aside his pain and struggled to steady himself before Keira came to help him dismount. He hoped she was quick for he desperately wanted to get into one of old Denny's surprisingly clean and comfortable beds.

Keira studied Liam closely as she helped him dismount. For the last few moments of their ride, he had looked so poorly she had been tensed and ready to hear his body hit the ground. He was still pale, but once off the horse, he no longer looked in danger of fainting. She did, however, keep close to his side as they entered the alehouse. A moment later, she heartily wished herself miles away as a fulsome, dark-haired woman cried out his name and nearly knocked him off his crutch with the force of her embrace. Liam had obviously passed this way before, she thought crossly.

He was cursed, Liam decided, as he gently, but firmly, extracted himself from the buxom Mary's rather tenacious embrace. Although he was willing to concede that he may have been greedy in his enjoyment of women, he did not think he deserved this amount of punishment for his sins. There was no need to look at Keira to know how she was taking this smiling proof of his somewhat intemperate past. He could almost feel the chill of her anger. This was going to make it even harder to convince her that Lady Maude was simply deluded.

" 'Tis good to see ye again, Mary," he said politely, his hands on her arms to hold her at a distance.

"Och, aye, 'tis good to see ye again as weel," Mary said. " 'Twill soon be e'en better, when we—"

"Allow me to introduce my wife," he interrupted hastily, not wanting Mary to get too precise in her reminiscing. Keira undoubtedly knew he had bedded this woman, but she did not need to know the how, the when, or the where.

Keira opened her mouth to heartily deny Liam's claim, but a quick, sharp look from him made her choke back the words. Her common sense told her there were some very good reasons for such a pretense. She would rather share a room with a man she was beginning to think was a rampant lecher, than sleep alone and unguarded. Some of the men gathered in the alehouse did not look as if they would be troubled much by a locked door or an unwilling woman. For all of his faults, Liam would never try to force her. It was going to be a long, uncomfortable night, however, she thought as she forced herself to briefly smile a greeting to a gaping Mary. When her mind added a lot of nasty qualifications after the woman's name, Keira hastily silenced it. It was not Mary's fault that Liam seemed unable to keep his breeches laced tightly against temptation. She just wished she could stop her mind from filling her head with painful images of Liam and Mary together, in a bed, naked.

"Married?" Mary screeched finally, then quickly took a step back and curtsied somewhat clumsily to Keira. "So that is where ye have been, Liam. Och, aye, and ye have been injured. Your cousins came here looking for ye, ye ken."

"When?" asked Liam.

"Oh, twice now. They last stopped here three, mayhap four, days ago." Mary grinned. "A fine-looking crop of braw laddies. We did have fun."

So, perhaps her mind was not wrong in naming Mary a whore, Keira thought. A pretty, cheerful one at that, and one who made no secret of her wanton ways. It did not matter. She knew men often sought out such women, some even after they were married. Her own kinsmen did so while they were free of all vows and bonds. It did not make it any less painful to know that Liam had done so or to have to look one of those women in the eye.

It does not matter, she sternly told herself. For a little while she had fooled herself, allowed herself to think she could be of interest to a man like Sir Liam. It was good that she had been awakened from that dream before she had done something there would have been no retreating from.

After gleaning what information he could about his cousins, Liam requested a room, a bath, and a meal. As a still chattering Mary led him and Keira to the small bedchamber they would share, Liam kept glancing back at Keira to make sure she was still with him. Her continued silence was making him uneasy.

There would be no wooing Keira this night, he thought as Mary ushered them into a bedchamber, still talking. Liam idly wondered if Keira would even speak to him, and for a brief moment, thought that silence might be welcome. He had never noticed how much Mary talked, but then, he had been too busy scratching an itch to care, he ruefully admitted. It pained him to admit it, even if only to himself, but his cousin Sigimor may have been right when he had said there might come a day when he paid for all that scratching. Liam just did not think he deserved to pay so dearly.

Keira remained silent as a bath was prepared for her. She would truly like to speak pleasantly and to act as if she cared not at all that Liam was a lecherous swine, but she feared what might burst out if she opened her mouth. When he left her to her bath asking only that she not take too long for he would also enjoy a wash with warm water, Keira sighed and began to undress. As she sank her weary body into the warm water, she sighed with pleasure and could almost feel sorry for Liam because he would not be able to enjoy this delight. It would be another fortnight before he could sink himself into a bath, and even then, he might need help getting in and out until his leg grew strong again.

Her mind suddenly filled with images of a naked Liam, and she was the one helping him bathe. She could almost feel the muscles and taut skin beneath her hands as she soaped his fine, broad chest. Keira shook her head and cursed herself for an idiot. Liam did have a fine, manly chest, but it was obviously one that had been touched by far more female hands than she cared to think about.

A strong urge to weep swept over her, and she scrubbed herself vigorously until it passed. The man was not worth her tears, although a few of her dreams had been so sweet she supposed they were worth grieving over. Worse, she had the sinking feeling it would be a long time before she could banish the man from her dreams. Keira doubted those dreams would be pleasant ones now either, for her mind seemed to have tenaciously grasped the thought of what Liam had done with all those other women and kept tormenting her with far too many clear images. Now she would probably find that her dreams of him were more like nightmares.

Somehow, she would find the strength to tear the man out of her heart and mind, she promised herself. It had been foolish to allow him to wriggle his way in, but she was through being a fool. From this moment on, Liam Cameron would simply be that man with a broken leg, someone she was helping in her capacity as a healer.

Keira hoped she could act with all the confidence she was bringing forth in these lectures to herself. Liam was hard to resist, even when she was angry with him. Even when fulsome brunettes flung themselves into his arms, she was more hurt and disillusioned than angry. Her gallant knight had feet of clay, and she could almost hate him for that.

Once done with her bath, Keira wondered what to wear as she dried herself. Since Liam had seen her in her night shift and robe many times, she decided to wear them. As soon as he was done washing himself, she would rinse her clothes out in the bathwater to rid them of the dust and the scent of horses gained from their ride.

She was just braiding her damp hair when Liam returned. He brought in a tray heavily ladened with bread, cold mutton, cheeses, oatcakes, and apples. It was plain fare, but Keira's stomach still growled with anticipation.

"Dinnae wait on me, lass," Liam said as he set the tray down on a table, inwardly sighing when her only reply was a cool, stiff nodding of her head.

Keira was just about to sit on the stool by the rough-hewn little table when Liam stripped to the waist. She had to clench her teeth to hold back an involuntary murmur of pleasure. The man was dangerous, she thought crossly as she hastily moved her stool so that her back was toward him.

Liam glanced at Keira as he washed and almost smiled. Her back was so stiff and straight he was surprised it did not hurt her to sit like that. That she was so angry with him was not amusing in the least, but the way she showed her anger was, if only just a little.

What troubled him more was that he had the strongest feeling he had disappointed her in some way. He doubted she was unaware of how men behaved, especially young men with no wife or betrothed, so exactly how he had disappointed her was somewhat of a puzzle. That she believed he had cuckolded Lord Kinnaird could be some of it, but he doubted all of her kinsmen were innocent of that sin. She had apparently formed some strange idea of him as some perfect, genteel knight, chivalrous and pure. Well, the last few hours had certainly shattered that image.

That, at least, was a good thing, he told himself firmly. If she had envisioned him thus, it was a role he could never play for long. He was better natured than many of his kinsmen, was more able to think before he acted, but he had as many faults as any other man. After living with him for a month, he was surprised she did not know that, but then, he had been on his best behavior.

He could explain Maude, and felt confident that he could get Keira to at least try to believe him. It irritated him that his word was not good enough, but that could be dealt with. If Keira had not met Mary, who had made it painfully clear that he and she had once been intimate, he might have already begun to win Keira to his side. Unfortunately, in Keira's eyes, that latest meeting had only added veracity to Lady Maude's claims.

Frowning a little as he sat by the tub and struggled to wash his hair, he wondered if it might be best to just let her stay angry. Everything within him immediately rebelled at that thought. He knew she deserved someone higher born, someone with a fuller purse and someplace fine to call home, but he was now determined to try to win her for his own. Although he was not sure what he felt besides lust, when he looked at her, he saw his mate, his partner, and the mother of his children. If in gaining that, he had to reach high and angered a few people, so be it.

After squeezing the water from his hair, he gave it a brisk rub with the drying cloth and then struggled to his feet. The way Keira started to turn, obviously moving to help him, and then visibly stiffened as she turned back to her meal, caused a flicker of hope to stir within him. She was not completely cold to him. Anger and disappointment he could deal with, bothersome as they were, but if she had utterly rejected him, he feared he would have been at a complete loss as to what to do.

He sat down across from her at the table and helped himself to some food and ale. Watching her closely as he ate, he felt that small spark of hope grow hotter. In the tense way she sat and in the way she would start to raise her head to look at him only to return slowly to staring at her food were proof that she was finding it hard to ignore him. If she were now completely cold to him, looking at him would not be a thing she would need to avoid so strenuously. Regaining her trust would be difficult, but he felt he could do it with hard work and patience.

A small part of him was angry that she would not simply accept his word, but he would do his best to smother that resentment. There was good reason for her to question the wisdom of trusting blindly in his word. In the past few hours, she had heard one woman claim him as her lover, making each harsh response he had made to Maude and his vigorous attempts to avoid the woman look like the actions of a callous man who used women mercilessly for his own pleasure. And then, she had been confronted with Mary, a woman he *had* bedded. If the situation was turned around, he suspected he would be angry as well. Violently angry, he thought with a little surprise, hastily banishing the images of Keira with another man. He just had to convince her that even though his past might be nothing to be proud of, if he pledged himself to her, he would hold to that vow.

Liam's eyes widened slightly when Keira made a noise that sounded very much like a soft growl and then abruptly stood up. She moved toward the bath, gathered up the clothes she had worn, and started to wash them in the bathwater. He slowly smiled and began to eat with real enjoyment, his lagging appetite fully restored. Keira Murray MacKail was most definitely *not* cold toward him. Let the battle begin, he thought, and nearly laughed.

Keira was disgusted with herself. She had been living with the man for a month. One would think she could easily conquer her need to look at him. When he had been too weak and injured to tend to himself, she had seen every part of him. True, he had not been quite so beautiful, but once the swelling had eased and the bruises had begun to fade, he had grown more handsome each day. She was sure he had reached the limit by now. Since she had been looking at him in this pleasurable guise for several days, it was past time to cease finding it such a delight.

As she wrung the water from her shift with a vigor she feared might ruin it, Keira admitted to herself that she had abruptly left the table because she was within a heartbeat of demanding that he put his shirt back on. That would have told him far too much about how she felt. Anger was something she could explain away. What woman would not be angry to discover that the man she had worked so hard to heal was little better than a hound constantly sniffing the air for a bitch coming into season? She also suspected that most women would be as hurt and angry as she felt for one of the reasons she was rather ashamed to admit to—this hound had not sniffed *her* out.

It hurt more than she cared to admit, far more than Duncan's sorrowful lack of desire for her. What that told her about the state of her feelings for the man was something she was too terrified to look at closely. He had been cloistered in a remote cottage with her for a whole month, and he had not even kissed her. Was it any wonder she felt such a strong need to weep she could barely swallow her food?

Something white flashed before her eyes and splashed into the bathwater. Keira stared down at Liam's shirt. Slowly, she picked it up. He obviously expected her to wash it. For a moment, she savored the image of pinning him to his seat and making him eat it. She glanced at him, seeing that he had already returned to the table and was calmly eating the last of the food. He smiled sweetly at her, and she glared at him before turning back to her washing.

Liam smothered a laugh. That glare had been so sharp he was surprised he was not bleeding. He had always thought his cousin Sigimor's tendency to stir people into a rage an odd way to sort out problems and conflicts, but he began to see some merit in it. Keira was definitely smoldering at the moment. If he kept poking at that fire, it would soon flare up, and then all those words she was choking back would come out. He suspected he would not like some of what she said, but at least he would no longer have to guess at what she was thinking.

He made a few idle attempts at conversation, but was glad when Mary and her two brothers appeared to remove the tray and the bath. Talking to Keira was no better than talking to himself or the wall, for what few responses she made were indistinct murmurs and something that came perilously close to a grunt. Then Mary began to speak of something from the past, a particularly lusty time when he and a few of his cousins from Dubheidland had stopped for a night. Liam quickly ushered the still chattering woman out of the room, but could see from the narrowing of Keira's eyes that it had probably been too little, too late. Inwardly cursing to himself, he sat on the edge of the bed and began to remove his boots.

"What are ye doing?" asked Keira.

Glaring at Liam, she tried to banish Mary's words from her mind. It was not easy, and Keira doubted it would get much easier for a long while. Mary had not said anything very precise, but she had said just enough before Liam had pushed her out of the room to give Keira a vague idea of what had gone on in the past. Now her far too keen imagination was running wild. She was going to have to strangle it, or she would never sleep again.

"Going to bed," Liam replied even as he settled down on the bed, idly arranging the pillow until it was in just the right shape.

"We cannae share a bed."

"I have kept my breeches on. And we have lived together for a month."

"We have ne'er slept in the same bed. Sharing the cottage was necessary, especially until ye began to heal enough to do some things for yourself. Sharing this bed isnae necessary. Ye can sleep on the floor."

"I have a broken leg, if ye recall. It isnae pleased that I have bounced it about on the back of a horse for hours. I am sleeping in this bed. If ye arenae able to trust me to restrain my lechery for a night, then ye can sleep on the floor." The way her eyes widened slightly told him that a little too much of his anger and frustration may have been revealed in his voice. "I will use the top blanket. Ye can wrap your wee self up in all the rest." He pulled the cover over himself and closed his eyes.

Keira hesitated only a few moments before shedding her robe and climbing into bed. Her knight could be ill-tempered and very ungallant, she mused. This was probably the best proof of how much his leg must ache. There was also the fact that he had never touched her in any overtly seductive way in all the time they had been together. Keira doubted any man could hold to any guise for so long without some brief glimpse of his true self slipping by his guard. Therefore, it was painfully evident that she did not rouse his lechery, even though it was becoming increasingly evident that Liam Cameron was very free with his favors. Tightly closing her eyes, she fought back the pain caused by that hard, cold truth and settled herself more comfortably upon what was a surprisingly comfortable, clean bed. She was almost grateful for the exhaustion that seemed to have settled into her very bones for it meant even her troubled thoughts and foolish, aching heart would not be able to rob her of much sleep.

"So, all your kinsmen were virgins ere they wed, were they?" Liam asked quietly as soon as he felt her relax beside him.

Now that was definitely a growl, he thought and grinned, not surprised when that furious noise was her only reply. Although he was willing to admit that he could have used a little more restraint in the past, he was not about to meekly accept being treated like a leper simply because he had not held himself inviolate until marriage. He had taken only what was offered, had made no woman any empty promises just to draw her into his bed, had never stolen a woman's virginity, and had never touched a woman who was betrothed or married to another. That last rule was going to be the one he would make Keira understand and believe in. In the confrontation he was pushing for, he would finally have a chance to explain all of that, and he knew a confrontation was coming.

Keira was definitely smoldering, and he found some hope for himself in her anger. It seemed impossible to him that a woman could be so angry over his past amours if she had no feeling for him beyond kindness or friendship. He would feed that anger, pile fuel upon that fire every chance he got until she popped like a roasting chestnut and all those words she was holding in flowed out. As he felt his exhaustion pull him into the comforting realm of sleep, he also decided that when she did pop, he would make sure no sharp weapons were close at hand.

CHAPTER 6

Smooth, warm skin heated the palms of her hands, and Keira murmured with pleasure. Liam did have a lovely chest. She had seen men's chests before. In her capacity as a healer, she had even touched a few. Yet she could not think of a one that was as fine as Liam Cameron's. It was the first time she had ever felt it so clearly in her dreams, however. Despite the nagging voice in her head that said it was time to wake up, she decided she would linger in this dream for a little while longer.

She pressed her cheek against his taut skin and smiled faintly as she heard the pace of his heartbeat increase. At least in her dreams she could stir his interest. In her dreams, she was always sultry and tempting, the sort of seductress that made men pant. To hear Liam's breathing grow louder and unsteadier was sweet music to her ears. She ignored the whisper that flitted through her mind, saying that Liam was a man who panted after anything in a petticoat. It might be true, but in her dream, all she cared about was that he panted after her.

Since this was a dream, she gave into the temptation to kiss, and then lick, that warm skin. A softly hissed curse tickled her ears. Keira smiled against his skin and murmured his name. It made her almost light-headed with delight to know she could stir the blood of such a handsome man.

Long fingers threaded through her hair. She sighed with pleasure. When those lightly calloused hands gently cradled her face and exerted a little tug, she freely obeyed the silent request and tilted her head back. Warm, soft lips pressed against hers, and Keira was astonished by how clearly she could hear, feel, and taste her dream lover. When he nudged at her lips with his tongue, she readily parted them. The feel of his tongue stroking the inside of her mouth roused a heat within her so strong and sweet, full consciousness began to intrude upon her dream. She clutched his trim hips to pull him closer, desperate to remain unaware, to ignore the harsh voice in her head that said she was not dreaming. If this was not a dream, she would have to put a stop to it, and she did not want to.

"Lass," Liam said, not surprised by the hoarse rasp of need roughening his voice, "if ye dinnae get your hands off me now, 'twill soon be too late to retreat from this."

The sound of that deep voice tore away Keira's lingering confusion, and she opened her eyes. She stared into Liam's eyes, noting what a warm blue color they were for a moment before the heat of a fierce blush burned her face. She pulled away from him so abruptly she paid no heed to how close to the edge of the bed she was. A soft screech escaped her as she struggled vainly to regain her balance and then hit the floor hard. Liam peered over the edge of the bed, his eyes alight with laughter, and she closed her eyes.

"It wouldnae be wise to laugh, Sir Liam," she said, embarrassment and anger at herself making her tone of voice impressively hard and cold.

Liam sprawled onto his back, closed his eyes, and did his best to suppress both his urge to laugh and the desire racing through his body. When he had first felt her soft caress upon his skin and had noticed that her eyes were closed, he had feared she thought she was abed with her late husband. She had not been a widow for very long, and while still asleep, such confusion was possible. Then she had murmured *his* name. The desire he had been fighting to control had abruptly snapped every bond he had put on it.

He had known then, and still knew, that it was far from gallant to take advantage of Keira when she was still more asleep than awake, but he felt no guilt. From the moment he had set eyes on her, he had wanted to taste that sensuous mouth. It had proven to be as sweet as he had thought it would be. Then his sense of honor had reared its troublesome head. Once it had cleared some of the lust from his brain, he had also realized that he did not want to trick her into his arms. He wanted her to come to him willingly and fully aware of what was happening.

The sound of Keira hurriedly dressing reached his ears, and he chanced a peek at her from beneath his lashes. He did not think he had ever seen a woman blush quite that brilliantly. She also looked very cross and a little distressed, but he hardened his heart to her upset. That kiss had verified all his tentative hopes and exceeded all of his expectations. She would not be allowed to turn back now. He might have to steal a few more kisses before she accepted the strength of the passion that flared between them, but he was up to the task. Since his intentions were honorable, he felt no guilt over his plan to seduce her. Brief though the embrace had been, it had given him a taste of a passion hotter and richer than any he had ever felt before, and he intended to claim it for his own.

Liam's silence only added to Keira's embarrassment. In the brief time in his arms, caught between a dream and reality, she had exposed her desire for him. There would be no denying it now. He simply would not believe her. Desperate to get away from him, to regain her wits and self-control, she started out of the room.

"I will return shortly with something to break our fast," she said and made her escape before he could reply.

Slowly, Liam sat up. He took a few deep breaths to banish the remnants of his lust, although he suspected his body would ache with unsatisfied need for a long while. His little bird had flown for now, but she would not go far. While he dressed and waited for her to bring them some food, he would carefully plan the first step of his campaign to woo and win her.

Keira held the tray laden with food and drink and stared at the door of the bedchamber. She had stayed away for almost an hour, earning a few curious looks from Mary. A brisk walk in the chill morning mists had cleared her head but little else. She could still feel the warmth of his skin on her palms, still taste his kiss, and it made her ache.

Lust, she decided, was a treacherous thing. She had been able to keep it a secret, use it only to sweeten her dreams, but that kiss had unleashed it. It wanted her to ignore every rule and all good sense. It did not care if her heart was at risk. It was a mindless hunger. Keira greatly feared it could easily make her become the greatest of fools.

Wishing it were his shin she was abusing, Keira kicked at the door. Liam opened it, but stared at her legs. He then looked up and down the hall.

"What are ye doing?" she asked.

"Looking for the verra wee person who knocked at the door," he replied.

Biting the inside of her cheek to keep herself from laughing, Keira gave him what she hoped was a very stern frown. With a faint but impish grin on his face and a glint of laughter in his eyes, the man was almost endearingly attractive. It was probably one of but many ways he seduced so many women, she reminded herself. Her anger renewed, she nudged him out of her way and marched into the room. Even if she was free to do as she pleased, she would still fight his allure, for she had no wish to be just one in a multitude of conquests.

Liam allowed her to hold fast to her silence for now. He had tasted her desire and seen that he could still make her laugh. One look at her face had told him that she was doing her best not to reveal her amusement over his little jest at the door. He had also seen how she had stiffened her spine and banished it.

As they ate and then gathered up their belongings, Liam made only a few attempts to stir her simmering anger into a rage. He could see it would not take much to accomplish that, and he did not wish to have the confrontation he sought here, in a tiny room in an alehouse, within earshot of a woman he had once bedded. Especially not within earshot of a woman like Mary, for he had no doubt she would repeat whatever she heard to anyone who would listen. As they continued on to Scarglas, he would have hours of privacy to goad Keira until she was too angry to keep silent.

How had she missed seeing how irritating this man could be? Keira asked herself as she and Liam made camp for the night. She felt nearly nauseous from all of the anger and hurt churning inside of her. The worst of it all was that if she repeated his words to anyone else, they would not understand what was making her feel so crazed. The words only had power because of their shared time together and the tumultuous state of her emotions. It was as if he were poking at an open wound. There were times when she felt certain Liam knew exactly what he was doing, and that only made her angrier.

He gave her only the smallest assistance in preparing their meal. Keira knew his leg hurt him for he was slightly wan and there was a pinched look on his face. That had not stopped him from helping her before, however. It was as if all his gallantry had vanished, had been left behind in the cottage. The more she thought about him, his legions of women, and how he would not leave her in peace so that she could turn her anger and hurt into a nice, icy cold distance, the angrier she got. It was almost impossible to swallow her food.

"A good meal, lass," Liam said and gently tossed his empty wooden bowl at her feet. "'Twill be good to reach Scarglas, however. There is a lass there named Mag who can make the finest rabbit stew ye have e'er tasted."

"Do ye ken any lasses whose names dinnae begin with 'm'?"

she asked, surprised she could speak at all with her jaws so tense and her teeth clenched.

"Weel, aye. A few." He watched Keira closely as he said, "Anne, Brenda, Clara, Deirdre, Ellen, Fiona, Gay, Helen, Ilsa, Jolene, Katie—"

"The whole alphabet? Ye have rutted your way through the whole cursed alphabet?"

Here it comes, he thought, and prepared himself to remain calm and reasonable in the face of the insults he suspected he would soon have to endure. "Weel, nay. I dinnae think I ken a lass whose name begins with an 'x' or a 'z'."

"Ye are a lecherous swine, sir," she hissed. "Oh, I should have kenned it e'en before that fool woman arrived. Any mon as bonnie as ye are was certain to be one who spent more time with his breeches down than up and laced tight."

"I wouldnae say that," began Liam.

Now that she had begun to speak, Keira was unable to stop herself. "Nay, ye wouldnae, would ye? Just like *all* men, ye think it great fun and sport, aye, and your right to rut yourself blind. Ye have no more control than a stoat!"

Keira leapt to her feet and started to pace, but it did not stop the words from pouring out of her mouth. She was a little appalled at some of the things she was saying, but she could not seem to shut herself up. Every thought she had had since Lady Maude had come banging on the cottage door was coming out of her mouth. They had obviously festered in her mind and heart long enough.

"Men can be such hypocrites," she said after a lengthy diatribe that maligned men's morals and intelligence. "They demand chastity, purity, and abject faithfulness in their women whilst they try to slip beneath the petticoats of every maid, wife, and widow they can find. Men would rut with a hole in the ground!"

Shock that she had actually said such a crude thing broke through the red haze of fury that had taken control of her mind and tongue. There was a choked sound behind her, and

Keira blushed. When she felt Liam's hands rest upon her shoulders, she only briefly tensed against his effort to turn her around. The moment she was facing him, she rested her forehead against his chest. Not only had she said a lot of things she should not have, but she also did not feel all that much better for having said them. Worse, she greatly feared she had revealed far too much about what she felt for this man.

Liam grinned at the top of her head. The lass had a true skill for ranting. Although she had directed most of her sharp, scathing remarks at men in general, he knew they were meant for him. Some of them had definitely left a bruise. Although he was willing to accept the charge that he had been less than temperate, he had to wonder how she could think he, or any other man, could be as licentious as she imagined.

"A hole in the ground?" he murmured and laughed softly when she flinched. "I have ne'er done that."

"Oh, hush," she said, embarrassed right down to her toes. "I cannae believe I said that."

"Ye said a lot of things."

Since she could not clearly recall everything she had said, and did not truly want to, Keira just nodded. "I let myself believe ye were better than most," she muttered.

That hurt, but Liam decided it was for the best if her illusions were muddied a little. It would be impossible to live up to an ideal. He wanted her to know him and want him despite his faults. If she was going to be disillusioned, better now than later, after he had claimed her.

"Lass, men start looking about for a willing woman at a young age, ere their beards e'en grow noticeable."

"That doesnae make it right." Keira winced, afraid she sounded annoyingly pious and self-righteous.

"Nay, it doesnae, but there are women aplenty who are willing to scratch that itch."

"And ye are an extraordinarily itchy mon, is that it?"

"Mayhap, though I doubt any mon could be as, er, itchy as ye were implying, not if he wished to live a long life."

Perhaps she had exaggerated a little, Keira thought, but if he expected her to admit to that, he would root where he stood.

"I dinnae seduce maids out of their chastity, and I dinnae touch women who are betrothed or wed to another mon." He was not surprised when she lifted her head to scowl at him.

"Lady Maude said—" she began.

"Lady Maude lied."

He sounded so certain of that, his every word holding the ring of truth, but Keira still felt uneasy. "But she is so beautiful," she muttered.

"And that means that she must be telling the truth?"

"Ah, weel, nay, but it makes one question her hunting down a mon who says he doesnae want her. I would think she wouldnae have to chase any mon. Men must chase her."

"Oh, they do, and mayhap, that is some of the trouble. I didnae." Since she had not moved out of his light embrace, Liam began to stroke her slim back gently. "Aye, I have had my share of women." He ignored her grumbled *and more.* "Howbeit, I dinnae trespass. Some of that is Sigimor's teaching, and some is due to my years of training to be a monk. Betrothed lasses and wives have said vows afore God. I will have no part in the breaking of them."

Liam sighed and pressed his lips to her forehead. She was listening, but her expression told him quite clearly that she was not sure she ought to believe a word he was saying.

"I confess to being, mayhap, a wee bit free with my favors," he said as he began to brush soft, light kisses over her face. "I like, um, rutting. 'Tis that simple."

"Ye have no obligation to explain yourself to me."

"Aye, I do," he said, although he had no intention of telling her all of the reasons he would do so. "Ye saved me and nursed me. Ye must be wondering why ye e'en bothered." He smiled against her soft, sweet-smelling hair when she muttered a denial. "Aye, I think ye now wonder if despite the weeks we spent together, ye truly e'en ken the mon I am."

"I shouldnae have e'en tried to think I kenned ye at all."
Keira closed her eyes as he touched a kiss to the hollow by her
ear. "Ye shouldnae be doing that."

"Hush now, and let me speak my piece. As I said, I like rutting. 'Tis one reason I left the monastery. And, aye, I was often
intemperate. Sigimor warned me that I might pay for that at
some time, and I have, for I have disappointed ye." Again she
murmured a denial, but a quick brush of his lips over hers silenced her. "I have. All I can say in my defense is that I gave no
woman a promise or a vow, and so I broke none; I never seduced a lass, and I have ne'er stolen a lass's innocence or
touched a woman lawfully claimed by another mon.

"Though I will concede that there are too many Marys in my
past, not once did I encourage Lady Maude. I have no idea why
she chases me so, for as ye have said, she is a beautiful woman
and can have near any mon she wants. I was most clear when I
turned away from her, but she chooses to ignore what I said.
She is why I left the king's court. I ne'er thought she would
hunt me down."

Keira was finding it a little difficult to concentrate on Liam's
words. The feel of his warm lips against her skin was not only
making her blood run hot but was also wrapping a thick haze
around her mind. This was more than a man trying to calm a
woman who had just had a glorious, screeching fit, she thought.
With more reluctance than she liked to admit to, Keira eased
herself free of his arms.

"If I was a suspicious person, I might think ye were trying to
seduce me into believing you," she said.

"Ah, ye *do* think poorly of me, dinnae ye? Nay, lass, I was but
trying to make ye stand still long enough to listen to me. I am
nay sure ye have."

"Oh, I have."

"Yet ye think I was trying to seduce ye?"

"Weel, what was all that kissing and stroking for, if not seduction?"

A good point, Liam mused, watching as she cleaned out their bowls. Since thoughts of seducing her were never far from his mind, Liam could not adamantly deny her accusation. This time, however, he had simply been enjoying the taste of her skin, the absence of anger, and the feel of her lithe body in his arms.

"I wasnae doing that to seduce ye." He shrugged and smiled when she frowned up at him. "That was just because your fine skin was so close to my lips I had to steal a wee taste of it. Ye taste verra nice, lass." He grinned when she blushed.

"Ye see? Ye just cannae help yourself, can ye?"

"Actually, I controlled myself verra weel during the years I studied with the monks," he said quietly, and then he went to spread out their bedding.

Keira had the feeling she had angered him, perhaps even insulted him, with her suspicions. His soft flattery had moved her, and she knew she ought to scoff at it. Such words probably meant little to him, were no more than pretty compliments he sprinkled about like dewdrops. Yet, it would be so easy to allow him to soften her heart with such words and to steal away all caution with his kisses.

She slowly shook those thoughts out of her head. It would be lovely to forget everything and roll about in the heather with him, learning all the secrets of passion. There was no doubt in her mind that Liam Cameron had learned a lot of those secrets. Unfortunately, she could not allow him to learn hers. Too many people depended upon her to help them. The people of Ardgleann had waited long enough for rescue. If she weakened and Liam discovered the truth, those people suffering beneath Rauf's boot might find that their torment had no end.

As Liam tended to the fire, Keira readied herself for bed, slipping beneath the blankets just as he moved toward his bedding, set barely a foot away from hers. When he began to shed his clothes, she quickly shut her eyes. She was feeling less angry and more confused, not sure of what to believe. It was not a good time to see any part of his far too attractive body.

A lot of what Liam had said was easy enough to accept, although jealousy was a bitter taste in her mouth. He was a free man, who could do as he pleased. Compared to many men, he did follow some very admirable rules. Or tried to. Keira still found it difficult to believe that a woman like Lady Maude would chase after Liam unless she had been given some reason to. A woman as beautiful as that lady surely had too much pride, even vanity, to pursue a man, no matter how handsome that man was.

The jealousy was truly what she had to deal with. It gnawed at her insides, feeding her anger and hurt. She had spit out a lot of that poison, but it could all too easily return. Every time she thought of Liam with another woman, it returned, stirred to life by her jealousy and turning her into a person she did not particularly like. She also suspected it would soon turn Liam against her, and even though she foresaw no future for them, Keira did not like the thought of that at all. When they parted, she would like to think that now and again, Liam would remember her kindly, perhaps even as a good companion or friend. And if that did not make her the greatest of fools, she did not know what did.

Liam looked over at Keira when he heard her mumble something about a fool. Since she was not looking at him, he decided she was talking to herself, and he grinned. Keira was one of those people who sometimes thought too much, worrying a problem to death, but this time he would not tease her about it. There was a very good chance she was thinking over all he had said, of how he had not denied his past or excused it. That, he hoped, would give the weight of truth to all he had said he was definitely *not* guilty of. On the morrow, he would begin his wooing again and let her know that he would stand her champion in the fight to regain Ardgleann.

"Good sleep, my delicious Keira," he murmured.

He does it on purpose, Keira thought as she banished the urge to reprimand him sharply for saying such things. "Good sleep, *my sweet prince*," she replied and grinned at his ill-tempered grunt. Two could play at this game, she decided and felt so pleased with herself she had no trouble going to sleep.

CHAPTER 7

"Liam!"

The hint of panic in that one whispered word yanked Liam from the grip of sleep. He had his sword in his hand, and was crouched by Keira's side before he realized they were alone. For a moment, he wondered if Keira was suffering from some bad dream, but even in the gray light of an early dawn, he could see that she was awake. Her eyes were wide with fright.

"There is no one here, lass," he said and then frowned as he recalled her special 'gift.' "Unless . . . have ye had some vision warning ye of danger?"

"Nay, there is something in my hair!"

"Are ye certain? I would swear that Denny's beds are free of vermin."

"Not that. There is something far bigger than a flea or nit moving about in my hair. It has fur!"

"Probably just a wee mouse."

"Get it off me!"

Liam wondered how she could put all the force and emotion of an hysterical scream into a soft, hissing whisper. He put his sword down and slowly leaned over her. When he saw that there was indeed some creature moving around in her hair close to her neck and that it was bigger than a mouse, he drew his dagger. As he plotted how best to strike, the movement ceased, and an odd sound began.

"I think there may be two beasties in your hair," he said.

Keira frowned as she listened to the noise originating so close to her ear, and then she began to relax. "It sounds like purring."

"Purring? As in what a cat does?"

"Aye, although whate'er is in there doesnae feel big enough."

Sheathing his dagger, Liam moved to her other side. Cautiously, not yet certain of what might have nested in her thick hair, he began to move it out of the way. Two pairs of eyes stared at him but made no threatening move, so he leaned a little closer and then grinned.

"Ye have kittens in your hair," he said as he gently picked them up.

Keira sat up and stared at the two small kittens trembling faintly as they huddled together in Liam's cupped hands. "How did they get there?"

"There is a wee burn a few feet from here. They may have gotten free of the drowning sack. Or, they could have just been set out here to live or die as God willed it. 'Tis clear they saw ye as both safe and warm."

Taking the kittens from him, she laughed softly as they snuggled up against her breasts. She gently scratched each one behind the ears, and they began to purr again. Although she understood why some people had to rid themselves of kittens and puppies when there were too many of them, she hated it. She smiled faintly when she thought of Old Ian at home who was too soft of heart to perform such a grim chore and so kept an alert eye on the females, isolating them the moment they went into season.

Liam watched her stroke the kittens and sighed. Not only did the soft look upon her face make him want to kiss her, but it also told him they would be taking the two tiny creatures with them. When she looked up at him from beneath her thick lashes and lightly bit her soft bottom lip, he felt the strong tug of lust. Instead of moving the kittens away from her breasts and burying his face there as he so desperately wanted to, he sighed and shook his head.

"I suspicion we could think of some way to carry them with us," he said, and the smile she gave him was so beautiful he felt his heart clench.

"Oh, thank ye, Liam," she cried as she stumbled to her feet, still holding the kittens. "I will make a wee nest for them in one of my saddle packs." She looked down at the two kittens. "Best I make it with something I care little about as they are so verra young I doubt they will let me ken if they need a patch of dirt." She started toward the shelter of some nearby bushes, then turned back to hand Liam the kittens, and impulsively kissed his cheek before hurrying away again.

Liam looked down at the two small animals that could each sit comfortably in the palm of his hand. The little white one stared at him with big blue eyes, while the silver gray one looked all around. It, too, had odd eyes, the iris encircled with a ring of color similar to his own eyes. If he were of a superstitious turn, these two would certainly send a chill through him. At the moment, however, he could almost kiss them. Maybe fate was giving him a little help in winning back Keira's regard and trust.

When Keira returned, he gave her back the kittens and made his way toward the burn, intending to linger in his ablutions long enough to give her a little privacy. His leg ached, but despite waking in the night with a cramp that had nearly made him bellow out in pain, he felt he had not damaged it. He had a few other aches as well, ones that strongly reminded him of the fact that he had not ridden a horse in a month and had done little long, hard riding for a long time before that.

"Och, aye, I will make her a fine champion," he grumbled as he finally made his way back to camp. He was in the middle of lecturing himself about how well he was healing and that he would soon be strong enough to help her when he walked by the kittens. They were greedily devouring something out of one of the bowls, and he peeked around their bent heads to

see what Keira had found to feed them. Liam's eyes widened
when he realized the cats were eating the cold mutton he had
packed for himself.

"Ye gave them our mutton?" he asked as Keira walked up to
stand at his side.

"They were hungry, and I didnae think they would like oatmeal," she replied.

"I prefer mutton to oatmeal, too."

"Aye, I suspicion ye do, but ye are a big, strong mon who can
do without for a wee while."

He frowned at her, but she paid him no heed. Liam watched
her take the empty bowl away to clean and then pack it. When
he looked back at the kittens, they were busy washing their
paws and faces.

"Aye, I am nay surprised ye enjoyed that. 'Twas the tenderest
mutton I have e'er tasted."

"It certainly was tender," Keira said when she returned to
collect the kittens. " 'Tis why I gave it to them. They are barely
weaned, I think, and cannae eat tough meat."

Following her to the horses she had readied for them, Liam
watched her settle the kittens into a well-padded saddle pack.
"Have ye already named them?"

"Aye—Thunder and Lightning."

"Verra grand names for two wee balls of fur." Liam slowly
moved toward her until he had her neatly caught between him
and the horse. "Now, I have agreed to let ye take these wee
beasties with us and didnae yowl too loudly when they ate my
mutton. I think I deserve a wee reward for all of this forbear-
ance I have shown."

"I said thank ye."

"Mere words. Easily said and oftimes not meant."

Keira knew he intended to kiss her. She should stomp hard
on his feet and push him away, but she stood still when he
placed his hands against her horse on either side of her. Although she was still fighting a burning jealousy over his past, a
voice in her head asked why she should deny herself a little

taste of what the man handed out so freely. She could still taste the kiss he had given her, and it definitely tasted like more. Keira decided the only one she would hurt by accepting a little of the delight he could give her was herself, and that was a foolish concern. Even if he had never kissed her, it would still hurt to leave him.

She looked into his eyes and noticed that they were more blue than green again. It was sign of his desire, she realized, and she felt her blood warm in response. It might just be a man's base hunger, the sort stirred by nearly any woman in reach, but she was still moved by it. No other man had ever looked at her in such a way. Keira cocked one brow in a silent question and challenge.

Liam nearly growled in response to Keira's unspoken challenge, his whole body taut with the need to taste again the sweet heat of her mouth. For reasons he did not even dare to guess at, Keira was not going to retreat. It was his chance to show her the passion they could share while she was wide awake and fully aware.

The first touch of his lips against hers made Keira feel so hot and needy, she had to clutch at his broad shoulders to steady herself. When she opened her mouth to welcome his tongue, she heard him groan softly and felt him wrap his strong arms around her. The feel of his lean body pressed so close to her made Keira shiver with delight. She put her arms around his neck and tried to get even closer to his warmth. She had the strangest urge to crawl right inside of him.

That strange haze only he could rouse began to curl itself around her mind again. It smothered all good sense and silenced all the warnings her more prudent self wished to make. All she could hear was the voice demanding that she take more, take all he wanted to give her and revel in it. It did not matter to that voice that Liam had undoubtedly given *it* to more women than she could count, so long as he shared it with her, too.

He slid his hands down her back until he was caressing her

buttocks. When he pressed his groin against hers, shifting himself against her in a promise of all he could give her, Keira heard herself moan softly. The fever he stirred was growing too strong to fight, and a reckless greed was taking hold of her.

Why not, her reckless self whispered in her mind. Who would know? Had her husband not failed her time and time again? Did she not deserve a little joy, a short time of blind selfishness before she had to fulfill her vow to Duncan? Facing Rauf and trying to free the people of Ardgleann could easily mean her death. Why not grab a little pleasure while she could, fleeting though it might be?

Keira was a heartbeat away from casting all caution to the wind and taking this man as her lover when the horse shifted, bumping into her and Liam. Although Liam quickly righted them, Keira knew the moment of danger had passed. Fighting a deep sense of embarrassment over her wanton behavior, she pulled free of his hold. Only the taut look of desire upon Liam's face and the way his breathing was fast and uneven saved her from utter mortification.

"That was thank ye enough, I believe," she said as she turned her back on him to pretend that she was carefully checking her saddle before mounting.

Liam took a deep, slow breath in a vain attempt to cool his blood. He could still feel her soft curves pressed against his body, fitting his embrace as if she had been made just for him. Moving even more awkwardly than usual, he walked to his horse, reluctant to climb up into the saddle. It was a relief when it took Keira several minutes to realize he still needed help to mount, for it allowed him a little more time to gain control of himself.

He may have shown her the passion they could share, but he had also discovered something. Keira robbed him of all control, stripped away all of the lover's skills he had gained over the years. He had thought the way that the morning kiss had affected him had been due mostly to waking from a somewhat salacious dream of her only to find her in his arms. It was now obvious that it was simply the feel of her in his arms, the taste of her, and even the soft murmurs of pleasure she made that enflamed him. He had suspected that the passion they could share would be hot and fine, but he had never truly expected it to be as all consuming as it was.

Once mounted and trying to ignore his discomfort, Liam silently led the way toward Scarglas. Unless there was some trouble, they should reach it before the gates were shut for the night, and he was glad of it. It would be best if he and Keira did not spend another night alone together, at least not until Keira no longer saw him as some lecherous dog who would sniff around any woman's skirts. When they finally made love and he was lying sated and happy in her arms, he did not wish to face her guilt or recriminations.

Thinking of making love to Keira only renewed his need, making it even more uncomfortable to sit in a saddle, so he pushed such tempting thoughts from his mind. It was time to begin his campaign to convince her that he was the perfect man to help her defeat Rauf Moubray. First, he needed her to tell him more about Rauf, Ardgleann, and her vow to her late husband. She had not been very forthcoming, and he had been reluctant to prod her to speak of the man to whom she had been so briefly married. It had been jealousy that had made him so reluctant, and it still was. Liam was a little surprised that he could be jealous of a dead man, but ruefully accepted that he was. Until he felt certain Keira was his and his alone, he suspected he could, and would, be jealous of anything and anyone who drew her attention away from him.

Slowing the pace of his horse, he waited until she caught up with him. "When ye were preparing to desert me back at the cottage, ye spoke of a vow ye had made and needed to fulfill. What did ye mean? Did ye speak of the one ye made to your husband?"

"I didnae desert ye," she said and then frowned. "How do ye ken that I made a vow to my husband?"

"Your cousin spoke of it for he worries o'er ye." He

shrugged. "I did wonder from time to time why ye didnae speak of it. S'truth, ye rarely spoke of your husband."

Speaking of her husband only reminded Keira of all the pain and embarrassment she had suffered during her short marriage. She did her best to try to remember Duncan only as a good but troubled man who had been cruelly murdered. Except for the good friends she had begun to make in her short time as Lady of Ardgleann, she tried to think of her marriage as little as possible. She certainly did not want to discuss it in any detail with a man who could make her feel feverish with only a brief, warm glance.

Yet she had to say something. Liam knew about the vow, and Matthew had undoubtedly told him about the trouble at Ardgleann. Keira decided that was what she would speak of, and that alone. What had happened between her and Duncan, the abysmal failure of her marriage, and the secret she was now forced to keep were not Liam's concern.

"My cousin told ye about Rauf Moubray and his crimes?" she asked.

"Aye. The mon now holds what is rightfully yours. He killed your husband, and considering the mon he is, he is undoubtedly making life a misery for all who live at Ardgleann."

"Ye ken the mon, do ye?"

"Nay, I have ne'er met him, only heard of him. Some verra dark things are said about him."

Keira nodded. "I am nay surprised, and I suspect those tales dinnae e'en begin to reveal his evil nature. He is a brute, vicious, cold, and deadly. He entered Ardgleann by stealth, having tortured to death several poor souls to gain the information he needed to do so." She shivered as the memories of that day came flooding back. "He and his men cut down anyone in their way as they poured into the keep. Duncan made me swear that I would help his people if Rauf won the battle. He did. He cut poor Duncan to pieces, making sure each wound was an agony, yet not immediately fatal. He *wanted* Duncan to suffer. He *enjoyed* it."

"And then he came after you?"

"Aye, but he wasnae planning to kill me. If not for his need to humiliate me and to show me what he had done to my husband, I probably would ne'er have escaped him. He was so enraptured by his victory and so certain no woman would have the wit to do aught but what he told her to, he didnae watch me closely."

"But he did hurt ye. Matthew told me ye were sorely wounded."

"I was. I tried to fight him, and that enraged him. I managed to get out of the keep and found help in getting away from Ardgleann. Since then, I have hidden away at the monastery."

"Ye needed to heal from your wounds," Liam said, even though he felt certain that simple truth would not be enough to ease the guilt he sensed behind her every word. "And what is your plan now?"

"I must think of a way to fulfill my vow to Duncan and help the people of Ardgleann. They are a gentle people, peaceful and interested only in their work. Weavers, carvers, and the like. Craftsmen, nay warriors. I have left them in Rauf's brutal care for too long. 'Tis past time I fulfill my oath to help them."

" 'Tis time *we* fulfill that oath."

"We?" Keira fought the urge to accept his aid readily.

"Aye. We. I am going to help you."

"Nay, this is *my* battle. I am the one who made the vow. I am the one who must face the risks."

Liam was not surprised that she was refusing his offer. Brother Matthew had told him that she did not even wish to draw her kinsmen into the battle. He was ready with his arguments. He was also prepared to stay close by her side whether she wanted him there or not.

"Lass, ye barely escaped alive from what your cousin told me. Ye need help."

"This isnae your fight."

"I am making it mine."

"Liam, ye have a broken leg."

" 'Tis nearly healed. It will be healed by the time men are gathered to fight Moubray and the necessary plans are made for the battle that must be fought. Sweet Keira, would ye deny a mon the right to repay ye for saving his life? Would ye deny him the chance to be your champion?"

"Aye," she said. "I would most certainly deny ye the right to get yourself killed."

"And if ye refuse all help, how do ye plan to rid Ardgleann of this brute? I doubt he will just sit still as ye creep up on him and bury a dagger in his heart."

Keira was not about to admit that she had no plan. Her thoughts had been centered mostly on how to keep her family from joining her in fighting Rauf. She had seen what the man did to anyone who had the courage to face him, and she did not want her family anywhere near the man. For many of the same reasons, she did not want Liam to play at being her champion. His life had become too dear to her, something she had no intention of letting him know.

"There is no need to be so snide," she murmured. "I will think of something. Mayhap when he tries again to rape me, I will just gut him," she muttered, then cursed herself for letting that small secret out.

Liam grabbed her reins and stopped her horse. "That is how ye were injured? He raped ye?"

"He *tried* to rape me. I was injured when I objected rather strongly. Then he decided I needed humbling, so he was going to do it in the village, forcing all the people to watch."

The urge to ride straight for Ardgleann and kill Rauf Moubray was difficult to subdue. Liam wanted the man to suffer for hurting Keira. He wanted the man to suffer very badly indeed for what he had planned to do to her. Common sense pushed aside his mad impulse. The only thing he would probably accomplish if he rode off in a blind rage was to get himself killed.

"*We* will fight Rauf," he said firmly.

" 'Tis not right to risk the lives of others when I was the one who made the vow and I am the one who gains if that mon is defeated."

"Aye, ye will gain, but so will many others. The people of Ardgleann will be free. I suspect the neighboring clans will also gain, if only in peace of mind. A mon like Moubray is a threat to more than ye, lass. Landless and poor, he was only a passing threat, but now he has a sturdy keep to shelter in and whate'er wealth he can bleed out of the lands and the people there. He has walls to hide behind and coin to hire men and arm them. He has now murdered a laird and claimed lands that arenae his. Now he is not only an outlaw of the worst kind but also a true threat to all around him. How long before he decides one victory and the gain it brought him isnae enough? How long before he hungers for more? Nay, lass, *we* will fight Rauf, and I have nay doubt there will be many men ready and eager to join us in that fight."

He was right in all he said. Keira knew it, and it made her heart ache. "I dinnae want anyone to die because of a vow I made," she whispered.

Liam leaned over and gently kissed her. "I dinnae want anyone to die either, but sometimes the fight is worth the risk. Aye, 'tis your land and your people, but that doesnae change the fact that such a mon is everyone's curse. Trust me in this, at least. Rauf Moubray will soon bleed Ardgleann dry and look for more. I promise ye, those who live upon the borders of Ardgleann are already preparing for him to reach out for them."

When Liam released her reins and started to ride again, Keira hurried to keep pace with him "Do ye think those clans will wish to join with us?"

"Unless they are blind fools or cowards, aye."

"Ye seem so certain that others will wish to march against Rauf," she murmured, still uneasy about others fighting what she saw as her battle yet unable to argue with any of Liam's reasoning.

"I *am* certain. Rauf Moubray is like a rotting limb that needs to be cut off ere it kills the mon. I have no doubt in my mind that many of my kinsmen will be eager to go against him. Aye, some will do so because they like a good fight, but most will do so for all of those other reasons I mentioned."

"That is why ye insisted we go to Scarglas, isnae it?"

"Aye, one of the reasons. One thing my cousins ken weel is how to fight and how to survive."

Keira prayed he was right, for she knew she would forever bear the weight of every injury and death in the battle ahead of them.

CHAPTER 8

"This is where Fiona lives?"

Keira stared at the keep they rode toward with a mixture of awe and trepidation. Everything about it made one think of defense and battle. Someone had spent a lot of time, effort, and coin to make Scarglas as impregnable as any place ever could be. Only constant threat could inspire such an effort, and she had to wonder exactly what sort of man Fiona had married.

"Aye, 'tis Scarglas. They have had some troubled years, but things are more peaceful now," Liam replied.

"It looks as if they thought themselves under constant siege."

"In some ways they were. The old laird had a true skill for making enemies. Ye havenae heard much from Fiona since she married?"

"Nay. Grandmere does, and cousin Gillyanne, but I have heard naught that would have prepared me for this fortress."

"Weel, the old laird may take ye by surprise as weel then. He is ill-tempered, and ere he wed his latest wife, he seemed intent upon breeding his own army. Just remember, when it comes to the old laird, he is more bark than bite. We may be lucky, and he willnae be there. Of late, he has taken to traveling to visit his children who dinnae abide at Scarglas. Fiona quickly won his heart for she stands up to him."

"Aye, she would. Liam, I really dinnae feel right asking aid from your kinsmen when I havenae e'en asked it of my own."

"Then 'tis past time ye told them of your troubles." He silenced her beginning protests with a wave of his hand. "Brother Matthew may think ye have written to your kinsmen and told them at least some of the truth, but ye havenae, have ye?"

Keira sighed and shook her head. "That was wrong and I ken it, but each time I tried to write, I faltered. I couldnae think of how to say just enough without saying too much or rousing their suspicions. I am a little surprised that none of my kinsmen arrived at the monastery, but they may have forgotten how close Matthew and I were as children. It was many years ago."

"Ye best tell them something soon, lass. They may have already heard of your husband's death. The truth will fret them less than dark rumors."

That was true, but Keira had no time to agree or discuss just what she should tell her family. The moment Liam led them through the gates, they were surrounded by people. There were so many big, strong men gathered to greet them, she felt a little uneasy. A big, handsome redhead swiftly pulled Liam from the saddle. A silent, dark man with a scarred face helped her dismount almost absently, for his attention was fixed upon Liam. They had obviously discovered that he had gone missing, and she suddenly thought of all the rumors her family might have heard about her by now. It was definitely time to send them word, she decided as she grabbed her saddle pack before a young boy led her horse away.

She relaxed a little when Liam pushed his way to her side, wrapped his arm around her shoulders, and began to introduce her to everyone. There were so many that she held fast to only a few names, including Sigimor, the laird of Dubheidland, and Ewan, the laird of Scarglas. The others would have to be learned more slowly.

Liam held her hand as they entered the keep and were led to the great hall. Keira knew it was not exactly proper for her to allow such a familiarity, but she felt a strong need for his support. His cousins were somewhat overwhelming.

"Keira? 'Tis really you?" called out a woman.

Even as Keira looked around to see who had spoken to her, a slender fair-haired woman rushed up to embrace her. "Fiona?"

Fiona stood back a little and smiled. "Aye, 'tis Fiona. Have I changed so much in but five years?"

"Och, nay, but I think a lot has happened to ye in that time that no one told me about." She lightly touched one of the little scars that marked each of Fiona's cheeks. "And not all of it good, aye?"

"True enough, but we can talk about that later." Fiona tugged her away from the men, leading her to the head table and gently pushing her down into a seat. "I suspect ye are hungry and thirsty. Here. Let me take your saddle pack."

"Oh, wait." Keira saw no signs of dogs in the great hall, so she carefully removed the kittens from her saddle pack. "We found these sweet things in the wood."

In between hearing all of Fiona's trials and triumphs over the last five years, Keira told her some of her own as they ate and fed the kittens. Keira found herself debating the wisdom of telling Fiona the one thing she had not told anyone else. Although she was both shamed and embarrassed by what had happened in her marriage, one she had had such hopes for, she found she was hungry for the opinion of another woman. She felt certain she could trust Fiona to keep her secret, but Keira finally decided to give herself a little more time to consider the matter.

It was just as she was teasing Thunder into sitting up to get the small piece of cheese she was dangling in front of him that Keira realized it had grown very quiet. She looked around to find all the men standing near or sitting at the head table watching her and Fiona play with the kittens, their expressions an interesting mixture of amusement and disbelief. The soft warmth in Sir Ewan's eyes as he looked at Fiona told Keira why the woman had married such a dark, scarred, and solemn man. Keira had to work hard to smother the pinch of envy.

"There are cats upon my table, Fiona," Sir Ewan said.

"Kittens, Ewan," Fiona said. "Wee, helpless creatures cruelly cast out into the wood, alone, motherless, hungry, and terrified." She sighed dramatically. "Were Liam and Keira nay kind to give them aid and shelter?"

"And ye think that means they can eat at my table?"

"Weel, just this once." Fiona grinned and kissed his cheek. "Especially since your father isnae here. Now, have ye assured yourselves that Liam is weel and safe?" She glanced at Liam as he sat down on the other side of Keira. "Except for that broken leg, of course. Keira told me how it happened. Angered some mon, did ye, Liam?"

"Actually, I begin to think it was the woman who sent those men to beat me and toss me off a cliff," Liam replied as he helped himself to some bread, cold grouse, and cheese, then scowled at Lightning, who moved to sit by his plate. "Ye ate all my mutton, ye wee white piglet. Ye are not getting any of this."

Keira frowned as she thought over all that Lady Maude had said back at the cottage, and then she gasped as she realized Liam was right. "What a verra odd thing for a woman who calls ye her sweet prince to have done to ye."

Liam groaned and glared at a widely grinning Sigimor. "Lady Maude is a blight upon my life. If she doesnae cease this mad game, one day her husband *will* kill me."

"We shall have to sort that out," said Sigimor. "We cannae have the mon killing our *sweet prince.*"

"Oh, dear," Keira murmured when she realized her words had given Liam's cousins fodder for many a teasing remark. "Sorry, Liam."

"So ye should be," he muttered as, unable to endure the way Lightning's big blue eyes followed each piece of meat from the plate to his mouth, Liam gave the cat some. "My problem isnae the most important, however."

"Nay, the battle to free Ardgleann certainly takes precedence over your romantic entanglements."

"There is no entanglement with Lady Maude, and ye weel ken it, Sigimor. She is married. Unfortunately, she has her husband believing there has been something between us. But as ye say, that irritant isnae important now. 'Tis Ardgleann and Rauf Moubray that concerned me the most."

Sigimor nodded and poured himself some ale. "He is a boil that badly needs lancing."

"Do ye ken who he is?" Keira asked.

"I have ne'er met the mon," Sigimor replied. "If I had, we wouldnae be troubled with him now. I have seen what he is capable of, however. The mon is naught but a rabid beast. It will be good to kill him."

Keira felt Fiona tense at her side. She turned to see the woman staring hard at her husband. It was a little astonishing to see such a big, dark man look uneasy beneath that steady feminine gaze.

"Ye are going to war?" Fiona asked Ewan.

"I am considering joining this fight, aye," Ewan replied. "'Tis a just cause. The mon murdered Lady Keira's husband, nearly killed her, and has stolen her lands, and from all Sigimor has told us, the people he doesnae kill will wish they were dead. I willnae be riding off on the morrow. This requires some careful planning."

Although Fiona slowly nodded, Keira could still feel the tension in the woman. Sir Ewan obviously did as well for he kept hold of his wife's hand, almost idly stroking the back of it with his thumb. This was one part of war Keira had not given much thought to. It was not just the men who actually fought the battle who could suffer. There were loved ones left behind to wait and pray for their man's safe return. She wanted to say there was no need for such concern as she would allow no one to fight this battle for her, but there was no turning back now. Liam had told the men everything, and as her father liked to say, their blood was up.

After a few moments of idle talk, Fiona escorted Keira to a bedchamber. The woman said very little, breaking the thick silence only when she introduced Keira to the children in the nursery. Keira felt guiltier with every step she took.

"I am verra sorry, Fiona," she said the moment they entered the bedchamber she was to use while staying at Scarglas.

Fiona looked at her in surprise. "What for?"

Setting the kittens on the bed, Keira sat down on the edge of it. "For drawing these men into my troubles."

"Och, nay, this isnae your fault." Fiona sat down next to her. "*I* am sorry if my brooding made ye think that I blame ye. Nay, I but hate the thought of my Ewan going to war, and always will. I will set it aside soon. This is what men do. I but thank God my husband chooses his battles most carefully and does all he can to avoid a fight. He isnae like his father, who seemed to make enemies with astonishing ease. Although the old fool did finally see the error of his ways. Nay, this isnae your doing. 'Tis the fault of that brutal swine who has stolen your lands."

"That is what Liam said. That 'tis a just fight and that Rauf is a mon who, now that he has a place to hide in and coin for men and arms, will soon seek to steal from others."

"Exactly. 'Tis best to stop him at Ardgleann. I think it best if ye send word to your family. They would like to have a part in this, I am sure. I think they would also like to ken that ye are still alive."

"What do ye mean?" Keira asked, her voice softened by shock.

"I have had several messages from them asking for some word of ye. They have heard that your husband was murdered and by whom. They have also heard that no one has seen ye since that day."

Keira closed her eyes and rubbed a hand over her forehead, cursing herself for not thinking of such a consequence of her silence. "I had hoped they wouldnae hear such rumors. Foolish of me. I should be flogged for my thoughtlessness."

Fiona laughed and then kissed Keira on the cheek. "I, too, have been guilty of causing my family worry. When I first met Ewan and he decided to hold me for ransom, I refused to tell him who I was. I also decided that this was a fine place to hide from that madmon who was hunting me. It was a long time ere my family kenned if I was dead or alive, and in the time I held silent, I gave only a passing thought or two to the worry my disappearance would cause Connor. I suspect Sigimor will make Liam verra aware of his displeasure over getting nary a word about where he was or what had happened."

"Ah, true, 'tis a common sin, I suspect. Is my family looking for me then?"

"Aye. They have been here once, and I feel they may soon come again."

"Then I had best get word to them as quickly as I can. 'Twill be better for me if they have a few days to calm down betwixt getting my news and seeing me."

"Bathe, rest, and sup with us first. We can send a lad off to take the word to them in the morning."

Keira nodded, and Fiona left to order up a bath for her. The speed with which it arrived told Keira it had been anticipated from the moment she had arrived at Scarglas. With the bath came a box of sand for her kittens and a lovely clean gown of deep green wool for her to wear. The moment the last maid left, taking all of Keira's clothes to be cleaned, Keira sank into the hot bath with a sigh of pure delight. She was little embarrassed to admit it, even to herself, but one of the things she most appreciated about this hot bath was that she had not had to ready it.

It was not until she was done with her bath and sitting before the fire to dry her hair that Keira realized there was one thing wrong with all of this comfort. Liam was not here, nor would he soon join her. She gasped slightly at the sharp bite of pain that realization brought her. The parting had already begun, and she was not ready for it. There would be no more quiet talks before the fire, no more unwitnessed chess games, no more listening to him breathe as he slept only feet away from her. They would still see each other until Rauf was defeated, but the loss of that close companionship they had enjoyed for a month was more devastating than she could ever have imagined.

She loved him, and if that was not the height of idiocy, she did not know what was. She had not protected her heart at all; she had simply lied to it. Keira fought the urge to hurl herself upon the bed and weep until she was too exhausted with grief to move. That would solve nothing. She could not afford to wallow in despair either, for it would mark her face and she was expected to join everyone in the great hall later. Somehow, she was going to have to face them all, to face Liam, and pretend that everything was just as it had been before she had come up to this room. Staring at the comb she held and realizing that her hands were shaking, Keira wondered where she would find the strength for such a massive deceit.

Liam cursed as Sigimor scrubbed his back with far more vigor than was necessary. "If ye wish to punish me for nay telling ye where I was, please just hit me. 'Twould be easier to bear than having all the skin torn from my back." Then he sighed as he stared down at the bathwater he stood in while Sigimor washed him off. "And I would think the humiliation I am suffering right now should be punishment enough."

"I beg your forgiveness for nay being the best of handmaidens, my sweet prince," drawled Sigimor.

"Say that again, and I will beat ye with my crutch."

Sigimor ignored the threat. "Dinnae ken what ye find so humiliating either."

"I havenae had to be bathed by anyone since I was an infant."

Pausing as he started to wash Liam's hair, Sigimor frowned at him. "Except for the lasses, aye?"

"Nay, not e'en the lasses. Weel, Keira did wash me down whilst I was bedridden, but 'tisnae the same."

"Ye, the great and profligate lover, have ne'er bathed with a lass?"

"Nay," replied Liam between clenched teeth, then briefly closed his eyes when Sigimor just stared at him, silently awaiting an explanation. "Bathing is a verra private thing, aye? 'Tis an intimate act, and ye are verra vulnerable whilst doing it."

"The same could be said for rutting with a lass."

"I didnae promise to make sense. 'Tis just something I dinnae do. I dinnae stay the night with a woman either. Nothing I say will make sense to ye. Jesu, it doesnae always make sense to me. 'Tis just some boundaries I set out for myself, and I ne'er cross them. Aye, I like the lasses, and I like the rutting. I am kind to the lasses; I dinnae scorn them for being free with their favors; and I make them smile, make them feel bonnie. Howbeit, I dinnae sleep the night with them or bathe with them." Liam shrugged. "I was only after a wee bit of pleasure, nay more, and I didnae want any of them thinking elsewise. I liked some more than others, but I didnae want them thinking there was more to be found with me than just a wee bit of fun."

"Do ye ken, in a strange way, it all makes sense." Sigimor began to wash Liam's hair. "Ye are vulnerable whilst bathing and sleeping. That implies a great deal of trust and all, doesnae it? Now that I think on it, ye dinnae bed any of the lasses who work or live in the keep either, do ye?"

"Not in any of the ones I plan to visit often, nay."

Sigimor rinsed Liam's hair and then helped him out of the bath. Liam's embarrassment over being rubbed dry by his cousin was fleeting, for Sigimor was brisk and impersonal. Once dressed in his braies, Liam sat on the bed as Sigimor replaced the now wet and still dirty slats and bandages on his leg with clean, dry ones.

"The leg looks good," Sigimor said as he poured them each a tankard of ale. "A wee bit pale, and it looks as if ye have lost a wee bit of muscle in it, but that can be regained. Ye were lucky."

"Aye, I was. If Keira and Brother Matthew hadnae found me, I would have died. Slowly." When Sigimor nodded, then sipped his ale and kept staring at him, Liam asked, "What is it?"

"Ah, I was just pondering on ye and the lasses again. Do ye ken? I think ye have always planned on taking a wife."

"Doesnae every mon plan to do so at some time in his life?"

"Most do, but most of them dinnae draw such a clear line in the sand when they start their frolicking. Ye did. Ye may ne'er have realized the full reason why ye did, or ye may have forgotten it, but I think ye did it because ye planned to marry one day. There will be no confrontations with maids ye have slept with in your own home, and there will be things ye can share with your wife that ye have ne'er done with any other woman. I suspicion there are a few other things ye havenae done with those women as weel." Sigimor smiled faintly when Liam actually flushed, and then he nodded. " 'Tis for the best, as I think ye have already chosen your bride."

"Mayhap I have, though 'tis a verra high reach I make. I get all the gain. She only gets me."

"If she fits, what does that matter? I married an Englishwoman, the daughter of a Marcher laird."

"Because she fit."

"Aye. Perfectly."

"Keira thinks I am a lecherous swine." Liam smiled faintly when Sigimor laughed. "I need to woo her, to gain her trust, which I lost when that fool woman chased me down. And I fear, when we stopped at Denny's tavern and Mary made me verra welcome."

"Weel, once ye are wed, ye can let Keira ken how many things ye are sharing with her, things ye ne'er shared with another. 'Twill ease the pinch of jealousy o'er your past. Now, let me help ye dress so that we might go down to the great hall and sup ere those MacFingals eat everything."

Liam got the feeling Sigimor had a plan. The man spoke as if a marriage between him and Keira was already settled. Before Liam could question his cousin, however, Sigimor began to help him dress, talking all the while on the battle they would soon fight. It was not until Liam was seated at the head table in the great hall waiting for Keira that he realized he had just been cleverly and thoroughly diverted.

He looked at Sigimor who just smiled faintly, making Liam immediately and intensely suspicious. Just as he was about to question his cousin, Liam was diverted again by Keira's entrance into the great hall. She wore a beautiful green gown that enhanced the color of her eyes. Her raven black hair hung down her back in long waves, only loosely tied back with a thick green ribbon. She looked every inch the fine lady, and Liam felt his determination to claim her falter a bit. Seeing her thus made him painfully aware of how little he had to offer her.

Keira blushed faintly beneath the warm look Liam gave her as he helped her take her seat at the table. She had finally calmed herself, tucking her newly discovered feelings for the man deep inside her. Until they actually parted, she would do her utmost to keep those feelings securely caged. It would certainly help if they only met at times like this, she thought as she ate her food without really tasting it. Surrounded by people and indulging in constant conversation should make it easier to keep her unruly heart tightly bound, her emotions curtailed.

"So, ye nursed our sweet prince back from the brink of death at the monastery, did ye?" asked Sigimor.

It was hard not to smile when Liam sighed heavily and his kinsmen snickered, but Keira remained solemn as she replied, "On the grounds, aye. The monks sent us to a wee cottage they have on the border of their lands."

"And the two of ye stayed there alone together? For a month?"

The way everyone looked at her and Liam so intently began to pierce the fog of calm Keira had wrapped herself in. "Liam was in verra bad shape for the first fortnight, but by then, all of his injuries save for his broken leg had healed weel."

"Sigimor," Liam growled.

"What? I but search for the truth, as will her kinsmen," Sigimor said.

"The truth is that she cared for my injuries."

"Aye, alone, in a wee cottage, for a month. Just ye and she. And, save for your poor, wee broken leg, ye were your old self within a fortnight. Weel, we all ken what your old self was like, aye? I suspicion her kinsmen have heard a rumor or two, for they often send some of their people to the king's court. Word of this will spread. Ye ken it as weel as I do. Ye ken what must be done to repair her good name, yours as weel, and to placate her kin."

"I dinnae believe the monks will run about telling tales."

"Nay on purpose, but her kin might finally recall Brother Matthew, aye? Then there were others who found ye, and they arenae cloistered monks. Ye ken as weel as I what will be said of her if 'tis learned that she spent so long with ye alone. 'Tis neither fair nor true, but that willnae matter. I dinnae think her verra large family will be pleased, and they will want matters set aright. As I see it, we have two choices—we prepare ourselves for a feud with the Murrays, or we prepare ye and the lass for a wedding."

Keira had listened to Sigimor in growing horror as the meaning of his words finally penetrated her hard-won calm. Everything he said was true, which made it all so much worse. She could see by the looks upon everyone's faces that they agreed with Sigimor, and she could not blame them for that. There were many reasons why a forced marriage to Liam was a bad idea, but one in particular immediately leapt to the fore of her mind—the wedding night. The realization of all the problems that could bring her finally freed her tongue.

"Nay!"

CHAPTER 9

"Aye!"

Keira looked toward the doorway of the great hall and nearly cursed out loud. Two of her brothers stood there. It was obvious from the looks on their faces that they had heard the entire conversation. She fought the urge to leap up and run very swiftly to some place where they could not find her. As they strode toward the table looking eager to pummel someone, Keira wondered in which direction Ireland lay.

Her brothers did not falter once in their march toward the head table, and Keira realized that their gazes were fixed firmly upon Liam, not her. They were not friendly looks either. In fact, they were murderous glares. She quickly stood up and put herself between Liam and her brothers. Artan and Lucas were known to hit first and discuss the justification later. At the moment, they clearly felt they had plenty of justification to beat Liam until he was no more than a smear upon Fiona's clean floor. Since she doubted Liam's kinsmen would sit idly by while her brothers pummeled one of their own, she decided she was protecting more than Liam.

"Move aside, Blackbird," said Artan, his blue-gray eyes looking almost silver, a sure indication that he was in a fury.

"Nay," she said. "Ye are guests in this keep, and this mon is kin to these people. It would be rude to beat him here."

"Rude?" muttered Lucas, his eyes matching Artan's to a

shade. "Weel, let it ne'er be said we lacked good manners. We will take the mon outside and beat him."

"Ye cannae do that either. It wouldnae be a fair fight. He has a broken leg."

Liam smiled when both men peered around Keira, and he shifted in his seat just enough to let them see his bandaged and splinted leg. For one brief moment, he had been annoyed by Keira's attempt to shield him, and then good sense had prevailed. He did not wish to fight with two men he suspected were very close kin to Keira, even if he had not been hampered by his broken leg. Any fight started would also quickly turn into a melee. Since he had done no more than steal a few kisses, he did not think he deserved a beating anyway.

He studied the two men as Sigimor calmly began the introductions, revealing that they were Keira's brothers, Artan and Lucas Murray. They were of a size with him and were probably near his age. They were also extraordinarily handsome, and the way the few women in the hall gazed raptly at them only confirmed Liam's opinion. Their hair was the same rich black as Keira's, a little long and very thick. As the tension in their lean bodies eased a little, the silvery glint in their eyes faded into a softer bluish gray. When they suddenly fixed stern looks upon Keira, however, Liam tensed. He hoped they would not be too harsh or unkind, or all Sigimor and Ewan had done to ease the anger and tension in the air would be for naught.

"Ye look hale, lass," murmured Artan. "Doesnae she, Lucas?"

"Aye, verra hale," Lucas said after carefully looking Keira over, "for someone we were told was probably dead."

Artan grasped both of Keira's hands and looked them over, too. "And she doesnae have any injury to these wee hands either."

"Nary a bruise that I can see."

"Strange then, that she didnae write to her family to tell them she was weel. A wee word or two such as, I am nay dead and rotting somewhere 'twixt Ardgleann and Donncoill," said Artan.

Keira winced and flushed with guilt beneath their glares. "I hadnae realized ye thought I was dead."

"Of course ye didnae, for ye ne'er sent word to find out what we may have been told."

"There are good reasons for my silence," she began.

"Sit," said Ewan, waving both younger men to a seat at the table. "Eat and quench your thirst. As ye do so, the tale can be told. There is a lot that must be said and decided upon."

"Aye," agreed Artan as he and Lucas took their seats, "such as when the wedding will be."

Liam quickly grabbed Keira by the hand when it looked as if she was going to flee. He gently but firmly tugged her back into her seat. This was not how he had wanted things to progress between them, but he could see no way out of this rapidly closing trap they found themselves in. He may have been able to convince his kinsmen to give him time to persuade Keira on his own, but he doubted her brothers would heed him.

As the tale was told from the time of Duncan MacKail's murder to his and Keira's arrival at Scarglas, Liam kept a close watch on Keira. He tried not to be stung by how pale and upset she looked as the talk turned to marriage. No one liked to be dragged into a marriage they were not ready for. Even he found it irritating, and he *wanted* to marry her. The wooing would have to come after the marriage, he decided. He soothed his unease by reminding himself of the passion she had revealed and that, before Lady Maude had arrived, he and Keira had been very compatible.

"There is no need for this," Keira said, trying not to sound as desperate as she felt. "We did nothing wrong."

"We believe ye," said Artan, "and so do these good people, but few others will. The mon is kenned to have a winning way with the lasses. He is nearly a legend in some places."

"How nice for him." Keira briefly glared at Liam before turning her anger back on her brothers. "And ye think it a good thing to marry me to a mon who is so profligate he is a near legend?"

"Profligate is a wee bit harsh," Liam murmured, but no one paid him any heed.

"I have only been widowed for a few months," Keira continued. " 'Twould be unseemly for me to marry again so soon. Aye, and widows are allowed more freedom than maids, are they not?"

"They are, if they are discrete. Sharing a wee cottage with a mon for a month isnae discrete. Nor is sharing a bedchamber at an alehouse or traveling alone together for three days."

"Ye were that close behind us?" Liam asked.

"Aye. We finally recalled how close Keira and our cousin the monk always were and hied ourselves to the monastery. Got there whilst the Kinnairds were still arguing o'er ye. There will be nay more of that once ye are wed to our sister," Artan added in a hard voice.

"There wasnae any of *that* with Lady Maude to begin with." Liam inwardly cursed when he could see by their frowns that neither of Keira's brothers believed him.

"Artan, what does it matter what might be said of me?" Keira asked. "As soon as Rauf is removed from Ardgleann, I will settle there. Any gossip or rumor about me will soon fade."

"Will it? Will it fade fast enough to keep many of your kinsmen from having to defend your honor?"

Keira felt her heart skip with alarm. She opened her mouth to argue with that statement only to close it again. All she could think of to say was that such a problem would never arise, but she knew that was a lie. She could not bear the thought that even one person could be hurt or, God forbid, killed because of rumors about her. The fact that her brothers already knew so much made it certain that there would be rumors about her and Liam. Mary had obviously given them an earful from all her brothers implied, and Lady Maude appeared ready and willing to spread the tale. The fact that Lady Maude was chasing Liam all over the country would not stop people from listening to the woman or repeating whatever she said. The fact that the supposed sins had been committed on the grounds of a monastery would only make the lies more intriguing.

It was all so unfair, she thought. She and Liam had not done anything wrong. Although there was some comfort in the fact that everyone gathered in the great hall believed her, sadly, Artan was right to say that no one else would. In all fairness to Liam, it was not even his reputation that was at fault. Not completely. It was enough for most people that a man and a woman had spent weeks together alone.

When Liam put his hand over her clenched one, she stared at their hands as they rested on the table. His touch, the subtle stroking of his fingers, worked to ease the tension within her. She wished that touch could smooth away all the troubles that lay ahead. There was one particularly huge complication just ahead, and Keira had no idea how to solve it. By the sound of it, she and Liam would be married tomorrow, which gave her less than a day to come up with some solution, one that would not betray her vow to her late husband or the vows she would soon exchange with Liam.

" 'Tis our clan's way to allow a woman some choice in marriage," she said, trying one last time to put a stop to the marriage. "Ye are nay giving me one."

"Aye, choice is best for all concerned," said Lucas. "Ye were allowed that the last time. Howbeit, there are times when it cannae be allowed, and this is one of them. In the past, there were similar situations, but the couple sorted themselves out ere force needed to be applied. With a battle facing us, we dinnae have time to play that game."

"Weel, have at it then," she snapped as she leapt to her feet. " 'Tis evident ye dinnae need me to help in all your grand plans for the rest of my life."

Liam joined the others in watching Keira stride out of the great hall, Fiona quickly following her. The way all the men looked wary and chagrined as they watched the small, delicate Keira leave in a fury would have been amusing at some other time. At the moment, Liam was too busy trying not to take her reluctance to marry him too personally. He turned to frown at Keira's brothers.

" 'Twould be better if I was given time to woo her," he said, holding out little hope that he would be granted that time.

"Aye, it would be," agreed Lucas, "but there is a battle to be fought soon. Though I am reluctant to say it, fearing I may curse us in some way, men die in battle. We cannae wait until ye woo her." He frowned, looking more puzzled than angry. "And if ye had a liking for our Keira, why havenae ye wed her already? Ye have had o'er a month together with her to get the job done."

"I am a landless knight, and though my coffers arenae empty, they are nay verra full either. It took me a while to decide I simply didnae care that she can sit higher at the table than I can. Then, weel, a few problems arose, and I had to start all over again."

"Problems named Lady Maude and Mary?"

"I have never touched Lady Maude!" Liam realized he had shouted that denial and took a deep breath to calm himself. He gave Sigimor a crooked smile. "Though the words fair choke me, I confess ye were right. I am paying dearly for all that scratching."

"Aye, I feared that may be the case," Sigimor said. "Howbeit, I ken ye will only scratch that itch with your wife once ye are wed."

The looks of confusion Keira's brothers wore as they listened to that small exchange suddenly cleared, and Artan said, "Ah, so ye are one to hold to vows made. Good."

"What? No threat? No warning?" Liam subdued an urge to curse both men heartily when they just grinned at him.

"No need," said Artan. "I dinnae think anything we could do will cause ye as much misery as Keira will if ye break with your marriage vows." He frowned slightly. "Although our wee Blackbird didnae seem quite herself just now. A wee bit of her fire was gone."

Lucas nodded. "She didnae try to hit us or throw something

at us." He scowled at Liam. "Have ye done something to hurt her already?"

"Nay, although she was a wee bit disappointed in me when my past was exposed ere I could tell her about it. Yet once she ceased brooding on it and let me ken what she thought, there was fire there aplenty." Liam cast a brief scowl toward the door Keira had just marched through. "Yet she did seem, weel, subdued."

Sigimor nodded. "She did. When the two of ye first arrived, there was that air about ye that made me comfortable about demanding this marriage as I kenned I must. When she sat down here to sup with us, something had changed in her, and I wasnae so sure anymore. 'Twas as if in donning that fine gown, she had enshrouded herself in some armor." He shook his head. "I grow fanciful."

"I think not," said Ewan. "When she first arrived, I saw a lass like my Fiona. Open, honest, easy to read, even if ye dinnae always understand the words written there. When she came down after a bath and a rest, that lass was gone, and she didnae start to appear again until the talk of marriage began. Instead of looking into her eyes and seeing all sorts of emotions, twists, and turns and mysteries, it was as if ye peered into a looking glass." He blushed faintly when he realized everyone was staring at him in slight amazement. " 'Twas just a thought."

Liam grinned at him. " 'Twas a fine one. Exactly right. Curse it, the lass did some hard thinking whilst she bathed and rested. I will probably drive myself mad trying to figure out what twist or turn that mind has taken now."

"Ah, aye, Keira is one to do a lot of thinking," said Artan. "Ye will need to learn the look."

"The look?"

"Aye, the one she gets when she starts thinking. If ye learn the look, ye will have time to start talking and get her talking instead of thinking. She is a clever lass, but she can think her way into a tangle. As my Da says, ye need to push yourself in there to snip the threads ere she makes a knot ye will need days to unravel."

It required a long drink of ale for Liam to drown his urge to laugh, especially when he saw the laughter brimming in Sigimor's and Ewan's eyes. "Weel, whatever tangle she has gotten into will have to wait until the morrow," he said. "Mayhap we best decide what little we can about getting Ardgleann free."

"There is no heir?" asked Ewan.

"Only Keira," said Artan. " 'Twas part of the marriage agreement. The mon was the last of his line. He sought a wife to beget an heir, but if that failed, Keira would be it. He felt she had kinsmen enough to help her hold the land and care for his people. Of course, now she will have a husband. I suspicion the people will be pleased with that."

"I hope so." And, Liam thought, I truly hope Keira does not think her lands are the only reason I married her.

"Best we rid the place of vermin first," said Sigimor, turning everyone's attention to the battle they would soon face.

Keira nearly slammed the bedchamber door behind her, but she decided that would be childish. She was just starting to pace, desperately trying to think of some way to get free of the plans everyone was making for her future when Fiona entered the room. The sympathy in the woman's expression was both comforting and irritating. Keira appreciated the sympathy, but what she really needed was a solution.

"He will make ye a good husband," Fiona said as she poured them each some wine.

"A reluctant one," Keira said as she accepted the drink Fiona served her.

"I am not so certain he is reluctant. He put up no real fight."

That was true, but Keira quickly beat down the hope that stirred within her heart. "He was sadly outnumbered."

"Dinnae ye want him?"

"Of course I *want* him. How can any woman nay *want* him?

How can she nay like him? How can she nay want to climb to the top of some high mountain and yell out to all the women of Scotland, 'Ha! I have him now and ye dinnae!'" She smiled faintly when Fiona laughed, but then she sighed. "But so many have, havenae they? Had him, I mean."

"Aye. Any mon that handsome will ne'er reach his marriage bed untouched, Keira. E'en my Ewan, who was so appalled by his own father's licentious behavior that he controlled his passions with an iron fist, couldnae be chaste all the time. Sigimor, too, was verra careful in his habits. Then we have my brother Connor who wed your cousin Gillyanne. He had three women in the keep itself whom he bedded whene'er the mood took him."

Keira nearly choked on the wine she had just drunk. "Och, nay, please dinnae tell me that I must face that!"

"Nay. As far as I can tell, Liam doesnae take lovers amongst the women who work or live within Dubheidland, or here, or e'en at his cousin's keep. Mayhap he always kenned he would take a wife some day and didnae want the trouble that can bring. Or mayhap he didnae want the trouble it could bring *him* whene'er he went home or visited his kinsmen."

"Or mayhap he just needed to give it a rest."

Fiona laughed so hard she had to set her drink down on the table. It was an infectious laugh, so much so that, despite her somber mood, Keira laughed a little as well. It was perhaps foolish to fret so over the past, yet she could not ignore what Liam's past said about him. The man had bedded a lot of women. Worse, he probably had not had to do much to gain those favors. Women were driven to hunting him down. It did not promise a happy future.

"Keira, the mon was, mayhap, a little quick to accept all that was offered," Fiona said, growing serious again. "And it *was* offered. I wouldnae be surprised if e'en those who require a coin or two for the giving would have bedded down with him for free. I truly doubt any mon would refuse such, er, gifts. Ye must forget it as, I suspect, he has. He ne'er wanted to marry any of them, was ne'er betrothed, and was ne'er faithful."

"And, mayhap, he ne'er can be faithful."

"Oh, aye, I think he can be. He behaved himself at the monastery for five long years, didnae he? He also held fast to rules few men follow—no innocents, no lies or false promises, and no wives or promised women. He believes in holding to a vow. Many of these Camerons do. As my brother Connor once told me, a mon seeks out a woman because he has an itch and wants a wee bit of warmth. If the wife gives a mon that, why look elsewhere? It simply isnae worth the trouble it can cause. Nay verra romantic, but 'tis the way most of these men think. I believe the men in your family are of the same ilk."

"They are." Keira finished her wine and frowned into the empty tankard. "Do ye *truly* think Liam will hold to his vows?"

"I do. Why, once Sigimor thought my Ewan had a mistress and followed him, intending to beat some sense into him."

"And Sigimor has reared most of his *lads*, hasnae he?"

"He has. And Liam didnae spend five years training to be a monk because he had no place else to go. He has a deep belief, just nay a true calling to cloister himself. Such a mon takes vows spoken to a priest verra seriously. Come, I doubt there is any woman alive who weds a virgin."

Keira almost said she was pretty sure she had, but hastily bit back the words. It might not be true. It was just one of far too many excuses she had made for her husband's lack of desire for her.

For a moment, she seriously considered telling Fiona the truth, but her vow to Duncan stopped her. It had been wrong of him to make her swear to live a lie, but she had accepted that burden. She would not break her word now simply because it was inconvenient. The only one she felt she could tell the truth to was Liam—after he became her husband. She just could not think of a good way to do so or even begin to guess what his reaction might be. Keira greatly feared he would think her the worst of liars, that she played some cruel game with them all, or that she was so greedy she was willing to make fools of everyone just to claim Ardgleann.

"Do ye still grieve for your husband?" asked Fiona. "Is that what troubles ye?"

"Oh, I do grieve for him, but only in that he was too young to die and that he didnae deserve such a cruel death. I liked him and thought we could have a good marriage, but nay more than that. Howbeit, he at least chose to marry me. Liam is being forced to."

"Nay, not forced. Persuaded. I have known these men long enough to ken that not one of them can be forced to do anything they dinnae want to. As I said, Liam didnae protest much at all. In truth, I cannae help but think he had already decided to make ye his wife if ye would have him."

"Fiona, we have only kissed twice, and we didnae e'en do that until we left the cottage. He certainly ne'er said or did anything to make me think he wanted to marry me."

"Of course he didnae. Ye have money and land. He has naught. Ye are higher born than he is as weel. I cannae explain how or why I believe it, but I truly do think he already had marriage in mind. I think he was slow to give ye e'en a tiny hint because he thought it wrong to reach so high, then thought to woo ye." Fiona grimaced. "I havenae got a gift for such things as our Gilly does, but she told me that I do have a verra strong intuition about people, and I have kenned Liam for many years. I just feel certain that at least a part of him wants this and that he will make ye a fine husband. Dinnae ye care for him at all? Is that it?"

There was one truth Keira felt she could entrust Fiona with. "Aye, I love him. I think the seed was planted when I first saw him, and he certainly wasnae verra bonnie then. I havenae told him, and I probably willnae for a while. Unless I feel certain there is some scrap of the same emotion in him, I cannae risk it."

Fiona nodded and gave Keira a brief, tight hug. "I understand that verra weel indeed. 'Tis that fear that ye might cause him such discomfort by confessing it that ye ruin what ye do have. Or e'en more chilling, all ye get in response to baring your heart is something devastatingly mild like, 'That is verra nice, wife. Thank ye.' " She smiled when Keira chuckled. "Dinnae fret o'er what cannae be changed. Ye *will* be married on the morrow. Ye will also begin that marriage with more good than bad, I am thinking. So, as I told Sigimor's wife when she was fretting, just love the fool. 'Tis all ye can do. 'Tis my feeling that ye will end up with something as fine as Sigimor's wife and I have found."

Except that the two of ye didnae go to your husband still holding true to a vow given a dead mon, Keira thought. A vow that makes ye a fraud. A vow that has chained ye to a huge lie.

"So, let us prepare for your wedding," said Fiona, grasping Keira by the hand and tugging her out of the bedchamber. "A feast, some music, and all of that. But, first, we will find ye a verra fine gown to wear."

Keira was more than willing to fall in with Fiona's plans. Preparing for the wedding would keep her too busy to brood on what would happen after it.

CHAPTER 10

"Mayhap she fled in the night." Liam ignored Sigimor's laughter as he stared at the doorway of the great hall, wondering why Keira had not yet entered through it.

"I ne'er thought ye would be nervous at such a time," Sigimor said. "Not Liam, the greatest lover in Alba."

Liam cursed and scowled at his cousin. "I am nay the greatest lover in this land."

"I think a lot of women would disagree."

"Mayhap, but mostly because they dinnae ken any better. I like the bedding. What mon doesnae? I like the feel of soft skin and womanly heat. I e'en liked most of the women I bedded, but that was easy enough, for it was often a fleeting alliance. I can string pretty words together, and I ken where to stroke them to make them ready. That is the sum of it. No great skills. No wondrous secrets. 'Tis this cursed face they bed down with, nay the mon behind it. My sin is that I kenned that weel yet still took whate'er was offered."

"As any mon will if the lass is fair enough and doesnae stink too badly."

Liam laughed and shook his head. "Sadly true, and if we are *itchy* enough, we will probably ignore the stink." He sighed. "She doesnae want to marry me."

"No one wants to be told to get married, but most are. Marriages are most often arranged by the elders for gain or alliances. I think ye and the lass start out with more than most. Ye lived together for a month and are still talking to each other."

"More or less. That cursed Lady Maude sorely hurt my cause. And that maid at Denny's alehouse has a verra loose tongue. Aye, the lass is talking to me again after she brooded for a while, but she doesnae trust me to hold to my vows. I dinnae mind a wee bit of possessiveness or jealousy, but I am nay sure how long I can patiently stomach my wife thinking that I cannae control my lusting at all, that I will be betraying her at every turn."

Sigimor nodded. "That *would* cause trouble. It could be that she is uncertain of ye and of herself. 'Twill take time to cure her of that. I fear that for a while, ye willnae have much time to work upon strengthening your marriage or easing your wife's qualms. There will be a battle to plan and to fight. When ye are settled at Ardgleann, working side by side to mend whate'er damage that swine has done, ye can sort it all out. As ye prove yourself a good laird to the people there, ye can prove yourself a good husband."

"Aye, true enough. I do wonder how she feels about my gaining so much by this marriage, mayhap e'en usurping a place she wanted for her own. Her husband claimed her as his heir yet we both ken that once the people there ken she has a husband, they will see me as the laird, nay her."

"Of course they will. Much better a strong mon with fighting skills than a wee lass. I would think she has the sense to see that for herself and understand it."

"She probably does, but it doesnae mean she has to like it."

"Then make sure all understand that ye are equal, that she speaks for ye and ye for her."

Liam was about to compliment Sigimor on that very good idea when Keira entered the great hall and he forgot everything he was going to say. She wore a gown of a deep wine red that complimented her every gentle curve. Her hair flowed over her slim shoulders in a river of soft, shining black waves, its rich depths decorated with cream-colored silk ribbons. The dress and her hair combined to make her skin look an even richer creamy color, soft and, at the moment, touched by the hint of a blush as everyone turned to look at her. Liam was moving toward her before he had even finished thinking about doing so.

"Here he comes," whispered Fiona.

"How do I look?" asked Keira. "I shouldnae have worn my hair down. I am a widow, nay an unwed lass."

"Cease your fretting. The mon cannae take his eyes off you."

"That doesnae have to mean he likes what he sees. He could be stunned with horror." She smiled faintly when Fiona laughed, but was too nervous to join in.

Then Liam was at her side, looking breathtakingly handsome in his black and gold doublet. Keira suspected this was some of the finery he wore when at court, and she could easily understand how it would affect the women there. He bowed to Fiona, then turned toward her, and Keira drew her breath in so sharply she nearly choked. His eyes were that warm blue color that appeared whenever he kissed her. Liam certainly did approve of how she looked.

That sign of approval, however, made Keira think of the night ahead of her, and she shivered. She had lain awake until far too late last night trying to think of a way to tell Liam her secret, all to no avail. Finally exhausted, she had fallen asleep telling herself that he would not notice. In the light of day, steps away from exchanging marriage vows with the man, she knew that was ridiculous. Liam may not have bedded any innocent maids, but she suspected it was something a man noticed, especially when the woman was one who had been married for three months.

" 'Twill be alright, lass," he whispered against her skin as he kissed her cheek.

Keira smiled and nodded as he took her by the hand and led her toward the priest standing at the far end of the great hall.

She wanted to believe his words of reassurance, but even she could not tell herself that big a lie. The foolish part of her liked to think that he would be pleasantly surprised tonight, but her good sense scoffed at that. Before or after, she was going to have to tell him the truth, and that would mean exposing her humiliation. Keira knew that was one reason she could not spit out the truth, could not simply say, *Excuse me, but although I am a widow, I fear I was ne'er really a wife.*

And would she even become one tonight? she thought, finally facing her greatest fear. Liam was stirred by her kisses, but Duncan had seemed to like them, too. It was in the bedchamber, as they had stepped beyond kisses, that everything had gone so horribly wrong. Inside her was a deep, gnawing fear that she would suffer that same humiliating rejection from Liam. It was clear that she had never really convinced herself that the problem had been Duncan's, not hers.

As they knelt on a pillow before the priest, Keira realized Liam did not have the slats of wood upon his leg. "Where are the splints?" she asked. "It hasnae been six weeks yet."

"It has been nearly five," he answered. "The binding remains. I wasnae able to kneel with all that wood on my leg. I will put the splints back on after we say our vows."

Keira suddenly wondered if they would have to forego their wedding night because of his broken leg, and she felt her spirits rise.

"And take then off again later," Liam whispered in her ear.

Her spirits plunged. She was just trying to think of a way to convince him that he could do irreparable damage to his healing leg if he indulged in something as strenuous as bedding his wife when the priest drew her attention to him. For one fleeting moment, Keira considered refusing to repeat her vows. Then she glanced at Liam. He was watching her warily out of the corner of his eyes. She sighed and cursed her too soft heart. She simply could not humiliate him so before all of his kinsmen.

* * *

"I thought women always smiled at weddings, especially their own."

Keira looked up at Artan as he stepped beside her. She did not need to look to her other side to know Lucas stood there. Her brothers were inseparable and always had been.

"This is my second wedding," she said. "*And* I didnae choose to have this one."

Artan shook his head. "Ye cannae tell me ye dinnae like the mon or want him."

She felt a blush heat her cheeks, but she ignored it. " 'Tis always better if there is some choice made freely."

"Weel, I think the choice would have been made eventually." Artan looked around at the men in the great hall. " 'Tis a good alliance. Aye, 'twas already there in some ways, but this makes it a more direct, stronger one. These are good men to have as allies."

That was a truth she could not argue with, but she was feeling particularly contrary at the moment. "I am so pleased I can bring ye that boon through my sacrifice at the altar," she murmured.

Lucas draped his arm around her shoulders. "Bury that resentment, Blackbird. If ye nurse it too long, it could breed a poison. He is a good mon who believes in vows spoken before a priest."

"So everyone keeps saying," she replied quietly, watching her new husband carry on an amiable argument with Sigimor.

"Then heed them for they have kenned the mon far longer than ye have. He will make a good laird for Ardgleann."

"Mayhap *I* wished to be the laird."

"And ye would have made a good one, but ye have the sense to ken that matters will go more smoothly with a mon sitting in the laird's chair. A wee lass as laird would seem a tempting target to many a mon, e'en the neighboring clans. A big, strong mon with a horde of big, strong kinsmen will make Ardgleann look strong."

"And help keep it the peaceful place it once was. I ken it, but that doesnae mean I have to think it is fair." She felt Lucas shrug and sighed. "Dinnae worry. I dinnae really care for I ne'er wished to be the laird. I agreed to the marriage settlements simply because I ne'er thought Duncan would die so soon after we were married. Nay, I am a healer, not a warrior. I am more than happy to set those responsibilities into Liam's hands."

"Something troubles ye, lass. I have seen it, and that look has lingered all day. 'Tis nearly time to sup, and I still see it. I cannae guess at what gnaws at ye, and I suspicion ye willnae tell me now either, but it wouldnae be wise to take it to your marriage bed." Lucas nodded toward Liam, who was watching them. "Aye, and by the look upon that mon's face, he willnae wait too much longer ere he takes ye there."

Keira blushed for she had seen that look upon Liam's face herself. It both warmed her and terrified her. The desire in his eyes was filled with promise, but she could not shake the fear that once alone in their bedchamber, that promise would quickly turn to ashes.

Lucas proved right in his prediction. Keira could feel Liam's growing impatience to be done with ceremony as they ate. He even quietly endured a lot of not so subtle teasing from his kinsmen, but his tension increased until it began to infect her. It was as Sigimor proposed a third toast that Liam finally lost his restraint. He leapt to his feet with surprising grace for a man whose leg was tightly splinted. Keira quickly set down her tankard of wine as he grabbed her by the hand, pulled her to her feet, and started to drag her out of the great hall. She was a little surprised to find that she was not the only one who blushed over some of the ribald remarks flung at them as they left the room.

There was one good thing about this marriage, Keira thought as Liam led her to their bedchamber. Because she was a widow, there would be no elaborate and embarrassing bedding ceremony. They were allowed to simply go to bed, she observed, and felt her stomach knot as they entered the room. That feeling intensified when she heard Liam shut and firmly latch the door. It was then that she realized she had no real idea of what she should do next.

"Ye look a wee bit confused, wife," Liam said as he slowly pulled her into his arms.

"Weel, I wasnae married verra long," she murmured.

Liam pressed a kiss to her forehead. "Although I gain from what your first husband left ye, I dinnae really want him in the bedchamber."

He kissed her, silencing the words she had almost said. Duncan was here whether Liam liked it or not. Keira allowed herself to become lost in the warmth of his kiss, too cowardly to face the truth now. The truth would be exposed soon enough, and she decided to take all she could before it was. Liam's desire might be a shallow thing, shared too often with far too many, but she wanted to bask in its warmth for as long as she could.

Liam kept Keira bemused with kisses as he unlaced her gown. The deep blush she wore when he finally had her stripped down to her shift made him think that Duncan had been one of those men who had bedded his wife in the dark. Knowing he could not continue until he had removed the wooden slats from his leg, Liam grasped her by the hands and pulled her toward the bed. He sat down on the side of the bed and began to remove the wood that was the greatest cause of his awkwardness.

"Liam," Keira said, "it hasnae been six weeks."

"So ye told me earlier," he replied as he continued to remove the splints.

"But ye could ruin all your healing if ye are nay careful."

As he tossed the last splint aside, he looked at her. "I willnae stomp about on it." Since his little jest had not eased her obvious concern, he said, "I feel verra strongly that it has healed

enough for this, love. It aches after a long day, and I can feel
that it has weakened, but nay more than that."

Since his other injuries had healed with a pleasing swiftness,
Keira thought it might be possible that the broken bone had
repaired itself a little more quickly as well. The healer in her,
however, continued to worry. She knelt at his feet and placed
her hands upon his leg, trying to feel if there was any reason
for her concern.

"My leg doesnae hurt that badly," Liam said, but when he
reached for her, she lightly slapped his hand away.

"Nay, it doesnae, but I wasnae looking for that. Now hush."
She grimaced at the abrupt way she had spoken. "Please."

Liam shrugged. She might not have set her hands upon him
to ease his pain, but it was eased. He hoped she had not taken
it into herself for he did not wish to go through the whole
ritual required afterward. He most certainly did not want to
spend even a small part of his wedding night sitting idly by
while she slept, not unless it was the sleep of a well-pleasured
wife. When she stood up, he saw no sign of the reactions she
had suffered before when she had laid hands upon his injury.

"Are ye weel?" he asked.

"Och, aye. I was only trying to, weel, see something, nay take
away the pain or the like."

"And what did ye see?" He braced himself for bad news.

"Nothing." She smiled faintly when he sighed, obviously relieved. "It appears that ye *have* healed, but it would be wise to
wear the splints during the day for at least another week and to
be cautious in how ye use that leg. The bone appears to be
mended, but the leg has weakened, and ye dinnae want to fall.
That could cause trouble."

He stood up, grasped her by her small waist, and sat her
down on the bed. Careful not to strain the leg she had just declared healed but weak, he knelt before her. He removed her
prettily embroidered shoes, her small, slender foot sharply reminding him that his wife was of a more delicate build than the
women he had known before. Taking the opportunity to stroke

her legs as he removed her stockings, Liam felt his blood grow recklessly hot. Her legs were surprisingly long considering her small stature, as well as slender and beautifully shaped. Beneath her soft skin, he could feel taut muscle. Delicate Keira might be, but she was obviously not weak.

Liam kissed each of her knees, then stood up and began to remove his clothes. He tried to undress without any obvious haste, but knew he was not completely successful in hiding his near desperate eagerness to be skin to skin with her. After tossing aside the last of his clothes, he looked at Keira and nearly grinned.

His beautiful little wife was blushing so fiercely, she looked feverish. After she looked him over, her wide gaze stayed fixed upon his erection. Liam did not know whether to be flattered or concerned. There was definitely a hint of uncertainty, even fear, in her eyes. Since he knew he was no bigger than most men, he began to feel certain that Duncan MacKail had indulged in only the most genteel bedding of his wife or had been one of those fools who believed one's lady wife should not be confronted with such things as a man's naked body and passion.

Keira nearly flinched away from his touch when Liam joined her on the bed and began to unlace her shift. Liam Cameron was a very fine-looking man from his thick coppery hair right down to his feet. She had not seen him naked for weeks, not since he had woken up in the cottage, and she had never seen him in *that* condition. Keira knew it was going to hurt her a little the first time a man possessed her, but she feared she would be far more than a little hurt when he stuck that into her. The healer part of her scolded her for being an idiot, but Keira could not stop herself from fearing she was soon going to be torn asunder in the name of passion.

Then he pulled her shift off and tossed it aside. Keira forgot all about his size and waited tensely for what would happen next. Her nudity was one of the things that had caused her husband such distress. Although she could not see his expression clearly, Keira did not think Liam looked even slightly distressed as he slowly looked her over from head to toe. She felt hope stir when he gently lowered his body on top of hers and only shivered a little. At least she thought it was him, but since she was shaking as if she had the ague, it was difficult to be certain.

"Ah, wife, ye are beautiful." Liam brushed a kiss over her mouth. "Dinnae frown at your husband when he pays ye a compliment. Ye *are* beautiful."

Liam could tell that she did not believe he truly meant those words, but he would do his best to make her believe he spoke only the truth. She was dainty in height and shape, but she had all the womanly allure any man could want. Her breasts might not be large enough to call her a fulsome lass, but they were plump, nicely shaped, and tipped with dark rose nipples that sorely tempted him. Her waist was small, her hips gently curved, and her backside was sized just perfectly for his hands. At the top of her slender thighs was a neat arrowhead of dark curls that pointed the way to paradise. And all that pale, creamy skin felt as soft as eiderdown against his, he thought as he kissed her. He would make love to her in a way that would prove he did not just mutter empty flatteries, and if it took many, many times of making love to get her to believe him, he was more than ready to oblige her.

When Liam covered her breasts with his hands, Keira nearly leapt from the bed. The feelings he stirred within her with his kisses and his touch were too intense. They made her want to run away at the same time they made her ache for more. When he took one aching nipple deep into his mouth, suckling her gently, she knew what at least some of that *more* was.

Soon she stopped waiting for him to flee her arms, unable to return and finish what he had started. The humiliation of the past was forgotten for a time, burned away by the heat of the passion Liam stirred within her. She tentatively stroked his back, and he murmured his approval. She rubbed her body against his ever so gently, and he groaned, then held her closer. Keira did not understand what was so different about her that this husband wanted her, but she saw no sense in arguing with the kindness of fate. At some point, Liam might begin to suffer as Duncan had, so she held him tightly and tried to hold fast to all the pleasure she could.

"Och, lass, ye make me burn," Liam muttered as he slipped his hand between her legs.

He ignored the brief tension in her and her fleeting look of shock, both which faded as he stroked her. Her marriage had been very short, and he was beginning to think her husband had been a very poor lover. It pleased Liam to think that he would be the first man to give her pleasure.

Deeming Keira ready and knowing he could wait no longer to possess her, Liam settled himself between her legs. It troubled him a little when she did not immediately wrap those slim, strong legs of hers around him, but again, he decided her husband was at fault. It took only a slight tugging on her legs as he tried to put them around his hips himself before Keira realized what he wanted, much to his relief. Then he kissed her even as he plunged inside of her, now desperate for the feel of her heat surrounding him. Liam felt her tense beneath him and realized in a small part of his passion-clouded mind that his entry had been less than smooth, so he forced himself to lie still. He looked at her as he fought to gain a little control of himself. She looked startled, he thought, but that made no sense at all.

Keira stared at Liam as he raised himself up on his forearms and looked at her. She had thought she had hidden her reaction to that brief slash of pain rather well, but the frown upon his face told her he had noticed something. Since he just looked a little confused, she decided he was not certain what he had felt, and she hurried to take advantage of that.

Wrapping her arms more securely around his neck, she kissed him using all she had learned from the way he kissed her. She tightened the grip of her legs, pushing him deeper inside and heard him groan low in his throat. When he began to move, she almost cried out in relief. As his thrusts grew fiercer, she felt something deep inside her begin to tighten and tried to urge him on with her own body. He slid his fingers between their bodies, down to where they were joined, and touched her in a way that made her feel frantic. When he did it again, she felt that tight knot inside her snap, sending pleasurable chills throughout her body. She clung to Liam as his movements grew briefly frenzied before he tensed and cried out her name. Keira felt the warmth of his seed and nearly wept with joy.

He collapsed in her arms, his breath hot against her neck. Her body still hummed with the pleasure he had given her, and she savored it. All too soon he would recover, and his mind would grow sharp and clear again. The knowledge she had briefly glimpsed in his eyes would return. Then all this pleasure and joy would be torn away by his anger and her painful memories of the past.

CHAPTER 11

Liam sat on the edge of the bed staring at the damp cloth he had used to clean Keira and himself of what he often jested was the sticky side of a good rutting. There was no explaining away the faint stain upon the linen. He may have been far less controlled than usual, but he had not been so fierce that he would have caused her to bleed. Despite the cloud of passion encircling his mind as he had kissed and caressed her, he had sensed a virginal unease at times. Now that his fever had cooled, he could also recall what he had felt as he had thrust inside of her. Her kiss, the feel of her lithe body wrapped around his, and his own blind need had briefly pushed that knowledge from his mind. His wife, a woman who had been married for three months, his little widow who should have had some experience in the bedchamber no matter how inept her husband, was a virgin.

Or had been, he quickly corrected himself. For a moment he felt extraordinarily pleased by that, savoring the knowledge that he was her first lover. Then, dark suspicion crept into his mind.

His wife, a word he realized he still liked the sound of despite the suspicions he now felt, sat up against the pillows. She held the sheet close to her chest and watched him, her eyes wide with distress. There was fear there, too, and he quickly smothered the urge to comfort her. Until he knew the truth, she had good reason to be afraid.

"My first question might be were ye ever e'en married, but I heard your brothers confirm it," he murmured. "So next I wonder, did ye refuse your husband his rights?"

He sounded so calm, so polite, and so absolutely furious that Keira had to take a deep breath to steady herself before replying, "Nay. Never. Duncan was verra forthright about his need for an heir, and I entered the marriage kenning that it would be my duty to try to grant him one."

"Did he think ye needed time to adjust to being his wife, for ye didnae love him, did ye?"

"Nay, I didnae love him," she whispered, wishing it did not sound so much like a guilty confession. "I liked him. He was a good, kind mon. Gentle really. There was no talk of waiting."

"Curse it, Keira, ye were a virgin. If ye didnae deny him your bed and he didnae think ye needed time to become accustomed to your new life, then how could ye still be a virgin?"

"Because Duncan didnae want me!"

"He married ye. He must have wanted ye. He picked ye, didnae he? The mon wouldnae pick someone he didnae want."

"He tried. Poor Duncan really tried, but he couldnae. I wasnae to his liking."

Liam sighed and rubbed a hand over his forehead. He needed to be calm. Either they were talking in circles, or she had not yet explained it all clearly enough. It was incomprehensible to him that her late husband had not wanted her. Until he had fully realized that he had rammed his way through a maidenhead that should not have been there, he had been enjoying a passion hotter and sweeter than any he had ever known and its delicious aftermath. And Keira had returned his passion in full measure despite it having been her first time with a man. Liam could not believe another man had been blind to the promise of her lithe body.

"Was he impotent?" he asked.

Keira frowned. "I dinnae think so. His, er, mon part did as it

should from all I could tell. Duncan didnae light as many can-
dles as there are in here so 'twas difficult to see much." Which,
she thought, was a good thing considering what had happened.

Turning to face her, Liam could see how distressed she was.
His dark suspicions eased a little. Something had happened in
her brief marriage that had made her think she was undesirable, at least to Duncan MacKail. Duncan had not been a bad
lover. He had been no lover at all. Liam desperately wanted
Keira to say something that would make him believe it had all
been Duncan's fault. He did not want to think Keira capable of
such a large deceit as marrying a man and, even though she
never allowed the marriage to be consummated, was now
claiming to be the man's true heir. Nor that she would be willing to risk men's lives to claim that false inheritance.

"Keira, do ye swear that ye went willingly to his bed?" he
asked.

"Aye, at first," she replied. "Then I stayed in the lady's bedchamber and waited for him to come to me when he felt he
could try again."

"Ye say he wasnae impotent, and ye didnae refuse him, yet,
Keira, I fear I simply cannae believe he didnae want ye. There
is a part of me that really doesnae wish to hear anything ye did
with another mon, but I think ye need to tell me about the bedding."

"Must I?"

"Aye, for I keep asking questions, but your answers arenae
helping me to understand this at all."

"Duncan wanted to wait until we reached Ardgleann before
we had our wedding night. So when we were bedded down together after the ceremony, he left me alone in the bed and
slept upon the floor. Before anyone came to help us prepare
for our journey to Ardgleann, he, weel, he made sure there
was a mark upon the sheets. The first night at Ardgleann, he
came to bed with me. He kissed me and removed my shift."
She shrugged. "He was trembling, and I thought it was because

he was feeling desire for me, and I felt a wee bit guilty because I felt little for him. Then he put his hand upon my breast. His trembling grew quite fierce, he groaned, and then he leapt from the bed and was violently ill."

Liam frowned as he studied her. She made no sound, but she wept, her tears dropping steadily upon her hands, which were clenched tightly together in her lap. He had to bend a little to see even that much, for her head was bowed and her long hair shielded much of her face. Such an appalling wedding night could easily have caused a couple to be reluctant to try again, but not, he thought, for three long months.

"Did he have the ague?" he asked.

"I wondered that myself at the time, fool that I was. I leapt from the bed to hurry to his side. He looked at me and just grew worse, screaming at me to get dressed. He couldnae get his own clothes back on fast enough and all the while he muttered about filth, ugliness, sin, and such as that. Then, when we were both dressed, I got beneath the bedcovers, and he took his place on top of them. He patted my hand and said I was not to worry, that it would just take time and that we would keep trying. We did, and it never got any better. 'Twas me. He couldnae abide e'en touching me, couldnae e'en try without emptying his belly."

Suddenly, Liam understood. Once or twice while at the monastery, he had met a man so tormented by what he saw as the sin of lust he would beat himself bloody in an attempt to banish the feeling. It sounded as if Duncan suffered something similar, had been scarred in some way so that even lusting after his lawful wife sent him into a paroxysm of guilt. Liam fetched a clean square of linen, returned to the bed, and turned Keira's face up to his.

"Keira, did I or did I not just bed ye most thoroughly?" he asked calmly as he dampened the linen in the bowl of water on the bedside table and gently bathed the tears from her face.

"Aye, but ye are—weel—ye will bed any woman," she murmured.

He sighed and rested his forehead against her for a moment. "Nay, I willnae. I would certainly ne'er bed a lass so foul she makes me vomit."

"But, if it wasnae me, what was it?"

"I cannae say for certain, having ne'er met the mon. There have been monks I have met who felt a mon's natural urgings were so foul, so sinful, they needed to be purged from the body by any means possible. Brother Paul suffered from that a wee bit, I think. Did Duncan have scars upon his back? Did he e'er have fresh wounds there?"

Keira frowned. "He did have some scars. Once I touched his back and felt a few, but 'twas only a fleeting touch for he fled from it. And once I did think he was in pain, but he wouldnae let me tend to him. He told me it was naught but a wee scratch he got whilst riding. From a tree branch, he said. I thought it odd that he wouldnae let me tend him as he kenned all about my gift, had been quite pleased about it. Told me it was a wondrous thing to bring to his people and that one day, it might e'en help him."

"Your touch wouldnae have cured what ailed him, love. 'Twas a sickness of the mind. Someone or something turned him that way ere ye even met him." He could see that she did not completely accept his words, but he would have to deal with that later. "Now, why didnae ye tell me of this ere I bedded ye?"

"Because of my vow. Duncan kenned that Rauf wanted Ardgleann, that he thought it weakly defended and with no heirs to make trouble if he took it. When he heard that the mon was in the area and was probably planning his attack, Duncan made me vow that I would tell no one that our marriage had ne'er been consummated and that if anything happened to him, I would take my place as his heir, get help, and free Ardgleann. One of the reasons he wed me was because he was certain I could gather enough people to fight Rauf and win, especially if they thought the mon had stolen what was rightfully mine." She shrugged again. "I felt I couldnae tell ye, not until ye were my husband. Then it was difficult to think of a way to tell ye."

"And, I suspect ye feared I would have the same difficulty as Duncan did."

"Weel, aye, but I was hoping ye wouldnae because ye—"

"Are a rutting, lecherous swine?"

"I wouldnae say that," she mumbled.

"Ye did say that once when ye were screaming at me that night we camped in the wood." He was pleased to see her glare at him, for it meant her despair had eased, the sad memories retreating for a while. "We shall have to discuss that soon, but for now, I must needs speak to Sigimor and Ewan."

Keira gasped and sat up straighter as he got out of bed and began to dress. "Ye cannae tell them!"

"I must. They are ready to ride into battle for ye and Ard-gleann. I willnae allow them to put themselves in front of a sword unless they ken the full truth."

When he put it that way, she had to agree. "I willnae be able to look them in the eye ever again," she said, flopping down onto her back and tugging the sheet over her head.

Once dressed, Liam tugged the sheet off her face and gave her a quick kiss. "I ken I will have to repeat myself many times ere your wee, stubborn mind grasps the truth, but the problem was with Duncan, not you."

"My wee, stubborn mind?" she muttered, but Liam was already out of the room and shutting the door behind him.

Shaking her head, Keira got out of bed. She added a little wood to the fire, then had a quick wash before donning her shift. Wrapping a blanket around her, she poured herself some wine and sat on the sheepskin before the fire to await Liam's return. When Thunder and Lightning appeared to curl up on either side of her, she smiled and took turns lightly scratching each kitten's ears.

She searched her heart for any guilt over telling Duncan's secret and breaking her vow, but found only a little. Poor Duncan's secret would remain safe, of that she had no doubt, but

Liam was right. She could not ask men to face a sword unless they knew the full truth, no matter how humiliating that truth was.

Liam's explanation for Duncan's difficulties also made sense, and she was strongly tempted to accept it. Her new husband had certainly revealed no reluctance to bed her. Yet Duncan had to have known how hurt and humiliated his rejection had made her. Why had he not even tried to explain or reassure her that it was not her fault? It annoyed her to admit it, but Liam could be right about that, too. It was going to be difficult to make her wee, stubborn mind accept that truth. Then again, she thought with a soft smile, if Liam was intending to use his lovemaking to prove his point, she would be a fool to complain.

Liam found Sigimor and Ewan in Ewan's ledger room. He patiently endured a few jests about new husbands fleeing their wives' beds before telling them all he had learned. Sigimor listened carefully, frowned, and then left the room, saying only that he would be back in a few minutes. Liam shrugged, poured himself some wine, and took a seat facing Ewan's worktable. He was just about to start discussing the problem with Ewan when Sigimor returned with Keira's two brothers, who looked as if they had been dragged from their beds.

"Tell them," Sigimor ordered.

Only briefly did Liam hesitate before doing as his cousin ordered. He found the wide array of expressions that crossed Artan's and Lucas's faces as he told them the story a little amusing. If Duncan MacKail were still alive, he would soon pay dearly for what he had put Keira through.

"Why didnae she tell us?" muttered Artan. "We could have gotten the marriage annulled."

"She was humiliated," said Liam. "Still is. It will be a long while ere she believes it wasnae at least partly her fault. Mayhap, if the marriage had lasted longer, she *would* have turned to her family."

"Mayhap," agreed Lucas, "but why did we need to hear of this now? The mon is dead."

"He named his wife his heir," said Sigimor, "but because the marriage wasnae consummated, the law would say she wasnae his true wife."

"Oh, aye, I suppose that is true." Lucas scratched his chin. "Dinnae think it matters. If I recall, the agreements signed give Keira Ardgleann if Duncan dies without leaving a legitimate heir. Verra simply put. No qualifications."

"And there is *no* other heir?"

"Nay. Duncan was the last of his line. Weel, except for the bastard."

Liam sat up straight. "Duncan's bastard?" For a moment, Liam feared he had been lied to, but did not want to believe it.

"Och, nay, his father's. A mon named Malcolm. My father wanted to make certain Duncan told the truth when he said there was no heir to question Keira's right to be named his, so he sent men out to verify the tale. He thought he *had* been lied to when he heard about Malcolm. Went to see the mon himself. Malcolm doesnae want to be laird. Ne'er has, ne'er will. He doesnae want it widely kenned that he is the old laird's bastard. My father had him sign papers and all, just to be sure. So, no heir."

"Duncan was the true heir, and he had the right to name whome'er he pleased to take his place," said Ewan. "Unlike the English, we arenae so concerned about direct lines or legitimacy. Duncan obviously felt Keira was the best choice because of the strength of her family and its allies."

Artan nodded. "My father said Malcolm said the same. Told my father that e'en if Duncan dropped dead climbing the stairs to his bed on the wedding night, he would still accept Keira as the lawful heir." Artan frowned. "Odd thing to say now that I think on it."

"Unless the mon was aware of Duncan's problems," said

Liam. "If he is, I will get the truth out of him. I think one reason Keira wouldnae fully accept my explanation or my assurance that it wasnae her fault is because I cannae tell why the mon was the way he was." He looked at his cousins. "So? Do we still go to war?"

"Aye," said Sigimor, and Ewan nodded in agreement. "Probably still would have, e'en if her right to the place was in question. Rauf Moubray needs killing, but it has always been difficult to find him."

"Ah, and now ye ken exactly where he is."

Sigimor nodded. "The fact that ridding the earth of that scourge will also make ye a laird just makes it all the more pleasing. Now, hie yourself back to your bride. On the morrow, we start our planning in earnest."

Knowing how meticulous Sigimor could be in his planning, Liam groaned and hurried back to his bedchamber. He smiled when he saw Keira sitting in front of the fire, a kitten curled up on either side of her. When he shut and latched the door, she turned to look at him, and he saw the concern in her eyes. Liam walked over to her, carefully moved Thunder to her other side, sat down beside her, and put his arm around her shoulders.

"Ye told them then," she said, feeling embarrassed all over again.

"Them and your brothers," he said. "Sigimor fetched them out of their beds so that they could hear the tale as weel."

Keira groaned and buried her face against his shoulder. "Where is a hole to crawl into when ye need one?"

Liam laughed and then hugged her. "Let me just say that if Duncan were still alive, he would be running for his life from your brothers. And if I judged Sigimor's and Ewan's expressions right, they would probably be right at your brothers' sides."

"Ewan and Sigimor actually had expressions ye could read?"

Ah, good, he thought. That tartness he liked was back. He tilted her face up to his. "Such impertinence," he murmured and brushed a kiss over her mouth. "Not one of them thought ye were at fault. Duncan should have told ye the same, should have at least tried to tell ye what troubled him."

"Actually, that is one reason I hesitate to believe your explanation. Duncan *was* a kind mon. How could a kind mon allow me to suffer such doubt about myself, such hurt and humiliation, when he could have eased it with a simple explanation? I have trouble believing he could be so cruel."

"Nay cruel, at least not intentionally. I think he was ashamed of his weaknesses, mayhap e'en feared he was sick in his mind. How could he speak of such things to his new wife? He *should* have told ye, if only because once ye kenned the truth, the two of ye could have worked together to cure him. Mayhap, given more time, that is just what could have happened."

A large part of Liam was glad Keira and Duncan had not solved their troubles. He felt a little guilty about that for the poor fool had suffered even before he had fallen into Rauf's cruel grasp, but he could not deny how he felt. Keira was all his; she had never belonged to another man. That he had been the one to take her virginity gave him a very primitive feeling of possession, satisfaction, and even a hint of victory. That she had found pleasure in his arms, despite the urgency that had caused him to act with less than his usual finesse, was even more satisfying.

"Poor Duncan," Keira murmured. "If what ye say is true, how he must have suffered, and probably for many years."

Then again, he mused, perhaps he did not feel so guilty. "Duncan is the past," he said firmly. "There is no helping him. However, the people of Ardgleann *can* be helped."

"There will still be a battle?"

"Aye. Sigimor and Ewan needed to hear the truth, not only because I couldnae allow them to act with a lie resting between us, but also because the fact that the marriage wasnae consummated could have meant ye had no right to Ardgleann. It was to answer that question that Sigimor dragged your brothers in to hear the tale."

"I think the agreements signed made me his heir even if we were only betrothed, so consummation shouldnae matter, should it?"

"That is what we all decided, although mention of a certain man called Malcolm caused a moment of hesitation."

"Malcolm doesnae want to be the laird, ne'er has. He doesnae e'en like anyone kenning he is the old laird's bastard." Keira smiled faintly. "Malcolm just wants to work with his woods and his metals. He makes such beautiful things."

"And he gives no thought to what his children might want or see as rightfully theirs?"

"He doesnae have any yet, but he and Duncan had an agreement that whate'er children Malcolm may have will be given the chance to be whate'er they want, except the heirs. That stands, unless I have no bairns. Then I could choose one of Malcolm's children as an heir, if the child was willing and able. The old laird ne'er claimed Malcolm, so he has only his mother's word that the old laird was his father, and she is dead now. No papers and no true resemblance. Duncan didnae e'en ken the truth until he was nearly full grown." She shook her head. "That was wrong. Bastard or nay, Malcolm was the old laird's child, and he shouldnae have been so callously cast aside."

Seeing the way she was eyeing him, Liam sighed. "I have bred no bastards, Keira."

"I ne'er said ye had."

"Ye didnae have to say the words." He carefully stood up and tugged her up to stand beside him, grinning at the disgruntled looks the kittens gave him. "And now, enough talk of battles and sad memories. I wish to take my wife to bed."

Keira blushed a little as he led her to the bed. "Weel, aye, it has been a long day. We could do with some rest."

"We could, and we will get some, later."

He grinned when she blushed even more brilliantly. After tossing the blanket she had wrapped around herself onto the bed, he removed her shift. Chuckling softly at how quickly she got beneath the covers, he shed his clothes and climbed in beside her. Despite her blushes, she did not resist at all when he pulled her into his arms and kissed her. This time he would go slowly, nurture her pleasure, and savor his own. He would not allow passion and need to overcome the skill and control he had acquired over the years.

Liam slowly raised himself up on his forearms and looked at Keira. She looked beautifully ravished. The sight both pleased him and made him inwardly shake his head in dismay. Where had all his carefully learned skills gone, all those little tricks of control and patience? He had started out well enough, but each touch of her hands, each kiss she had given him, had driven him into an undisciplined frenzy.

Of course, she did not look as if she had minded that at all. Liam was also certain that she had gained her pleasure. Not only had she cried out his name and drummed her little heels against the backs of his thighs, but he had felt her body clench around him as he had spent himself inside her. His wife was a very passionate woman, he thought with a sigh of satisfaction.

He kissed her, and although she kissed him back, he could tell she was more asleep than awake. The fact that despite his lack of control, he had exhausted her with his lovemaking pleased him. He moved to lie at her side and then tucked her up against him. When she snuggled up closer to him, pressing her taut little backside against his groin, he felt himself begin to respond and grinned. Keira had made him insatiable, and he thought that a fine thing.

As he rested his cheek against her hair and tried to think of ways he could convince her that the failure of her first marriage was all Duncan's fault, he discovered he was too sated and too exhausted. All he wanted to do was lie there enjoying the feel of Keira sleeping in his arms until he, too, fell asleep. That was a new feeling for him for he had never spent a full night with a woman nor wanted to. His mind did not really want to consider why it should be different with Keira. When she took his hand and settled it beneath her cheek, he smiled. It was going to be nice having a wife. Very nice indeed.

CHAPTER 12

Keira opened her eyes to find herself kissing her husband's taut stomach. She was feeling a little feverish, and that ache she now recognized as need was already well begun, so she knew she had been mauling him in her sleep—again. The hope that he was not awake faded quickly when she realized that one part of him at least was very much awake. It was nestled between her breasts, and he was subtly rubbing it against her. She had thought that once married, she would cease to have lust-filled dreams about him, but now, she simply acted out those dreams. Every morning for a week now, she had awakened to find herself taking willful advantage of him.

Blushing faintly, she lifted her head to look at him. "Sorry."

"For what?" He grabbed her under her arms and dragged her up his body until she was seated astride him. " 'Tis a fine way to greet the new day. Mayhap on the morrow, I shall be a verra lucky mon, and ye will be a wee bit slower in waking up."

Before she could ask what he meant by that, he kissed her, and all ability to think clearly fled. There was a fierce hunger in his kiss that told her she had probably been ravishing him for a while, and it quickly infected her. When he slid his hand over her stomach and between her legs, it took only a few strokes of his clever fingers to have her aching to feel him inside her. She started to move off him, but he grasped her by her hips and held her in place.

"This way, love," Liam said, his voice low and husky with need.

Keira frowned a little, uncertain of what to do. "How does this work?"

"I will show ye this time."

He did, and Keira shuddered with pleasure. She raised herself up until he was almost out of her and then ever so slowly lowered herself back down again. It was not only how it felt, but also the fact that she could control the movement that made her sigh with delight. She played with him for a little while longer until he growled, grabbed her by the hips again, and moved her at the pace he wanted. Realizing that she, too, could not endure much more idle play, she quickly caught on. With his husky words of praise and encouragement inspiring her, she took them both to the heights, their cries of pleasure blending perfectly in her ears. She collapsed on his chest and stayed there trying to catch her breath until she felt him soften and slip away from her.

Embarrassment over her wantonness returned as she moved to lie at his side, burying her face in the crook of his neck. Although she hated to think of him sharing such things with other women, she now understood better how he would be loathe to refuse any favors offered him. Such pleasure was a temptation it was hard to turn away from. If she had had even a small taste of it in her sad marriage, she doubted her time together with Liam in that cottage would have been so innocently spent.

Liam stroked his wife's slim back and grinned into her hair. It was a strange morning ritual between them, but he had no intention of putting a stop to it. He would wake to find Keira making love to him in her sleep, bold, exciting love. Then something would wake her up, and he would have to act fast to keep embarrassment from chilling her passion. Once sated, she would feel embarrassed again. It was obviously going to take some time before she realized he adored that wanton side of her, the one that seemed to run free in her dreams. He would heartily welcome that woman wide awake and as a permanent part of his lovely wife.

"Ye have some verra intriguing dreams, I am thinking," he said and laughed when she groaned.

"Be glad I dinnae have your wealth of knowledge, or ye would be in real danger."

He nudged her face out of the crook of his neck and turned on his side to face her, nose to nose. "Now, heed me closely, wife. Aye, I was a greedy fellow, but I dinnae have a wealth of knowledge."

"But—"

"Hush. I havenae spoken about this because to me, it isnae important; 'tis but the follies of a greedy lad, but *'tis* important to you. I dinnae have a wealth of knowledge. I dinnae have any wondrous skills. I dinnae e'en have any fond, lasting memories. The lasses bedded me because of my face, and any feeling I had for them was as shallow and fleeting as theirs was for me. Nay a thing to be proud of, but I cannae change it now, and I will *never* go back to my old ways.

"As for how ye are in the morning? Weel, there is obviously a verra wanton wee lass skipping through your dreams. Whene'er ye wish to bring her out and present her to me, wide awake and willing, ye can be verra sure that I will welcome her with wide open arms." He gave her another brief kiss, slapped her lightly on the backside, and climbed out of bed. "I may e'en do a wee dance about the room," he said as he yanked on his clothes. "Naked. Aye, I think that wee lass would like that. Mayhap she would e'en join me. Just two happy, lusty creatures cavorting about in the clothes God gave them. Now there is something to dream on." Before he laughed at the wide-eyed look upon Keira's face, he escaped the bedchamber.

Keira stared at the door her husband had just shut behind him. She did not know whether she wanted to laugh or get dressed, hunt him down, and kick him. There was no doubt in her mind that she would be plagued by visions of Liam dancing naked, probably for days. If she did not know better, she would think he knew that he was always naked in her dreams. After all, when a man looked as lovely as he did naked, why bother with clothes?

A young girl arrived with a bowl of hot water for her morning ablutions. Keira murmured her thanks, and the moment the girl was gone, she hopped out of bed to wash before the water cooled. After taking care of her more personal needs, she washed herself down and then dressed in one of her own gowns. Fiona had been more than generous with her gowns, allowing Keira to always look her best when she went to the great hall to sup. During the day, however, Keira preferred to wear something less rich and elegant so that she could lend a hand in all of the work that needed doing.

She thought over what Liam had said about the women in his past as she combed and braided her hair. He was right to say that being so callous about something so intimate was nothing to be proud of. On the other hand, she did find some comfort in it. It appeared that there was no love or past infatuation, no ghost to fight. A wife could only be thankful for that. The way he had so forcefully declared that he would never go back to bedding any woman who gave him a welcoming smile was certainly good to hear. Keira was just not sure she fully believed it.

If he loved her, she might believe it, she thought and sighed. She was following Fiona's advice and just loving him, but she was not able to tell if it was having any effect upon his heart. His passion for her was certainly strong, but they were still new lovers, so she was not sure she could depend much upon that as a sign of his deeper feelings. She was beginning to think he cared for her in some ways, but her own uncertainties made that conviction falter several times a day.

Shaking her head, she decided to answer the demands of her stomach. As she headed to the great hall to break her fast, she thought about what Liam had said concerning her morning assaults upon his person. There was indeed a very wanton Keira skipping through her dreams, a woman free of doubt and immune to embarrassment. Keira suspected the way she kept acting out her dreams while caught in that misty time between waking and sleeping was her mind and heart urging her to let that Keira free. It was an intriguing thought. Of course, she mused and grinned, when and if that Keira broke free of her restraints, she would definitely ask Liam to dance naked.

"What are ye grinning about?"

Keira realized she was already at the head table in the great hall facing Fiona. Without thinking, she replied, "Watching Liam dance naked."

Fiona dissolved into a fit of the giggles. After a hasty look around to reassure herself that no one else had heard her, Keira was able to laugh as well. She sat down next to Fiona and filled a plate from what was a rather astonishing array of food, considering no one else was in the great hall. Espying hot, thick porridge, she spooned some into a bowl, dribbled a little honey and milk on it, and began to eat. As she did so, she watched in growing amazement as Fiona ate, and ate, and ate.

"Um, Fiona? Why do I get the feeling that all of this food was actually intended for you?" Keira asked as, done with her porridge, she looked around for something to put on her piece of bread.

Setting a bowl of herbed butter in front of Keira, Fiona sighed. "Because it is. I am with child."

"Oh, Fiona, how wonderful for you!" Keira ruthlessly beat down a sudden attack of envy.

"Aye, but if ye tell Ewan, I will have to beat ye."

"Why will ye not tell him? Wouldnae kenning it make him remain here at Scarglas? Ye dinnae really wish him to ride off to battle, do ye?" Keira tentatively tasted the butter and then spread it thickly on her bread.

"Nay, but he wants to go. If he kens I am with child again, he will stay, but his heart and mind will be with the others. So I have sworn all who have guessed to silence upon pain of dark, unmentioned torments." Fiona briefly grinned when Keira laughed and then sighed again. "Since one sure sign that I am carrying is that I eat enough for ten men, I have been stealing these feasts on the sly whene'er Ewan isnae about. In a day or two, I willnae have to hide the fact that I am ravenous near all day long."

It took Keira a moment to grasp the meaning of that statement. "A day or two?"

"Aye. Liam will probably tell ye soon for ye are to go with them. They would rather ye didnae, but ye ken the people there and they dinnae, so they need ye with them. They also think it best if ye and Liam step right into the laird's place once they get Rauf out. Ah, ye are frowning." Fiona cut up an apple and began to eat the slices. "Liam hasnae told ye much about their plans, is that it?"

Keira nodded and then grimaced. "I havenae asked about them either, so he may think I dinnae want to hear anything about it all."

"Ye will probably hear about naught else tonight. Some more Camerons have arrived, as weel as some of your clansmen. The great hall will be filled with braw men ready for a fight. Ach, that sounded unkind. They are eager because they see it as a just cause. Few men have seen Rauf Moubray and lived to tell about it, but they have all heard tales of him or seen what cruelty he is capable of. This presents a good chance to rid the country of him. A few of my brothers' men have come, along with my brother Nanty, and a few of our allies, the Dalglishes and the Goudys. By taking a few from here and there, no one is risking all of their good fighting men or leaving their lands too lightly guarded."

"Verra clever," Keira murmured.

"Aye, I thought so, too. And Sigimor has men already creeping about near Ardgleann, seeing what they can find and talking with the lairds of the neighboring clans. Sir Ian MacLean has already sent word that we are welcome to camp upon his land and that we have his full support. We havenae heard from any others."

"There is only one other close enough to be worried, and I doubt ye will hear from him. He is so cautious, he sidles close to cowardliness. The mon will sit back, let others take all the risks, and just enjoy the benefits. I wouldnae be surprised if one of his sons brings a few men and joins the fight."

"That would be good. They can meet Liam and, by fighting at his side, declare their acceptance of his place as laird of Ardgleann." Fiona looked closely at Keira. "Are ye certain that doesnae trouble ye?"

"Oh, I willnae say I dinnae feel a wee pinch of resentment now and again, but not against Liam. 'Tis against the whole world, I suppose. That world that cannae accept a lass as laird, that sees it only as proof of a weakness they can take advantage of."

"By the whole world, ye mean men."

"Aye, men."

They both scowled for a moment, realized what they were doing, and then laughed. For a while, they talked about all the work that needed to be done at this time of the year and Fiona's children. Replete and in need of something to do, Keira decided to go and work in the herb house. Since Fiona was beginning to find the strong scents in there too unsettling, she was more than happy to let Keira do the work.

On the way to the herb house, Keira met the men sent by the Murrays who were standing with her brothers. Since most of them were her cousins, they all felt free to lecture her about not telling them where she was and how she was faring for so long. She endured the scolding for a little while, for she felt it was deserved, but only for a little while.

When she finally broke away from them, her brothers followed her into the herb house, and she inwardly cursed. Keira had the sinking feeling that they wanted to talk to her about Duncan. She had been expecting it, but as the days had slipped by with nothing being said, she had thought they had decided that nothing really needed to be said. It was now obvious that they had been spending the days trying to think of what to say and how to say it.

"Ye should have told us ye were having trouble with your husband," Lucas said.

Keira sighed as she carefully checked the progress of several scents Fiona was mixing. "It was *my* trouble and *my* husband. I didnae feel it would be right to run to Maman about it all, especially as I chose him, didnae I?" She gave them both as stern a frown as she could muster. "And I dinnae want to talk about it."

"Mayhap if ye had talked about it, ye wouldnae have filled your head with all sorts of foolish ideas."

"When a mon vomits every time he touches ye, 'tis nay hard to get *foolish* ideas, as ye call them."

Artan grunted. "We could have told ye that the fault was his, nay yours."

"And why should I listen to your assurances?" Keira asked. "Ye are my brothers. Ye are bound to take my side and blame him."

"We wouldnae lie to ye about something like that. There was something wrong with the mon. Aye, ye arenae the sort of fulsome lass who is quick to draw a mon's eye, but there is naught a thing wrong with ye."

" 'Tis plain your new husband doesnae find anything wrong with ye," said Lucas.

Keira turned to face them, leaned back against the worktable, and crossed her arms over her chest. "Nay, he doesnae appear to. And mayhap soon that will ease the sting of what happened with Duncan. I ken ye mean weel, and I thank ye for your concern, but I have to sort this all out myself. I suffered through three months of humiliating rejections. Let us just say that it left some bruises, and they need time to heal."

Artan nodded. "Aye, they would. Weel, your new husband will certainly help ye with that. A fine, lusty fellow Liam is."

"Aye, verra lusty. Just ask half the women in Scotland." She almost grinned at the way both of her brothers grimaced.

"He was a free mon." Artan shrugged. "A free mon takes what he can when he can. Sorry, lass, but few men would turn aside freely offered favors because they want to save themselves for their wives."

"I ken it, ye hypocrites. Ye certainly expect your chosen wife to have done so."

"Time to leave," said Lucas even as he headed for the door. "I scent a lecture filled with complaints about men."

Artan winked at her and turned to follow Lucas, only to frown when his brother did not move out of the open doorway. "Are our cousins squabbling with the MacFingals again?"

"Nay," replied Lucas. "They are bringing two men this way. A young monk who looks as if he has endured one too many fasts and a big mon with a bad squint."

Keira started to walk to the door even as she told herself the monk could not possibly be the one she was suddenly thinking of. "Does the monk have light brown hair? Oh, and has he stumbled yet?"

"Three times," replied Lucas. "The big mon seems to have a firm hold on him though. Just keeps holding him up until he gets his feet back in the right place."

Nudging her way past her brothers, Keira stepped outside the door just as her cousins arrived with the monk and the soldier. She blinked, unable to believe her eyes. It was indeed Kester. The big man at his side was not someone she had ever seen at the monastery. It was not clear whether he was supporting Kester or Kester was supporting him. Even though Kester was standing upright and steady, the man still held onto the boy's arm.

"M'lady, we have come to join ye in your fight to regain your lands," Kester announced.

It would have been a grand announcement if Kester had not swung his free arm out wide at that moment and caught Keira's cousin Colin right between the eyes. A blushing Kester hastily apologized, but when it looked as if Colin was going to retaliate anyway, Keira hurried to get the boy and his friend into the keep. As she ushered the odd pair along, her widely grinning brothers following her, Kester introduced his friend as Sir Archibald Kerr. Keira had not taken many steps before she realized that Sir Archibald had very poor eyesight, but she said nothing until they were all seated at the head table in the great hall, sharing the remains of the feast that Fiona was still nibbling at.

"First, Kester, I would like to ken why ye have left the monastery," Keira said as she poured him and Sir Archibald some cider. "I cannae believe the monks approved of ye running off to battle."

After hastily swallowing the large piece of bread he had shoved into his mouth, Kester replied, "They didnae, but when I heard about all your troubles from Brother Matthew, I wanted to help."

"That is most kind of ye, but—"

"I dinnae want to be a monk!" the boy abruptly said and blushed. "I was sent to my uncle because my father didnae want me about. I was sent to the monastery because my uncle didnae want me about either. He said I was more of a danger to his men than the cursed English. My father didnae want me back, so the two of them sent me to train to be a monk. I thought that mayhap if I can help ye, ye could find a place for me and Sir Archie at Ardgleann. I wouldst do most anything. S'truth, I wouldst rather be a swineherd than a monk."

Keira exchanged a glance with Fiona and saw the same sympathy for the boy that she herself was feeling. Even her brothers had stopped grinning. She inwardly sighed, knowing she could not send the boy back to a life he so obviously loathed. Not only would he be hurt by her rejection, yet another in what appeared to be a sad succession, but she also knew it would be condemning him to a very unhappy life.

"And ye, Sir Archibald?" she asked, watching closely as Kester handed the man his tankard and then, after the knight had had a drink, helping him guide it safely back onto the table.

"Weel, I am nay of much use to ye, but I am as willing as the laddie to help," he said, his voice a deep rumble in his broad chest. "I am having a wee bit of trouble with my eyes, but my sword arm is still good."

"Are ye losing your eyesight then?" she asked gently.

"Lost it. Weel, nearly. Things arenae verra clear. Helps if I squint. Took a blow to the head a few months ago, ye ken."

"I found him in the woods as I was following ye and Sir Liam," Kester said. "He was talking to a tree."

"Thought it was a mon," Sir Archibald muttered. "Squinting didnae help much that time."

Keira was very proud of her brothers when they both quickly shoved food in their mouths to stifle their laughter. A boy who could stumble over his own shadow and a knight who could not see clearly were of no use to her, but she could not bring herself to say so. Somehow, she was going to have to find something they could do, something that would not cause them to hurt someone or themselves. All she had to do was to get Liam to agree with her.

"Keira, they will be more of a threat than a help," Liam said. "Kester is a good lad, but I ne'er met one as clumsy as he is. And that Sir Archie is nearly blind."

"A sad end for a fighting mon," murmured Sigimor as he stared into his tankard of ale.

There was a look of sympathy upon Liam's face, but no welcome. Sigimor and Ewan's expressions were as difficult for her to read as ever. Keira had hunted the men down in Ewan's ledger room after everyone had supped. It had been impossible to discuss Sir Archie and Kester with any privacy until now. Worse, even though she had had hours to think of how to present her arguments in their favor, she had come up with very few.

"I ken that they will be little help," she said, "but they have nowhere else to go."

"Kester can return to the monastery." Liam grimaced when Keira slowly shook her head.

"He doesnae want to be a monk, Liam. His own father and uncle sent him there, making it all too clear to him *why* they did so. He doesnae have the calling. Better than anyone here, ye ken what that means. I cannae send him back, kenning that he will be trapped there, unhappy for God alone kens how many years. There must be something—"

"Take them," said Sigimor, smiling faintly when everyone stared at him in surprise. "She is right. There is nowhere else for them to go. The lad will be miserable as a monk, or he will run off somewhere else and get himself killed. He is a good lad, and I can see a strong, trustworthy mon in him. Just needs to grow into his feet."

"And Sir Archie who sees so poorly he talks to a tree thinking it is a mon?" Liam asked.

"Is a good mon, but will soon be dead if he cannae find a place to live out the rest of his life safely. We are blessed. If we suffered as he does, we would have shelter and family to aid us. He has no one. The lad and the mon together do weel enough. Young Kester is Sir Archie's eyes, and Sir Archie keeps the lad from falling down too often. And although Sir Archie cannae make his living by his sword any longer, he did so for a score or more years. He has skill and knowledge. Ye will need some of that to train new men to mon your walls." Sigimor winked. "So long as no one stands within reach of his sword, the mon can still show ye how he used it to stay alive so long as a mercenary."

Pushing aside the grief she felt over how many good men had died at Rauf's hands, thus necessitating the remanning of Ardgleann's walls, Keira said, "Mayhap they should stay here until we regain Ardgleann."

"Nay, take them," said Sigimor

Liam frowned at his cousin. "Since they cannae fight, why do ye think we should take them with us?"

"No real reason. Yet. If naught else, they can tend to the horses and guard Keira." Sigimor frowned. "Now why do ye look as if I just knocked ye offside the head?" he asked Liam.

"I was just recalling how Kester tended our horses every day when we were at the cottage," replied Liam. "He ne'er stumbled, ne'er had e'en the smallest accident whilst in the stables.

E'en Gilmour, a verra contrary beast, ne'er gave Kester any trouble."

Sigimor nodded. "He has the touch. That may be your answer."

" 'Tis a hard step down for a weelborn lad and a knight, mercenary or not."

"Nay as hard as the first step into a grave."

"Good point. Verra weel." Liam smiled crookedly when Keira hurriedly kissed his cheek, frowned when she did the same to Ewan and Sigimor, and then shook his head when she dashed off to give the news to Kester and Sir Archie. "And now, Cousin," he said, turning his attention back to Sigimor, "ye can tell me the other reason ye want us to take those two with us."

"What does Rauf Moubray do to any strong, hale mon he thinks might be a threat?" asked Sigimor.

"Kills them."

"Aye, just so, but no mon alive would e'er see young Kester or Sir Archie as a threat, would he?"

"Nay, he wouldnae," Liam said slowly. "Ye have a plan?"

"Only possibilities, but if one presents itself, I would like to have the proper tools close at hand."

CHAPTER 13

The aroma of roasting meat filled every corner of Scarglas. There would be a huge feast tonight, but Keira felt no joyous anticipation. In the morning, they would ride out and head for Ardgleann. No swords had been drawn yet, but the battle had truly begun. She pushed aside the guilt and doubt that assailed her. This was all Rauf Moubray's fault, not hers, and she let her anger at the man stiffen her spine as she went looking for Fiona.

When she and Liam joined the army they had gathered, there would be little privacy, so she had decided to treat this night as the eve of battle. Keira wanted it to be memorable for him as well as for herself, even if those memories made her blush right down to the soles of her feet. Since Fiona had been married for several years now, she rather hoped the woman could give her some ideas and advice. She was not sure that some of the things she did in her dreams were the sort of things men liked or would want their lady wife to indulge in. Keira also viewed such a discussion with Fiona as a good test. After all, if she could not even talk about behaving wantonly, there was little chance she would actually be able to do so.

To her delight, she found Fiona in her solar alone, cursing softly over her needlework. "Not going weel?" she asked as she sat beside Fiona on a well-cushioned bench beneath the window.

"Och, nay, 'tis going weel enough," Fiona replied as she set her work down and smiled at Keira. " 'Tis just that I like the results, but I dinnae much like doing the work."

"I ken that feeling verra weel indeed."

"Weel, spit it out."

Keira looked at Fiona in surprise. "How did ye ken I have something I need to, weel, *spit out*?"

"Saw the look upon your face as ye walked over here. It was an *I can do this* sort of look. Trouble?"

"Nay, nay trouble." Keira took a deep breath to shore up her lagging courage. "Since we ride for Ardgleann in the morning, once weel, we are with this army we have gathered, Liam and I will have verra little privacy, I rather thought that tonight—"

"Ye would give him a night to remember? Make his toes curl?"

Keira laughed. "Something like that. Since ye have been married for several years, I thought ye could advise me a little."

Fiona nodded. "Ye want me to give ye the knowledge I may have gathered, the value of my experience, so to speak."

"Exactly. Also, I have these dreams in which I act rather freely, but I am nay sure if what I do in those dreams is something a husband would wish his wife to do."

"I doubt ye do anything in your dreams that would shock Liam." Fiona got up to pour them each a tankard of cider. "If it makes ye feel good when ye do it in your dreams, I suspicion it will make ye both feel verra good indeed if ye do it for real." Fiona served Keira her drink, then sat back down beside her. "So let us talk." She winked at Keira. "This will be much more interesting than needlework."

" 'Tis what we expected," Sigimor said as he watched Liam pace the ledger room.

"I ken it," said Liam, tossing the message they had gotten from one of Sigimor's men onto the worktable. "I but hoped for something better."

"Some wee bit of stupidity on Rauf's part that would let us just tiptoe inside," said Lucas as he slouched down even more in one of the heavy oak chairs Ewan was so fond of.

"Aye, something like that," said Liam as he stared down at one of the drawings Keira had made that showed Ardgleann and how it was situated. "There is no way to cover ourselves if we must make a direct assault. 'Tis open land all 'round the cursed place, and since it sits upon a rise, the men on those walls will see us coming from a long way off."

" 'Tis why I chose to go now," said Sigimor. "In a few days' time, it should be the full dark of the moon."

Liam nodded, silently complimenting Sigimor's careful planning. As he fought to calm himself so that he could think more clearly, he studied the other ones gathered in the room with him, Sigimor, and Ewan. Nanty, Fiona's brother, sat on a stool near the hearth, idly cleaning his sword. Keira's brothers both sat in heavy oak chairs, their long legs stretched out, their ankles crossed, and their hands lightly clasped together and resting on their stomachs. At a glance, one would think them bored with it all, but he had known them long enough now to know they were as far from that as any man could be. Kester sat next to Ewan at the worktable, diligently making copies of the maps Keira had drawn of the inside of the keep. They would need those if they ever found a way inside. Sir Archie sat next to the boy, his back straight, his hands fisted on his knees, and a scowl on his face as he listened closely to every word said.

"The mon gained his prize by stealth and treachery," said Kester as he shook sand over the map he had just finished drawing. "He would expect everyone else to do the same, and he will have a keen eye for all the ways it can be done."

There was obviously a fine mind inside that tousled head, Liam mused, even as he murmured in agreement, "Hence the sealing up of all the bolt-holes."

"Nay," said Sir Archie, startling everyone. "A mon like that doesnae live as long as he has by cutting off all his routes of escape. Aye, he has closed himself up inside those walls to protect himself, but somewhere in there is a way for him to get out if all his defenses fail him."

Liam was glad Sir Archie's eyesight was so poor for his pride would have been badly stung by the looks of surprise cast his way. Only Sigimor and Kester looked as if the man's insight was just what one should expect. It galled Liam to admit it, but his cousin had been right again. Sir Archie might not be able to see clearly with his eyes or be a skillful fighting man ever again, but his years as a mercenary had left the man with a wealth of useful knowledge.

"Aye, ye are right, old mon," Sigimor said. "The question is where? And will anyone else ken about it?"

"Moubray willnae think so, but someone always kens," said Sir Archie. "Someone he is too arrogant to see."

"Keira kens where all the bolt-holes are, but we cannae risk testing each one."

"A waste of time," said Artan. "It willnae be able to be opened from outside the walls."

"So we are back to where we started," said Liam.

"Not exactly," murmured Sigimor. "We just need to have a wee bit of luck. And a plan."

After exchanging a grin with Ewan, Liam started for the door. "Weel, I am for bed. A mon I ken once told me that bedding one's wife until her eyes crossed was what a husband needed to do to keep her happy." He winked at Sigimor. "I think I will give it a try." He shut the door on Ewan, who was saying that he thought that sounded like a very good plan to him.

Keira scowled at the bedchamber door and then finished off her wine. If Liam did not join her soon, she was going to be either too annoyed or too drunk to carry out her plan. She suddenly grinned for she suspected there was another wife in another bedchamber feeling much the same. By the time she and

Fiona had ended their talk, Fiona had been making plans for her husband as well.

She was glad she had worked up the courage to talk to Fiona. Although she had been a little dismayed to discover that Ewan had told his wife all about Duncan and the humiliation she had suffered during her marriage to the man, it had helped in some ways. Not only had Fiona known that Keira had no previous experience and little knowledge, but in many subtle ways, she had also made Keira begin to truly believe that none of it had been her fault. So, too, had Fiona convinced her that her dreams were nothing to be ashamed of. Indeed, Fiona had been absolutely certain that Liam would be a very happy man if the woman who Keira was in her dreams greeted him in the bedchamber this night.

Looking down at herself, Keira realized she was no longer concerned about greeting Liam in what was little more than a thin veil of linen draped over her naked body. Fiona had called it a night shift, but Keira thought that implied a substance it simply did not have. Every night shift she had ever owned had been intended to keep one modestly covered and warm. This wisp of blue smoke she wore did neither. She poured herself another drink of wine to drown that faint pinch of modesty she still felt.

When the door to the bedchamber opened and Liam walked in, she nearly gulped down all the wine to drown a sudden onslaught of nervousness. The look on his face halted her for it banished that unease better than any drink could. The smile he wore slowly turned into openmouthed astonishment. His eyes grew wide as he hastily shut and locked the door. Even from where she stood, she could see his eyes turn that warm blue color that signaled his growing desire. He licked his lips, and she fought the urge to preen a little. Fiona had spoken the truth. Men did like to see a woman as good as naked, but not quite. And, she thought as she gave Liam a slow smile, if Fiona was right about that, the woman was probably right about everything else she had advised. As he walked toward her,

Keira found herself wondering if she ought to ask him to dance naked now or later, and almost laughed. That wanton lass who skipped through her dreams had definitely stepped to the fore.

Liam finally recovered enough of his wits to approach Keira. He was almost afraid to speak, as if that would break whatever spell she was weaving. Placing his hands upon her shoulders, he slowly moved them down her arms, pausing only to take the drink from her hand and set it down on the little table she stood next to. He took her hands in his and looked her over again. The linen shift she wore revealed enough to torment him and concealed just enough to make him want more.

"Where did ye get this?" he asked.

"Fiona has granted me the use of it for this one night," she replied.

"Now I ken why one actually sees the dour Ewan smile now and then. Mayhap ye can discover where she found linen so fine."

Deciding she had reveled in his flattering words and looks long enough to make her nearly vain, Keira tugged her hands free of his and began to unlace his doublet. "Mayhap I will. Of course, it isnae verra warm."

"We could build the fire up."

Keira could tell by the faint smile upon his lips that he was not just referring to the one in the hearth. As she slowly removed his clothes, the glint of curiosity in his eyes turned to one of challenge. She was in the mood to meet it. Recalling Fiona's advice concerning the value of anticipation, Keira took time to place each piece of his clothing carefully on a chair after she removed it. The way he stood there and allowed her to play her game excited her.

"Tell me, wife, are ye wide awake?" Liam asked when he was finally relieved of all his clothes.

"Oh, aye, wide awake." She looked him over as slowly and carefully as he had done to her.

"And how much wine have ye drunk?"

"Just one tankard and a wee bit." She placed her hand upon his chest and slowly caressed each rise and hollow. Beneath her palm, she could feel his heart beating as swiftly as hers was. "Did ye fear drink was making me act this way?" She stroked his taut stomach. "Nay, not drink," she whispered against his skin as she kissed the hollow at the base of his throat.

"Then 'tis that wanton wee lass who skips through your dreams."

"Mayhap. Are ye going to start dancing?"

"Mayhap. Later."

He was not surprised when that last word came out in something perilously close to a squeak for Keira had curled her long, elegant fingers around his erection. She had never touched him there before, and despite how badly he had wanted her to, he had forced himself to be patient. The way she was stroking him as she spread warm kisses over his chest was going to make patience very hard to grasp hold of this time, however.

He was trembling with anticipation by the time she knelt in front of him and began to caress and kiss his legs. It was hard to believe his wife, the virgin widow who apologized for kissing his stomach, was going to do what he now desperately wanted her to do. Liam had enjoyed the pleasure once, but the woman had so clearly thought herself the master of him that he had made it one of those things he did not do. It required a level of trust he simply had not felt toward the women he had bedded over the years. He trusted Keira completely, he realized. He especially trusted her only to give or share pleasure and never to use it to gain power over him.

When the warmth of her lips finally touched his erection, he shuddered with the strength of the desire that raced through his body. He groaned softly and threaded his fingers through her hair to encourage her, to let her know her daring was most welcome. The ferocity of the passion that took hold of him as she kissed him and stroked him with her tongue, all the while caressing his backside and thighs with her soft, little hands nearly made him dizzy. Keira would never use the passion they shared to gain power over him, but he realized she already held it. He was just thanking God that the one woman he could not resist had too gentle a soul and too much honesty to play such games when Keira took him into her mouth. Liam had to lock his knees to keep standing, and had only enough of his wits left to keep alert for the moment when he would have to step back.

That moment came far too soon for his liking. "Enough, love," he said as he grasped her by the arms and tugged her to her feet. "I dinnae want to finish there. Nay tonight."

Tonight he wanted to fill her with his seed as often as he could before they both collapsed from exhaustion. Liam did not really feel as if he would be facing death any time soon, but that risk existed whenever a man went to war. He had a keen desire to try to plant a child in his wife on this eve of battle.

As he carefully removed the delicate, borrowed night shift she wore, Liam was yet again surprised by his bride. The slightly dazed look she wore and the fine tremors rippling through her revealed that she had been as aroused by what she had been doing as he had been. It had been a lovely gift she had given him, but it was obvious she had fully shared in it, and he felt an odd clenching near his heart.

Picking her up in his arms, he took her to their bed, pausing only to satisfy his need to kiss her several times. Gently setting her down on top of the bed, he crouched over her. He doubted he would ever tire of seeing her delicate body, the way she looked with her long, dark hair spread out beneath her. After taking several deep breaths to regain some control over his lusts, he kissed her. There was something he knew all about but had never done, and he was eager to try it. Now it was his turn to give.

Keira moaned softly as Liam feasted upon her breasts. She was not sure how much she could endure as her need to feel him inside her was already strong and very demanding. Making love to him had stirred her far more than she would ever have imagined, even in her dreams.

As he kissed his way down to her stomach, he caressed her legs. Keira was so caught up in how good that felt that it took her a moment to realize he had subtly spread her legs. A touch of embarrassment born of a modesty she feared she might never fully conquer cooled her passion just a little. When she realized he was looking at her there, that she could actually see him doing it, she tried to divert his attention before that embarrassment she felt growing inside of her killed all the delicious heat in her body.

"Liam, I am nay sure I can endure much more play," she said, gripping the sheets in her hands as he kissed the inside of her thighs, his soft hair brushing over her woman's flesh in a caress that sent waves of desire rolling through her body.

"Be strong, wife," he said and gently nipped her thigh. "Think of scrubbing pots."

She opened her mouth to say that that was a foolish thing to say to her, but all that came out was a squeak of shock as he kissed her right *there,* in that place he had been staring at so intently. Her whole body tensed so much she lifted herself off the bed a little ways. Just as she was thinking it was because she could not tolerate such an intimacy, he stroked her with his tongue. Keira had the fleeting thought that she had just uttered a blasphemy when all ability to think left her and she became a creature of only feeling, heat, and need.

One tiny flicker of sanity came to her when she realized she was about to shatter. She cried out to him, asking him to join with her, but he ignored her. A heartbeat later, she felt her release tear through her with a strength that left her shaking. Liam gave her no time to recover, however, using his intimate kisses to drive her mad all over again, but this time, when she called out to him, he gave her what she asked for. The joining was fierce, and the ride hard and fast. Keira reveled in every too short minute of it.

* * *

Keira cautiously opened her eyes, frowned in confusion for a moment, and then blushed as memory came flooding back. She closed her eyes again, but it was too late. Liam already knew she was awake. He kissed her, and then she knew he was staring at her. When she opened her eyes again to find him grinning at her, she gave him a severe frown. He laughed, pulled her into his arms, and rolled onto his back. Sprawled on top of his naked body as she was, Keira found it a little difficult to remain dignified, especially when she found herself remembering how very good he had tasted.

"Has my wanton fled again?" Liam asked as he idly rubbed her back.

"She should be hiding under a rock, cringing in embarrassment," Keira replied.

Liam grinned again for even as she said that, she was running her fingers over his ribs in a soft caress. That wanton part of Keira might retreat a little now and then, but he had the feeling it would never be completely leashed again. He was feeling quite proud and vain for having loved her into a swoon. As he had waited for her to open her eyes, he had realized that something had been slightly different about their lovemaking.

Although Keira's passion had always been hot, beautifully matching his own, it had needed coaxing, and embarrassment or modesty had often intruded, making that climb to passion's heights a little rocky at times. The only hesitation this time had been when he had given her that most intimate of kisses, and it had been so fleeting as to be unimportant. In freeing herself to be as bold and daring as she seemed to be in her dreams, Keira had also fully unchained the sensuous woman inside of her. She had allowed herself to revel freely in every touch, every kiss, and it had been a wonder to behold. He had thought the desire they shared the best he had ever tasted, but now knew it could be even better. Liam would not let her hide that side of herself again.

"Och, nay, bring her back," he murmured as he combed his fingers through her hair, easing the tangles caused by their lovemaking. "She has naught to be embarrassed about."

"I am certain she broke several of the church's rules." Keira discovered that a very large part of her did not really care if she had. Liam was her lawful husband, after all.

"Nay doubt, but having studied all those edicts, I believe that there are far too many rules. At times, I begin to think the men who make them simply wish to be certain that no one finds any joy in the life God gave us."

Keira stopped kissing his chest and studied his face for a moment. "Is that one of the reasons ye decided ye couldnae bear a life in the church?"

"Aye, one of them. Just as there is in the world outside the church, within it, there is hypocrisy, greed, and a lust for power. I didnae have the calling strong enough to go on despite that, nay like your cousin has."

"He sees all of that, too?"

Liam nodded. "But this isnae the time for such solemn thoughts. Nay, not when I have that wanton lass from your dreams within reach."

Keira smiled a little. "The one ye were going to dance naked for?"

To her astonishment, Liam nudged her off him and got out of bed. He winked at her and then began to sing and dance. Keira laughed. The man did not have a modest bone in his body. He also had a very good voice. After watching him for a moment, she stopped laughing, although a smile lingered upon her lips. It was a silly thing to do, yet the man had such strength and grace in his body, it was a pleasure to watch him.

"I believe I also said I was certain that wee, wanton lassie would probably dance with me," he said as he grabbed her hand and tugged her off the bed.

For a moment, Keira felt both foolish and a little embarrassed, but then he began to sing again. It was a song she loved, and she was quickly singing it along with him. They danced a very courtly dance for a little while, the careful, measured steps and moves taking on a whole new meaning when danced naked. Then Liam started to sing a slightly risqué, more common tune, and they were soon cavorting around the room like two children, laughing, singing, and dancing as if they did not have a care in the world.

Keira was not sure who was the first to realize that joy had stirred up a very hot need, or if it struck them both at the same moment, but she suddenly found herself staring at Liam. He was staring right back, and she suspected the heat she could see in his eyes was reflected in her own. She licked her lips. He licked his.

Still feeling a little playful, she darted away when he reached for her. The chase was short, however, for she wanted to be caught. She screeched in surprise when he tossed her onto the bed, but welcomed him with wide-open arms when he joined her there. When he kissed her, she felt how fierce his need was, and hers rose up to equal it. It was rather nice to be a lusty, wanton lass, she thought just before passion burned away all clarity of mind.

CHAPTER 14

Subtly, Keira rubbed her sore backside. Two very long days in the saddle had left her aching and loathe to ride a horse ever again. What she would really like was a long soak in a hot bath, but it would be days yet before she could enjoy such a luxury. She would, however, take a good, hard wash in the burn they were camped near as soon as Liam returned.

And just how long could it take to get a look at Ardgleann? she thought. It was not far away, and since it was still light out, there was no chance of searching out any weaknesses without risking being captured. What really troubled her was how adamant Liam, Ewan, Sigimor, and even her brothers had been about her not going along with them. Keira supposed that could simply be because it was too dangerous to draw so close to Rauf. She had the distinct feeling, however, that they were afraid of what she might see, yet no one had brought them any news since they had stopped on the far eastern border of Ardgleann.

"M'lady, I have brought ye some cider."

Keira turned to smile at Kester. "Ah, thank ye kindly," she said, accepting the tankard and taking a deep drink of the surprisingly cool cider. "Perfect for clearing the dust from one's throat."

She glanced down and realized that Kester's monk's robe had been pulled up a few inches from the ground. When she looked up a little, she saw that he had bunched that extra length up above the rope belt he wore. Keira suddenly realized that Kester had brought her a full tankard of cider and that there was no sign upon him or the tankard that he had spilled even one drop of it. Although she doubted shortening the length of his robe would completely cure him of his youthful clumsiness, it had obviously helped.

"I could cut that extra length off, if ye want," she told him.

"Och, nay, but thank ye," Kester said. "Laird Sigimor did this, but he told me nay to cut it. Nay yet, he said."

And it was obvious that as far as Kester was concerned, Sigimor's word was law.

"He told me once Ardgleann is yours, I can have breeches to wear," Kester continued.

"But nay yet."

"Aye, Laird Sigimor says nay yet."

"I dinnae suppose he told ye why he wants ye to wait." She was not surprised when Kester shook his head, and she turned to look in the direction of Ardgleann again. "They have been gone quite a while."

"Nay so long as that, m'lady. Laird Sigimor said they were going to do a wee bit of watching. I suspicion good, careful watching can take time, if ye do it right."

Sigimor had clearly become Kester's new hero. She had to admit that the man was very patient with the boy. After having been cast out so callously by his own blood, Keira was a little surprised at how eagerly Kester accepted the guidance of the older men. There was hurt there, but no real anger or resentment that he then turned upon any adult male. She would have to find the right path for him to take, one that would make him a man to be reckoned with. Kester might not be angry with his kinsmen, but she was; one day, she would dearly like them to see how big a mistake they had made in throwing this boy away.

"I am o'er here, Sir Archie," Kester said and started waving his arms. "If ye walk straight toward me, there is naught in your way." Kester glanced at Keira. "He can see this movement, ye ken."

A moment later, Sir Archie had safely crossed the distance from the horses to them, and he patted Kester on the back. "Ye are a good lad."

The wind tousled Sir Archie's long hair, and Keira got a glimpse of the ragged scar that ran from his hairline just past the side of his right eye. "Ye said ye had trouble with your eyes after ye had a knock on the head?" she asked Sir Archie.

"Aye," replied Sir Archie. "Took a long time to heal, it did. Thought my sight would get better when it did heal, but it didnae."

"Did it fester a lot?"

"Lady Keira is a healer, Sir Archie," Kester said. "A verra good one."

"Nay sure any healer can fix this, but, aye, it did fester for weeks," he replied. "The poison didnae spread, however."

It might not have spread, but Keira was not certain all the poison was out. "Might I have a look at it?"

When he nodded, she carefully looked over the barely healed wound. It was rough, too rough. Keira feared there was something stuck beneath the closed skin, perhaps even in the bone. There were also signs that it still seeped poison from time to time. Aside from opening the wound up again, she could tell no more just by looking. With so many men she did not know well wandering close by as they settled into their camp, she did not dare use her gift either.

"I think, sir, that the wound needs to be reopened and thoroughly cleaned out," she said.

"Do ye think that if ye do that, it will make me see more clearly?"

"Nay, I cannae promise that." Although she thought there was a chance there could be some improvement, she was not going to raise the man's hopes. Until she got a very good look at that wound, she could not really be sure anyway.

"Then leave it as it is for now, m'lady. Once all is settled and ye are back where ye belong, I will think on it."

"I will be certain to remind ye of that, sir," she said and turned to frown in the direction of Ardgleann again. "What could possibly be taking them so cursed long?"

"A mon likes to look hard at his enemy's defenses," said Sir Archie, " and that takes time."

There was obviously nothing wrong with the man's hearing, Keira mused. "Weel, I hope they get back soon as I am growing keenly anxious to ken what they have seen."

"We cannae let Keira see this," whispered Liam as he stared in horror at the walls of Ardgleann.

He had not noticed anything at first; he had been too busy noting such things as the richness of the land they were crossing and the size of the village. It had been Sigimor's and Ewan's sharply indrawn breath and the whispered curses of Keira's brothers that had drawn his attention. At first, he had not recognized what he was looking at. When he did, he had had to struggle hard not to empty his belly. Dangling from the parapets of Ardgleann's walls were bodies. They were strung all along the wall like some gruesome necklace.

"I suspect they are the men who tried to defend their laird and their home," murmured Sigimor. "Rauf must think it will strike fear into the hearts of his enemies."

"And ye dinnae think it will?"

"Some, but then others will feel as I do. Angry. Verra, verra angry."

"The village is too quiet," said Lucas, drawing everyone's attention away from the walls. "And has anyone seen or heard any animals? 'Tisnae night yet. Why no sounds of cows, sheep, or those cursed, noisy fowl?"

Liam looked around and realized Lucas was right. It was too still and quiet. With light to see, someone should have been moving around. There was not even a mongrel dog to be seen.

"He has already stripped the place bare," said Ewan.

"Either that, or he is hoarding everything inside those walls," said Liam. "When Sir Ian comes, he may ken more."

"Aye, and if the mon has seen what Lucas has, it would explain how quickly and eagerly he allied with us."

"Rauf's rather like those locusts in the Bible."

"Verra like, now that I recall the tale. No thought to the future either. If he has been feasting each and every meal, slaughtering livestock without a thought to breeding more, he will have to reach out for the lands and possessions of others just to keep from starving." Glancing toward the quiet village, Ewan added, "And he will care naught that he has condemned all of them to death with his greed."

"I told ye he needs killing," Sigimor said and turned to start back toward their camp.

The others were quick to follow him, but Liam stared at the keep for another moment. If this was the sort of thing Sigimor had seen as the result of Rauf Moubray's work, it was no wonder he was so eager to rid Scotland of the man. Liam was also certain that this was not the only atrocity the man had committed. There was no way he could hide all of the truth from Keira, and he worried about how he would keep her from drowning in guilt she had not earned. He crossed himself, bowed his head, and said a prayer for the souls of the men on the walls awaiting a proper burial. When he turned to follow the others, he found Sigimor waiting for him.

"Havenae completely shaken free of the monastery, have ye?" Sigimor said as he fell into step beside Liam.

"Oh, aye, I have," Liam replied. " 'Tis just,"—he shrugged—"they needed a prayer."

"Aye, they did. She will find out, ye ken. There is no hiding all of this from her."

Liam nodded. "I ken it, but I will try to hold back the ugliness for as long as I can. She doesnae need to see it either, for her to bury herself in guilt."

"Guilt for what?"

"For nay being here, for taking months to return to help them."

"Fool lass. If she had stayed, she would have been dead or wished she was. As for waiting? Weel, she needed to heal, and 'tis only just now the season for battle. I see no cause for guilt."

"Neither do I, but it may take more than those truths to cleanse her of it."

" 'Twill fade when she sees that none of those who survive will be blaming her."

"Ye dinnae think they will?"

"A fool or two might, aye. There are e'er people who need someone to blame for every ill. But, nay, I doubt many will think ill of her. She is just a wee lass. I suspect a lot of them will be fair amazed that she actually came back to help them. After all, she was only the lady of Ardgleann for a few months."

Liam slowly nodded. "True. There was no time for any real bonds between the lady and the people to form."

"Now, ere we reach the others, I have a question I must ask ye. It has been gnawing at me since we left Scarglas."

"Weel, ask it then."

"Did I really hear singing and stomping coming from your bedchamber that night?"

"It wasnae stomping. It was dancing." Liam had to bite back a grin at the look Sigimor gave him.

Sigimor grunted and shook his head. "When ye left us earlier that night, ye had said ye were going to love your wife until her eyes crossed."

"Mayhap that is why I was singing and dancing. With my wife. Naked."

This time, Liam could not hold back his laughter. Sigimor looked both intrigued and as if he feared Liam had gone utterly mad. "Aye, it was a great foolishness, but it was strangely, weel, freeing. Come, there must be something ye do with Jolene that would make others think ye mad yet makes ye feel carefree, exuberant even."

"Swimming. Swimming naked with her." Sigimor nodded.

"Felt like a fool all the while I did it, but 'tis why I made that wee pond. Water is warmer in there, ye ken."

Liam thought of the pond that had slowly appeared over the course of a year. He had thought Sigimor had made it to hold fish or to attract wild fowl for the table. Not once had he ever thought Sigimor and Jolene were sneaking out there now and then to swim naked together. It would explain the rather high stone wall that almost completely surrounded it. That was not to try to keep predators away as he had thought, but to give the laird and his wife some privacy as they cavorted in the water.

"I wonder if Keira can swim," he murmured and grinned when Sigimor laughed.

Keira heard laughter and relaxed a little. Ewan and her brothers had looked so grim when they returned, she had felt afraid. Their answers to her questions about Ardgleann had been suspiciously vague. So she had returned to watching for Liam, certain that he would tell her the truth. Hearing that laughter, she could not believe that things could be as bad as she had feared.

Liam saw Keira and felt all his good humor flee him in a rush. Sigimor was right to say he could not hide the truth from her forever, but he was determined to do so for as long as he could. He smiled at her, put his arm around her shoulders, and kissed her cheek.

"I dinnae suppose a ray of light from the setting sun pointed out the way to sneak into Ardgleann," she said, exchanging a nod with Sigimor before he went to join the other men.

"I fear not, love," replied Liam. "It all looks just as high walled and sturdy as your drawing showed it to be."

"Ye went there to make sure my drawing was accurate?"

"That was one reason, though a verra small one. Ye did a verra fine, verra precise drawing, but looking at the keep still helped us get a feel for the place. Aye, 'tis all open ground around the keep, but it looks as if it hasnae been grazed or scythed for months. That could provide a wee bit of cover if we keep low. Together with the fact that 'tis the dark of the moon, it could be enough."

"But it would be much better if ye could slip inside the keep itself and begin the fight right in the heart of your enemy's lair."

"Aye, it would be."

"Then I think we must seek out Malcolm," she said and prepared herself for an argument.

"Nay, there is too much risk of being seen," Liam said, shaking his head.

"Malcolm may ken something that could lead us to that bolt-hole ye are all so certain is still there."

"And Malcolm may be dead." He sighed and kissed her forehead when she paled. "Sorry, lass."

"Nay, 'tis but the truth. Howbeit, I think it worth a try. His home is at the end of the village nearest us. Unless Rauf has posted guards at every turning, we should be able to get to Malcolm safely."

"I dinnae like it."

"Neither do I," said Sigimor as he stepped up to them and handed Liam a wineskin, "but 'tis too good a chance to not take it. Malcolm may weel ken about which bolt-hole has been left unsealed. E'en if he doesnae, he will have information we might make use of."

Liam continued to argue for several minutes, but saw that it was a waste of breath for they were right. "Can we trust this mon Malcolm?"

"Aye," replied Keira. "He is a good, honest mon."

"Good and honest enough to have held true to his loyalties e'en whilst under Rauf's boot?"

"I believe so. I told ye, all Malcolm wants in life is to live quietly with his wife Joan and make beautiful things. He would loathe a mon like Rauf. I am verra certain of that."

"We saw no guards about the village," Sigimor said.

Keira thought that odd but kept her attention fixed upon

the matter at hand—convincing Liam that they should go and speak to Malcolm. "For the sake of all these men and the others who will soon join us, I think we should try to get to Malcolm. He may not be a warrior, but he was trained as a knight. He might have seen something over these last few months, some weakness ye can use against Rauf."

That was a truth Liam could not argue with, although he dearly wished he could. The fact that Sigimor thought it a good idea only made arguing more impossible. Liam knew his cousin would never allow a woman to put herself at too great a risk. That Sigimor was agreeing with Keira meant that the man felt that the risk of her going was probably not that great or that it was worth it for all they might gain. Liam sincerely hoped it was the former.

"When it is full dark, we will give it a try," he said, unable to keep his reluctance out of his voice. "For now, we shall busy ourselves building a wee shearling to shelter under."

"I dinnae mind sleeping outside, Liam," Keira said.

"I dinnae want ye sleeping in the midst of an army. Verra soon there will be men here we dinnae ken weel."

Considering how many of her cousins and his were there, Keira did not think that would be such a great problem, but she said nothing. The way Liam scowled at the amusement Sigimor did nothing to hide told her that silence was probably best for the moment. In truth, she would prefer a little shelter, even one of sticks and mud, just in case the weather turned against them. She did not mind sleeping outside, but she was not fond of it when she was cold and wet.

In the end, they had a lot of help. Keira got the feeling that her kinsmen and his thought it a good idea, despite how they teased Liam. A messenger arriving from Sir Ian MacLean saying he would be arriving with his men in a few hours and another from the other laird's son offering himself and ten men apparently prompted so much assistance. When Keira saw the results, she decided not to complain about their overprotective attitudes. The walls were a mix of stone and branch, and the roof was of oiled cloth. It was only high enough for her to sit up in, but it would certainly protect her from all but the fiercest of storms. With another oiled cloth hung over the opening, she and Liam would actually have some small measure of privacy.

It was not until well after they had supped that Liam decided it was dark enough to attempt a visit to Malcolm. He yet again offered his opinion that no one could be certain Malcolm could still be trusted, even if he was still alive, but no one heeded him. Reluctantly allowing Keira to lead the way, they started toward the village.

Liam was so busy looking for any signs of trouble, he did not pay much heed to the path Keira led him along. It was not until he heard her give a soft, strangled cry that he realized they had come within sight of Ardgleann keep. Cursing softly, he hurried over to take her in his arms. She clung to him, pressing her face against his chest, and wept.

Looking at the keep, Liam cursed again. Torches upon the walls cast light upon Rauf's gruesome battle trophies. The bodies looked even more horrifying than they had when he had seen them in the light of day. That Keira, a softhearted woman and a healer, should be subjected to such ugly brutality was reason enough to kill Rauf Moubray.

"I should ne'er have left them," Keira said in a hoarse, unsteady voice.

"Dinnae be a fool, love," he said, pushing aside his sympathy for her grief and forcing himself to sound firm. "If ye had stayed, ye would probably be just another bead strung upon that gruesome necklace."

Keira moaned and nearly threw herself out of his arms. "I am going to be sick."

That did not surprise Liam. He had come very close to it himself. Ignoring her demands for him to go away, he supported her as she retched. When she was done, he tugged her back into the shelter of the wood, away from the sight of Ardgleann. It troubled him when she sat silent, trembling faintly as he bathed her face with water from the wineskin she carried. He then forced her to rinse her mouth with a few sips from the wine he carried in his. He was now glad he had made them carry such things, even though they were going only a short way, simply because he always prepared for the worst. Still not sure this trip to Malcolm was a good idea, he had wanted to be ready to make a run for their lives, one that would, by necessity, have been in the opposite direction of their camp and kinsmen.

Sitting beside her, he put his arm around her shoulders and held her close. "I hadnae wanted ye to see that."

Taking a deep breath to steady herself, Keira said, "That is why Ewan and my brothers looked so grim when they returned from seeing Ardgleann, isnae it?" She felt him nod, his cheek rubbing against her hair with the movement. "Why would anyone do such a thing?"

"To terrify the ones still living."

"Is that why ye think Malcolm is dead? Do ye think he is up there?"

"I think those are the ones who tried to defend their laird and their home."

"Did none of them survive?"

"Some. Sir Ian said there are some people from Ardgleann sheltering on his lands. A few of the fighting men, who will come with him, and some of those who worked and lived within the keep. That is how we ken that all the bolt-holes are sealed. Four men ran for one only to find some of Rauf's men guarding it. Only two escaped to try for another. One lass hid herself away for nearly three days until she was able to sneak away. She told Sir Ian and others how Rauf had ordered all of them sealed tight."

Keira looked in the direction of the keep, knowing she would see that horror for the rest of her life. For a moment, she wanted to turn around and go somewhere, anywhere else, and never return, but she quickly shook that cowardly thought aside. Duncan had failed her in many ways, but she would not fail him. Nor would she fail the people who were suffering under the rule of that beast who called himself Rauf Moubray. She might have to depend upon men to actually rid Ardgleann of Rauf, but she would see to it that it was restored to all it had once been. There would probably always be ghosts there, but she would learn to live with them.

"We will kill him, aye?" she asked as she stood up and brushed off her skirts.

"Aye, love," replied Liam. "We will kill him."

"Good. Now, let us go and talk to Malcolm." As she started on her way again, she ignored Liam's muttered complaints.

CHAPTER 15

"Are ye sure the mon will still be there? Or willing to help?"

Liam pretended not to hear Keira's sigh as he crept along behind her. He knew he was repeating himself, but he could not fully banish a growing unease. A small voice in his head kept reminding him that she had not known these people very long and that they had been under Rauf's boot for months. She was wagering her life on what could be no more than a brief acquaintance with the man. The village also gave him a bad feeling. Lucas was right; it was far too quiet. E'en though it was now late, he did not think it should be so still, so silent and dark. Aside from his fear for her life, he was concerned that if she saw many more signs of Rauf's cruelty, she would be weighted down with a guilt he could not talk her out of.

"He will be here," she whispered back, "if he is still alive, and he *will* help."

Keira understood Liam's concerns. She shared them. These people had suffered for several months beneath the rule of a man more cruel than she had imagined. She could not know how cowed they were. She could not even be sure Malcolm was still alive. The man was a survivor, but Rauf might have learned of Malcolm's true heritage, and could easily have seen him as a threat. Rauf made a quick end to any threat. She truly had not needed to see such gruesome evidence to know that fact. Her reassurances to Liam were said as much to calm herself as to still his very reasonable concerns.

She crept up to the small door hidden cleverly by a rough stone chimney and thick ivy. Silently praying that she was not leading both of them to their deaths, Keira rapped upon the door using the series of knocks Malcolm had taught her. Lacking Duncan's optimism, Malcolm had quickly taken her aside when she had arrived at Ardgleann and had shown her this secret entrance. It had aided her when she had fled Rauf, and she hoped it could provide help now.

As the door slowly opened, Keira felt Liam move up close behind her. She did not need to look to know he had his sword at the ready. He took his duty to protect her very seriously. That ought to make ye happy, she scolded herself as she studied the shadowed man peering at her from around the edge of the door.

"Malcolm?" she whispered, not sure this somewhat timid man could really be her friend.

"M'lady? 'Tis really ye? Sweet Mary, we all thought ye had died!" He started to fling open the door, then abruptly stopped when he saw Liam behind her. "Who stands with ye?"

The hard, angry suspicion in Malcolm's voice stung a little, but Keira pushed aside her hurt. She had left these people at the mercy of Rauf for months, had not even tried to send word that she had survived. He did not know her well enough to know she would never betray him or the rest of the people of Ardgleann.

"My new husband—" she started to reply.

"Ye have married again?"

" 'Twas, weel, unexpected."

Liam edged forward slightly. "The light falling from your open door and all this whispering could draw attention we dinnae need. Best we sort this all out inside."

"Of course, I am but stunned into stupidity," Malcolm said. "Come in."

Ushering Keira in before him, Liam carefully looked around

what appeared to be a very dimly lit workshop of some sort. When Malcolm lit another candle, Liam realized the shapes he had seen were pieces of finely carved wood and beautifully marked metal, a few looking very much like silver. Even the wooden goblets were of a quality no man would be ashamed to set upon his table.

He said nothing as the man led them to a smaller room, waving them toward benches flanking a table. Liam sat next to Keira and watched Malcolm gather three goblets and a jug. There was a strange awkwardness to the way the man held the jug in his right hand. As Malcolm set it down on the table, Liam inwardly cursed. The man's hand was scarred, his fingers crooked.

"Oh, sweet heaven," Keira cried. "What happened to your hand, Malcolm?" She reached out to touch the gnarled hand Malcolm rested on the table, but he allowed her only a fleeting touch. It was enough, however, to tell her that he was probably in constant pain from broken bones that had healed badly.

"Rauf Moubray happened," Malcolm replied as he poured them all some ale.

"He kens who ye are?"

"Nay, I dinnae think so, or I would be dead. He didnae do this because of who I am. He did this because I tried to stop him from taking my wife."

"Och, nay. Nay. Not Joan."

"Aye, my Joan. She is up at the keep. They took many of the lasses up there, e'en wee Meggie, the cooper's daughter, who is barely thirteen."

Keira covered her face with her hands. Her cowardice had cost the people of Ardgleann far more dearly than she could have imagined. She felt Liam gently rub her back, but that touch gave her little comfort. Forcing herself not to give in to the urge to weep, she looked at Malcolm.

"I am so sorry. I should have returned sooner."

"To do what? Die? Be raped by those brutes? Ye were sorely injured when I last saw ye. I suspect it took ye a while to heal."

Malcolm shook his head. "Nay, lass, ye have naught to be sorry for."

"Nay? Whilst I hid safely at the monastery, ye lost your wife and your livelihood." She briefly touched his injured hand again. "I ken how much ye loved your work."

"Still do."

"Ye can still carve and all with this hand?"

"Och, nay, but it doesnae matter. Ye see, m'lady, I hide it weel for some still think it the mark of the devil, but, weel, I favor my left hand. Always have." He smiled fleetingly and then sighed. "I would let the bastard take my carving hand if it would give me back my Joan. I dinnae care what the men have taken from her, if ye ken my meaning, save that it will hurt her in body and soul. I just want her back. Without her, I cannae see the beauty in the wood or metals, cannae bring it out."

"We will get her and the others back," Liam said, the man's sharp look telling him that Malcolm had heard the vow weighting every word.

"Ye have fighting men with ye?" Malcolm asked.

"Some and more to come."

"Rauf and his men are good."

"We are better." Liam smiled. "We also have men with us who could steal the shroud off a corpse e'en as the dead mon's kinsmen lower him into the grave. And get clean away."

"I am nay sure that is something to be so proud of," Keira murmured.

"Mayhap not," agreed Liam, "but 'tis useful."

"And then ye will be our laird?"

"Keira tells me that ye are the true heir although ye be bastard born."

"I dinnae want to be the laird. Ne'er have. Told m'lady's father the same when he asked. I just want to be with my Joan and search for the beauty in the woods and the metals. Nay, if ye rid us of Rauf Moubray, ye are more than welcome to be our laird. Duncan kenned that I didnae want that duty. 'Tis one reason he sought a wife. Aye, and we were all willing to accept her as our laird if aught happened to Duncan."

"But a mon as the laird would be so much better, of course," muttered Keira, and then she almost smiled when both men eyed her warily.

"Weel, aye, if only to keep others from trying to claim Ardgleann," said Malcolm. "Just who are ye?" he asked Liam.

"Oh, sweet heavens, I ne'er introduced ye to each other, did I?" Keira shook her head. "Malcolm, this is Sir Liam Cameron of Dubheidland, my husband, as I said. Liam, this is Malcolm MacKail, Duncan's half-brother, though 'tis evident he still wishes to keep that a secret from most people." As the two men nodded to each other, she continued, "He is also kin to the MacFingals of Scarglas." She briefly smiled at Malcolm's look of confusion. "They are Camerons, too, but the old laird had a falling out with his kinsmen and gave himself a new name. It is still being argued over."

"A tale I shall wish to hear when this trouble ends. Who are the reivers?"

"The MacFingals," Liam replied. "They are fine fighters as weel, mayhap e'en better than my kinsmen, though I risk a lot in saying so. Most of them have spent near all their lives surrounded by men eager to kill them."

"And yet they still live."

"Exactly."

"How many fighting men do ye have with ye?"

"Forty, give or take a few. Camerons, MacFingals, MacEnroys and a few of their allies, and some Murrays."

"And Kester and Sir Archie," said Keira. "Ye forgot them."

Liam exchanged a brief look with Malcolm, and the man nearly smiled, revealing that he understood there was a good reason Liam had not included them in his tally of fighting men. "Dinnae fear, lass; I will yet think of a way to make use of them, one that willnae hurt their pride and yet give them a goodly chance of surviving the battle."

Keira grimaced. Kester and Archie had courage and honor,

but Liam was right to exclude from his count of good fighting men. Kester was showing improvement and revealing some skills that could make him a valuable asset in the future, but he was still a beardless boy who spent far too much time sprawled on the ground. And poor Sir Archie, she thought with a sigh. He had skill and knowledge, but unless she could find a way to help him see the world as more than a blur, he would be as great a threat to his allies as to his enemies.

"What do ye need from me?" asked Malcolm.

"Information," replied Liam, and he immediately began to ask Malcolm about the defense of Ardgleann and the strength of Rauf's forces.

As she listened to the men, Keira felt her fear stir to life, and she struggled to bury it again. In the weeks since he had taken hold of Ardgleann, Rauf Moubray had strengthened its defenses. The man obviously had a keen eye for any weakness that could be made use of by an enemy. It did not surprise her that the first thing Rauf had done was seal off all the hidden entrances to the keep. The only way into Ardgleann still appeared to be over the high walls or straight through the gates. Such battles would cost an attacker dearly in men, dead and wounded. Keira wanted to put a stop to it all, but she knew that was impossible.

Her sense of guilt was like some live thing writhing inside her. If she had come sooner, Rauf would not have been so securely settled within the walls of Ardgleann, poor Malcolm would not be maimed, and the women of Ardgleann would not be suffering so grievously. No matter how many reasons she gave herself, it was mostly fear that had kept her hiding at the monastery.

In an attempt to push aside the bitter taste of failure and thoughts of her own cowardice, she studied Malcolm's hand and then reached for it. He started slightly, but Liam held his attention. Keira knew Duncan had told Malcolm of her gifts, but she suspected Malcolm had nurtured doubts, perhaps even some fear. For now, however, the man seemed willing to allow her to do whatever she wished, and Keira took quick advantage of it.

It was not until she released Malcolm's hand and opened her eyes that Keira realized the men had ceased talking. Malcolm was staring at her in wide-eyed astonishment, but she saw no sign of fear or horror. Liam, however, had his hand on the man's forearm, holding it firmly in place. She had been so lost in Malcolm's pain and her struggles to discern the extent of his injuries, she had not even noticed that at some point, he had obviously made an attempt to pull free of her grip.

"Do ye have any bread, honey, and cider?" Liam asked Malcolm when he saw Keira sway slightly and grip the edge of the table to steady herself.

"Aye." Malcolm started to stand up, but Liam was already on his feet, and he held him in his seat with one hand upon his shoulder.

"Nay. 'Tis best if ye stay seated. Tell me where it is."

Liam quickly served Keira the bread, honey, and cider, silently urging Malcolm to have some as well. He ignored the man as he urged Keira to concentrate, whispering to her as he helped her to picture cool water washing away the pain now resting in her hand. Then he sat down and, ignoring her weak protests, took her onto his lap and held her close. He smiled faintly when in less than a minute, she slumped against him, sleeping deeply.

"Duncan was right," Malcolm said in a soft voice as he stared at his hand. "She has the touch. Duncan was so pleased by that."

"Aye." Liam absently kissed the top of Keira's head. "She doesnae often use it so fully. It costs her dearly to do so, as ye can see." He looked at Malcolm's hand. "Ye should be eased of most of your pain for a day or more. 'Tis nay healed, ye understand."

"I ken it, but a respite from the pain, nay matter how short-lived it is, is gift enough."

"When she wakes, here or later at camp, she will probably tell ye if there is any hope of mending it, e'en if only a wee bit."

"She was seeing the damage beneath the skin, wasnae she?"

"Aye, in a way I doubt I will e'er understand. Just why was Duncan so pleased with her gift?" Liam wondered if this man knew the whole ugly story of Keira's failed marriage.

"He hoped she could heal him."

"He was ill? She has ne'er said so."

Seeing that he and Keira had finished the cider, Malcolm poured Liam and himself some more ale. "Duncan's first interest in wedding the lass was to gain a strong alliance with her clan for he kenned she would be able to call them to her side if needed. When she told him of her gifts, he was e'en more eager to make her his wife as he hoped that some day, she could cure him." Malcolm grimaced and took a deep drink of ale before he said, "He had a weakness in his male parts."

Liam stared at the man for a moment. "Ye ken the whole truth, dinnae ye?"

"That the marriage was ne'er consummated? Aye, but the trouble was ne'er with his body. It was in his mind, I think. Mayhap in his heart."

"He wasnae impotent. She told me how he behaved each time he tried to bed her. Was he mad?"

"Aye and nay. He had desires, felt a deep lusting for the lass, but he couldnae act upon it. I blame his parents. Aye, his mother mostly, but his father was near as bad. I willnae trouble ye with all they did to the lad, the many ways they worked to breed the troubles he suffered from, but they succeeded in making him unable to bed a lass. They and that vile priest they kept at Ardgleann for many years. Lust was sin, filth, a sure road to the flaming pits of hell, and so many other sad things, including beatings and other hard punishments. The poor lad couldnae feel a fine, healthy lusting without being tormented, made nauseous e'en. If the marriage had lasted longer, it may have worked. After all, marriage and the begetting of children is no sin, aye? But the fates decided it wasnae to be."

"Yet his father must have felt such urgings and acted upon them, or Duncan wouldnae have been born and ye wouldnae be here."

"True, but the mon also whipped himself bloody for such sin, and he did so often. His wife often used my presence as proof of the loathsome foulness of men and their bestial urges."

"Ye need say no more. I had thought it so. I studied to be a monk for a while and met some men of that ilk." Liam felt the last of his jealousy of Duncan drown in a torrent of sympathy. "The mon's childhood must have been a constant torment."

"Sadly, aye, it was. I feel certain he ne'er told me e'en half of the things they did to him whene'er they suspected he was e'en thinking a lustful thought."

"He ne'er told Keira. She thinks he found her undesirable, that it was her fault he couldnae bed her. I dinnae think I have really succeeded in making her believe otherwise."

Malcolm shook his head. "Poor lass. I told Duncan that he should be fully honest with her, but he was slow to work up the courage. And then, his chance was gone."

"How many ken this truth?"

"Only a few, and they will ne'er speak of it. She is a good lass, and those who ken the truth are more than willing to accept her, and thus her clan, as laird. Ye may need to prove yourself. Although if ye can rid us of that foul demon now holding the keep, 'twill undoubtedly win ye everyone's loyalty."

Liam slowly shook his head. "Mayhap, but much more than defeating that swine will be needed to make Ardgleann what it once was. Signs of the mon's brutality and greed are everywhere. I am a wee bit surprised he left ye with any of your finer pieces."

Malcolm glanced toward the room where his work was displayed, then looked at Liam. "He took a few, but what matter that? He robbed me of my greatest treasure, of my heart and soul when he took my bonnie Joan," he finished softly in a faintly choked voice. "I cannae sleep for thinking of what my wee lass may be suffering, and I feel as if I am damned because

I can do naught to help her. I stare at that keep and think of how I ache to kill that bastard. Too many times, I have started toward it, determined to confront Rauf, only to be halted by my own cowardice."

"Your own good sense," said Liam sharply and then softened his tone. "Do ye really think it would aid your wife if she had to watch ye slaughtered before her eyes? How much more would she suffer if her hell included seeing your corpse rotting in chains and hung from the battlements like those other poor souls?"

Paling slightly, Malcolm shuddered and whispered, "They werenae all dead when he hanged them there."

Liam cursed softly and profusely. "He needs to die." He smiled, and if Malcolm's slightly uneasy look was any indication, it held all the fury and loathing he now held for Rauf Moubray. "I shall be sure to tell my cousins and Keira's brothers about that."

"That will matter to them, will it?"

"Oh, aye. It will enrage them. They have all the reason they need to want that bastard out of that keep. He has stolen from one of their own and left her a widow. But this will harden that calm resolve into a cold, intense one. Seeing the bodies hanging from the walls began that. This tale will finish it nicely."

Malcolm stared at his hands. "I am no true warrior, but I can wield a sword, m'laird."

A sense of pleasure rippled through Liam at Malcolm's form of addressing him. The battle had not yet been fought, but this man was clearly stating that he had already accepted Liam as laird of Ardgleann. A lot of people would scowl over his sudden rise in power and prestige, but only the opinion of the people of Ardgleann truly mattered. This first step toward their acceptance was a heady one.

"Then ye are welcome to join us. All we need now is a plan," he added lightly as he absently kissed the top of Keira's head.

"Ye love the lass, dinnae ye?" Malcolm said and briefly grinned when Liam blushed faintly.

"I believe I might," Liam replied and grimaced. "She didnae really choose this marriage." He told Malcolm a very succinct version of all that had happened to bring him and Keira to this point. " 'Tis slow work to convince her that I will be a faithful husband and that all these riches I have gained arenae the reason I wanted her."

"Aye, 'twill be hard work, I am thinking. Poor old Duncan's troubles left her wounded in some ways, I suspect, since he ne'er gave her the true reason for them."

Liam nodded and then turned the conversation to the battle facing them. It was clear that Malcolm had the sort of knowledge that could prove vital in the days ahead. When the man made it clear that he was more than willing to leave his home and join them, Liam did not waste any more time. Within moments, he was leading the man away from the village, the fact that he had to carry a still sleeping Keira not slowing his pace at all.

Keira blinked, looked around, and then frowned. When and how did she get back to their camp? She slowly sat up as Liam approached her and held out a tankard she recognized as one of Malcolm's. Smiling her thanks, she drank down the cool cider as he sat down beside her.

"Is that Malcolm o'er there talking to Sigimor?" she asked.

"Aye." Liam draped his arm around her shoulders and held her close to his side. "He asked to join us, and his knowledge of who is inside the place, and sometimes where, is valuable. Unfortunately, he cannae be sure which bolt-hole might be the one Rauf would choose for his own."

"The battle will begin soon?"

"As soon as the others arrive, or soon thereafter."

"There is no turning back now, is there?"

He kissed her cheek. "Nay, lass. After all ye have seen here, would ye truly want us to walk away?"

Keira slowly shook her head. " 'Tis just that I only want Rauf

Moubray and his dogs to be hurt, and such a clean justice isnae really possible in the battle to come."

"Probably not. Yet, if a mon must die, 'tis best if he does so in a fight to rid the world of such filth. Aye, and the men from the neighboring lands who are joining with us come because they ken that a mon like this will soon bleed his stolen lands dry and look to theirs for more gain. As Sigimor says, this man is a boil that must be lanced."

"I should have heeded those in my family who expressed concern about the marriage," she muttered.

Liam took her face in his hands and forced her to look at him. "Ye must shed this guilt that gnaws at ye, lass. None of this is your fault. Duncan was intent upon getting himself a wife. Rauf has wanted Ardgleann for a long time. Those hard truths were there ere ye e'en met Duncan. If nay ye, he would have wed another lass. At least ye had the wit and strength to survive and return with an army."

"Too late. I—"

He stopped her words with a brief, hard kiss. "By the time ye were healed of your own wounds and certain Rauf wasnae hunting ye down, it was already too late to stop the worst of his cruelty. Give up the guilt, Keira. Ye are the only one who thinks ye have earned it."

"Mayhap." She rested her head against his chest. "Have ye come up with a plan? Something better than a direct assault upon the walls?"

"Soon. 'Tis brewing. And I promise ye, wife, 'twill be a verra cunning plan indeed."

CHAPTER 16

"That is your brilliant, cunning plan?"

Keira stared at Liam, Sigimor, Kester, Malcolm, and Sir Archie in utter disbelief. She suspected she looked as appalled and angry as she felt, for all five men looked wary, although Sigimor also looked amused. The plan to send Kester and Sir Archie into the keep to find a way to let the rest of them in was utter madness, yet none of these men seemed to think so. How they could possibly think a clumsy boy and a man who saw the world as if through a thick mist could accomplish anything other than getting themselves killed, she did not know. Unfortunately, she could not say that aloud. Kester and Sir Archie had their pride. Worse, they looked eager to take on such a dangerous task, to be such an important part of this battle.

"Liam, if I might speak with ye privately?" She was not sure why her cold, angry request should make Sigimor grin so, but she had already decided that he was a bit odd.

For a moment, Liam hesitated. There was really nothing to discuss. The plan was set, and all had agreed that it was their best chance to avoid a serious bloodletting. Then he saw the fear in her eyes. If nothing else, he needed to soothe her concerns for their two friends, and that would require a little privacy. Things might need to be said that could hurt Kester's and Sir Archie's feelings or batter their pride.

"Aye, lass," he said as he took her by the arm, "but we cannae argue o'er this for too long."

"I said I wished to speak with ye, nay argue," she protested as he led her toward a large tree at the far edge of their camp.

"I suspicion we will be doing a wee bit of both."

The moment they halted and faced each other, she snapped, "Are ye insane? How can ye e'en think to send those two into that place, right into Rauf's bloody grasp? 'Tis like sending lambs to the slaughter. E'en ye have spoken of how Kester cannae walk a yard without stumbling, and Sir Archie has been kenned to attack a shrub, thinking it a wild boar."

"Exactly."

She frowned. "What do ye mean?"

"They willnae be seen as a threat."

"That doesnae mean they will be safe. It just means Rauf willnae raise a sweat in the killing of them."

Liam took her in his arms and rested his chin on the top of her head. "Aye, there is danger facing them. I cannae lie to ye and say there isnae. Howbeit, Rauf kills only the strong, only those who are a threat to him. Or those who anger him. No mon could e'er see Kester and Sir Archie as a threat, save that they might fall on him."

"How can ye be sure of that?"

"I cannae be, nay fully, but I am certain enough to risk two lives. Kester and Sir Archie seem witless, harmless fools unless ye take time to speak to them, come to ken who they are. Together, they make one verra clever fighting mon. Kester is Sir Archie's eyes, and Sir Archie is Kester's strength. They will go in there claiming your cousin sent them to speak to ye, and Rauf will at least hesitate ere he kills them. He will want to plot out the best way to keep your clan from coming 'round, at least until he can strengthen his defenses e'en more."

Keira stepped back to frown at him. "But how can they use that to help all of ye slip in behind the walls? Rauf watches everyone, and the men he has are as vicious and wary as he is."

"Two things will give Kester and Sir Archie a chance. They

will appear helpless to Rauf, no threat at all, so he probably willnae bother to confine them. And Kester can make himself sound like Rauf."

"Weel, aye, but he cannae make himself look like him."

"Sir Archie can. There will be no moon tonight. E'en Malcolm says that in the shadows, he could pass for the mon." Liam lightly kissed her when she continued to frown. "Kester and Sir Archie have practiced so that when Kester speaks, Archie moves his mouth. I have advised them to nay try anything if they ken the risks are too great, to only look about and tally the number of men, what arms there are, and where there may be a weak spot."

"And they badly wish to do this," she murmured.

"Verra badly. If this doesnae work, our only other choice is a direct assault upon those walls."

"Which could cost far more than just two lives."

"Aye. Everyone is willing, but invading the nest of this adder in the dark of night would be far better." He stroked her cheek with his knuckles. "And, nay, there is no turning back from this. Ye must needs cease wavering in your commitment, sweet Keira. We have gathered the army needed. Now, we must act."

She nodded and then looked around at the men camped amongst the trees. There were some of her kinsmen and their allies and some of Liam's. Little by little, more men had gathered during the short time they had been camped there. Last night, in the short time she and Liam had been with Malcolm, their army had visibly increased. It astonished her that Rauf still seemed unaware of the army gathering on his border. They were camped only a short march away on MacLean land, and that should not have made them invisible.

"How can they not ken that we are here?" she muttered. "Does the mon do naught but huddle behind those walls?"

"That appears to be his strategy. There have been scouts, but they are easily evaded." Liam smiled faintly. "Or were sent running by the men Sir Ian has set all along his border with Ardgleann. If Rauf suspects any trouble, that will be the mon he expects to bring it. Since Sir Ian's clan is a small one and isnae kenned as one eager to get into a fight, I doubt Rauf is worried about them at all." He put his arm around her shoulders again and started to walk her back to the others.

Once back with the other men, Keira listened closely to the whole plan. Kester and Archie would go in as emissaries from the monastery, sent out by Brother Matthew to search for her. They would claim that no one had seen her for months but that they had heard that her husband had died and that she had headed back to her kinsmen. It would make Rauf believe she was dead and that word of his crimes had not yet spread over the land. Since Kester and Sir Archie would approach Ardgleann just before the gates were closed at sunset, it was assumed that they would be invited to remain at Ardgleann until morning. If they could not find a way to let the others slip inside under the cover of a moonless night, they would leave in the morning after gathering all the information they could.

It all sounded so clever and well thought out, but Keira could not help but be afraid for Kester and Sir Archie. A man like Rauf could not be counted upon to do what was expected of him. She said nothing, however. The intense pride Kester and Sir Archie felt over being chosen for this little sortie was almost painful to see. To express her doubts would hurt them.

The sky was just turning the colors of the sunset when Sir Archie and Kester set out. Sir Archie rode an aging cart horse, and Kester trotted along beside him on a hardy Highland pony. They certainly did not look threatening. She was a little startled when Sigimor stepped up beside her and patted her on the head.

"They will be back, lass," Sigimor said. "Hale and puffed up with pride in a job weel done."

"Ye sound verra certain of that," she said.

"I am. They have the wit, the courage, and the need."

"The need?"

"Aye, the need to be a part of Ardgleann once ye and Liam

claim it. Aye, and the verra great need to be seen as worthy and useful."

Keira watched the man stride away, pausing only once to knock down a grinning MacFingal. "That is a verra odd mon," she murmured as Liam took her by the hand and led her toward their part of the ever growing camp.

Liam laughed softly and nodded. As he crouched by their small campfire to stir the pot of mutton stew she had begun earlier, he attempted to explain Sigimor. When he finished his string of tales, he wondered what the frown she wore meant. Sitting by her side, he kissed her cheek and then her hand.

"He married an Englishwoman?" Keira said and sighed with a false exasperation when Liam laughed. "I think I may have been told that, but either I didnae listen close or it slipped my mind."

"She is a wee, bonnie lass who stands up to him. Jolene doesnae tolerate any nonsense, though he can still stir her into a fierce anger at times. 'Tis a rough place I come from, full of rough men, but there is none better to my way of thinking."

"Rough but close. He is a good mon for all his odd ways. Ne'er think I meant elsewise. Aye, and thinking on all ye have told me, he truly is like a father to his clan." She smiled faintly. "And he is right in what he says about Kester and Sir Archie, curse his eyes. They *need* to do this. They need to win a place here, nay just have it given to them."

"Sigimor is often right. 'Tis one of the more annoying things about him." He grinned when she laughed, pleased to see that her fears had eased for the moment.

"In all your planning, did ye decide what I am to do?"

"Stay here."

"But—"

"Ye will stay here, lass. If I can, I will send Kester and Sir Archie back to be your guards, or someone will be left behind to do it, but here is where ye will stay until I can come and get ye." He grasped her by the chin and gave her a quick, hard kiss.

"And if anyone flees this way, ye will hide. The mon tried to rape and kill ye. Dinnae give him a chance to succeed."

Keira opened her mouth to argue with him and then shut it. There really was nothing she could do to help while the battle was being fought. In truth, she could easily endanger them, for they would feel compelled to keep a close guard on her. Watching out for her instead of watching out for the enemy could get men killed. Her time would come when the battle ended and there were wounds to tend. It would be hard to sit and wait, however, wondering all the while how those she cared for were faring.

After sharing their meal with Sigimor, Ewan, Malcolm, and her brothers, Keira crawled into the small shelter Liam and the others had built for them. It had proven a good shelter from the chilly wind and mist that had seeped into the area during the night. She had wanted to stay with the men while they talked, but it had become painfully clear that her presence had restricted what they said. Since they were in many ways fighting for her, she had quietly left them to make their plans.

Curling up beneath the blankets, she hoped Liam would not think she was always so meek and accepting. She also hoped he did not linger too long with the other men. Despite the uncertainties that still plagued her concerning their marriage, she was sure of one thing. She did not like to sleep without him at her side.

"Weel, I ne'er thought to see the day," said Artan, looking at Liam with mild wonder, "but it appears ye have tamed our Blackbird."

"Dinnae believe it," said Liam. "She didnae want to leave, but is a wee bit cowed at the moment by a burden of guilt and a heavy sense of debt for what all these men are going to do."

"She has naught to feel guilty about, and I dinnae think anyone here expects her to feel indebted to them."

"True, but 'twill take time ere she believes that."

"If anyone should feel indebted, 'tis ye," grumbled Lucas, nimbly ducking when Sigimor swung at him. " 'Tis true."

"Aye, it is," agreed Liam. "I reached high. I ken it. I also ken that I gained the most from this marriage."

"If ye make her happy, none will care."

Liam inwardly sighed. It was obviously going to take time for Keira's brothers to accept him fully, even though they had forced the marriage. The other Murrays in the camp seemed content to accept him as Keira's husband, although they had made it clear that he had better be a good one. If he stepped wrong, he had better start running, Liam mused. A quick glance at a grinning Sigimor told him his cousin was thinking much the same. Liam also knew that if he shamed or hurt Keira, the Murrays would be hard-pressed to get to him before Sigimor did.

"I intend to be a good husband," Liam said firmly. "I have given ye my word already, I believe. Now, shall we discuss what lies ahead one more time?"

"Is it not difficult to make plans when ye arenae certain what Sir Archie and Kester might accomplish?" asked Malcolm.

"Some," agreed Sigimor, "though 'tis always best to have more than one plan."

"Ye dinnae think we will need more than one, do ye?" asked Liam, recognizing how calm his cousin was and what that meant.

"Nay. I feel certain they will succeed, if nay in getting us in tonight, then in bringing us vital information." He looked at Keira's brothers, whose doubt was clear to see on their handsome faces. "As I told your sister—they have the wit, the courage, and the need. They are eager to make a place for themselves at Ardgleann."

"But Keira has already given them a place here," said Artan.

"Aye, *given* them one. Tastes a wee bit too much like charity, and there will be those who see it that way. Ah, but now, despite their obvious weaknesses, they have marched right into the lion's den, and they will be the ones who breach those defenses."

"Devious. 'Tis a verra devious mon ye are."

"Thank ye. I do my best." Sigimor then began to relate his very exact plans for the battle ahead.

When Sigimor was done and what little discussion there was began to wane, Liam stood up. Keira's brothers immediately fixed him with a look that was not quite a glare. He suspected that some of their lingering unease with him was due to the fact that he was bedding their little Blackbird.

"Where are ye going?" asked Artan.

"I am going to my bed where mayhap, I will be a good husband," Liam drawled and almost grinned at their ill-tempered grunts.

Sigimor laughed and stood up. "Everyone should try to get a wee bit of rest. We may need to move fast and fight hard soon."

As soon as everyone left, Liam put out the fire. With so many men around, it did not need to be kept lit to hold any animals at bay. Just outside the opening of the crude shelter he and Keira shared, he stripped down to his braies, had a brief wash with the water Keira kept in a bucket just outside the opening, and then crawled inside. It was so dark he had to grope around until he found a way to slip beneath the blankets, and then he removed his braies. Turning onto his side, a light touch revealed that he was behind Keira. He slipped his arm around her and tugged her close to him. The way she murmured his name and pressed close to him, fitting her lithe shape against his body, had him ready and eager in a heartbeat.

He had always been a man of healthy appetites, but Keira made him ravenous with just a smile. Once this battle was over, he was going to do his best to make her see that, to make her understand that he neither needed nor wanted another woman. Thinking of the battle ahead, he grew even hungrier for her. Although he still felt no premonition of impending death, he knew he would soon be facing it. It made him nearly desperate to make love to her, to try again to leave her with child. Kissing her neck, he slid his hand beneath her shift.

Keira awoke to the feel of a lightly calloused hand upon her breast, long, skillful fingers gently teasing her aching nipples. She could feel Liam's aroused body pressing against her back. For a moment, she savored the heat he was stirring inside her, but then she recalled where they were.

"Liam," she said, placing her hand over his, "we may be hidden from view, but any sound we make will be heard by every mon out there."

"Then ye had best be verra quiet," he whispered as he tugged her shift up to her waist.

A gasp escaped Keira as he stroked his way up her inner thigh, all the while kissing her neck. When he slipped his hand between her legs, she tensed, but the clever play of his fingers over her heated flesh banished her lingering embarrassment over such an intimacy. Since she had let her wanton side make an appearance, a lot of her unease had disappeared. She clapped a hand over her mouth when she started to make those soft, little humming noises she was unable to hold back.

"Liam," she finally whispered, shaking with the need to feel him inside her, "I must turn round now. I need—"

"Hush, my lass, I can give ye what ye need." He gently cocked her leg back over his and slowly entered her, delighting in the shiver that went through her as he pushed himself in as deeply as he could.

His slow thrusting drove Keira wild. She reached around and lightly dragged her nails over the back of his thigh, something she had quickly discovered that drove Liam wild. His movements grew gratifyingly fiercer. Then he slid his hand down from her breasts and with but a quick touch sent her tumbling into bliss. She retained only just enough of her wits to clamp both of her hands over her mouth. A small part of her was aware of Liam pressing his face against her shoulder to muffle his groans as he released his seed deep into her womb.

It was several moments before Keira recovered enough to realize that Liam had pressed her legs together, holding himself trapped with her. "Um, Liam?"

"Let me linger a wee while, sweet wife. 'Tis a fine place to be."

"Oh. I didnae ken that there were three ways to do this," she said, and she was glad of the dark when she felt herself blush. She was even gladder of it when she felt him grin against her shoulder. "There are more?"

"Aye, and after I have rested, I will show ye another."

"Shouldnae ye be resting in case ye are needed later?"

"That is what I *am* doing." He nibbled her ear when she giggled. "I can think of no better way to spend the time before a battle than wrapped tight in your arms."

Keira wanted to believe his sweet words. In fact, she wanted to believe him so badly, it made her very aware of her weakness for the man and helped her keep a firm grip upon her wariness. If he wished to spend the hours before a battle in her arms, making love until neither of them could move, however, she was willing to be a full partner in that plan. Just thinking of what could happen to him in the coming fight chilled her to the bone, and she pushed away those dark thoughts. Then she thought of what, even now, could be happening to Sir Archie and Kester.

"They will be safely returned to us, will they not, Liam?" she suddenly asked.

Since he was concentrating on the lovely curve of her neck and trying to decide where to kiss it, it took Liam a moment to understand the meaning of her question. "Aye, my tenderhearted wife, they will be. Remember, they have three weapons to use."

"Of course—wit, courage, and need. I pray they are the strong shields your cousin thinks they are."

"They are." Liam slipped free of her body and turned her around to face him. "Now, to banish your worry, I believe 'tis time we tried a fourth."

"A fourth what? Oh my. That fourth."

* * *

Kester waited until the door of the tiny room he and Sir Archie had been shown to was shut, then collapsed onto one of the small beds. He was barely fifteen years of age, and he had just looked death in the face. It was not a pleasant experience.

"Are ye unweel, lad?" asked Archie as he stumbled into the side of the other small bed and sat down.

"Nay, I am terrified."

"Wheesht, cannae blame ye. 'Tis ne'er easy on a mon's innards to be set in the heart of the enemy's camp."

Sitting up and resting his back against the wall, Kester looked at the man who was rapidly becoming more of a father to him than his own had ever been. "Ye do look a wee bit like him. In the dark, if I give ye the voice, few would guess ye werenae him. In the dark, none could see those eyes, anyway."

"What is wrong with his eyes?"

"They are, weel, yellow. Like some cat's, I think, but he has the cold, unblinking stare of an adder."

"Cats have an unblinking stare."

"Weel, aye, but mostly when they are hunting. And I have ne'er feared cats. Ne'er thought them evil as some do. Evil creatures wouldnae be so helpful in keeping the vermin down or be so loudly happy for a pat or a wee scratch on the ear." He smiled faintly when Sir Archie chuckled. "This mon is evil. If we hadnae appeared so helpless, e'en foolish, he would have just killed us, and probably nay quickly. He thought us so little a threat, he didnae e'en take your sword. One look in his eyes, and ye ken that the coldness there runs deep. The lost look, the despair upon the faces of the women there, few of whom were free of bruises, only confirms that. Nay, these men are naught but rabid beasts, and 'tis past time they were killed."

"And they will be. As soon as we are able, we will begin our search for a way to help our allies do that without having to hurl themselves against weel-defended walls."

Kester began to speak and then shut his mouth when Sir

Archie suddenly tensed and began to ease his sword out of its scabbard. "What is it?" he whispered.

"I swear I can hear something in the walls," Sir Archie whispered back.

"Rats?"

"Psst!"

Sir Archie smiled faintly. "I dinnae think rats say 'psst!' "

Even though Sir Archie appeared to have relaxed, Kester pulled his dagger free from the sheath strapped to his arm where it was hidden by the sleeve of his monk's robe. He peered around the dimly lit room and saw a faint line of light in the middle of the far wall. Just as he started to creep toward it, the thin line widened, revealing an opening in the wall and a small, pretty face surrounded by tangled red hair.

"Come, I can show ye a way out," the girl said.

Wary of a trap, Kester asked, "Why should we wish to leave?" He frowned when she rolled her big, brown eyes and gave him a look of utter disgust.

"Because ye want to find a way to let those men in to kill that bastard Rauf. I ken a way. I be Meggie, the cooper's daughter. I took to hiding in these walls when I was dragged here by those swine. I have slipped away a few times and saw the men gathering at the border of Ardgleann lands, and I saw Lady Keira."

"But we were told Rauf had sealed all the secret ways out of here."

"How could he when he didnae ken where they all were? Nay many do."

"Then how do ye ken it?"

"Because I have been slipping in and out of these walls since I got here. Some of the other women hide with me now and again, but they didnae want to let that bastard ken there were any hiding places, so 'tis only me what stays in here."

"Why havenae the women used them to escape?"

"To what? They cannae go home, and they also ken that their family will suffer for it. One lass who fled had to watch her father killed. I didnae because Rauf and them dinnae really care that I am gone."

"Now, two of the ways out of here arenae sealed tight. One he didnae find, and one is just barred from the inside." She held out her hand. "Come."

"Go with her, lad," said Sir Archie. "Unbar that door that is secured. Then hie yourself back here." Archie looked at the girl. "Can ye go to where the men are camped and tell them all ye have learned? Lead them in here?"

"Aye," Meggie replied, "but why would ye stay here?"

"To be sure there isnae anything stopping the men from entering at this end. Ye get them in from the outside, and we will get them in from the inside."

Just before he followed Meggie, Kester gave Sir Archie a brief, crooked smile. "Weel, it appears we have accomplished our mission without doing much of anything. I am sure that one day, I will be able to gracefully accept sharing this victory with a wee lass." He shut the door on Sir Archie's soft laughter.

CHAPTER 17

"Time to buckle on your sword, lad."

Liam blinked, stared at the hand wrapped around his ankle, and then grimaced. He nodded at Sigimor, who quickly disappeared, but it was too late to keep the call to arms a secret from Keira. Even as he moved to dress and arm himself, she was tugging on her clothes. She said nothing, however, until they were both outside their little shelter, watching Sigimor talk to a little red-haired girl.

"Where are Kester and Sir Archie?" Keira asked, almost relieved to have something else to fix her worry on, aside from the fact that the man she was helplessly in love with was about to go into battle.

Hearing her question as he approached them, Malcolm replied, "Still inside. The wee lass is Meggie, the cooper's daughter. She has told us how to get inside. Kester and Sir Archie stayed to make certain no traps could be set for us."

"So Rauf didnae hurt them or imprison them?"

"Nay, m'lady. He thought them naught but harmless fools, and from what Meggie tells us, he is busy planning some tale of your fate with which to send them on their way in the morning."

"And Joan?" Keira asked, feeling certain Malcolm would have asked the girl about his wife.

"Alive," was all Malcolm would say before striding away to join Keira's brothers.

Seeing how upset Keira looked, Liam wrapped his arm around her shoulders and held her close. "Alive is the most important thing, lass. All the rest can be healed with time. At least the wee lass Meggie seems to have come away unharmed."

Keira nodded, watching the young girl talking so seriously with Sigimor and the other men. "What shall we do with her whilst we go into Ardgleann?"

"We?" Liam stepped back and shook his head at her. "Nay, wife, ye will stay here."

"Here? But 'tis *my* battle. Since ye willnae have to hurl yourselves at the battlements as we feared, then I can come with ye."

The look on Liam's face told her there was little chance he would bend in this, but she felt compelled to try to change his mind. Slipping into the keep unseen and surprising the enemy could not be as dangerous as a full assault against the walls. She had heard that said time and time again. Since it would not be as dangerous for them, then it would not be as dangerous for her. Keira said as much to Liam, but the over my dead body look on his face did not change at all. The man she was hopelessly in love with obviously had a wide stubborn streak.

"There will still be fighting, wife," Liam said, struggling to deny her without sounding arbitrary, for he knew she could turn contrary on him if he played the overbearing husband. Keira had a habit of bristling when given a direct command. "Aye, fate has smiled upon us and given us a way inside those thick walls, a chance to surprise our enemy. But that enemy isnae going to surrender en masse, is it? If naught else, they have too much innocent blood on their hands, and they ken it weel. They will believe there will be no mercy shown them, even if they do lay down their arms."

"And so they will decide to die fighting," she said and sighed when he nodded.

"Some will try to flee, and some will succeed, but most will see their choices as few. Die by hanging, or die by fighting. They are going to fight hard, and I dinnae want ye in the middle of it. 'Twill be difficult enough trying to ensure no inno-

cents die in the battle to free them. I suspicion that is one reason Sir Archie sent the lass here to tell us how to get inside—to
get her outside."

"So I must still wait here and just worry about all of ye."

"Aye." He pulled her into his arms, silently praying that he
would soon return to hold her this way again. "Stay here with
wee Meggie."

"Will Meggie nay have to lead ye to the places where ye can
get inside?"

"Mayhap, but she will be sent right back here to wait with ye.
Within the keep, there will be few safe places. We may get in
unseen, but there is no kenning where everyone is inside the
place. We have all carefully studied the map ye drew us, but
from that lass, Kester, and Sir Archie, we can only learn where
everyone *should* be or *may* be." He stepped back a little and
gave her a brief, hard kiss. "Stay here, my wife. Keep a close
watch. If ye see anyone approaching this camp, warn the
guard, then hide fast and stay hidden. If 'tis one of us, ye will
ken it soon enough."

Although it felt as if every part of her ached with the need to
stay close by his side, Keira nodded. It was the wisest and safest
thing to do for all of them, but she hated it. The thought of
how she would spend the rest of the moonless night, waiting to
see if Liam, her brothers, and all the rest of the men she cared
about returned safely, sent a shiver of dread through her. Common sense told her she would be more hindrance than help,
that the only thing she could do to keep him safe was place her
body between him and a sword, but she dearly wished it were
not true.

She walked with Liam as he went to join the others. Ignoring
their grumbles, she hugged each of her brothers. Since they
heartily returned the embrace, she knew their complaints
about foolish women were false. She even hugged Malcolm,
Ewan, and Sigimor. The last two startled her by how vigorously
they returned the embrace. It was not until Liam yanked her
away from Sigimor and glared at both widely grinning men

that she realized they had acted so oddly just to stir his possessiveness.

Before she could say anything about indulging in such foolish games when they were facing a hard battle, the men were
all leaving. She was just thinking that she needed to hug her
cousins when she found herself alone. In only a moment, the
darkness had swallowed them all. Even the sound of so many
armed men moving through the shadows swiftly faded. Keira
wrapped her arms around herself and shivered, praying that
was not some omen. The touch of a hand upon her arm drew
her out of her dark, frightening thoughts, and she looked at
Meggie. The girl had obviously not been needed to show the
men the way.

"They will win, m'lady," Meggie said. "Ye have some braw
allies and kinsmen. My father said 'twas one reason the laird
chose ye as his bride and as the one to stand in his place if
aught happened to him. Of course, ye are bonnie, too."

"Thank ye." Keira was a little surprised that everyone knew
Duncan had sought a wife for such reasons.

"Aye, my father said that made ye an e'en better choice for
ye would soon marry again if the laird died, giving us a strong
mon to care for the land. And ye did, didnae ye?"

"I certainly did. A strong mon with an army of verra strong
kinsmen." She smiled faintly. "And of course, he is bonnie,
too." Her smile widened a little when Meggie giggled.

"Dinnae worry. He will be back as bonnie as ever."

"I dinnae much care if he is still bonnie, just as long as he is
still alive."

"Och, he will be."

The confidence of youth, Keira thought. " 'Tis what I pray
for."

Meggie frowned and stared down at her feet as she scuffed
one foot in the dirt. "M'lady, is that lad Kester really a monk?"

Despite the worry she was plagued with, Keira almost smiled
again. "No longer. He was sent to the monastery by his kinsmen who didnae want him, but Kester doesnae have a true call-

ing. When he learned what I was going to do, he followed me to Scarglas, the keep of my husband's kinsman. He found Sir Archie along the way. I am nay sure what they will do, but they have a home with me now." When Meggie smiled at her, Keira gave her a wink. "Kester needs a wee bit of growing yet, but I think he will be a braw laddie one day."

"Aye, he just needs to grow into his feet."

"Ah, ye have a brother, dinnae ye?"

"Three." Meggie glanced toward the banked fire in the middle of the camp. "I dinnae suppose there is aught to eat, nay with so many men about."

"I think we can find something." It was not until they were seated by the fire, with Meggie devouring some bread, cheese, and rabbit stew, that Keira dared to ask, "How are the people in the keep? Has it been verra hard for them?"

"It has been hell, m'lady," Meggie said and shivered. "Rauf and his hounds are vicious. They take whate'er lass is near to hand whene'er they choose. Complaining just gets ye beaten. When Malcolm asked about Joan, I was that pleased that I could tell him she only suffered in the first week and that she isnae that sad. Rauf discovered she was a good cook. From that day onward, she was left alone. The brute likes his food more'n he likes raping women. The only thing that saved me was that I havenae grown much in my chest, ye ken. The bastards were so busy squabbling o'er who would get which more fulsome lass after they had grabbed us all that I was able to slip away. I think they just forgot about me after that."

Keira put her hands over her eyes and fought the urge to be violently ill.

"Here now, m'lady, dinnae weep. 'Tis soon o'er, isnae it? And my father says any mon who scorns a woman because of what she has suffered in there will have some good sense knocked right into him."

It took Keira a moment to shake free of her grief long enough to realize what Meggie's words implied. "Ye have seen your father since ye were captured?"

"Aye, twice. Once when he brought some barrels to the keep and once when I slipped away. He had to go into hiding, or he would be in this fight. Aye, my brothers, too. He o'erheard two of Rauf's dogs asking after my eldest brother, saying the lad was imper—, impertee—"

"Impertinent?"

"That be the word. Weel, my father kenned what it meant. Kenned it meant my brother was a dead mon, too, so he and my brothers took to the hills fast as they could. I would have gone, too, but I thought I best stay in case ye did come back and needed a way inside." Meggie shoved the last piece of bread into her mouth and rolled her eyes as she chewed it. "Rauf was enraged. Beat those two fools of his near to death for failing to bring him my brother to kill."

"I should have come sooner," Keira whispered. "I am such a coward."

"Wheesht, no one thinks that," said Meggie as she licked her fingers clean. "Truth is, most ne'er expected ye to come back at all. Some thought ye dead, too. When I told Joan about the men gathering and how I saw ye with them, she was that surprised. Then she cried. Happy tears, ye ken."

"Ye told Joan?"

"Aye. Shouldnae I have? She willnae tell anyone."

"Nay, of course she willnae, but does Joan ken what ye have done this night?"

"She does. Had to tell her as I didnae want her looking for me as she is wont to and worrying if she couldnae find me. Told her she might try to get as many people as she can to someplace safe. She said she would."

"What a wonder ye are." Keira smiled when the girl blushed so deeply that it was clearly visible in the faint light from the fire and then frowned. "Why didnae the women slip out of there when ye found a way for them to do so?"

"Because Rauf would kill their families. Killed one lass's father when she managed to flee out the gate one day, and she didnae get verra far either."

"Sigimor is right—that mon needs killing."

"Och, aye, and 'tis a shame ye cannae kill him a few times o'er."

"Aye, a verra big shame. How would ye like to work in the keep?"

"As what?"

"As whate'er suits ye and whate'er skills ye have."

"Once that vermin is gone, I would like that. Ye did say Kester was staying with ye, didnae ye?"

Keira nodded, and the girl gave her a very adult, very feminine smile. Poor Kester did not have a chance.

Liam winced when Kester opened the door, and the light in the room stung his eyes. He stumbled into the room, somewhat pleased to hear the men with him do the same, indicating that he was not the only one affected by the long, slow walk in the dark passage. When his vision cleared, Liam realized that several women were with Kester and that they had entered what looked like a large storage room. Just as he was about to ask Kester why the women were there, Malcolm rushed by him, whispering his wife's name. Seeing the woman who now clung to Malcolm, Liam was a little surprised. The way the man had talked about his wife had made Liam think she was a beauty. Joan was short, thin, and somewhat plain.

" 'Tis good these women are safe," Liam said, "but ye took a risk in telling them about us."

"I didnae," replied Kester. " 'Twas Meggie. She told Joan, and Joan has been bringing women down here for the last hour. Seems Meggie slipped away and saw us at the camp. She kenned who we were and that we were trying to find a weakness."

"Aye, she is a clever wee lass."

"Aye, 'twould seem so. Rauf and his men have had no warning, if that worries ye."

"It did for a moment." Seeing that the room was now crowded with the men who had come with him, Liam moved toward Malcolm and lightly patted him on the back. "We must move now. We cannae be cornered here, or all our good fortune will be for naught."

"Aye, m'love," Joan said, pulling free of Malcolm's embrace. "Go. Clean Ardgleann of this plague."

"Kester, ye stay here to make sure none of these swine have the chance to escape," Liam ordered. "And to guard the women. I suspicion more will gather here soon." He looked at Joan, who nodded.

"Ye dinnae think I can fight, do ye?" Kester muttered.

"Ye have ne'er been bloodied in battle, lad. Aye, ye need training. There is no shame in admitting that. And I have given ye a most important part to play. Guarding the escape route and the women is verra important, and I have no doubt ye will do it weel."

Even as Kester stood straighter and nodded, Liam began to lead the men out of the room. With only the slightest whisper of a signal from him, the men started to move away. In groups of two or three, they would all make their way through the halls, and using Keira's map and little Meggie's information, they would hunt down Rauf and his men. For as long as they could, they would stealthily cull the ranks of their enemy.

Liam usually considered a dagger thrust from the shadows murder, not a battle tactic, but he felt no such qualms now. As they had made their way to the keep, Sigimor had told Liam all that Meggie had told him. Even in telling them where the men might be, the girl had revealed a lot. Rauf and his men had turned the once peaceful Ardgleann into a living hell. He wanted the keep washed clean of this vermin as quickly as possible.

As Liam and Malcolm left a room where there now rested two dead men, they met up with Sigimor. Pausing only to send a woman to where Joan and the others hid, Liam then turned to his cousin. Sigimor's dagger was bloody, but he looked so calm that no one outside would believe the man had been creeping through the halls of the keep killing. Liam suspected

Sigimor felt it was all a justified punishment, and one that was long overdue.

"I cannae believe no alarum has sounded yet," said Sigimor.

Sigimor had barely finished speaking when a half-naked man dripping blood from a shoulder wound stumbled out of a room yelling out a warning to Rauf and his men. Liam looked at Sigimor and shrugged. Muttering about fools who could not even silence an unarmed, sleeping man, Sigimor strode toward the wounded man. Liam heard his cousin ask the man if he surrendered. The man's reply was grossly profane as he struggled to unsheathe his dagger. Sigimor killed the man with one clean thrust of his dagger. He then stood there, spread his arms wide, and let out a battle cry that caused Malcolm to jump, then mutter a few curses in an unsteady voice.

"The mon has a fine set of lungs," Malcolm said.

Liam laughed even as he listened to the results of the alarum and Sigimor's battle cry. No more was there only a whisper of sound as Keira's army slipped through the halls. Now one could hear the sound of running feet, men calling out to others to join them, and then, finally, the sounds of swords clashing. Now the battle had truly begun.

"Keep Malcolm close," Sigimor ordered. "That bastard may have left a few of the MacKail men alive, and we will need him to recognize them. Dinnae want to kill the wrong men. Now let us hunt down Rauf the Rat."

"Your cousin is a wee bit odd, isnae he?" murmured Malcolm as he and Liam hurried to keep up with Sigimor.

"Och, aye, just a wee bit. I warn ye, if ye e'er meet his wife, ye will fall over in shock."

"Ah, then she isnae some large, buxom warrior woman."

"Nay, a wee, black-haired Sassanach." Liam had just enough time to laugh at the wide-eyed shock on Malcolm's face before the battle began in earnest.

It soon became clear that Rauf Moubray's men had been trained to do one thing well—protect Rauf Moubray. While others dealt with the men in the bailey or upon the walls, Liam joined Ewan, Sigimor, Malcolm, Sir Ian, and a few others in cutting down anyone who tried to stop them from reaching Rauf. The few people they met who were of Ardgleann were shielded until they could flee the danger. Sigimor sent them to Sir Archie, and Liam sent them to Kester and Joan.

Liam confronted one of Rauf's men within feet of the entrance to the great hall. With Malcolm guarding his back, Liam fought relentlessly, slowly driving the man back one step at a time. As they passed through the doorway, Liam stumbled slightly and heartily cursed his still somewhat weak right leg. That awkwardness could have cost him dearly, except that the man he was fighting also faltered, stumbling over the huddled body of a terrified child. Screeching out a vicious curse, the man raised his sword, clearly intending to kill the child. Even as Liam hurried forward, knowing he would be too late, a knife buried itself in the man's throat. The child cried even harder as the man's life's blood came pouring out, and he collapsed, dead at the feet of the child he would have murdered. Liam looked at Malcolm, unable to hide his surprise.

"I thought ye said ye were no warrior," he said as Malcolm calmly retrieved his knife.

Malcolm shrugged. "I can only wield a sword adequately. However, I am verra good with a knife."

"So I see." Liam suddenly saw the man they all wanted to kill standing at the far end of the great hall behind eight well-armed men. "See that the child gets to safety, Malcolm."

"I should watch your back," Malcolm said.

Glancing back at the doorway, Liam saw Ewan, Sigimor, Sir Ian, and Keira's brothers standing there. "No need to worry about that now. See the child safely away, and come back if ye are eager to join the fight."

Malcolm nodded, grabbed the child, and hurried out of the great hall. Liam started toward Rauf and his men, hearing his allies quickly step up behind him. He knew what the positioning meant. Once Ardgleann was free, he would be laird here, and they were signaling that fact by this show of deference. The look that crossed Rauf's broad face told Liam that that man understood it, too.

"Do ye surrender?" Liam asked, halting just out of sword reach of Rauf and his men, although it did not look as if Rauf intended to be at the fore of this fight.

"And just who are ye? What right do ye have to come and take what is mine?" demanded Rauf.

"Sir Liam Cameron. I have married Lady Keira Murray MacKail."

"That bitch is still alive?"

"If ye are thinking of surrendering, it might be wise to cease insulting my wife."

"I will do more than insult her! If I e'er get my hands on the little whore, I will kill her—slowly! Look what she did to my face!"

Liam hid his surprise when he looked at the ragged scar on Rauf's left cheek. Keira had said she had struggled with the man. She had never mentioned the fact that she had torn open half his face. He was going to have to teach her to be a little more specific when she told him things, he decided, then smiled coldly at the man he so badly wanted to kill.

"I will ask ye but once more—do ye surrender?"

"Nay! Kill them!" Rauf ordered his men.

As the men moved forward, Rauf grabbed the backs of two men's jupons and held them in place in front of him like a human shield. Liam was surprised Rauf did not see that he had just robbed himself of the one small advantage he had—his eight men against their six. He then turned all of his attention upon the man he must now fight in order to get to the one he really wanted.

The man who confronted him proved to have little skill, and Liam quickly dispatched him. He looked around to see if any of his allies needed assistance and, for a brief moment, marveled at their skill. Keira's brothers were surprisingly skilled, even graceful, as they went about their deadly work. Then, even as Liam was turning back to face Rauf, one by one, Moubray's men died. The two left standing with Rauf realized they would be sacrificed next, and a thin coat of sweat appeared on their pale faces.

"Cease cowering behind those fools, and face me," demanded Liam.

"Oh, nay, I think not," Rauf said and laughed softly.

" 'Ware your backs!" cried Ewan, even as he turned to fight the man rushing at him from behind.

Cursing, Liam found himself locked in a fierce battle, he and his allies outnumbered almost two to one. It was only a matter of moments before Keira's cousins and a few MacFingals arrived, but Liam knew that help had come too late. When the last of Moubray's men lay dead, Liam looked to where Rauf had once stood, but he was not surprised to find the man had fled.

He started out of the great hall determined to find the man, pausing only long enough to send Keira's brothers and Sir Ian to the room Sir Archie held for them. "The bastard may weel ken where at least one escape route is. As Sir Archie said, he is the sort to be sure he has one," he told them, then with Sigimor and Ewan right behind him, he raced to where Kester and the women were hiding, Malcolm appearing at his side even as they started down the steep steps leading to the bowels of the keep.

They had barely started down the stairs when they heard a lot of screaming. Liam raced down the steps, ignoring the increasing pain in his leg. When he stumbled into the storage room, he felt his heart sink. They were too late. Rauf's two men lay upon the ground, but Rauf was gone. Even though he knew it was useless, he tried to open the door, but the man had bolted it from the other side.

"We can break it down," said Sigimor.

"That will take too long." A quick look at Rauf's two men revealed that they were dead, and Liam realized the screaming they had heard had been born of fury, not fear. "Jesu," he whispered as he suddenly knew without a single doubt which way Rauf was headed. "Keira."

CHAPTER 18

"Do ye think the battle is o'er yet?" asked Meggie as she wrapped a blanket around herself.

" 'Twould be nice if it was over so quickly. E'en nicer if none of the men were hurt or killed. 'Tis verra hard to sit here and just wait."

"My father says that be why women have a more patient, sweeter nature than men."

"Because we must just sit and wait for our men to return from battle?"

"Aye, that and other things. Women do a lot of waiting."

"True enough. Yet mayhap God gave women a more patient, sweeter nature so that we dinnae strangle all the men."

Keira chuckled when Meggie giggled so hard she tumbled over sideways. The girl had proven to be good company, helping her to keep the worst of her fears from overwhelming her. Meggie had a very quick mind as well as a lot of spirit and courage. Keira was determined to nurture that once she returned to her place as the lady of Ardgleann.

Looking around the deserted camp, Keira shivered slightly. It surprised her that not one man had remained behind to guard the supplies and the horses or even to watch over her and Meggie. She felt certain Liam, Sigimor, or Ewan would have wanted that. Even her brothers would have wanted at least one armed man here. Either someone had disobeyed orders, or in the confusion of rushing off to battle, those orders had never been given. It was too late to worry about that now, she thought. She just hoped no one suffered too badly for what she was sure had been just a simple mistake.

Meggie yawned and, staying curled up on her side, wrapped the blanket more securely around herself. "'Tis so verra quiet, isnae it?"

"Aye, and ye are so verra tired. Rest, lass. Ye have worked hard this day."

"I should keep ye company in your waiting."

"Ye have done a fine job of it, but rest now. I dinnae think it will be verra long now until we hear of what has happened. I have confidence in the wit and skill of our men, for all I cannae stop worrying about them. No need of ye suffering for my foolishness the whole night long. And if I should wake ye and tell ye to go hide, do it without question."

"Aye, I will, m'lady. I am verra good at hiding."

A weary smile crossed Meggie's face, and a moment later, the girl was asleep. Keira sternly told herself it was foolish to suddenly feel so all alone. The girl had worked hard, and all of it to their benefit. Although barely more than a child, Meggie had seen terrible things, yet she had retained the courage and wit to help where she could and to recognize the chance for Ardgleann's salvation when it came. It astonished Keira that although the girl had been able to flee the keep at any time, she had stayed in the hope that rescue would come so that she could show them the way inside. When Ardgleann was free, Keira was determined to make sure everyone knew what an important part the cooper's daughter had played in it all.

In fact, she thought with a little smile, if they won the fight against Rauf, they owed it, in large part, to three very unlikely heroes. A boy who was as clumsy as any she had ever seen, an aging warrior who was as good as blind, and a thin girl. If anyone had told her before the battle that such people would be so important, Keira knew she would have thought them mad. *When* they won the battle, she hastily corrected herself, immediately fighting back any hint of uncertainty. Keira knew she had to cling to such confidence, or she would become frantic with fear and worry.

She turned her thoughts to Liam in an effort to stop thinking about what was happening within the walls of Ardgleann. It was almost frightening how much she loved the man. Putting restraints upon that feeling had proved utterly fruitless. The best she had done was keep herself from telling him several times a day. She was not sure how much longer she could keep those words locked up inside her. They rushed into her mouth every time he even smiled at her.

He was a good husband, just as Fiona had said he would be. Although he had all the usual manly faults, he tempered them with kindness and understanding. When he gave an order, he did not expect her to leap at his command; instead, he explained himself and even allowed her to argue with him. Even better, he truly listened to what she had to say. Keira had no doubt that he would be a good laird for Ardgleann, working hard to provide for and protect all who would depend upon him.

He was also a wondrous lover, one who promised to be hers alone. And that, she mused, was one thing that could still cause her a few doubts no matter how often she told herself that it was unfair to him, that she judged him guilty before he had even committed the crime. Yet she could not stop herself from wondering just how long a man could resist temptation when it was constantly thrust into his path. Women were drawn to Liam like bees to clover, and she feared her whole life would now be spent constantly pushing aside adoring, willing women. Even worse was the knowledge that she could not always be there to push them away.

"If only I kenned how he felt about me," she whispered as she added a few sticks to the fire.

That was the true crux of her problem, she decided. Liam desired her, of that she no longer had any doubt, and it had soothed a lot of the hurt Duncan had unwittingly dealt her.

Unfortunately, she was far too aware of the fact that a man's desire did not have to be bred in his heart. Liam had certainly bedded a lot of women, yet he claimed he had had no true attachment to any of them. How a man could be so intimate with a woman he cared little for, she did not know, but it was a truth she could not argue with.

Taking a sip of wine from Liam's wineskin, Keira decided to look very carefully at what she was sure of. She was alone for the first time in weeks, except for a sleeping Meggie, and it was a perfect time to sort out a few things in her mind. He was possessive of her, she realized. Though it was true that men could be possessive of a favorite tankard, Liam's possessiveness concerning her should not be ignored completely. He enjoyed her company. Of that she had no doubt. He talked with her, discussed many things, and never acted as if he thought her poor woman's mind was too weak to understand. Even her grandmother had stressed the importance of that. He was always touching her and giving her kisses. Keira blushed as she thought of how he made love to her. Despite his past, she could not believe that he could be so tender, so concerned that she find pleasure too, then hold her close all night if he did not feel something more than simple desire.

A sound caught her attention, yanking her out of her thoughts. Someone was running hard, straight for the camp. Since sound could carry far distances in the night, Keira could not judge how close the person was. She shook Meggie awake.

"Hide. Now," she ordered.

It astonished Keira when Meggie not only did as she was told, but also did it so very quickly and efficiently. One moment, the girl had been sound asleep; the next, she had completely disappeared into the darkness. Leaping to her feet, Keira sought a place to hide herself, one far away from Meggie. Even as she started for a tree at the far corner of the camp, thinking to climb it and conceal herself amongst the leaves, she knew she had lost her chance.

A man stumbled into the camp, and for a moment, Keira did

not recognize him in the shadows. Then he laughed, and she felt a deep chill flow through her body. It was Rauf Moubray. Keira beat down the blind impulse to run for her life. It would gain her nothing, except giving Rauf a chance to grab her from behind, something he would heartily enjoy.

"So I finally have fate smile upon *me* this night," he said. "Not only have I found ye, but horses and supplies as weel."

"Ye wouldnae be running through the wood like a frightened hare if ye hadnae lost the battle," she said. "Since ye are obviously so eager to save your own miserable hide, I suggest ye keep on running."

Keira watched his cold eyes narrow and his lips draw back in a silent snarl. It was, perhaps, pure madness to speak so insultingly to the man, but she doubted it would make any difference to her fate in the end. He may not have run this way expecting to find her, but now that he had, she had no doubt that he would kill her. She could only try, in some small way, to make it difficult for him and pray that he was in too great a hurry to save his own life to linger over the deed. Just thinking about how cruelly he had killed others made her so afraid that she felt her stomach rise up into her throat, and she fought the urge to be ill. It might be passingly enjoyable to vomit on the man, but she knew he would recognize that to be the result of terror, and she refused to let him know how afraid she was.

"Och, nay, nay, my wee black-haired bitch," he said, his voice hard and cold. "Ye and I have a debt to settle between us."

"Debt? What debt? Ye think I owe ye something for slaughtering my husband and many of his people? For nay allowing ye to rape me? In public? If there is any debt atween us, 'tis all yours for ye have stolen from me. Sadly, since most of what was stolen is the lives of those dear to me, it can ne'er be repaid, except with your death."

"Ye should be dead, ye whore!"

"Oh? Weel, I do so beg your pardon for nay dying from the wounds ye dealt me." Keira found it both amazing and intriguing that as Rauf grew more enraged, she grew more chillingly calm.

"And look what ye did to my face!"

The ragged scar on the side of his face nearly made her wince. She could still recall his scream of rage and pain and the smell of blood as she cut his cheek open with a dagger. Keira dearly wished she had that dagger now. As a healer, the act of hurting someone, of spilling blood, was sickening, but she was more than willing to do this man some injury. She only had to think of poor Duncan, of the men hanging from the walls of Ardgleann, and of the sad fate of the women trapped within the keep to feel absolutely, coldly murderous.

" 'Tis an improvement, if ye ask me."

That proved to be one insult too many. Keira barely had time to notice that he drew neither his sword nor his dagger before he was on her. The feel of his body slamming into hers, followed by her body hitting the ground hard, robbed her of breath. She fought to get some air back into her lungs, almost uncaring of the hands cruelly mauling her. When she could finally breathe, she realized that her hands were free, and she started punching Rauf in the head. He actually endured several hard blows with no more than a grunt before he reacted to them.

He put his big, calloused hand around her throat and slowly tightened his grip until Keira found herself struggling to breathe all over again. "I can take my fill of ye, be ye dead or alive, woman. Makes no difference to me."

Keira was so shocked by those cold words, she stopped clawing at his hands and gaped at him. When she caught the shadow of movement behind Rauf, she was almost glad she had revealed how his words had so appalled her. Within a heartbeat after she had glimpsed that shadow, a thick piece of wood slammed into the side of Rauf's head. He grunted and fell to the side. Keira reached for the hand Meggie was holding out to help her stand, but the faint sound of movement at her side made her tense.

"Run, Meggie," Keira tried to scream, but her words came out as a hoarse croak, and the warning was too late anyway.

With a roar of fury, Rauf leapt to his feet. Meggie tried to hit him again, but he tore the rough club from her small hands and threw it aside. Then he grabbed Meggie, oblivious to the girl's fists and feet as he got a firm hold on her.

"I ken who ye are," he said. "The cooper's brat. Weel, that coward fled with all his wee laddies, didnae he? Saved his disrespectful son, but left his wee bitch behind. So be it. I will kill ye as I wanted to kill that fool brother of yours."

Ignoring how her body ached, Keira scrambled to her feet. She threw herself onto Rauf's back, wrapping her legs around his waist and one arm tightly around his neck. With her free hand, she hit him again and again.

"Let her go, ye filthy bastard!" she cried. Hearing how soft and hoarse her voice was, Keira feared he might have damaged something in her throat, and that made her even angrier. "Let her go, or I shall scratch out your eyes!"

A deep, rumbling growl escaped the man. "I could just snap her wee neck."

"Aye, ye could do that, and her dying will be the last thing ye e'er see for I *will* blind ye. I swear it."

For a moment, Keira feared he would actually follow through on his threat. Then he yelled out a curse so loudly her ears hurt and hurled Meggie away like some dinner bone. Keira cried out when the girl hit the ground hard and did not move. She had no time to grieve or even see if it was necessary, for with his hands now free, Rauf proceeded to do his best to tear her from his back.

Keira quickly realized she could not hang onto the man for very long. It was all she could do just to shield her head from the blows he tried to inflict by simply keeping her head tucked hard up against the back of his. Even the awkward, glancing blows he struck her, however, were more than she could bear. Yet she did not know how she could fling herself from his back and move quickly enough to escape, let alone protect Meggie as well. Then he grabbed her legs in a painful hold and started to pry them from his waist.

Just as she began to fear he would actually break her legs, a sword entered her field of vision, and it was pointed straight at Rauf's throat. She stared in surprise at Liam. Behind him, she could see Sigimor helping an unsteady Meggie to her feet. Then, two large hands grasped her around the waist and pulled her back, away from Rauf. She glanced behind her to see that it was Ewan who had put an end to her dilemma. Behind Ewan stood her brothers.

"Ye are a verra stupid mon, Rauf Moubray," said Liam, backing up a step. "Ye could have escaped, mayhap e'en lived a few more days ere we hunted ye down. Instead, ye stop here to torment two wee lasses."

"Ye think I didnae ken I was a dead mon already?" Rauf asked. "Mayhap I just decided it would be fair to make ye pay some price for taking Ardgleann."

It was over, Keira thought, and slumped against Ewan. Her whole body ached, and her legs felt too weak to hold her upright for much longer. She was just about to ask why someone did not hurry up and kill Rauf so that she could get some rest when Rauf drew his sword and no one did anything to stop him. Taking a deep breath in the hope of making her voice louder and firmer than it had been so far, Keira intended to tell these fools that a man like Rauf Moubray did not deserve a chance to die in honorable combat. It was her opinion that he should be gutted like the pig he was. Before she could utter one single word, however, a large hand was gently, but firmly, placed over her mouth.

"Hush, lass," Ewan whispered in her ear. "This way is for the best. Liam can explain the way of it all later."

All Keira could think of as Liam and Rauf began to fight was that the explanation had better be very good. Ewan started to remove his hand, but she placed hers over his to hold it in place. Even though she knew full well that crying out in any way as a man was engaged in a fight could dangerously distract him, Keira was not very confident that she could remain silent. She felt Ewan nod, revealing that he understood her concern.

Despite the fact that Liam was obviously suffering some pain in his leg, the fight was over very quickly. Rauf was good, but Liam was much, much better. No matter how good Liam was, however, Keira swore to herself that she would try her utmost never to watch him in a fight again. Her heart simply could not bear the strain.

Liam wiped his sword clean on Rauf's jupon and sheathed it before moving toward Keira. His leg, having decided it could take no more abuse this day, buckled beneath him after only a few steps. He managed to catch himself just enough to be saved from the humiliation of sprawling gracelessly in the dirt. Liam managed a smile for Keira as she knelt by his side. Now that his fear and anger had eased, he was all too aware of the pain in the leg. He had pushed himself too hard and asked too much of it in the last few days.

When he had realized where Rauf was headed, Liam had felt terrified for Keira, but also for himself. He feared losing her, feared never hearing her laugh again, never hearing those soft murmurs and humming noises she made when her passion was running hot, and never knowing if she loved him. Ignoring all the advice to be calm, he had raced for the camp. Sigimor grabbing his reins had been what stopped him from loudly announcing his approach to his enemy. The only thing that had kept him from feeling utterly humiliated by his blind recklessness was the knowledge that both Sigimor and Ewan had suffered the feeling themselves and understood.

The stealth he had needed to reach Rauf before the man saw or heard him had been hard-won when he had seen how the man was trying to hurt Keira. Telling himself over and over again that she was alive was all that kept him moving slowly and silently. He even took a moment to start planning the lecture he would give Keira for not hiding and for attacking a man a foot taller and several stone heavier than she was. Now, however, he could take his ease; rest his throbbing, overworked leg;

and perhaps, bask a little in the warmth of her gratitude and praise for a job well done.

"Ye idiot!" Keira began to unlace his boots, terrified that he had damaged his leg in some way. "Your leg is barely a week healed, and ye are leaping about getting into sword fights."

Concern for his well-being was almost as good, he told himself. Then he frowned. There was something wrong with her voice, and he did not think it was so soft and raspy because she was fighting tears.

"What has happened to your voice?" he asked.

Relieved from finding only a little swelling when she finally bared his shin, Keira replied, "Rauf decided to show me how easily he can strangle a wee lass with only one hand."

She pushed away his hand when he attempted to look at her throat, hidden from his view by her hair. Studying Liam's face, she saw all the signs that he was suffering badly. The least she could do for him after he had freed Ardgleann and saved her life was to take away his pain. She rubbed her hands together. That was obviously enough for him to guess what she planned to do for he grabbed both of her hands in his.

"Lass, we are nay alone," he said quietly. "Ye risk your secret."

"My brothers already ken it, and ye trust your kinsmen, dinnae ye?" He nodded, even though he still frowned. "And I think we can trust Meggie to keep a secret." She smiled at the young girl who had moved to stand on the other side of Liam. "Ye will swear to keep what I do now a secret, aye, Meggie?"

"Aye," Meggie agreed, "although if ye are talking about your healing gift, it isnae such a great secret here."

"Duncan told ye?"

"Weel, he told a few people, nay everyone. Thought it a wondrous dowry. Said we shouldnae trouble ye about it though, because it weakens ye to use the gift." Meggie frowned at Liam's leg. "It doesnae look hurt."

Shaking herself free of the shock of knowing her secret was not such a secret anymore, Keira said, "I cannae heal with a touch, Meggie. I can take away pain and sometimes see with my hands what ails a person."

" 'Tis still a wondrous gift."

"Thank ye. I would still prefer that it doesnae get talked about too much. Some dinnae see it as a gift." Keira took a deep breath to steady herself, closed her eyes, and placed her hands on Liam's leg.

Liam felt her hands start to work their magic. He softly ordered Keira's brothers to try and find some food and drink, cider, honey, and bread being the preferred choice. Since Keira often carried such things with her, he told them to check her saddle packs first. Then he sat at the ready to catch her when she was finished, carefully planning all he would say to aid her in ridding herself of the pain she was taking into her body.

No one spoke as Keira worked her magic. Her brothers were quick to hand her food and drink when she was done. Liam had to move quickly as well in order to grab himself a little of the bounty before she devoured it all. As soon as she was done, Liam held her close and whispered a tale of cool spring rains and fields of heather. When he felt her begin to relax, she murmured a very polite thank you and then slumped against him, sound asleep.

"Does she always do that after she does her healing?" Meggie asked, finally breaking the silence.

"What? Eat like a starving piglet and then fall asleep?" Liam grinned when the girl nodded. "Aye. The healing steals her strength. She takes a lot of the pain into herself and must then try to make it go away. 'Tis a costly gift."

Meggie slowly nodded. "Nay one she can use all the time. A good reason to keep it as secret as possible."

"True." Liam looked around the camp and realized someone had already tossed Rauf's body over a horse. "I think Keira and I will finish the night here."

"Aye, that might be best," said Sigimor. " 'Twill give us time to clear away the bodies."

"And remove those poor souls from the walls?"

"That was already being done as we raced out of the keep."

"Good." Liam frowned at Artan as the man crouched by Keira and worked through her thick hair to expose her throat. "What is it?"

"Just wanted to see what damage that bastard did," Artan replied. "It might need tending."

Everyone cursed, including Meggie, when even in the dim firelight, the bruises upon Keira's slim throat looked livid. Liam was sorry he had not just gutted Rauf, had allowed the man to die like the knight he never was, but he had been determined to do nothing that might raise questions concerning his possession of Ardgleann. He winced as Artan rubbed some salve on the bruises.

"Can she nay heal herself?" asked Meggie.

"Nay," replied Liam, "but she obviously brought salve, and she will ken what she may take to soothe her throat."

"Sir Ian and his men will nay doubt pass through to collect their horses and supplies," said Sigimor. "I will tell him to make sure he gives ye fair warning. Let the lass have a goodly rest for her skills will be needed when she gets to Ardgleann. A few small wounds. Only two dead, and they were Sir Ian's men. It was a good victory."

Even as he murmured in agreement, Liam had to wonder how Sigimor had found the time to make that tally. The man never ceased to astonish him, Liam thought as he watched the others leave. As soon as he and Keira were alone, Liam carried her to their small shelter, undressed her, and tucked her into their rough bed. Just as he was about to join her there, Sir Ian and his men arrived. The man wished to discuss the battle and exchange words of gratitude, much to Liam's dismay. The sun was beginning to rise before he was able to join Keira.

As he slipped beneath the blankets and pulled her into his arms, Liam breathed a sigh of relief. The last of his fear for her faded away as she snuggled against him, fitting her slim back perfectly against his front. He ached to make love to her, but he knew she needed her rest. He had the feeling Rauf had done a lot of damage to Ardgleann in the few months he had been there, and he knew Keira would want to restore as much as she could as quickly as she could.

"Liam, we arenae back at Ardgleann, are we?" Keira asked.

"Nay, love, we are still at the camp." Sensing that she was more asleep than awake, he kissed her cheek. "Rest."

"But there is such a lot of work to do."

"Ye can start it later. It isnae going anywhere."

" 'Tis going to break my heart, isnae it?"

"Aye, I ken it might. But it and the keep will mend."

CHAPTER 19

Keira looked around the bailey of Ardgleann as she clung tightly to Liam's hand. He had let her sleep for hours, and it was now past noon. Although he had been sleeping for most of that time as well, it did not make her feel any less guilty about it. The fact that she dreaded seeing the people of Ardgleann tasted too much like cowardice, and she feared it was one reason she had lost herself in sleep. She had the strongest urge to run back to the little shelter in the wood, but she fought it. Ardgleann was her home now, and it was her duty to cleanse it of Rauf's stench and all the memories.

It did look as if a great deal of work had already been done outside. There was little sign of the battle that had been waged, but Rauf's mark upon the place was still clear to see. He had had no true feeling for Ardgleann, and neither had his men. There would be many hard weeks of work ahead to clear away the filth and fix all those things that had suffered from careless or thoughtless, destructive hands.

"He was a pig," murmured Liam. " 'Tis sad, but it can be mended."

"Aye." She looked at the doors to the keep, thick, oaken doors covered in fine carvings. "They didnae hurt the doors."

"They are good, thick doors by the look of it. Good for defense."

"Of course."

"Ye have to go inside sometime, love," he said gently. "Best to get it over with."

She nodded and, still holding his hand, entered the keep. It took only a moment for her to realize why the heavy doors had been left partly open. Months of rough men living like pigs left an odor. Keira feared some of that smell could also have come from the corpses left to rot upon the outer walls. She shivered and then stiffened her spine. That scourge was gone from Ardgleann now. There would be the loss of some beautiful things to grieve over, of that she had no doubt, but the lives lost were of far more importance. Ardgleann could be repaired and scrubbed clean. The dead could never be replaced.

"The great hall first, I think," she said, and Liam led her to it.

Even as she took the few steps down into the great hall, Keira looked around in a mixture of shock and surprise. There were half a dozen women working hard to clear away the filthy rushes upon the floor and scrub everything clean. Some of the furniture had obviously been lost, but the elegant tapestries upon the walls looked as if they had not been damaged. When Joan led the women over to her, Keira tensed, unsure of her welcome.

"M'lady, we had hoped to have the great hall and mayhap a few other rooms cleaned ere ye came," said Joan.

Relaxing a little when she saw only welcome upon the women's faces, Keira said, "Ye didnae need to set to work so soon, Joan." She could see bruises on several of the women, and she felt her heart clench with sorrow over how they must have suffered. "Ye need time to heal, to be with your families."

"We are healing, m'lady," Joan said firmly. "Getting rid of every sign of those pigs *is* healing to us." All the women behind Joan vigorously nodded and muttered their agreement.

"Scrubbing this place down is one of the ways to do it," said Claire, the laundress. The woman suddenly brushed at her skirts and patted her hair. "Is this the new laird then?"

A little stunned, Keira introduced Liam. She almost wept at

the way he greeted each woman as if she were the finest lady. As she watched him learn each one's name, her place in Ardgleann, and even her family, she felt someone gently tug on her arm. She turned to look at Joan and let that woman pull her a few steps away from where Liam was working his magic.

"Dinnae look so sad, m'lady," said Joan.

"But they have suffered so," began Keira.

"Aye, they have, and there are some deep wounds that will be a long time healing. But dinnae ye see? *All* the women of Ardgleann have suffered. We give each other comfort and strength now, just as we did whilst we were trapped here. Aye, a few escaped, but verra few."

"Are there many widows?"

Joan nodded and sighed. "Verra few of the men within the keep survived. The men of Ardgleann who did survive have welcomed their women back, and that was a fine thing. 'Twill come about, dinnae ye worry. We see it all as a trial by fire, and we survived."

"I should have—"

"Done just as ye did. Run—far and fast. We all ken what that beast had planned for ye. He ranted about here for days about nay being able to do it. Ye came back, m'lady, and we were all surprised. Ye were a verra wee lass married to a sad, troubled mon for but a few months. We were naught to ye. Hadnae had time to be, had we? But ye came back with as fine a group of men as I have e'er seen and sent that demon straight to hell where he belongs."

"Ye truly didnae expect me to come back?"

"Why should ye? Aye, and we feared ye had died since ye were so hurt and all on your own. From time to time, we hoped ye were alive and might think of a way to help us. We also hoped Sir Ian would see what a threat Moubray was and want to get rid of him. But, wheesht, we ne'er expected our hell to end in only a few months."

Keira felt the guilt she had carried for so long begin to lift from her heart. Joan was saying what everyone else had tried to tell her time and time again. Since Joan had been one of the ones to suffer at Rauf's hands, however, the woman's words carried far more weight. Keira could be certain they were the truth, and not simply words of comfort.

"Your husband is a bonnie lad," said Joan, "and my Malcolm says he is a good mon, too. Ye have brought us a fine laird."

"Oh! Malcolm!" Keira grasped Joan by the hand. "I forgot to speak to Malcolm about his hand."

" 'Tis a sad thing." Joan looked around to make sure no one was near enough to overhear her and added, "But ye do ken that it isnae his working hand. It pains him though, and I hope Moubray suffers a thousand torments in hell for that."

"I looked at his hand, Joan. I think I can help him. It will probably ne'er be as it was, but I think I can make it better than it is, make it hurt him less." She grimaced. "Unfortunately, I would have to cause him pain to do so."

"What would ye need to do?"

"Break his fingers, and set them properly." She nodded when Joan winced. "The pain and the way his hand has become crabbed like that is because the bones didnae heal right. It shouldnae be left too much longer though."

Joan nodded. "Do it ere it sets wrong permanent like. Makes sense. I will speak with him, m'lady. A quick pain that could end most of the constant pain sounds a good thing. If he says aye, I will find someone to do the breaking, and then ye can do the setting."

"His hand would be near useless for six weeks or so."

" 'Tis near useless now, and I will be there to help him."

Keira took a deep breath to steady her sinking courage. "I ken how ye all suffered here, and, weel, if any of ye find yourself with child and cannae bear to keep the bairn because it will remind ye too much of your torment, bring it to me."

"Ye dinnae think the bairn will carry the taint of its sire?"

"No more than I believe that a raped woman getting with child means she had to be enjoying herself. Nay, just because the mon is a brute and does things so cruel it turns one's stomach doesnae mean his child will be of the same ilk. Nay, if he doesnae have the raising of that child. I dinnae believe Rauf was mad either, and 'tis odd, but I find that makes it all the more chilling."

"I ken what ye mean. He had more a sickness in the soul than in the mind. I will tell the women, but I think there will-nae be too many bairns born of this, and e'en fewer who will-nae be able to abide the child. Aye, especially when I tell them that what Moubray and his men were was a pack of wild dogs, but a pup can be trained to be a fine companion if treated with a loving hand. S'truth, 'twill be the men who will have the hardest time accepting a bairn born of this time."

"M'lady! 'Tis good that ye have come!"

Turning to see Kester hurrying over to her, Keira started to smile until she saw the worried look upon his face. "What is it, Kester?" she asked as he stumbled up to her, Meggie close at his heels.

" 'Tis Sir Archie," Kester replied. "He has cracked his head again."

"No one told me that he had been wounded during the battle."

"A mon or two asked him if he was hurt, and he told them all that it was naught but a scratch, but I think his old wound has been opened. Two of Rauf's men tried to escape through the room Sir Archie was guarding. One of the women was verra good at helping Sir Archie find his target, and the other mon was dealt with by the others hiding themselves inside Sir Archie's chambers. But Sir Archie did take a blow to the head ere he dealt with that pig."

"Where is he?" she asked as Liam stepped closer to her, listening carefully.

"In the wee bedchamber we were given when we first came here."

"Weel, I wanted to get a good look at that wound, and I thought to open it to clean it. At least I dinnae have to do the opening of it." She looked around at all the work that needed doing. "Is he bleeding badly?"

"Go take care of the mon," said Liam before Kester could answer. "I can start dealing with some of the work, although it appears that these ladies dinnae need much direction. Go. Meggie and Kester can help ye get what ye need. And ye may as weel look at who else is wounded at the same time." When she still hesitated, he gave her a quick kiss. "Ye go and do what ye are so verra good at, and let me survey the damage. I may be just a mon, but I think I can tell what needs cleaning."

Keira laughed softly and then went off with Kester and Meggie to help her gather what she would need to tend the wounded. Liam hated to think that any of those who had helped retake Ardgleann were suffering, but he *was* pleased that Keira would be thoroughly caught up in healing people for a while. He wanted to confer with the women about what damage they had seen and what they felt needed to be done first. As soon as Keira had disappeared, he turned to talk to the women, only to find them all gathered together watching him.

" 'Tis better if ye take an accounting, m'laird," said Claire. "We didnae have a chance to ken the wee lass verra weel, but we do ken that she has a soft heart, and what that mon did here will grieve her sorely."

Joan nodded. "And add to her guilt." Joan looked at the other women. "Fool lass thinks she failed us by nay getting back here sooner."

Liam listened to the women exclaim in surprise, and then Claire looked at him. "Dinnae worry, m'laird. We will soon shake that nonsense from her head. Now, will ye be needing something to tally or write with to record it all?"

"Aye, something to write with and on would be most helpful," Liam replied, fighting to contain the delight he felt, for he was certain these women would indeed finally remove the burden of guilt Keira had carried for so long.

Claire hurried off to get him what he needed, and Joan said, "The kitchens are in no need of work. The men rarely stepped inside the room. We have also scrubbed clean a bedchamber for ye and our lady. There are three women up there now putting it back to rights."

"I suspicion Rauf Moubray used the laird's bedchamber."

"Aye, he did, so we have cleaned the lady's bedchamber for ye. None of the men slept in there as it was used by Rauf's woman." Joan nodded to a very fulsome brunette with world-weary brown eyes. "Hattie slept in there. When that demon asked who was the laird's whore, she bravely stepped forward, kenning that the mon intended to act the laird here. She also taught us a few things that helped us survive, being as she has, weel, dealt with a lot of men in her life." Joan blushed.

To Liam's surprise, Hattie laughed, and the women quickly joined in. "Weel, Hattie, if ye e'er decide ye would like to stop dealing with men, just let me ken it." He could tell by the widening of Hattie's eyes that she understood him, and he suspected he would hear from her soon. "Are there any other people who need tending to?"

"I suspicion our lady will be seeing to that soon," replied Joan. "Those two big lairds went right down into the dungeons to free the poor souls Rauf had put in there, and most of them will be with the few men wounded in the fight. The truly grim work is done. Those poor souls that pig hung from the walls have finally been put to rest. Rauf and his men were stripped of all that was worth anything and were buried in a pit dug by your men and e'en a few of Sir Ian's who lingered here for a wee while. So did the laird MacKay's son Adam and his men. They all made quick work of it, and I fed them weel ere they left. When they saw what had been done here, weel, to a mon, the MacLeans and the MacKays were verra pleased that ye had come to rid this land of Moubray."

Which meant that he would get no argument from his neighbors for claiming Ardgleann as his own because of his wife's short marriage to Duncan MacKail, Liam thought. In one stroke, he had won lands and a fine keep and secured allies. It had all gone so well, he was sure it would be quite a while before he fully believed it. Claire returned, and Liam set his mind to making a list of what needed doing and what might need replacing. He was just settling into what had been Duncan MacKail's ledger room, one thankfully used little by Rauf and his men, when Sigimor, Ewan, and Keira's brothers joined him.

"We will be leaving in the morning," announced Sigimor as he leaned against the heavy worktable at which Liam sat.

"Ye ken that ye all have my hearty thanks," said Liam.

"Aye, but we dinnae need them. This needed doing. Ye gaining this place just sweetens it all a wee bit more."

"And we would have come because of Keira," said Lucas. "We are verra pleased that we didnae have to fight for what was hers all by ourselves."

" 'Tis bad?" asked Ewan, glancing over the listing Liam had set in front of himself.

"Nay verra good," replied Liam. "Ye were right about the feasting. The mon gave nary a thought to what would happen when he and his men had eaten everything. The people managed to save a few cows, sheep, and fowl, but 'twill be a long time ere we can replenish what was sacrificed to his gluttony."

"We can help there. A few small contributions from each of us willnae leave any of us suffering, but they will help ye keep the wolves from the door come the winter."

"Aye," agreed Sigimor, and Keira's brothers nodded. "We all gain from this, and at little cost to ourselves. Ye now have more horses than ye will e'er need or want. Use them to barter with your neighbors for what ye *do* need."

"Ye dinnae want any of them?" asked Liam.

"Weel, there are one or two I think ye should keep, and I will be seeking stud service or a colt or two if ye do, but no more." When Liam nodded, Sigimor said, "I will show ye the ones I mean ere I leave this place."

"How fares my sister?" asked Artan.

"It grieves her to see what was done to what is a verra fine keep," replied Liam, "and, e'en more, what all of the people here have suffered through. Howbeit, that will pass, and if all feel as the women cleaning the great hall do, Keira will finally let go of all that guilt she has clung to for so long."

Artan cursed softly. "We all told her she had naught to feel guilty about, but 'tis clear she didnae heed us."

"Aye, but then we werenae the ones suffering, were we? Those women telling her to cease being a fool carries far more weight than anything we did or could have said. S'truth, I could almost see the weight of it lift from her whilst she talked with Malcolm's wife."

"Good," said Sigimor. "Now, tell us if there is aught we and the men can do now. No sense in wasting the chance to put so many strong backs to use."

"Aye," agreed Ewan. "Hard work will also help me decide how to act when I get home to my pregnant wife."

"Fiona is with child again?" asked Liam. "I am surprised ye still joined us for this fight."

"Had to. I kenned it was why she worked so hard to keep it a secret from me." Ewan shook his head. "Near everyone at Scarglas kens it, and since not one of them believes she would e'er carry out any of the rather bloodcurdling threats she used to keep them quiet, it wasnae long ere I heard about it. I just have to decide whether I should act surprised or scold her for trying to keep secrets from her laird and husband."

Liam laughed along with the others. When they all turned their attention to what work might be done before they left, however, Liam often found his thoughts distracted. As soon as the others left him, he sought out Keira before joining in the work that was being done. Ewan's announcement that Fiona carried his child made Liam think of Keira, of how she might soon be carrying his son or daughter, and he felt a strong need to see her.

It was a while before he found her sitting in the lady's solar. The room looked as if it was another one that had mercifully escaped the taint of Moubray and his men. Keira sat on a cushioned bench near one of the surprisingly large windows. He walked over to her, sat down beside her, and took her hand in his. It was only then that he noticed she was studying a long, thin piece of metal.

"What is that?" When she held it out to him, he took the piece from her hand and studied it carefully. "It looks a bit like some piece of a flail or what some men might stick in a club to make it a more dangerous weapon."

" 'Tis exactly what it is," Keira said. "It was in Sir Archie's head."

"Jesu. It must have been a constant source of pain."

"I think so, too, but he insists that it wasnae so verra bad. I also think it may be why his vision was so blurred, but I willnae be certain of that for a wee while yet. The wound did need a lot of cleaning, but that thing was a great surprise. I had to get one of my cousins to pull it out for 'twas stuck in the bone. Sir Archie is sleeping now, but once he wakes, I will ken better if getting that out will help his eyesight improve."

"And what of the others ye tended to?"

"The battle wounds will heal. They werenae so verra bad. The poor souls Rauf had locked away in the dungeons will need some careful tending for a while. Some suffered from beatings, some were tortured, but mostly, they werenae fed much or given enough water. They needed washing ere I could e'en see their wounds."

"They survived it. They are clearly strong, and they have the will to live."

Keira nodded. "Ah, Liam, they were all so grateful," she whispered. "They were so verra pleased that I had come back, and in their eyes, I did so more quickly than they would e'er have thought I could."

"So will ye now believe me and all the others who have tried to make ye understand that ye have naught to feel guilty about?"

She smiled and rested her head against his shoulder. "Aye, I will. 'Tis odd, but when Joan spoke of how surprised they all were that I had come back at all, let alone in only a few months' time, 'twas as if unseen hands had lifted a huge weight from my shoulders. And from my heart. Now, it just aches for the lives lost, the pain the living still suffer, and the ill done to a place that was all beauty and peace."

"Good. 'Tis as it should be." Liam looked around, yet again noticing the elegant touches that seemed to run throughout the keep, from a beautiful tapestry upon the wall to the carpet upon the floor. "The MacKails had a taste for fine things, aye?"

"Aye, they did. A lot of these things are made here, ye ken. A long time ago, the laird here began to gather fine craftsmen into his fold. Since word spreads quickly amongst such people, more came here for 'tis usually a peaceful place, and the land is surprisingly good here. Ye will find wares from Ardgleann at every market. Unlike so many others in this land, Ardgleann is quite a profitable place for all of its people. I think that is why I found it so verra hard to bear that Rauf would come here. All these people wished to do was to make beautiful things. To have such a mon come here seemed an abomination."

"Weel, we shall put it to rights, and it will be peaceful again." He told her of how certain it was that strong alliances had been made with the neighboring clans; of the horses that could be used for barter; and anything else he could think of that could be considered good news, no matter how small.

Keira smiled as she listened to Liam talk. He was trying so hard to turn her eyes toward all that was good and to keep her from grieving on all that had been hurt or lost. She almost laughed when he sighed heavily and muttered a curse, for she knew it meant he had run out of good news.

She sat up, took his hands in hers, and gave him a brief kiss. "That all sounds wonderful, and we are most fortunate in our kinsmen. Now, tell me all the bad news."

He did, and it was bad, yet Keira realized it was not quite as bad as she had feared. Rauf Moubray and his men had been crude brutes, but it appeared that Rauf had kept the destruction of the finer things in Ardgleann to a minimum. He had wanted to play the laird, and thus he had seen such things as the tapestries, the glass in the windows, and rugs as the trappings of a laird. It had obviously never occurred to him to do his very best to keep the people who made those things alive, if only just to keep his purse full.

"The worst, aside from those who died, is the loss of so much food and the delay in the planting of the fields," Keira said when Liam was done. "Howbeit, it appears our kinsmen will save us this year."

"As Sigimor and Ewan said, they have gained by this, too. Another laird in the family, more allies, and a stronger bond made with some old ones."

"Such practical men," she teased and stood up. " 'Tis time to go to work. If naught else, we need to find a place to sleep."

"We already have one. Nay, not the laird's bedchamber," he said when he saw the consternation she could not hide. "The lady's bedchamber. Only Hattie stayed there. Do ye have any trouble with that?"

"Why? Because she is a whore? Nay." She smiled faintly. "She was a verra clean whore. I just wonder how she got herself in here." Her eyes widened as Liam told her what Hattie had done, as well as the offer he had made to the woman. "I hope she accepts that offer. I always got the feeling that she was what she was because there was naught else she could do, or thought she could do. And I think if she does step away from that life now, she will be accepted by the other women. She could have a new life."

"I believe she will. If naught else, she seems a clever woman, and she will see all of that for herself."

"Shall we get to work then?" She hooked her arm through his.

Liam kissed her and whispered against her lips. "It will be alright, love."

When she stared into his blue-green eyes, Keira could almost believe him.

CHAPTER 20

Liam grinned as he stepped into the area where the kitchen gardens were. Keira and Joan were working side by side on their hands and knees, weeding the garden. What made him smile was that each had a cat riding on her back. Keira's two cats had arrived with the supplies from Scarglas a month ago, and they had quickly become two very spoiled animals. Rauf, it seemed, had loathed cats, and he had had his men kill every one they could find. Most of the dogs had fallen victim to cruel games as well. Only two cats had survived, both females, although one of them was rather old. Lightning was going to be one happy tom when he finally came of age.

It had only been two months since the battle, but Ardgleann was nearly as good as it had been. There was still some grief and unseen wounds, but the healing had begun. There were signs that a few of the men from the neighboring clans had their eyes on the widows of Ardgleann. Life goes on, Liam thought as he walked over and picked Light-ning off Keira's back, giving an exaggerated sigh when the cat draped itself over his shoulder and purred. Thunder hopped off Joan and draped herself over his feet, obviously trying to purr louder than her brother. Very spoiled cats indeed, he mused.

Keira sat back on her heels and laughed softly. "They dinnae believe all of your scowls and grumbles."

"This isnae dignified," Liam said, idly scratching Lightning's back just to see if he could get the cat to purr louder. "A laird shouldnae be draped in cats." Both women laughed, and Liam enjoyed the sound of the continued healing of Ardgleann. "I have just discovered another skill in our Kester. He is verra good at catching rabbits. He has a string of them and wonders what to do with them now."

Joan got to her feet and brushed off her skirts. "I will see to that, m'laird. They will make us a fine meal tonight." She hurried off toward the kitchen.

Liam held out his hand, and when Keira frowned at her own rather dirty hand and hesitated to offer it to him, he grabbed it to pull her to her feet. "I am draped in shedding cats, Keira. A wee bit of dirt willnae matter. If ye would be so kind as to take that cat off my feet, we could sit beneath the apple tree for a wee while."

Picking up Thunder, Keira walked with Liam to the rough stone bench beneath the apple tree. She sat down beside him, setting the cat on her lap. "I should finish clearing away the weeds."

"We will both return to our work soon." He put his arm around her shoulders and held her close. "Do ye think there is enough time left in the growing season for ye to gain a good harvest from your garden?"

"If winter is kind enough to come a wee bit late this year, aye. Otherwise, we will get a harvest, but things will be much smaller than they usually are."

"Aye, 'tis what the men say about the fields planted," he murmured, "but 'twas worth a try. Howbeit, e'en the MacKay laird says that for this first winter, he will help if we need it. But there is hope yet, for we seem to be getting an equal share of sun and rain, which is good for the growing. Or, so the men in the fields tell me." He smiled. "I nod in all the appropriate places."

Keira laughed. "They are right if that is what ye are wondering. As I keep saying, we are most fortunate in our kinsmen and allies. They willnae allow us to go hungry, and 'tis a great comfort to ken that. 'Tis also comforting that our fighting men have been replaced. Sir Archie is verra pleased with them."

"As am I. They begin to act as one now, as they should."

"And ye are verra pleased your cousin Tait has come to be your second. Ye can admit it," she teased. "I vow to tell no one."

Liam lightly tugged her braid in gentle punishment for her teasing. "Aye, I am verra pleased. I was only a little hesitant because I feared there was some unhappy reason he came here, such as a falling out with Sigimor. But it is as he said. Sigimor has more men than he needs, and brothers and cousins are plentiful. Tait thought I might have need of another one."

"And here he isnae just one of many," Keira murmured. "Here he can be more than just another younger brother to the laird."

"There is some truth in that. 'Tis also no sin to have a wee bit of ambition. At Dubheidland, Tait was really no more than another one of the men at arms. Here, he is my second, and he has some command o'er the men. Once I kenned Sir Archie's sight had been restored, I had thought of asking him to be my second, but I hesitated for he didnae seem to want to do more than train the men. I am glad now that I did falter for Sir Archie's warm acceptance of Tait revealed that I was right. Sir Archie likes what he is—a good soldier and a good trainer of men. Oh, did ye ken that he has been courting Hattie?"

Keira nodded, enjoying the rare warmth of a sunny day almost as much as she enjoyed sitting with Liam and being held close to his side. "Hattie isnae sure what to do. She told me there is a part of her that is verra happy living in her wee cottage, making her dyes, and not having to deal with men, but there is another part that grows lonely."

"Ah, but is that part lonely for Sir Archie?"

"Hattie feels certain it is. When she told him that she had been a whore for five years and had bedded down with a lot of men, he said he had been a mercenary for fifteen years and had probably put more men in the grave than she could bed in a lifetime. He said they would both probably go to hell but at least they could be there together if they were married." Keira smiled when Liam laughed, but she quickly grew serious again. "Hattie also thinks that she is with child."

"Is she?" There had been only six women so far who had found themselves with child after their ordeal, but as yet, none seemed to think they would need to accept Keira's offer to give up the child to her care.

"Aye. She still doesnae believe it e'en though I told her two and thirty isnae too old and nothing outside of complete abstinence can guarantee that a woman willnae conceive a child. Sir Archie says he doesnae mind at all, e'en though it is surely Rauf's child. I thought myself free of the superstitions concerning bad seeds and all of that, but I did suffer a moment of unease when she told me. Poor bairn will probably suffer for it, too, at least a wee bit."

Liam nodded, having just suffered that same unease. "Ye need to pause and remind yourself that 'tis as much who does the raising of the bairn as who did the breeding that makes a mon. Or woman. One only needs to look at Kester to be reminded, too. Ridiculed and cast aside by his own blood, hard, unkind men, and yet he is a good lad."

"I think that in some ways, it was good he went to the monastery, that those kinsmen didnae have the full raising of him."

For a little while, they sat in the sun, quietly enjoying a moment of peace together. Liam soon decided that Keira was not ready to tell him that she was with child. There was a small chance she had not noticed yet, even though she was a healer, being either too busy or too blind to the changes in her own body. He had noticed, however, if only because it had suddenly occurred to him that there had been no interruption in their lovemaking since the day they had married. If she was not suffering any of the other ills that afflicted a woman with child, it was possible that she had not realized it yet. It was getting harder and harder not to just ask her, however.

Deciding he had better return to work before he did just that, Liam took Lightning off his shoulder and set the cat down, ignoring the animal's disgruntled look. "I had best return to work," he said, kissing Keira before he walked away. One more week, he told himself. He would give her one more week to tell him.

Keira watched her husband walk away, admiring his grace as he walked and, she was no longer ashamed to admit, the shape of his legs. Since it was a fine day, he wore what he called the Ardgleann plaid over a rough linen shirt and his deer-hide boots. The deep greens, blues, and touch of black in the plaid suited him. She had teased him the first time he had donned the outfit, claiming he was too shy to show his bare legs, and he had told her that he wore his boots because there were too many things upon the ground he did not wish to have oozing up between his toes. Keira understood that well enough, but she also knew that her husband was a very fastidious man.

She sighed, set Thunder on the ground, and returned to her weeding. Very soon she was going to have to tell Liam that he would be a father in about seven months. It still embarrassed her to think of how long it had taken her to realize it. For far too long, she had excused the uneasiness in her stomach by telling herself she was working too hard or was too concerned about Ardgleann and its people. When she had finally faced the fact that she carried Liam's child, she had been delighted and then dismayed.

For almost a fortnight now, she had come close to telling him, only to choke on the words. It was probably foolish, but Keira wanted to know how he felt about her before she became the mother of his child. Since she could not discern how he truly felt about her when it was just the two of them, she doubted she would ever figure it out after he knew about the child she carried. The only way she could know what he felt then would be if she asked him outright, perhaps even told him all she felt. Keira did not have the courage to do that yet, and she suspected it would be a long time before she did.

"Ye didnae tell him, did ye?"

Blushing a little, Keira looked up at Joan. "Weel, nay." She sat back on her heels and shrugged. "It shouldnae be so hard, should it, but it is. 'Tis so foolish, yet, 'tis almost as if I am jealous of my own child. I have no doubt in my mind that Liam will be most pleased, and probably, verra caring, e'en too much so."

"And ye would like it if he was that way for just you, nay ye and what rests in your womb."

"Aye, that says it rather weel."

Joan grabbed Keira by the hand, pulled her to her feet, and started to lead her toward the bench. " 'Tis time ye and I had a wee talk, woman to woman."

"I have already spent too much time sitting," Keira protested softly. "The weeds—"

"Will still be there." Joan sat down and then nodded when Keira finally sat down next to her. "Ye have a good mon there, m'lady."

"I ken it, and if we are to talk woman to woman, should ye still be calling me m'lady?" Keira had to look away from Joan's scowl before she blushed with guilt over her thin ploy to try to halt the lecture she knew was coming.

"Dinnae try to turn my thoughts down another path. Ye have been wed to that mon for o'er two months, and now ye carry his bairn. 'Tis time to stop wondering and sighing and *thinking* so cursed hard about it all."

" 'Tis good to think o'er a problem verra carefully."

"Wheesht, that is true, but ye think it to death. Ye love the mon, dinnae ye?"

"Oh, aye," Keira answered softly. "I love him so much that sometimes at night, I can be happy just lying near him, listening to him breathe."

"And I suspicion it has been that way from the beginning."

"Quite possibly, though I was quite successful in lying to myself."

"It hits some of us hard and fast like that. I took me one look at Malcolm and thought, this one is mine." Joan winked at Keira. "I was ten at the time. Malcolm was six and ten. E'en when he left the village for five long years, went away to learn how to make beautiful things with the metals, I ne'er lost faith. Ye need to have faith."

"I have faith in what *I* feel, Joan. And I have faith in Liam—as a good mon, a kind mon, one who will ne'er turn from what is his duty. 'Tis what he might feel for me that I lack faith in. He is so bonnie and learned—"

"And ye think he cannae care for a wee lass like ye? Ye arenae still fretting o'er your troubles with Duncan, are ye? I though Malcolm told ye all about that poor mon. It wasnae ye. It was ne'er ye. Ye do ken it now, dinnae ye?"

Keira nodded. "I ken it. The poor mon had been, weel, damaged ere I met him. The verra ones who should have loved him and nurtured him destroyed him."

" 'Tis always sad when that happens," Joan agreed. "So, 'tis that ye have no faith in yourself." Joan crossed her arms and frowned at Keira. "And why is that, eh? Why would a bonnie lass like yourself feel she isnae good enough for any mon?"

"Ye havenae seen the sort of women Liam can draw to himself," Keira muttered, wanting to deny Joan's insight, yet unable to. She had to wonder just when she *had* begun to lose faith in herself and why.

"I am sure some of them were beauties, but ye are far from plain, lass. Ye have bright, beautiful eyes. Your hair is lovely, long, and thick. Aye, ye arenae a verra fulsome lass, but ye have flesh enough on your bones and in all the right places." She glanced down at her own reed slim body and smiled faintly. "More than me, and my mon has ne'er complained. 'Tisnae the body that holds a mon at your side either, but the heart, the spirit of ye, and ye have a hearty serving of both."

Keira was a little surprised when Joan handed her a scrap of clean linen, and then realized she was crying. "This is so verra foolish," she said quietly as she wiped the tears from her cheeks.

" 'Tis the bairn. Weel, some it is. Now, ye listen to me ere ye go to take a wee rest—"

"Take a rest?" Keira said, but Joan ignored her interruption.

"Ye have yourself a verra good mon. He is the laird and your husband, but he listens to you. 'Tis a verra fine thing that. He has made it verra clear to all of us that ye *and* he are the laird here, that ye speak for him as he speaks for ye."

"Oh. I didnae ken that."

Joan nodded firmly. "To share his authority with his wife is no small thing for a mon to do. And we ken he shares your bed each and every night. I suspicion he keeps it verra warm indeed." Joan laughed softly when Keira blushed. "The mon cannae keep his hands off ye, m'lady. He is always having to touch ye or give ye a wee kiss when ye are in reach. We can all see that he cares for ye. I cannae understand why ye cannae see it. Wheesht, a bonnie lass of your good birth must have been wooed dozens of times."

"Nay, I wasnae. 'Tis one reason I was quick to accept Duncan e'en though I didnae ken the mon as much as I would have liked to. I was o'er twenty, and I had ne'er been seriously wooed." She sighed. "I so wanted children, ye see."

"What I see is that, weel, how to put this? Did ye ne'er consider that ye just didnae see the attempts to woo ye for what they were because ye werenae really interested in those men? It sounds to me as if ye had already decided to accept the verra first mon to approach ye or your kinsmen and then along came our Duncan. A mon decides to take himself a wife, and he is verra apt to, er, test the water first. If there is no welcome, he will go elsewhere. I think that ye ne'er gave a mon any sign that ye would welcome their wooing, that ye didnae e'en ken that ye were being wooed. So they moved onto the next lass."

Keira sat up a little straighter and began to consider that, suddenly recalling things said to her by her own family that had been very similar. Unfortunately, she would have to consider that matter later. Joan clearly had more to say.

"And, think, m'lady, ye are a wondrous healer with a blessing from God resting in those wee hands. Ye left here wounded and alone, yet ye got yourself to a safe place, healed, and regained your strength, then brought us what we needed to be free of that bastard Rauf. Aye, and ye were sorely tested by your marriage to a mon who was so scarred and crippled in his mind, he ne'er should have taken a wife. But ye held fast, and we who ken what Duncan's troubles were truly believed ye could have helped him. There just wasnae enough time. Ye healed Sir Archie. My Malcolm doesnae suffer unending pain in his hand, and 'tis near as good as it was. All because of ye. Ye healed that husband of yours, and because of ye, he is a laird, a mon with lands and power, instead of just another cousin to a laird. All that he is now is due to ye."

"But what does all that have to do with his feelings for me, or if he e'en has any deep ones?"

"Naught. It does have to do with how ye seem to think ye arenae good enough for him. Aye, most of us think he was born to this, that it would have been a sad waste if he had remained just another cousin, but he gained this because of ye. Ye love him; 'tis easy to see that ye warm his bed to his satisfaction, he treats ye as a true equal in all of this, and ye are about to give him a bairn." Joan shrugged. "I cannae think of anything more to say. What ye need to do is have a hard look at yourself, and see the good in yourself, for I dinnae think ye do, nay clearly." Joan stood up and tugged Keira to her feet. "And ye might think on just telling him."

"Oh, I do intend to tell him about the bairn soon."

"Good, but I was meaning that mayhap ye should just tell him that ye love him and see where that leads ye. Now, get some rest."

It was not until Keira was in her bedchamber cleaning the dirt from her hands that she realized she had just been sent to her room like a naughty child—by her cook. She laughed and shook her head. Lectured thoroughly, told what to think hard about, and then sent off to do so.

Keira sighed; she was forced to admit that Joan was right about many things. She had lost faith in herself. It was also very possible that she had simply not noticed any attempts to woo her because she had not been interested in any man enough to notice. That utter lack of interest would certainly have turned away any number of men. Many of her kinswomen had tentatively said the same. She had noticed Duncan, but that could have been because she had decided that she needed to marry and Duncan had been the first man after that to step to the fore. It was all rather sad. Recalling how she had felt when she had first seen Liam, even bruised and swollen as he was, she knew she had had no real interest in a man before that. It was easy to see how her feelings, or complete lack thereof, had turned aside any who had even thought to woo her.

Peering at herself in the looking glass, Keira saw yet again how much she looked like her grandmother, several of her aunts, and many of her cousins. And yet, had she not always thought them handsome women? she thought. Somehow she had neglected to carry that appreciation over to her own face. Surrounded by so many who looked similar to her, she supposed it was easy enough to begin to think herself very ordinary. She was not the great beauty Lady Maude was, but there was nothing to shame her in her looks.

Or her body, she thought, as she glanced down at herself. She was small and slender, but there were no unsightly parts she needed to hide. She was also strong and healthy. And she had good teeth, she thought and laughed.

She stripped to her shift, gave herself a more thorough wash, and went to lie on the bed. It was only a few hours until they all gathered in the great hall to sup, and it was probably a good idea to rest a little before she had to help with the meal. Keira placed her hand over her still flat stomach and smiled faintly. She always told women to rest a lot when they were carrying a child. It was time this healer took a little of her own advice.

It would be best if she was well rested, she decided as she closed her eyes, for she intended to confront Liam tonight. Even if she could not find the courage to tell him she loved him, she would tell him about the child. It would be wrong to wait so long that he discovered it on his own or, worse, from someone else.

Liam fought the urge to crawl into bed with his wife when she finally responded to his soft calls and slowly opened her eyes. There was such a soft, welcoming look in her eyes. He could almost believe it was a look filled with love, but he quickly smothered that hope. Until Keira told him how she felt, he would only drive himself mad trying to guess what each look, smile, or kiss might mean.

"I would love to crawl in there with ye, love," he said and kissed her, "but Joan has worked hard to prepare our meal, and Kester is eager to see how she prepared the rabbits he caught."

Keira blinked, realizing suddenly that Liam really was leaning over her. She had thought it a dream. Her hand was still touching his cheek, and she could almost taste the words *I love ye* on her tongue.

"Och, aye," she mumbled, slowly sitting up. "Kester must be feeling verra proud of himself."

"That he is." Liam frowned for if she was not with child, this weariness could be a sign of some illness. "Are ye feeling unweel?" he asked, a tingle of fear tripping through his body at the mere thought of Keira falling ill.

"Nay, I am fine. Just fine. I think it was spending so many hours pulling weeds in the sun." She smiled. "We get so few warm, sunny days, 'tis nay wonder I am not accustomed to them."

Liam kissed her again. "I will meet ye in the great hall."

Keira nodded, watched him leave, and then fell back onto the bed with a soft groan. She had almost told him everything. Although she was planning to do so, a better time and place was needed. And she had better choose her time and place very soon, she told herself sternly as she got out of bed and began to dress. It was cowardice holding her silent, and that could no longer be allowed. Keira knew that even though Liam might not return her feelings in full, he would never treat her vow of love as unimportant or as a burden.

After thoroughly looking herself over, Keira deemed herself ready. She wore her best gown, she had brushed her hair until it gleamed and had only loosely braided it for that was what Liam preferred, and she had touched her skin very lightly with lavender oil. Tonight, after the meal was done, she would get Liam to walk her out into the garden, and she would tell him her secrets. Or at least half of them, she mused as she started out of the room. Cowardice being difficult to shake free of, Keira did not want to promise herself too much.

A smile curved her lips as she walked into the great hall. It was filled with men laughing, talking, and even arguing. It was a strange mix of men. Some had come from her kinsmen's lands, some from Liam's, the few MacKails who had survived, and even some from the MacLeans and the MacKays, but Liam was right. They were beginning to act as one. It was good to hear laughter inside Ardgleann again. Even the few women there no longer held that frightened look while in the company of the men. Keira felt laughter was one thing that would cleanse the place of Rauf's evil better and more thoroughly than any scrubbing could.

Keira smiled at Tait Cameron who sat on Liam's right as her husband helped her into the seat on his left. With a different shade of copper-colored hair than Liam's and ivy green eyes, Tait was quite handsome. It seemed odd to her that the man had little to do with the women working inside Ardgleann. Perhaps, she thought as she filled her plate with a page's assistance, Tait held to some of the same rules Liam did. She would be pleased if that was so. At the moment, she was just pleased that the man was not as odd as his elder brother Sigimor.

As the pages and the maids removed the remains of the last course and began setting out fruits and other sweets, Keira reached out to take Liam's hand in hers. She was opening her mouth to ask him to take her for a walk in the garden or to come to the solar with her if the weather had turned sour when a loud disturbance from outside the great hall's doors pulled her attention away from Liam so swiftly it made her a little dizzy. Then she recognized the voice of the woman arguing with Liam's men, who wished her to wait somewhere quietly. She yanked her hand away from Liam. This time, it was not cowardice that would halt her confessions, but fury.

Keira turned to glare at Liam as a sweet, feminine voice cried out, "Liam, my sweet prince, where are ye?" Keira also came very close to repeating the foul curse Liam spat out.

CHAPTER 21

The look Keira gave him should have slain him in his seat, Liam thought. He was almost surprised not to see his life's blood pooling at his feet. Liam did wince, however, although he was not sure how much of that reaction was due to Keira's look and how much to Lady Maude's shrill voice echoing too sharply through the halls of Ardgleann. When he heard Tait murmur the words *sweet prince,* Liam gave his cousin a hard glare of reproof before Lady Maude raced into the great hall.

"Oh, Liam," Lady Maude said, pausing a few feet inside the hall to clutch her dainty hands together as if in prayer and press them against her heaving breasts, "at last I have found ye, my dearest love."

Keira watched every man and boy in the great hall fix their gaze upon Lady Maude's breasts and nearly screamed. A calm, reasonable part of her attempted to make her take careful note of the fact that Liam was not one of that crowd, that he looked at the beautiful Lady Maude as if she were a rat in the meal. She ignored that voice, too angry to care. Not only was Lady Maude's arrival a stark reminder of Liam's past, but it also had ruined the careful plans she had made for the evening. Keira had to wonder if it was an omen as well.

Here was her future as the wife of a man like Liam, a future filled with women trying to pull him away from her or tempt him to betray her. She was almost certain Liam had told the truth when he had claimed he had never been the woman's lover, but that did not matter. Keira might believe him now, but what about the next time? She could not feel certain she would not slowly turn into a jealous shrew, and whatever hope she had for a long, happy marriage would quickly disappear. The fact that she might never have the knowledge that he loved her to quiet her doubts made it an even greater possibility.

When Lady Maude ran up to Liam and nearly hurled herself into his lap, Keira gritted her teeth so hard her jaws ached. Liam grasped the woman by the arms and held her away from him, but his quick rejection of the woman's embrace did not make Keira feel any less violent. She had the urge to run to her bedchamber and lock herself inside before she gave in to the aching need to pull out every strand of Lady Maude's golden hair. Stiffening her spine, Keira forced herself to stay in her seat. She would not allow herself to do anything that weak, that spineless, and that undignified before the people of Ardgleann.

"Curse it, Maude, what are ye doing here?" demanded Liam as he pushed her into the seat one of the men had hastily brought over for her.

"Looking for you," she replied and then took out a delicately embroidered scrap of linen to dab at the tears that suddenly began to glisten in her big eyes. "My husband locked me away after he dragged me home from the monastery where I came to you, m'love. It took me weeks to get free so that I could be with ye again. Och, my bonnie lad, my husband was such a brute to me."

"Mayhap having his wife gallop about the country hunting down another mon irritates him a wee bit," murmured Keira. She found it almost funny when Lady Maude somehow managed to glare surreptitiously at her yet hold firm to her air of distress and lovesickness. " 'Twas just a thought."

"Who is that, my love?" Lady Maude asked Liam.

"This is my wife, Lady Keira," Liam said. "I am a married man now."

This was all a game to the woman, Keira realized. Although she truly had begun to believe that Liam had never bedded the woman, she had remained torn concerning how responsible he was for Lady Maude's apparent adoration. Now she doubted the woman loved Liam at all. Lusted after him, perhaps, for what woman with blood in her veins would not wish to bed Liam if he wanted her or if she was daring enough to take a lover. But loved him? No. What Keira could not even begin to understand was why would the woman play this game at all?

"I would suggest ye return to your husband, m'lady," Liam said, praying this could all be solved so simply, but doubting he would be so lucky.

"To Robbie? But, my sweet prince, he was so cruel to me. Why, he quite terrified me." She gave a little shiver that immediately drew nearly all the men's gazes back to her breasts. "Ye would ne'er be able to guess how horribly he has treated me."

Looking around at the men gathered in the great hall as Lady Maude proceeded to relate tale after tale of her husband's barbarous treatment of her, Keira decided the woman was too caught up in her game to even notice when she went too far. Except for Tait and Liam, most of the men initially had looked outraged by her tale and even sympathetic to her plight. Kester, Malcolm, and Sir Archie began to look skeptical very quickly, and then, one by one, Lady Maude lost the others. Even the most besotted man had to doubt the woman's claims when she sat there looking so beautiful, so healthy, so strong, and so very well dressed. The survivors of Rauf's brutal, but thankfully brief, reign at Ardgleann and those who had seen them before their wounds had healed began to look particularly disgusted with Lady Maude. They knew all too well the look of a woman beaten often or a body made to suffer from little food or water for days on end.

"Ye accuse your husband of some hard crimes against ye, m'lady," said Liam. "Mayhap ye best take your tale to your own kinsmen." He glanced at the three men who had entered with her. "If ye feel a need for more protection, I believe we can find a few men to assist yours."

"But how can ye cast me out so heartlessly?" asked Lady Maude. "Ye ken I will simply be taken back to Robbie if I go to my kinsmen. They willnae protect me from my husband." She started to weep. "They cannae understand the ways of love. Robbie was such a fine choice they will tell me as they take me back and place me into his cruel, unloving hands. Rich, power-ful, and possessing some verra fine lands. That is all they will care about."

As the woman sniffled and complained, Liam rubbed at his right temple where a sharp ache was rapidly growing. Out of the corner of his eye, he watched Keira watch Lady Maude. Keira ate slowly, rarely taking her gaze from the woman. Liam could sense Keira's fury in every taut line of her face and body. Lady Maude seemed completely unaware of it, which Liam found totally incomprehensible.

"Please, m'love," begged Lady Maude, "let me stay here with ye."

"I willnae shelter ye from your lawful husband, m'lady," Liam said.

"But after all I have told ye—"

"Ye must give me leave to doubt some of your claims." The way her tears seemed to dry very quickly told Liam that he had just angered her. "As I said, I can give ye some men for added protection on your journey—"

"But, Liam, my dearest, the sun has set, and the weather has turned most foul."

A quick glance at her men revealed that that at least was the truth. The men looked wet, muddy, and very tired. Since Lady Maude did not look as if she was even damp, Liam had to as-sume that she had ridden in a covered cart or that all the men had been forced to sacrifice their oiled skins for her comfort.

"Then ye may stay here for the night," he said.

The words were still falling from his lips when Liam realized he had just made a very big mistake. He should have driven the

woman out of Ardgleann, offered her a cottage at the far corner of his lands, or even paid for a bed for her at the alehouse
in the village. His sympathy for the men Lady Maude dragged
around with her had prompted his invitation, but he noticed
they were giving *him* a look of sympathy now. The way everyone
in the great hall nearly gaped at him, however, told him that
his explanation would be doubted. Liam did not even look at
Keira for a moment. He would almost swear he could feel her
gaze burning a hole through his clothes. To his relief, Lady
Maude's attempt to enfold him in an embrace was thwarted by
the arm of the chair just long enough to give him a chance to
hold her back.

"As soon as the weather eases, ye will leave," he said firmly as
he pushed the woman back into her seat. "I refuse to be caught
up in the middle of whate'er game ye play with your husband."

"Oh, how cruel ye can be," she murmured.

Liam noticed that his cruelty did nothing to dull her appetite as she helped herself to whatever food was within her
reach. Quietly, Liam instructed one of the scowling serving
women to see that Lady Maude and her men were served
something heartier. He then turned to look at his wife.

"Her men need a rest," he said.

"Of course," Keira replied. "They look verra worn out.
Tired, hungry, and irritated." She looked at Lady Maude, making it very clear whom she felt was fully responsible for that.
"Courtesy demands that we dinnae send them out into the
dark and the storm."

"Aye, it does." There was something in the tone of Keira's
voice that told Liam not to get his hopes up, that this was not
the polite, meek acceptance it sounded like.

"Courtesy doesnae demand that I like it, however."

Liam sighed as he watched Keira walk out of the great hall. He
was astonished, however, when every other Ardgleann woman
also left. Even Meggie left Kester's side.

"I do believe the battle lines have just been drawn," murmured Tait, and he grinned when Liam glared at him.

Turning his glare upon the one he felt was fully responsible for his troubles, Liam snapped, "I believe this game has gone on long enough, Lady Maude. I grow verra weary of it. I dinnae ken what ye think ye will gain from this, but it starts to cost me verra dearly. I am now a married mon—" he began.

"Aye, so I heard. So I can see," Lady Maude replied as she looked around the great hall. "Ye have done verra weel for yourself. Despite your many charms, I ne'er would have thought ye would be allowed to reach so high." She smiled and stroked his hand, appearing oblivious to the way he yanked that hand away. "Now it will be easier for us, my love. Ye are now a laird with an army at your command. We can defy anyone and everyone in the name of our love. Is that nae wonderful?"

He did not really think she was insane, but Liam could not begin to guess exactly what was part of her game and what she might actually believe. "Nay, it isnae wonderful. I dinnae ken what strange dream ye are caught in, m'lady, but ye willnae pull me into it with ye. I have told ye—I will be no partner in adultery. I will hold to vows I have made with my wife. These are the rules I follow, ones weel-kenned by many people. Why would I break them for ye?" To his surprise, she looked briefly, intensely furious.

"Why would ye nae do so? Ye certainly didnae follow your virtuous, wee rules when ye bedded down with my sister Lady Grace."

"Lady Grace MacDonnell?"

"Aye. I see that ye recall her weel enough."

"Of course I do. I spoke with her husband Edmund many times, e'en supped with him and his wife on occasion. I ne'er bedded down with his wife, however." The invitation had certainly been there, but Liam had held fast to the rules he had set for himself. He also considered Edmund a friend, and he would never betray him so.

"She told me—"

"I dinnae care what she told ye. I *never* bed down with a married woman. Ye have believed a lie and have let your beleaguered husband believe e'en more lies. And just when can we expect Laird Kinnaird?"

Lady Maude stared at him for a full minute, then shrugged slightly. "I cannae say. He wasnae at home when I freed myself from my prison and sought ye out." She sniffed. "Only to have ye break my poor heart as usual. I dinnae ken what to do next. I have no one to turn to in my time of trouble. Truly, life has become such a weary burden for me, so full of pain and disappointment, I ofttimes wonder if I should continue to struggle through another day."

"Weel, if ye finally make up your wee mind and the answer is nay," said Liam as he stood up and pointed east, "the river is that way."

He heard her gasp, but it was quickly drowned out by Tait's laughter, a laughter that quickly spread to the other men in the hall. It was tempting to leave the keep and ride away, far away, and not return to Ardgleann until he was absolutely certain Lady Maude Kinnaird had left it. Looking up the stairs, Liam sighed and started up them. There was a part of him that felt he should not have to placate his furious wife, that she had no right to be furious with him. He had done nothing wrong, had never bedded the woman whose sanity he now seriously questioned, had never even encouraged her.

Then he recalled how lovely Keira had looked tonight. She had obviously taken extra care with her appearance. After the way she had touched his cheek and smiled at him when he had roused her to come down to the great hall to sup, he believed she had decided to tell him about the child. That belief had been enhanced when she had taken his hand in hers at the table. There had been that soft, warm look in her eyes again. Unfortunately, whatever Keira had intended to say or do had been lost when Lady Maude had, yet again, intruded upon their life.

"The woman is a curse," he muttered and then stopped just outside of the bedchamber he shared with Keira.

For a moment, he tried to think of what to say, but it was useless. He was not exactly sure of what she was angry about or who she was most angry with. Liam shrugged, grabbed the door latch, and tried to open the door. He tried several times before he accepted the fact that Keira had locked him out.

"Keira!" he yelled as he banged on the door.

"What?" his wife called back.

"Let me in."

"Nay, nay tonight. I need to think, and I dinnae get much of that done when ye are about."

That sounded good, but the thinking alone sounded very bad. Liam suddenly recalled what Keira's brothers had said about the danger of letting her think. He had thought their remarks funny at the time, but he felt no inclination to laugh about them now. There was no telling what path her thoughts might lead her down. Liam could all too easily think of several conclusions she could reach that he would suffer for.

"I think it would be better if we talk."

"Nay, we can talk about it when I am done thinking."

Liam stared at the closed door. He considered getting a few burly men and some very sharp axes and turning the door into a pile of splinters. It was a pleasant thought, but he sternly repressed the urge to do just that for two reasons. It would be undignified, and he had the sudden thought that Lady Maude would find far too much enjoyment in it.

"Fine then," he snapped. "Ye think. I will go find something else to do and someone else to do it with."

That was a stupid thing to say, he decided as he hastily retreated to his ledger room. He wanted Keira to trust him, and he had just left her thinking he was running off to be the rutting swine she had once called him. When he found his cousin Tait waiting for him, he almost ordered him out of the room, but then he saw the large jug of wine and the two tankards set on the worktable.

"I had a wee suspicion ye might hide away in here," said Tait as he poured them each some wine. "And that ye might appreciate something to drown your sorrows."

Liam threw himself into his chair and drank half the wine in the tankard before saying, "She has locked me out of our bedchamber."

"Did she happen to say exactly why she has barred ye from the room?"

"She says she has to think."

"That sounds ominous."

"Aye, and as I left, I gave her e'en more to ponder." He told Tait what he had said.

Tait grimaced. "That wasnae particularly wise."

"That was stupid is what that was. Utterly and astoundingly witless."

"What do ye think she needs to think about? Ye? Lady Maude? Or ye and the Lady Maude together?"

"All of it, I suppose." Liam frowned as he sipped at his wine. "I just wish I kenned what game Lady Maude plays with us."

"Are ye so certain it is a game she plays?"

"More and more with each thing the woman says and does. I just cannae be certain who is declared the fool in this game— me or her husband?"

"Mayhap both of ye," said Tait after he frowned in thought for a moment. "Do ye think she really will leave Ardgleann in the morning? She seems the tenacious sort, and one who is verra good at hearing only what she wishes to hear."

"She may not leave in the morning, but she *will* leave on the morrow ere the sun sets. Then I go and get that cursed door unlocked. I willnae spend more than one night alone."

Keira almost unbarred the door as Liam's parting remark echoed through the room, but she forced herself not to give in to that weakness. He had told her that he would hold true to the vows they had taken. She had to trust in that. And if he was the sort of man to break those vows simply because they were having an argument, it was best if she knew that, too.

"Do ye think he meant that?" asked Meggie as she sat on the edge of the bed and scratched Thunder's belly.

"Nay, of course he didnae," said Joan. " 'Twas an empty threat thrown out in anger, one said to try to make m'lady fret in retribution for locking him out. Are ye certain this is what ye should do?" she asked Keira.

"Aye," replied Keira. "I need to think, and that mon can make thinking verra difficult at times."

"Just what do ye need to think about? Him and that woman? I would believe him when he says he ne'er bedded her. If he had, it would have been before ye were married, and so there wouldnae be any reason for him to deny it."

"Oh, I believe him, too," Keira said and realized she spoke the truth. "Yet there has to be some reason for the woman to act this way. When I first came up here, I was angry—at him, at her, at the whole situation. I thought I wanted to think about how this was a bad omen for my future with that mon. Yet now that I have calmed down a little, I discover that isnae what I am thinking about."

"What are ye thinking about?"

"I cannae really put my finger on the why of it, but something tells me that Lady Maude isnae as daft as she would like us to think she is. Nay, not at all. In truth, I begin to think she is playing some game with us all." Keira scowled into the flames as she let that thought rest in her mind for a moment and discovered that it felt right.

"A game? What sort of game?"

"I dinnae ken. That is one of the things I must think about now. I truly believe that she doesnae love Liam as she keeps claiming she does. So why does she do this? It makes no sense at all. It appears that Liam's rules about not cuckolding a mon are weel-kenned, so Lady Maude cannae be so vain she thinks she will be the one who can make him break those rules."

"Weel, I thought she seemed vain," said Meggie. "Just look at how she kept drawing attention to her big breasts."

"Oh, that doesnae have to mean that she is vain," said Keira.

"She just kens that most men appreciate such bounty and uses it to draw their attention to her. Some women think that nonsense is flirtation." Keira put her hands on her hips and slowly shook her head. "Nay, I grow more certain with each passing moment that that woman plays some game, and Liam is but a pawn in it. She is probably the one who had him beaten, ye ken."

"Weel, that certainly sounds like the act of a jealous woman," said Joan. "So, would that nay mean that she does care for him?"

"Not necessarily, although it gave me pause. Jealousy can be bred from many things, however. Who can say? Mayhap she hoped Liam would believe her husband had it done, and then Liam would break his own rules so that he could bed her as a form of revenge against her husband. She could have e'en ordered it done in a fit of temper because Liam wasnae playing her game in the way she wished him to."

Joan shook her head. "I dinnae ken how ye think ye can untangle this. The woman just might be as daft as she seems."

"Daft or not, she is clever enough to keep finding Liam. And there is one consistency in all of this. In a verra short time, her big husband and his equally big men will be here, and Laird Kinnaird will be screaming for Liam's blood."

Meggie frowned. "That happens every time?"

"As far as I can tell, aye," replied Keira. "Ye would think that a woman who is clever enough to slip free of a watchful husband and hunt down a mon who doesnae wish to be found could do so without leaving a trail her husband can so easily and quickly follow, wouldnae ye?"

"Aye, ye certainly would. So the question I would like answered is, which mon does she want dead?"

Keira stared at Meggie in astonishment. She noticed Joan doing the same. Try as she would, Keira could not argue away the keen insight Meggie's question revealed.

"Meggie, ye have a wondrously clever and devious mind," Keira said.

"Is that a good thing?"

"Oh, I certainly think so. I but pray it stays sharp and devious as the night wears on."

"Why?"

"Because we need to find the answer to that question ere Laird Kinnaird comes bellowing at our gates."

CHAPTER 22

"How long are ye going to allow Keira to think?"

Liam scowled at his grinning cousin. The fact that Tait had caught him standing in the bailey glaring up at the window to the bedchamber Keira had locked herself in annoyed him. Now it would be impossible to act as if the fact that his wife still would not speak to him or see him did not bother him at all. Even worse, Tait's grin told Liam that his cousin knew he had absolutely no idea of how to solve this problem.

"In two hours, it will be exactly sixteen hours since she started pouting—"

"Thinking," Tait said.

Ignoring that, Liam continued, "—and if she doesnae open the door to me, then I will break it down." He glared at Tait again. "Laugh, and I will grind ye into the mud."

"I will laugh later when ye cannae hear me." Tait shook his head. "Sorry, Liam, but after years of watching the lasses grow faint at the sight of ye and listening to ye charm e'en the most ill-tempered old crone, I cannae help but find this amusing."

"Ye find it funny that my wife thinks me a rutting swine? That she is undoubtedly hurt by all of this?"

"Och, nay." Tait crossed his arms over his chest, glanced up at the window Liam had been glaring at, and then looked at his cousin again. "Actually, I dinnae think she believes that woman."

"If she doesnae believe Maude, then why has she locked me out?"

"She told ye. She needs to think." Tait chuckled when Liam growled. "Mayhap, Cousin, she needs to decide if she has the strength to endure this nonsense for a lifetime."

"I told her I would hold to my vows."

"Aye, but have ye told her that ye love her?" Tait asked quietly.

Liam opened his mouth to tell his cousin that that was none of his business, but then he sighed and dragged his fingers through his hair. He did love Keira; he had known it for certain from the moment he had thought Rauf would kill her, but he had never told her so. Coward that he was, he wanted her to say it first. There was a chance he was now paying dearly for that timidity.

"What makes ye think I do?" he asked, ignoring the way Tait rolled his eyes.

"Everything. Dinnae forget, I have watched ye with women for years. Oh, ye are kind, and ye say pretty things to them, but little more than that. And I am certain ye made sure they got pleasure out of the rutting or thought they did. But again, nay more than that. Ye just, weel, liked them in some fleeting way as ye like most women. When Sigimor told me that ye had found your mate, the right one—"

"The one that fits," Liam said quietly.

"Aye, the one that fits. Weel, I wasnae sure I believed it. I was here but one day, and I did."

"Ye thought I had married her for this place, for the chance to be a laird?"

"There is naught wrong with that, Liam. At least ye would be a good husband to her. I had *no* doubts about that." He smiled faintly. "I also believe that ye *fit* her, but, I suspect, she hasnae told ye either."

"So why should I bare my soul to her?"

"Because she needs to ken it and believe it more than ye

need it. Aye, I suspect 'tis difficult to nay ken how your wife feels about ye, but ye have had enough experience with women to ken enough of how she feels to keep ye waiting patiently for the rest. That wife of yours may ken the ways of men, but nay in this situation, nay in love or lust. I am afraid ye must be the one to go first."

Liam cast one long last glare at the bedchamber window. "May I throttle her first?"

Tait laughed and shook his head. "Ye will have to be satisfied with threatening it."

"M'laird!"

Even as Liam turned in response to that call, Kester stumbled to a halt at his side, his shadow Meggie close at his heels. The lad looked concerned. Meggie also looked concerned, but there was anger in her expression as well. He had a sinking feeling he knew what was wrong.

"There is that mon—" began Kester.

"Cameron, ye bastard!"

Liam sighed and shook his head as Kinnaird's bellow echoed through the air. "I truly fear that the only way this will end is if I kill that fool." He caught Meggie opening her mouth to say something, but the girl quickly closed it and pressed her lips together. "He will drive me to it, lass, if only to stop him from killing me."

"I dinnae think 'tis that fool who holds the reins, m'laird," she muttered and then ran off.

"Now what did she mean by that?" asked Kester, frowning after Meggie.

"I was about to ask ye the same thing," Liam murmured.

"Cameron, ye cuckolding swine, come out here!"

"Do ye think we can talk any sense to the fool?" asked Tait as he joined Liam and Kester in walking toward the front bailey where Sir Kinnaird was bellowing out insults and challenges.

"It hasnae worked yet," Liam replied.

"I was afraid ye would say that."

* * *

Keira stood in the doorway of the bedchamber that had been given to Lady Maude Kinnaird, Joan at her side. She, Joan, and Meggie had finally given up trying to guess what twisted game this woman played with them all and had sought their beds. When she had been awakened a few hours ago, Keira had felt tired, her head had ached, and her stomach had finally ceased being merely uneasy in the morning and had openly rebelled against her. As she had struggled to settle her stomach and get dressed, determined to keep a close watch on Lady Maude, she had begun to doubt her own conclusions about the woman. Now, standing there watching the woman smile down at her raging husband, Keira lost all doubt.

She marched over to the woman, grabbed her by the arm, and twisted it up behind the woman's back. "Enjoying the wee play ye have written, m'lady?"

"Release me this moment!" Lady Maude demanded. "Who do ye think ye are to handle me this way?"

"The lady of this keep ye forced your way into. The wife of the mon your husband seeks to kill. The woman who is going to break your arm if ye dinnae answer my questions promptly and truthfully."

"I dinnae ken what ye are talking about."

Keira twisted the woman's arm a little more and winced at Lady Maude's screech of pain. She waited for the healer in her to be appalled by how she was behaving, but she found no hint of regret or revulsion in her heart. Keira decided that this was because she was so very certain that this woman had plotted all of this, that Lady Maude had worked very hard to put these two men at sword point. If in hurting this woman, she could stop two men from killing or maiming each other, she would be content, and her conscience would be at peace.

"Dinnae press me too hard, m'lady," Keira said. "I am nay in a verra good humor. My head aches, and my stomach is nay too happy about that rose scent ye have poured all over your

scheming body. Now, answer me this—which mon do ye wish
to see dead and why?"

"Ye are talking utter nonsense."

"I can break your arm. Dinnae doubt me."

"Aye," said Joan, chancing a look out the window. "She had
all of my mon's fingers on one hand broken."

Keira almost grinned when Lady Maude grew pale. Joan had
chosen a brilliant way to give weight to Keira's threat. She
spoke only the truth, so her words held the appropriate tone of
conviction. Lady Maude could not know that it had been done
so that Malcolm's fingers could be set correctly and the hand
healed.

"Nay, ye dinnae understand. Liam and I—"

"Did naught," Keira snapped. "Liam made himself a rule to
ne'er take part in adultery, and he has ne'er broken it. Did ye
think he had spent five years in a monastery because he liked
the robes? He believes in God's laws, and he *can* follow rules,
e'en those he makes himself. Aye, he was a lecherous wee
piglet for several years, but he was *never* a cuckolder. So, let us
try again with the truth, shall we?"

"He bedded my wedded sister! She told me so!"

"She lied."

" 'Tis obviously a trait that runs rampant in the family," Joan
murmured.

"Oh, what do ye ken about it? Ye dinnae ken my sister
Grace," Lady Maude said, her voice roughened by tears of pain
and, Keira suspected, fury. "She can have any mon she wants.
She had my husband!"

"Ah, I see," said Keira. "That is why ye tried to cuckold him
with Liam."

"And why not? If he can, so can I, but, och nay, suddenly, Sir
Liam Cameron dons the armor of the saintly. And fool that I
was, I believed him. Then he bedded Grace, who is married.
He turned me aside, but nay her."

"So ye made certain your faithless husband kenned all about

your pursuit of my husband. Now, why do I think Liam was nearly killed because ye heard your sister's lies?"

"He wasnae supposed to be killed!"

"Nay, of course not. Just punished." Keira looked at Joan. "I think that is enough. Are the men fighting yet?"

"Nay, but I think it willnae be long now," replied Joan. "I think your husband is trying to talk sense to her husband, but the fool isnae listening. He just keeps bellowing insults. I dinnae think our laird will be able to stomach many more."

Keira showed Joan how to hold Lady Maude's arm in a grip that could be painful, could even be used to break the arm, but that was also a very useful means of restraint. With Joan firmly holding Lady Maude, they headed out of the room, Keira pausing to pick up the sword she had leaned against the wall just outside the door. In the mood she was in right now, she could probably use it, Keira thought as they made their way out of the keep.

Liam shook his head as the word *coward* still echoed in the now utterly silent bailey. If he were not standing on his land, surrounded by his closely watching people, he might have let that insult pass unchallenged, just as he had all the others. He knew it was not true. Most of the people watching knew it was not true as well. Unfortunately, he could not simply stand there and keep reasoning with this fool now that he had said that. It was one of those insults a man was expected to respond to with his sword. As a laird, that was even more true. Yet, he still waited until Sir Kinnaird drew his sword before he drew his own.

"I am nay a coward, sir, and weel ye ken it," Liam said quietly. "I but hate to draw blood, yours or mine, o'er a lie."

" 'Tis probably what ye say to all the men ye cuckold," said Kinnaird.

"There are a lot of things I would say to some husbands. One being that they ought to take a wee bit of time to come to know their wives better. If ye had done so, ye would ken that she is lying and probably why."

"My Maude was an angel ere ye caught her in your web, ye lecherous swine," snapped Kinnaird, shoving one of his men aside when the man tried to talk sense to him.

It was obvious to Liam that at least some of Kinnaird's own men questioned their lady's tales, but Lady Maude had certainly convinced her husband. The man was blind with jealousy and, Liam began to suspect, hurt. Justice would be better served if Lady Maude was the one having to fight for her lying, manipulative little life instead of him or her poor, besotted husband. She had brought them to this point, and he dearly wished he knew why.

Just as Kinnaird started to swing his sword, and Liam tensed to parry the blow, the man went very still, and his eyes widened. Liam gradually started to see more than just his opponent and the sword in the man's hand; he realized every man, woman, and child in the bailey was wide-eyed as well, and many of them were gaping. Then the women began to smile. It took another blink of his eyes before Liam dared glance away from Kinnaird for long enough to see Joan holding a pale, yet furious, Lady Maude in front of her. Realizing he was in no danger of being attacked by Kinnaird at the moment, Liam wondered where Keira was. He leaned a little to the side to see behind Kinnaird's back and knew he now looked as astonished as everyone else. Keira stood behind the man, the point of the sword she held touching the small of the man's broad back.

"Wife, this is a matter of honor ye meddle in," he said calmly.

"There is no honor in this," snapped Keira, angry at the insults she had heard Kinnaird hurling at Liam, who was trying so hard to make peace. She was sorely tempted to give the man a few painful jabs with the sword. "Tell them the truth, Lady Maude," she ordered.

"My sweet prince," Lady Maude began, looking at Liam, "your wife has sorely abused me—"

"Joan?" Keira nodded with satisfaction when Joan pulled at the woman's arm and she screamed.

"Here now," protested Kinnaird, "ye have no right to hurt her." His last word ended on a soft grunt as Keira gave him a quick, painful, but insignificant poke with the sword.

"Hush. Dinnae press me too hard, m'laird," said Keira. "I have an aching head."

The dire tones Keira used to announce that nearly made Liam laugh, but he hastily swallowed the urge. Kinnaird looked astonished, but he also remained very still. It was clear that Keira had uncovered something that would finally put an end to this macabre game.

"Now, m'lady, shall we try again?" asked Keira, hoping the woman would cease her attempts to keep lying for the sword was heavy and her stomach was acting very strangely. Keira just wanted to lie down.

"I ne'er took Sir Liam as my lover," Lady Maude began again.

"I believe ye meant to say that my husband ne'er took *ye* as *his* lover."

"Ow! Ye will break my arm if ye dinnae stop!"

"Aye, that could happen. Joan is a wee bit stronger than I am, I think."

"Alright! Sir Liam refused to be my lover. He claimed he ne'er bedded down with married women. Hah! I should have kenned that he lied as all men do, for he bedded Grace, didnae he, and she is married." She glared at her husband. "How does it feel to ken that your lover is as faithless to ye as ye are to me?"

"What are ye babbling about?" demanded Kinnaird. "I was ne'er faithless to ye."

"Grace told me all about the two of ye! Dinnae lie to me! She told me all about your many trysts!" She briefly turned her glare upon Liam. "Aye, and yours."

Kinnaird stared at his wife, then at Liam, and then at his wife again. "She lied, and, I am thinking, ye have been lying, too."

He sheathed his sword as he looked at Liam again. "I assume it is your lady wife poking me with a sword or a dagger."

"Aye," replied Liam as he also sheathed his sword. "Keira, ye may cease poking Sir Kinnaird in the back now."

"Tell this woman to release me," demanded Lady Maude as Keira stepped out from behind Kinnaird.

"Nay, not yet," said Kinnaird as Liam opened his mouth to tell Joan to let go of Lady Maude. "Verra clever," the man said as he studied the hold Joan had on his wife. "Hurts, I suspect, eh, Maudie."

"Robbie, how can ye allow this woman to abuse me so?" asked Lady Maude in a tearful voice.

"It seems it makes ye tell the truth, something that has obviously been a stranger to ye for a while."

Not wanting Joan dragged into the middle of this, Liam looked at Keira. "Perhaps ye could—" he stuttered to a halt when Keira held her arm out straight, her hand palm out toward his face.

"Nay. I am done with this. I was up half the night trying to figure out that woman's twisted, wee mind. I am tired, and my head aches. All I want to do is lie down and mayhap, nibble on an oatcake or two and drink goat's milk. I am sure Joan doesnae mind assisting ye in untying the knots this wretched woman had tied ye all up in." When Joan murmured her agreement, Keira nodded. "Good. Have at it then." She left them, praying every step of the way that she could make it to her bedchamber before she was ill.

Liam, along with everyone else in the bailey, watched Keira disappear into the keep, still clutching the sword, although the tip of it was dragging in the dirt. It would be nice if all Keira had brooded on was what plot Lady Maude had been hatching, but Liam doubted he would be so lucky. He looked at Kinnaird at the same time the man looked at him.

"A Murray lass to the bone," Kinnaird said. "Ye will have your hands full with that one." He scowled at his wife. "And ye will have no more trouble from this one. Your sister is a lying whore, Maude, and ye are a great fool for believing her. Aye, and ye have made me a fool. I have been trying to kill a mon who hasnae done me any wrong." He briefly glanced at Liam. "S'truth, I could have been killed. Was that your plan?"

"Nay, m'love, I—"

"Hush. Just hush." He looked at Liam again. "I regret she pulled ye into this. I offer my apologies."

"For trying to fight me honorably or for having me beaten near to death?" Liam asked, not surprised when Sir Kinnaird looked shocked and confused over that latter accusation, for Liam was now certain that Lady Maude had ordered the beating. He would not let her hide that truth from her husband. "So it wasnae ye who set those men on me?"

"The insult was to me, and my honor demanded I avenge it myself. Or rather, the insult I thought ye had inflicted." Kinnaird scowled at his wife again. "Ye had him beaten? For what? Refusing to cuckold me?"

"He cuckolded Edmund," Lady Maude said.

"Nay, I think not." Kinnaird looked at the men who had come to Ardgleann with his wife. "Ye should have told me what she had done. I wasnae precise enough in my orders to ye, I can see. Ye will continue to accompany her wherever she goes, but now ye will tell me more than the where. Ye will tell me everything she does, everyone she meets, and everything she says. Take her to the cart."

"But, m'love—" protested Lady Maude as the men took her from Joan.

"Best ye keep silent for now, woman. I will speak to ye later." The moment she was taken away, Kinnaird turned back to face Liam. "Ye must allow me to make reparations for what she has done, for that beating and all the trouble she has caused ye."

"Nay, there is no need. In a way, it served me weel." Liam smiled faintly. "I met my wife because of it." He glanced around at Ardgleann. "I gained a lot more than I lost."

"I heard ye had to fight to claim it and ye rid Scotland of a scourge in the doing of it."

"Luck was with us, and the battle cost us little."

"From what I saw as I rode here, that bastard left a hard mark on the place. I will send ye a few things to help fill your larder for the winter."

Knowing they could use such largesse and that Kinnaird felt a need to do something to make amends, Liam said, "I thank ye. It will be a most welcome gift."

Kinnaird bowed and walked away. Within a few minutes, he, his wife, and all of his men were gone from Ardgleann. Liam sighed and shook his head. That man had a hard road ahead of him. Beneath the anger and disappointment in his wife, there had definitely been pain. The woman could have been trying to get her husband killed, and Kinnaird knew it.

"Weel, your wife obviously *was* thinking hard," said Tait as he moved to stand next to Liam. "Lady Maude isnae quite sane in her jealousy of her sister. I wonder how Keira found that out."

"I suspect she started to have suspicions the same as we did. The arm-twisting probably gained her the rest."

Tait grinned. "A fine thing to teach a wee lass."

"It wasnae me. I suspect it was her brothers. Or some of her many cousins."

"I believe her allotted time for thinking is over now. Might be best if ye get to her before she turns that clever, wee mind on ye."

Liam frowned. "Might be best, although she still seemed verra angry."

"That might prove useful. Sigimor finds it so."

Nodding slowly, Liam started toward the keep. By the time he reached the foot of the steps leading to the floor his bedchamber was on, he was feeling very ill-used. He had been insulted and held at sword point in his own bailey all because of a woman's jealousy and lies. His wife should be standing at his side, supporting him and soothing him, not sulking in her bedchamber.

And, he thought as he reached the door, she was too quick to believe lies about him. From the moment he had met her, he had done nothing to abuse her trust, yet she refused to give it to him. She was with child, yet she did not see fit to inform him of the fact. The looks she gave him at times hinted at the deeper, richer feelings he wanted and needed from her, but she said nothing.

His temper barely leashed, Liam began to lecture himself on the many ills caused by losing one's temper. He tried to open the door to the bedchamber. It was locked again. Liam felt every restraint he had just put on his temper snap, and he pounded on the door.

CHAPTER 23

"Open this door!"

Keira opened one eye and glared at the door, wincing at the sound of Liam's fist pounding on it. She had barred it to keep anyone from interrupting the rest she so desperately needed. Her peace had not lasted very long, she thought crossly.

"Open it now, Keira, or I swear I will have it chopped down!"

Her eyes widened as she slowly got off the bed. Liam sounded furious. She unbarred the door and hastily stepped back in case he threw open the door as angry men often did. When the door was opened almost gently and her husband stepped into the room with his usual grace, she began to feel a little uneasy. When he quietly shut the door and latched it, Keira looked up at his face and had to fight down the urge to go hide under the bed. Liam was very furious indeed. Her even-tempered, pleasant-speaking husband obviously had a true redhead's temper hidden beneath his calm.

"Are ye done sulking yet?" he asked.

"I wasnae sulking," she protested. "I was thinking."

"Aye, all about your rutting swine of a husband?"

Keira opened her mouth to refute that, but Liam gave her no chance to do so.

"Aye, I was somewhat of a lecherous fool for a few years," he said as he paced the room in front of her. "I have admitted it. I have e'en admitted that it wasnae weel done of me. But do ye listen when I swear I never bedded that madwoman? Nay! Do ye listen when I tell ye that I never bedded any married or betrothed woman, never bedded an innocent maid, never seduced or lied my way into a woman's bed, and never gave one single woman one tiny promise? Nay!"

"Liam, I—" she started to say, only to fall nervously silent when he halted in front of her, put his hands on his hips, and scowled at her.

"I am most definitely at my wit's end with ye, Keira," he said. "I took solemn vows with ye, but ye dinnae believe I meant them, do ye? I swore to ye that I would be faithful, and ye doubt my word on that, too, dinnae ye? I give ye pretty words, and ye just shrug them aside. I have done things with ye that I have ne'er done with another. All this, and ye still eye me as if I am about to grab the nearest lass and rut with her on the table!"

"Oh, nay, I most certainly do not," she protested, but his scowl stopped her from saying anything else in her defense.

"I told myself to be patient, that I am the one who gained the most from this marriage of ours. Weel, I have been patient, and I am done with it. Ye will cease thinking that I am about to betray ye at every turn. E'en if I wanted to, I wouldnae, for I have made vows before God and mon. A solemn oath. But I dinnae want to betray ye with anyone, ever, yet I cannae think of how to make ye believe that."

An almost plaintive note entered his voice, and he started to pace again. Keira opened her mouth to assure Liam that she had begun to believe him concerning the lady Maude, but some inner voice made her quickly shut her mouth. Liam was ranting, and she knew all too well how much one could expose one's inner feelings and thoughts while caught up in a rant. It might be wise to just stand there silent and let the man ramble on.

"I try to tell ye all this when we make love, but ye cannae see it. 'Tis there though in my every touch, my every kiss. Yet still ye remain blind. Ye hold part of yourself away from me, guarding it like some great treasure I might loot and destroy. Since I have ne'er much cared what lurked in a woman's mind or heart, I find I have no skill at reading yours. If I cannae make ye see that my desire is for ye alone, how can I e'er make ye understand that my heart is yours as weel?" He shook his head. "I ne'er thought to fall in love. After being with so many women, I felt I must be immune. E'en worried from time to time o'er the lack. Yet now, I sometimes wish I truly were a mon who couldnae love. I—"

Liam grunted as Keira threw herself against him and hugged him tightly. He blinked and looked down at the top of her head as he tried to think of all he had just said. It was obvious he had said something right while he had been ranting, and it would serve him well if he could recall just what it had been.

His eyes widened slightly as he wrapped his arms around her slim body. At some point during his rant, his anger had begun to fade, and he had begun to feel sadly defeated. He had realized that he had no more ideas of how to make his wife at least trust him, let alone how to make her love him as he loved her. Liam had the distinct feeling that he had told Keira that he loved her somewhere within his litany of complaints. It appeared that Tait was right. He had needed to go first.

Keira did not think she could hold Liam close enough. She was trembling, and her heart was pounding, but it was sheer joy pounding in her veins. Liam loved her. The knowledge spread through her, warming every part of her from her head to her toes. She felt as if she had drunk a full jug of wine.

The declaration had not come during some sweet moment of passion or even in the sort of romantic moment she had always envisioned. Nor had he looked her right in the eye and declared his heart in clear, precise language. She knew he had said it, however. It had been there amongst all the complaints about how blind she was and how she never listened to him. Oddly enough, it was that that made her believe him.

"Oh, Liam, I love ye, too," she said and tried to hug him even tighter.

Liam tilted her face up to his and kissed her. It was a ravenous kiss, hungry and demanding, and Keira met it and matched it. She was not sure who started removing their clothing first, but soon, they were both naked. They fell onto the bed in a tangle of limbs. Keira gave herself over completely to the wild passion she and Liam had stirred in each other with their words of love. Liam caressed and kissed every inch of her, and she lovingly returned that gift, giving all she knew how to give and holding nothing back from him. He brought her to the very edge of bliss time and time again until she began to curse him for denying her, instead of begging him to join with her. Then he was deep inside her, and Keira clung to him as he fiercely pushed them both off the precipice.

Trying not to move much for Liam seemed to be sound asleep on top of her, Keira looked around the room and grinned. There were clothes scattered everywhere. She tried to recall when they had knocked the table over, but her memories were still pleasantly clouded with thoughts of the pleasure and joy they had found in each other's arms.

Keira frowned a little. Liam had not said the words clearly yet, although his reaction to her declaration was certainly all any woman could want or hope for. He had made her repeat the words again and again as they made love as if he could not hear enough of them. Keira had no doubt that her love was wanted, welcomed eagerly.

She felt as if her heart had been unchained. Liam's past only caused her a twinge now and she was certain that too would soon fade. Despite the pretty words he had given them and how kindly she was sure he had treated them, Liam had used those women in his past as much as they had used him. There had been no real depth of feeling, only lust. There really were no ghosts in his past that she had to compete with or banish from his memory.

And he did have a right to some of his complaints, she silently conceded. She had heard his words, but had not really listened or believed. She did wonder what he had done with her that he had never done with anyone else, however. In the hope of rousing him so that he could answer that question, she began to trail her fingers up and down his back.

Liam opened one eye, saw the curve of his wife's lovely breast, and had to kiss it. His wife loved him. He had made her repeat the words several times during their frenzied lovemaking. Liam did not think he could ever hear it often enough. In a way he did not truly understand, it made him feel whole. It also made him feel strong and ready to face whatever the future held.

"Liam?"

He smiled. He liked the husky note that lingered in Keira's voice after they had made love. "M-m-m?"

"When ye were ranting—"

"I wasnae ranting. I was merely discussing a few things with ye."

"Of course. Weel, when ye were discussing these few things with me, ye said ye had done things with me that ye had ne'er done with another. Being that I am nay as worldly as ye are, I cannae think of what those things might be."

Hearing no lingering anger in her voice when she spoke of his past, he lifted his head to look at her. "Curious, are ye?"

"Weel, aye. Ye ken all that I havenae done with another since I was a virgin. And since all I ken now I have learned from ye, how could I guess what is new for ye as weel?"

"Verra true." He began to trail kisses over her still slightly flushed face. "I have ne'er slept the night with a woman. I have ne'er bathed with a woman." He grinned at the blush that warmed her cheeks as she obviously recalled those times they had shared a bath. "And I have ne'er praised a woman's body with kisses as I have yours." Her blush deepened to such a brilliant shade that he knew she understood exactly what he was referring to and he laughed softly.

"So it was truly just a rutting," she murmured.

Realizing that she was trying to finish putting his past firmly in the past, he agreed. "I followed my rules; I said pretty words to make them smile; and I took my ease with them." He brushed a kiss over her mouth. "I do wish I could have come to you as pure as ye came to me."

"Oh, that would have been nice, but 'tis probably for the best that one of us had had a little practice."

Thinking of the embarrassment and fumbling that had constituted his first time with a woman, he silently agreed. "I am still learning," he said.

Keira had to laugh. "Nonsense. A mon as weel, er, practiced as ye has naught left to learn."

"Oh, aye, he does." Liam studied her face, idly brushing strands of hair off it. "I have learned a lot since I married ye. I have learned the taste of a woman." He winked when she blushed. "I have learned that some of those positions I caught a glimpse of in the less saintly books some of the monks have can really give one pleasure. I had but the two before." He bit back a grin for he could tell by the still look on her face that she was hastily counting up all the positions they had tried. "And I have learned how complete it makes me feel to be one with the woman I love," he added in a soft voice. "How loving the woman I am with makes all other times meaningless, empty, for none could e'er equal the pleasure she gives me."

Keira wrapped her arms around his neck and pressed her face against his throat. "Ye said it clear. I was wondering if ye would."

"Ye said it clear. And verra loudly once or twice," he murmured and laughed when she lightly pinched his side. "I dinnae want ye to e'er doubt it, lass, though I may lag a wee bit from time to time in saying it."

"I ken ye would ne'er say such a thing unless ye truly meant it, Liam."

"And do ye trust me now, love?"

She lifted her head to smile at him. "Oh, I think I have for a while. That woman just made me so angry, and I wasnae sure why or if some of it was aimed at ye. I would like ye to remember that, Liam. I trust ye to hold to your vows. I trust in your love for me and in our marriage. I just dinnae trust all those women out there who look at ye and want ye and think to walk right o'er me to get at ye. I will get angry. I cannae promise I willnae. But e'en if I snap and snarl at ye, 'tisnae because I think ye will be rushing off to the nearest bed with whate'er woman is ogling ye at that moment."

"I think I understand what ye are trying to say. 'Tis the situation, nay me."

"Aye. I cannae always just punch them in the mouth, but there is that anger sitting there in my belly and—"

"There I am. If we didnae live so sheltered here, ye would have to deal with the same from me, lass." He kissed her when she frowned. "Trust me, ye would be heartily pursued if ye e'er went to the king's court."

Keira just smiled, not believing a word of it, but flattered that her husband found her so beautiful he feared other men would pursue her. "There is something I have been meaning to tell ye, Liam," she murmured, her gaze fixed upon his chest as she idly ran her finger over the muscles there.

It was difficult not to reveal his knowledge, that he knew she was about to tell him of the child they had made. "Ah, a deep, dark secret?"

"I have no deep, *dark,* secrets, Liam. Where would I get them? I have spent my whole life living in a place much like this. My time at the monastery was a grand adventure." She smiled when he laughed and then added very quietly, "But I think I may soon have another adventure. In, oh, mayhap seven months."

Even though he had known what she was about to tell him, Liam still felt deeply moved. She looked a little uncertain, and he kissed her. "We shall have a wee lass with black curls and dark green eyes," he said as he stroked her stomach.

"Nay, a lad with dark copper hair and eyes that can be blue and can be green." She laughed and then stroked his cheek. "Ye are pleased? Ye ne'er said much about wanting a bairn or two."

"Ah, love, how can ye ask? I have thought of ye as the mother

of my children since before we were married. I could see it so
clearly almost from the start. Wee black-haired lassies I could
spoil and ye would have to discipline."

"Thank ye."

"My pleasure."

"Oh, dear. I just had a thought."

"Your brothers warned me about letting ye think too much,"
he teased.

"Wretches. Nay, I just realized we shall have to name Sigimor
as godfather."

"Ye dinnae think that would be a good idea?" He knew she
was not quite sure about Sigimor, but now that she had spoken
of naming him godfather to their first child, he knew he
wanted that very much.

"Oh, nay, it would be wonderful. I just thought of how utterly spoiled a lass would be with ye as a father, my brothers as
her uncles, and Sigimor as godfather."

He laughed and hugged her. "We shall have a verra good
life, my love. A very good life indeed."

Please turn the page for an exciting sneak peek of
Hannah Howell's newest Highland romance
HIGHLAND LOVER
coming in June 2006!

Scotland, Spring 1475

"Oof!"

Oof!? Dazed and struggling to catch her breath, Alana decided she must have made that noise herself. Hard dirt floors did not say *oof*. It was odd, however, how the rough stone walls of the oubliette made her voice sound so deep, almost manly. Just as she began to be able to breathe again, the hard dirt floor shifted beneath her.

It took Alana a moment to fully grasp the fact that she had not landed on the floor. She had landed on a person. That person had a deep, manly voice. It was not dirt or stone beneath her cheek, but cloth. There was also the steady throb of a heartbeat in the ear she had pressed against that cloth. Her fingers were hanging down a little and touching cool, slightly damp earth. She was sprawled on top of a man like a wanton.

Alana scrambled off the man, apologizing for some awkward placement of her knees and elbows as she did so. The man certainly knew how to curse. She stood and stared up at the three men looking down at her, the light from the lantern they held doing little more than illuminating their grinning, hairy faces.

"Ye cannae put me in here with a mon," she said.

"Got no place else to put ye," said the tallest of the three, a man called Clyde, whom she was fairly sure was the laird.

"I am a lady," she began.

"Ye are a wee, impudent child. Now, are ye going to tell us who ye are?"

"So ye can rob my people? Nay, I dinnae think so."

"Then ye stay where ye are."

She did not even have time to stutter out a protest. The grate was shut, and that faint source of light quickly disappeared as the Gowans walked away. Alana stared into the dark and wondered how everything had gone so wrong. All she had wanted to do was to help find her sister Keira, but none of her family had heeded her pleas or her insistence that she could truly help to find her twin. It had seemed such a clever idea to disguise herself as a young girl and follow her brothers, waiting for just the right moment to reveal herself. How she had enjoyed those little dreams of walking up to her poor, confused brothers and leading them straight to their sister. That had kept a smile upon her face and a jaunty spring in her step right up until the moment she had realized she not only had lost her brothers' trail, but also had absolutely no idea of where she was.

Feeling very sorry for herself and wondering why her gifts had so abruptly failed her just when she needed them the most, she had been cooking a rabbit and sulking when the Gowans had found her. Alana grimaced as she remembered how she had acted. Perhaps if she had been sweet and had acted helpless, she would not be stuck in a hole in the ground with a man who was apparently relieving himself in a bucket. Maybe it would be wise to tell the Gowans who she was so that they could get some ransom for her and she could get out of here. Appalled by that moment of weakness, Alana proceeded to lecture herself in the hope of stiffening her resolve.

Gregor inwardly cursed as he finished relieving himself. It was not the best way to introduce himself to his fellow prisoner, but he really had had little choice. Having a body dropped on top of him and then being jabbed by elbows and knees had made ignoring his body's needs impossible. At least the dark provided a semblance of privacy.

He was just trying to figure out where she was when he realized she was muttering to herself. Clyde Gowan had called her an impudent child, but there was something in that low, husky voice that made him think of a woman. After she had landed on him and he had caught his breath, there had also been something about that soft, warm body that had also made him think of a woman despite the lack of fulsome curves. He shook his head as he cautiously stepped toward that voice.

Despite his caution, he took one step too many and came up hard against her back. She screeched softly and jumped, banging the top of her head against his chin. Gregor cursed softly as his teeth slammed together, sending a sharp, stinging pain through his head. He was a little surprised to hear her softly curse as well.

"Jesu, lass," he muttered, "ye have inflicted more bruises on me than those fools did when they grabbed me."

"Who are you?" Alana asked, wincing and rubbing at the painful spot on the top of her head, certain she could feel a lump rising.

"Gregor. And ye are?"

"Alana."

"Just Alana?"

"Just Gregor?"

"I will tell ye my full name if ye tell me yours."

"Nay, I dinnae think so. Someone could be listening, hoping we will do just that."

"And ye dinnae trust me as far as ye can spit, do ye?"

"Why should I? I dinnae ken who ye are. I cannae e'en see you." She looked around and then wondered why she bothered since it was so dark she could not even see her own hand if she held it right in front of her face. "What did they put ye in here for?"

Alana suddenly feared she had been confined with a true criminal, perhaps even a rapist or murderer. She smothered that brief surge of panic by telling herself sharply not to be such an idiot. The Gowans wanted to ransom her. Even they were not stupid enough to risk losing that purse by setting her too close to a truly dangerous man.

"Ransom," he replied.

"Ah, me too. Are they roaming about the country plucking up people like daisies?"

Gregor chuckled and shook his head. "Only those who look as if they or their kinsmen might have a few coins weighting their purse. A mon was being ransomed e'en as they dragged me in. He was dressed fine, although his bonnie clothes were somewhat filthy from spending time in this hole. I was wearing my finest. I suspect your gown told them your kinsmen might have some coin. Did they kill your guards?"

Alana felt a blush heat her cheeks. "Nay, I was alone. I got a little lost."

She was lying, Gregor thought. Either she was a very poor liar, or the dark had made his senses keener, allowing him to hear the lie in her voice. "I hope your kinsmen punish the men weel for such carelessness."

Oh, someone would most certainly be punished, Alana thought. There was no doubt in her mind about that. This was one of those times when she wished her parents believed in beating a child. A few painful strokes of a rod would be far easier to endure than the lecture she would be given and, even worse, the confused disappointment her parents would reveal concerning her idiocy and disobedience.

"How long have ye been down here?" she asked, hoping to divert his attention from how and why she had been caught.

"Two days, I think. 'Tis difficult to know for certain. They gave me quite a few blankets; a privy bucket, which they pull up and empty each day; and food and water twice a day. What troubles me is who will win this game of ye stay there until ye tell me what I want to know. My clan isnae really poor, but they dinnae have coin to spare for a big ransom. Nay when they din-nae e'en ken what the money will be used for."

"Oh, didnae they tell ye?"

"I was unconscious for most of the time it took to get to this keep and be tossed in here. All I have heard since then is the thrice daily question about who I am. And I am assuming all these things happen daily, not just whene'er they feel inclined. There does seem to be a, weel, rhythm to it all. 'Tis how I decided I have been here for two days." He thought back over the past few days, too much of it spent in the dark with his own thoughts. "If I judge it aright, this may actually be the end of the third day, for I fell unconscious again when they threw me in here. I woke up to someone bellowing that it was time to sup, got my food and water, was told about the privy bucket and that blankets had been thrown down here."

"And 'tis night now. The moon was rising as we rode through the gates. So, three days in the dark. In a hole in the ground," she murmured, shivering at the thought of having to endure the same. "What did ye do?"

"Thought."

"Oh, dear. I think *that* would soon drive me quite mad."

"It wasnae a pleasant interlude."

"It certainly isnae. I am nay too fond of the dark," she added softly and jumped slightly when a long arm was somewhat awkwardly wrapped around her shoulders.

"No one is, especially not the unrelenting dark of a place like this. So, ye were all alone when they caught ye. They didnae harm ye, did they?"

The soft, gentle tone of his question made Alana realize what he meant by *harm*. It struck her as odd that not once had she feared rape, yet her disguise as a child was certainly not enough to save her from that. "Nay, they just grabbed me, cursed me a lot for being impudent, and tossed me over a saddle."

Gregor smiled. "Impudent were ye?"

"That is as good a word for it as any other. There I was sitting quietly by a fire, cooking a rabbit I had been lucky enough to catch, and up ride five men who inform me that I am now their prisoner and that I had best tell them who I am so that they can send the ransom demand to my kinsmen. I told them that I had had a very upsetting day and the last thing I wished to deal with was smelly, hairy men telling me what to do, so they could just ride back to the rock they had crawled out from under. Or words to that effect," she added quietly.

In truth, she thought as she listened to Gregor chuckle, she had completely lost her temper. It was not something she often did, and she suspected some of her family would have been astonished. The Gowans had been. All five men had stared at her as if a dormouse had suddenly leapt at their throats. It had been rather invigorating until the Gowans had realized they were being held in place by insults from someone they could snap in half.

It was a little puzzling that she had not eluded capture. She was very fast, something often marveled at by her family; she could run for a very long way without tiring; and she could hide in the faintest of shadows. Yet mishap after mishap had plagued her as she had fled from the men, and they had barely raised a sweat in pursuing and capturing her. If she were a superstitious person, she would think some unseen hand of fate had been doing its best to make sure she was caught.

"Did they tell ye why they are grabbing so many for ransom?" Gregor asked.

"Oh, aye, they did." Of course, one reason they had told her was because of all the things she had accused them of wanting the money for, such as useless debauchery and not something they badly needed like soap. "Defenses."

"What?"

"They have decided that this hovel requires stronger defenses. That requires coin or some fine goods to barter with, neither of which they possess. I gather they have heard of some troubles not so far away, and it has made them decide that they are too vulnerable. From what little I could see whilst hanging over Clyde's saddle, this is a very old tower house, one that was either neglected or damaged once, or both. It appears to have been repaired enough to be livable, but I did glimpse many things either missing or in need of repair. From what Clyde's wife said, this small holding was her dowry."

"Ye spoke to his wife?"

"Weel, nay. She was lecturing him from the moment he stepped inside all the way to the door leading down here. She doesnae approve of this. Told him that since he has begun this folly, he had best do a verra good job of it and gather a veritable fortune, for they will need some formidable defenses to protect them from all the enemies he is making."

Alana knew she ought to move away from him. When he had first draped his arm around her, she had welcomed what she saw as a gesture intended to comfort her, perhaps even an attempt to ease the fear of the dark she had confessed to. He still had his arm around her, and she had slowly edged closer to his warmth until she was now pressed hard up against his side.

He was a very tall man. Probably a bit taller than her overgrown brothers, she mused. Judging from where her cheek rested so nicely, she barely reached his breastbone. Since she was five feet tall, that made him several inches over six feet. Huddled up against him as she was, she could feel the strength in his body despite what felt like a lean build. Considering the fact that he had been held in this pit for almost three days, he smelled remarkably clean as well.

And the fact that she was noticing how good he smelled told her she really should move away from him, Alana thought. The problem was, he felt good, very good. He felt warm, strong, and calming, all things she was sorely in need of at the moment. She started to console herself with the thought that she was not actually embracing him, only to realize that she had curled her arm around what felt like a very trim waist.

She inwardly sighed, ruefully admitting that she liked where she was and had no inclination to leave his side. He thought she was a young girl, so she did not have to fear him thinking she was inviting him to take advantage of her. Alone with him in the dark, there was a comforting anonymity about it as well. Alana decided there was no harm in it all. In truth, she would not be surprised to discover that he found comfort in it, too, after days of being all alone in the dark.

"Where were ye headed, lass? Is there someone aside from the men ye were with who will start searching for ye?" Gregor asked, a little concerned about how good it felt to hold her, even though every instinct he had told him that Alana was not the child she pretended to be.

"Quite possibly." She doubted that the note she had left behind would do much to comfort her parents. "I was going to my sister."

"Ah, weel, then, I fear the Gowans may soon ken who ye are e'en if ye dinnae tell them."

"Oh, of course. What about you? Will anyone wonder where ye have gone?"

"Nay for a while yet."

They all thought he was still wooing his well-dowered bride. Gregor had had far too much time to think about that, about all of his reasons for searching for a well-dowered bride and about the one he had chosen. Mavis was a good woman, passably pretty, and had both land and some coin to offer a husband. He had left her feeling almost victorious, the betrothal as good as settled, yet each hour he had sat here in the dark, alone with his thoughts, he had felt less and less pleased with himself. It did not feel *right*. He hated to think that his cousin Sigimor made sense about anything, yet it was that man's opinion that kept creeping through his mind. Mavis did not really feel *right*. She did not really *fit*.

He silently cursed. What did it matter? He was almost thirty years of age, and he had never found a woman who felt *right* or who *fit*. Mavis gave him the chance to be his own man, to be laird of his own keep, and to have control over his own lands. Mavis was a sensible choice. He did not love her, but after so many years and so many women without feeling even a tickle of that, he doubted he was capable of loving any woman. Passion could be stirred with the right touch, and compatibility could be achieved with a little work. It would serve.

He was just about to ask Alana how extensive a search her kinsmen would mount for her when he heard the sound of someone approaching above them. "Stand o'er there, lass," he said as he nudged her to the left. "'Tis time for the bucket to be emptied and food and water lowered down to us. I dinnae want to be bumping into ye."

Alana immediately felt chilled as she left his side. She kept inching backward until she stumbled and fell onto a pile of blankets. She moved around until she was seated on them, her back against the cold stone wall. The grate was opened, and a rope with a hook at the end of it was lowered through the opening. The lantern this man carried produced enough light to at least allow them to see that rope. Gregor moved around as if he could see, and Alana suspected he had carefully mapped out his prison in his mind. She watched the bucket being raised up and another being lowered down. As Gregor reached for that bucket, she caught a faint glimpse of his form. He was indeed very tall and very lean. She cursed the darkness for hiding all else from her.

"We will need two buckets of water for washing in the morn," Gregor called up to the man, watching him as he carefully lowered the now empty privy bucket.

"Two?" the man snapped. "Why two?"

"One for me and one for the lass."

"Ye can both wash from the same one."

"A night down here leaves one verra dirty. A wee bucket of water is barely enough to get one person clean, ne'er mind two."

"I will see what the laird says."

Alana winced as the grate was slammed shut and that faint shaft of light disappeared. She tried to judge where Gregor was, listening carefully to his movements, but she was still a little startled when he sat down by her side. Then she caught the scent of cheese and still warm bread, and her stomach growled a welcome.

Gregor laughed as he set the food out between them. "Careful how ye move, lass. The food rests between us. The Gowans do provide enough to eat, though 'tis plain fare."

"Better than none. Perhaps ye had better hand me things. I think I shall need a wee bit of time to become accustomed to moving about in this thick dark."

She tensed when she felt a hand pat her leg, but then something fell into her lap. Reaching down, she found a chunk of bread, which she immediately began to eat. Gregor was obviously just trying to be certain of where she sat as he shared out the food. She did wonder why a small part of her was disappointed by that.

"Best ye eat it all, lass. I havenae been troubled by vermin, but I have heard a few sounds that make me think they are near. Leaving food about will only bring them right to us."

Alana shivered. "I hate rats."

"As do I, which is why I fight the temptation to hoard food."

She nodded even though she knew he could not see her, and for a while, they silently ate. Once her stomach was full, Alana began to feel very tired, the rigors of the day catching up to her. Her eyes widened as she realized there was no place to make up her own bed; she doubted there were enough blankets to do so anyway.

"Where do I sleep?" she asked, briefly glad of the dark for it hid her blushes.

"Here with me," replied Gregor. "I will sleep next to the wall." He smiled, almost able to feel her tension. "Dinnae fret, lass. I willnae harm ye. I have ne'er harmed a child."

Of course, Alana thought and relaxed. He thought she was a child. She had briefly forgotten her disguise. The thought of having to keep her binding on for days was not comforting, but it was for the best. Thinking her a child, Gregor treated her as he would a sister or his own child. If he knew she was a woman, he might well treat her as a convenient bedmate or try to make her one. She brutally silenced the part of her that whispered its disappointment, reminding it that she had no idea of what this man even looked like.

Once the food was gone, Gregor set the bucket aside. Alana heard him removing some clothing and then felt him crawl beneath the blankets. She quickly moved out of the way when she felt his feet nudge her hip. After a moment's thought, she loosened the laces on her gown and removed her boots before crawling under the blankets by his side. The chill of the place disappeared again, and she swallowed a sigh. Something about Gregor soothed her, made her able to face this imprisonment with some calm and courage, and she was simply too tired to try and figure out what that something was.

"On the morrow, we will begin to plan our escape," Gregor said.

"Ye have thought of a way out of here?"

"Only a small possibility. Sleep. Ye will need it."

That did not sound promising, Alana mused, as she closed her eyes.

ABOUT THE AUTHOR

Hannah Howell is an award-winning author who lives with her family in Massachusetts. She is the author of nineteen Zebra historical romances and is currently working on a new Highland historical romance, *Highland Lover*, which will be published in June 2006. Hannah loves hearing from readers and you may visit her website: *www.hannahhowell.com*. Or write to her c/o Zebra books. Please include a self-addressed stamped envelope if you wish a response.